AMERICAN ROYALS III: RIVALS

ALSO BY KATHARINE McGEE

RIVALS

AMERICAN ROYALS III

KATHARINE McGEE

Random House  New York

For William

Text copyright © 2022 by Katharine McGee and Alloy Entertainment
Jacket art copyright © 2022 by Carolina Melis

All rights reserved. Published in the United States by Random House Children's Books, a division of Penguin Random House LLC, New York.

Random House and the colophon are registered trademarks of Penguin Random House LLC.

Visit us on the Web! GetUnderlined.com

Educators and librarians, for a variety of teaching tools, visit us at RHTeachersLibrarians.com

Produced by Alloy Entertainment
alloyentertainment.com

Library of Congress Cataloging-in-Publication Data
Name: McGee, Katharine, author.
Title: Rivals / Katharine McGee.
Description: First edition. | New York: Random House Children's Books, [2022] | Series: American royals; 3 | Audience: Ages 14 and up.
Summary: In an alternate America, Beatrice, now queen, and her siblings, Samantha and Jefferson, struggle to untangle their personal lives and settle into their new political roles while the country hosts the world's monarchs at the League of Kings conference.
Identifiers: LCCN 2021048199 (print) | LCCN 2021048200 (ebook) |
ISBN 978-0-593-42970-9 (hardcover) | ISBN 978-0-593-42971-6 (library binding) |
ISBN 978-0-593-56743-2 (international) | ISBN 978-0-593-42972-3 (ebook)
Subjects: CYAC: Kings, queens, rulers, etc.—Fiction. | Princesses—Fiction. |
Princes—Fiction. | Congresses and conventions—Fiction. | Dating (Social customs)—Fiction. | Courts and courtiers—Fiction. | LCGFT: Novels.
Classification: LCC PZ7.1.M43513 Ri 2022 (print) |
LCC PZ7.1.M43513 (ebook) | DDC [Fic]—dc23

Printed in the United States of America
10 9 8 7 6 5 4 3 2 1
First Edition

1

BEATRICE

Beatrice pulled her arms overhead in a stretch. She wondered if all brides felt like this when they returned from their honeymoons: flush with a warm, relaxed pleasure.

Except that Beatrice—Her Majesty Beatrice Georgina Fredericka Louise, Queen of America—wasn't a normal bride. Actually, since she hadn't gotten married, she wasn't a bride at all.

She glanced at Theodore Eaton, the man she was supposed to have wed earlier this year. His hair was an even brighter blond after three weeks in the Caribbean sun, his skin burnished to a golden tan. Beatrice knew she looked just as relaxed and well rested.

Not that it would last, with everything that lay ahead.

In the weeks following their non-wedding, Beatrice had remained in the capital, dealing with the aftermath of her decision. She had reviewed infrastructure bills and ambassadorial appointments, and had studied foreign legislation and trade policies in preparation for the upcoming League of Kings conference. It was all the tedious, unglamorous work of being a monarch—the work Beatrice *should* have been doing since her father died, if she hadn't allowed herself to be sidetracked with planning her wedding.

Porcelain platters were scattered on the table before her and Teddy, laden with the remnants of their scrambled eggs and fruit. Franklin, the golden Lab puppy that she and Teddy had adopted together—not a puppy much longer—nuzzled her leg, whining. Beatrice surreptitiously broke off a piece of toast and passed it to him under the table.

"Glad to be back?" Teddy asked.

Beatrice leaned down to rub Franklin's velvety-soft ears. "Glad to see this guy again," she said, and sighed. "Though I have to say, I already miss our bungalow."

Beatrice had never really been on a *vacation* before. She'd traveled all over the world, but always for a diplomatic visit or state business. Even on family trips she'd been too busy skiing, or sailing, or catching up on school assignments to relax. It was a trait she'd inherited from her father. King George IV had never taken a day off work in his life. And now that he was gone, Beatrice wished that he had.

A knock sounded at the door. "Yes?" Beatrice called out.

"Your Majesty," the footman announced, "the Lady Chamberlain is here to see you."

Surprised, Beatrice checked her watch: a platinum one that her father had given her on her eighteenth birthday, its hands starred with tiny diamonds. It wasn't like her to be running late. She'd gotten too accustomed to island time—all those mornings when she and Teddy had lingered over breakfast, only to end up falling into bed again afterward.

Beatrice glanced at the footman, struck with an idea. "Why don't you tell Anju to come on in?"

"Into the breakfast room, Your Majesty?"

"Why not?" Beatrice's relationship with her former chamberlain, Robert Standish, had been stiff with formality. But beneath the incessant bowing and *Your Majesty*-ing, Robert hadn't respected her at all. He'd been silently undermining Beatrice's authority, trying to keep her from exerting any real power.

Robert had been far too stuffy and old-fashioned to even *consider* sitting down in the Washington family's private breakfast room, which was precisely why Beatrice had suggested it. She was determined to do things differently this time around.

"Bee." Teddy cleared his throat. "Do you think you could run some of my thoughts past Anju, see if we can get moving on any of them?"

She nodded. "Of course."

America had never had a king consort before. The only real precedents for Teddy's position were the eleven queens consort who'd come before him—most recently, Beatrice's mother, Queen Adelaide.

So Teddy had drawn up some ideas for responsibilities he could take on. He'd been trained as a future duke, after all; he had a great deal of experience in allocating budget, looking out for the good of his people. Beatrice knew he wouldn't be happy doing what queens consort traditionally did—cutting ribbons, arranging tablescapes.

Of course, it wasn't fair that the queens had been limited to domestic roles in the first place. Beatrice's mother was one of the smartest people she knew. And, like Teddy, Adelaide had been trained to rule a duchy someday—*two* duchies, in fact. But once she'd married King George, she'd been relegated to a position that was more ceremonial than political. That was just the way the monarchy worked.

Until now.

Beatrice was determined to change all of that, to show people that a woman could rule as effectively as any man. Still, she didn't want Teddy to feel purposeless. He was too talented to sit around waiting for her to need him. Even if that was, technically, the only item in his job description.

"Thanks. I'll catch up with you later." Teddy stood, dropping a kiss on Beatrice's forehead as the Lady Chamberlain walked in.

After she'd fired Robert Standish, Beatrice had launched a full-scale search for a new chamberlain. She'd interviewed dozens of options before settling on Anju Mahali, who, as the former CEO of a software company, might have been the unlikeliest candidate of them all.

"Are you sure you want to hire her? She knows next to nothing about politics," Beatrice's mother had warned.

Honestly, Beatrice thought, the royal family *needed* someone with a fresh perspective. And anything Anju needed to know about politics—not to mention the intricacies of protocol—she could find in Robert's binders and file folders. He'd certainly left enough of them.

At least Anju had some experience managing public opinion. When Beatrice had called off the wedding of the century, offering no more explanation than a vague security scare, she'd expected a public reaction. There was always a reaction to every last one of her decisions, no matter how insignificant they seemed to Beatrice. She'd met with a congressional leader at his office rather than summoning him to hers—was that a gesture of respect, or of disdain? (In reality, the palace's air-conditioning had been out that day.) She'd worn a pair of amethyst earrings—surely that was a silent cry for help, since amethysts were known to have healing vibes. (Beatrice had been especially bemused by that claim; she'd worn the earrings because her stylist thought they matched her purple dress.)

The scrutiny had only gotten worse after her controversial decision to postpone the wedding. All summer, people had been speaking out against her, in op-eds and on talk shows and in social-media rants. *It's not that I'm antifeminist,* they would begin, *but—*

As if that single *but* absolved them of anything they said next. *But she's so young and inexperienced. But it's hard to imagine she could ever live up to her father. But she called off her own wedding; don't you worry that's a sign of emotional instability?*

For the first time in both their lives, *Samantha's* approval

4

ratings were higher than Beatrice's. Sam had just completed a successful royal tour, while Beatrice was the woman who'd left America's favorite duke at the altar. The magazines that used to rave over "Queen B" now piled criticism on "Runaway B."

In Beatrice's opinion, their puns were getting worse.

"Welcome back, Your Majesty," Anju said with a brisk nod. That was another thing Beatrice liked about her: she didn't bother curtsying.

"Have you eaten?" Beatrice gestured to the breakfast spread before them. Anju ignored the food but poured herself a coffee and added a heaping scoop of sugar before taking the seat opposite Beatrice.

"As our first order of business, I'd like to review Teddy's suggestions for ways to shape the role of king consort," Beatrice began.

Anju hesitated. "With all due respect, Your Majesty, that's not very time-sensitive. And many of Teddy's suggestions—that he meet with ambassadors on your behalf, or help manage your briefings by the Trade Commission—would require congressional approval. I think we should focus on the League of Kings conference for now."

"Right, of course." Beatrice swallowed against a sudden panic.

The imminent convocation of the League of Kings would be her first great test as a ruler.

The League had been founded in 1895, ending the War of the Three Peters: Tsar Pieter of Russia, King Pedro IV of Spain, and Emperor Peter of Austria. In Europe it was still known as the Cousins' War, since all three Peters were cousins through the Hapsburg line.

At its inception, the League of Kings had been something entirely new: a multinational treaty, in which all the signatory nations swore to maintain international peace and security.

They agreed that every five years they would meet at one of their palaces—no politicians, no press, just the kings and their sons—to discuss issues of global importance.

Now the League of Kings comprised the monarchs of nearly every nation in the world, except a few holdouts in the Pacific who didn't see the need to sign, like Singapore and Hawaii. Now the attendees were not only kings, but queens and empresses and sultanas, though all efforts to rename the coalition as anything but the League of Kings had sputtered out and died. And now the conferences were held all over the globe, not just in St. Petersburg or Sandringham.

The League of Kings hadn't met in America since Beatrice's grandfather was king. But this fall, America would be hosting the conference again, in the very first year of Beatrice's reign.

The rotation of League of Kings hosts was a contentious and highly delicate act of international diplomacy, more prestigious—at least to the monarchs—than hosting the Olympics. Already the King of Ghana and the Emperor of Japan were fighting over the location of the conference in 2045.

Months ago, at the funeral reception for Beatrice's father, King Frederick of Germany had asked Beatrice if she'd like to withdraw as this year's host. "No one will blame you for stepping out of the lineup. Why don't you let me have everyone to Rumpenheim instead?"

She knew Frederick meant well. At eighty-four, he was the current chairman of the League of Kings, and he'd been something of a mentor to Beatrice ever since she'd lived at Potsdam one summer in college, studying German.

Beatrice shook her head. "Thank you, but I need to see this through. My father was so eager to host this year's conference." She tried to ignore Frederick's look of consternation as she added, "He was planning to bring his climate accord to a vote again. I'd like to finish what he started."

"The climate accord?" Frederick repeated, frowning. "Beatrice, your father tried to pass that proposal for years, but he could never get enough people on board."

"Only because they kept quibbling over the details."

Climate change was one of those issues that the League of Kings agreed upon in theory, but not in practice. Whenever King George had brought it up, the discussion devolved into accusations and finger-pointing. Each monarch insisted that everyone *else* was a grievous offender. Why should they have to devastate their economies fixing other people's mistakes?

"Besides," Frederick had added hastily, "you can't propose new business your first time at the conference. It simply isn't done."

"This isn't my first conference." As her father's successor, Beatrice had attended the League's most recent meeting in China, as well as the previous one in France.

There had been a few raised eyebrows that first time: most monarchs waited for their heirs to graduate from high school, or at the very least middle school, before bringing them to the conference. Twelve-year-old Beatrice had worked tirelessly and frantically to prove herself. At the heirs' info sessions, she had scribbled notes until her hand cramped, trying not to feel intimidated when she was partnered up with the Prince of Wales, who was almost twice as old as her father.

"It's your first time attending as a *ruler*," Frederick amended. "You're in the driver's seat now, Beatrice."

Like her grandfather, Beatrice would host the League of Kings at Bellevue, the royal family's palace in Orange. The League of Kings never took place at a monarch's main residence, but instead at a summer palace or minor estate. It would have been too risky, gathering so many world leaders in a busy capital city.

Located on a private island, Bellevue was the most secure of the Washingtons' various homes. It had been built by the French, as a wedding gift from King Louis XX when his daughter Thérèse married King Andrew. And, in typically French fashion, it had never been connected to the mainland by a bridge. One had to cross either by boat or by helicopter. When Louis had given the estate to the newlyweds, he'd included a gilded ferryboat, complete with a captain named Gaston.

Thanks to its eighty guest rooms and dozens of outbuildings, Bellevue could accommodate almost everyone onsite. Of course, the coast would still be swarming for miles. People always flooded the area around a League of Kings conference: journalists desperate for a story, activists protesting an issue, royal enthusiasts who hoped a bit of glamour might rub off on them.

Beatrice had only been to Bellevue a handful of times in her life. Her family had never loved going there; it was so grand in scale and splendor that it felt like trading one palace for another. They were much happier at their country house, or the Telluride cabin—somewhere cozy, where they could make pancakes and watch TV as if they were an ordinary family.

And so, while Bellevue's state rooms and gardens were open to the public, the rest of the estate was largely shut up, hidden behind dust cloths and curtains. Until now.

Beatrice tried to remember the last time she'd been at Bellevue, almost two years ago, when Connor Markham had still been her Revere Guard. So much had happened since then: she and Connor had started dating in secret, until Beatrice had lost her father and everything had changed. Or, really, *she* had changed. She'd realized that she and Connor didn't belong together. That she loved Teddy—even if she wasn't ready to marry him.

"I've brought hard copies of everything. Shall we begin with your schedule?" Anju asked, reaching into her briefcase for a stack of binders. Their spines were labeled with phrases like PROTOCOL & CEREMONIES or NORTH ATLANTIC TRADE ROUTES & TREATIES, or even YOUNGER SONS OF THE ROYAL HOUSES OF THE WORLD.

Beatrice slid the binders eagerly across the breakfast table. The sight of all those color-coded plastic tabs felt oddly comforting. Studying was something Beatrice had always excelled at.

"Let's get started," she agreed, turning to the first page.

If Beatrice could fulfill her father's dream and get the climate accord passed, maybe America would start taking her seriously. Maybe the press would actually discuss her accomplishments, instead of her fashion choices or her relationship with Teddy—would stop lamenting that she wasn't the ruler her father had been.

This conference was her chance to start building a legacy as queen.

2

SAMANTHA

"I can't believe this is the end of our tour." Samantha glanced at her best friend, Nina Gonzalez, who was seated across from her on the royal family's private jet. "How many flights have we been on now, seventy?"

"More like a hundred."

Nina leaned down to press a brass button on the side of her seat. A hidden drawer popped out of the chair's base, revealing neat rows of candy and peanuts. "The M&M's are back!" she exclaimed, ripping open the corner of a bag. "I wonder whose job it is to restock the plane after our flights. They're probably sick of buying more M&M's every time."

"I'm sure they started buying in bulk once they realized what an M&M monster you are," Sam teased.

"I prefer M&M *enthusiast*, thank you." Nina passed her the bag, but Sam shook her head. Her stomach was too knotted with anticipation to handle any sugar.

Understanding flashed in Nina's eyes. "Are you nervous about staying with the Davises?"

"Well, yeah." Sam's words tumbled out in a sudden rush. "What if Marshall's parents don't like me? And how am I supposed to act around them, anyway? Do I call them Lord and Lady, or by their first names, or—"

Nina threw an M&M that landed squarely in Sam's chest,

silencing her. "Quit freaking out. Just act like you do around my family, and you'll be fine."

"Somehow I doubt the Duke and Duchess of Orange want to sing show tunes in matching sweatpants."

"That's because they haven't heard your rendition of 'Mamma Mia,'" Nina said, and Sam smiled.

The thing was, she'd never stayed with a boyfriend's family before. She'd never even *had* a boyfriend until this year, when she'd started dating Lord Marshall Davis, heir to the dukedom of Orange. There had been men in her life—a number of men, if you counted all the names the tabloids had linked with hers—but those relationships had all quickly fizzled out.

And this time, the attention was more intense than ever. America couldn't stop talking about her and Marshall, whether in disapproval or obsessive adulation. Sam had never gotten so much hate mail, or so much fan mail. There was even *gear*: coffee mugs printed with their faces, tank tops that said TEAM SAMARSHALL, and a rather terrifying set of rag dolls, with Sam's and Marshall's palms sewn together so that they were forever holding hands. Her brother, Jeff, kept joking that he would buy one and leave it on Sam's bed for her to find, at which point Sam had threatened to commission one of him and Daphne. Jeff hadn't mentioned it again after that.

Sam wished she and Marshall could get a little more breathing room. But they had always been in the spotlight—at first, that had been their *goal*. They'd originally gotten together for show, just to make their respective exes jealous. Only later had they realized that their feelings were real. It wasn't exactly a normal way to start dating.

But then, dating was never normal when you were Princess of America and heir to the throne.

Sam looked back at Nina, who'd curled her bare feet beneath her, a book in her lap. The bag of M&M's was propped on the leather armrest as Nina absentmindedly popped one candy after another into her mouth. Sam felt an overwhelming burst of affection for her.

"Thanks for coming with me this summer," she said. "You know I couldn't have done this tour without you."

Nina glanced up from her book. "Please, you would have done just fine without me. Though you would've been forced to hold your own koala."

Sam smiled at that. "Ah, Maxine the koala. What an icon."

During their visit to the Phoenix Zoo, one of the animal handlers had offered Sam a koala to hold. "Thank you! I'm sure my friend would like to hold her," she'd replied, dodging the offer. Before Nina could protest, the koala was thrust into her arms. Poor Maxine must have been even more anxious than Nina was, because she promptly peed down the front of Nina's color-blocked dress.

"Are you sure you can't stay another few days?" Sam added. "It's going to be so long before I see you again."

"You don't want me crashing your time with Marshall." Nina raised an eyebrow. "Besides, you *do* have your own plane. You can always come see me if you get bored of the League of Kings conference and need an escape from all the stuck-up princes and princesses."

"Speaking of the plane, are you sure you won't take it back to the East Coast?"

"Absolutely not." No matter how adamantly Sam had insisted upon it, Nina refused to take *Eagle III* without her. She'd booked a commercial flight back to Washington for later that afternoon.

"You're the only person I know who would turn down a private plane. Which, I should point out, is fully stocked with M&M's."

"Ooh, good point. I should steal more while I still can."

Nina marched over to the other six seats on the plane, cheerfully grabbing M&M's from the snack drawer beneath each of them.

A ding sounded through the cabin, and the seat-belt light overhead turned bright orange. "Your Royal Highness, Miss Gonzalez," came the pilot's voice, "we're beginning our descent. Please take your seats."

Sam pressed her face against the window. As their plane sank toward the private airstrip, she noticed a bright red SUV parked alongside the runway. A tall Black man leaned against the door with deceptive casualness, wearing commercial-grade headphones and sunglasses.

"Marshall's here!" Nina exclaimed, staring out her own window.

"I told him not to pick me up at the airport," Sam replied, though she was grinning.

"This isn't just picking you up at the airport; it's meeting your plane. He will be there right as our door opens." Nina's eyes met Sam's. "I know you're not a romantic, but for the record, this is an expert-level romantic gesture."

Sam pretended to scoff, though her heart wasn't in it.

Not a romantic. That used to be true, but not anymore.

♛

Marshall tugged at Sam's wrist, pulling her onto the back porch. Row upon row of vines receded into the distance, their pale green grapes peeking out from beneath waxy leaves. "Come on, my little polpetta!"

Sam gave a breathless laugh. "*Polpetta?*" Ever since she and Marshall had started dating, he'd called her an increasingly ridiculous series of nicknames—panda bear, Skittle, love muffin.

"It's Italian for 'meatball,'" Marshall explained. "I ran out of nicknames in English, so I looked up some in other languages. To be fair, I don't actually know if *polpetta* is a romantic nickname or what parents call their babies," he added. Sam couldn't help but smile.

As they started down a gravel path, the wind pricked at Sam's arms. Seeing her shiver, Marshall unzipped his fleece and handed it over. She laughed when she saw the orange T-shirt he wore beneath, the words STATE CHAMPIONSHIPS written above a cartoon grizzly bear.

"You do realize that your shirt has a hole in it. Multiple holes," she amended, tugging at a rip along the hem.

"Hey, this shirt is a *relic*! It's not like I can go to championships again to get another one. My high school water polo career is over." Marshall sighed in mock sorrow.

"If only I'd known you then. I clearly missed out on your glory days." Sam tilted her head. "Do you think we would've liked each other, if we'd met in high school?"

"I doubt it. You wouldn't have put up with my shenanigans."

"Like what?"

"You know, stupid guy stuff. Driving the Jeep when I was fourteen, skipping school and heading to the beach, playing beer pong with the Orange State Cab. Fun fact: red wine and beer pong do *not* mix," he added.

It didn't sound all that different from what Jeff and his friends used to do. Except— "What's the Orange State Cab?"

"My family has been growing the same cabernet for over a hundred years. We always serve it at official state functions. You didn't drink any at Accession Day?" Marshall asked.

Sam made a face. Red wine was such an *old people* drink.

Seeing her expression, he laughed. "Come on. You have to at least try some."

Marshall led Sam farther down the path, to an enormous

brick structure. "The crush facility," he explained, when one entire side of the building retracted upward like a garage door.

Lights flicked on at their arrival, illuminating rows of massive steel cylinders, each affixed with a label: PINOT NOIR LOT 12 or RIDGE PROPERTY MERLOT. Marshall grabbed a paper cup from a nearby water cooler; then they wove through the tanks until they reached one labeled OSC. He turned a spigot, filling the cup with a dark purple liquid.

Sam took an eager sip—and nearly spat it onto the floor.

"What *is* that?" she gasped, thrusting the cup back toward Marshall. The wine burned her throat so fiercely that she could practically feel it in her eyes.

"Yeah, it's not quite ready to drink. It'll be smoother once the fermentation is done." Marshall shrugged, then tipped back the rest of the cup and drained it in a single gulp. *Show-off,* Sam thought affectionately.

"I can't believe you and your friends played beer pong with this," she told him.

"I was a teenage boy. My body could run for days on monster tacos and adrenaline."

"Right, because you're so much older and wiser now." Sam glanced around the crush facility, amused. "So, this was your go-to move? You invited girls here for a 'private tasting' of your family's wine?"

"Please. High school Marshall had zero moves." His tone softened, grew more serious. "You're the first girl I've brought to the Napa house. You know that, right?"

There was an eager swoop in Sam's chest. She squeezed his hand in answer, not sure she trusted herself to say the right thing.

Marshall showed her around the rest of the facility: a machine room with strange-looking equipment, then down a narrow staircase into the barrel room, where a damp, vegetal scent hung heavy in the air. Sam nodded, only half listening to his explanations, content simply to be near him after so long apart.

Finally they headed back to the house and collapsed onto a porch swing, rocking back and forth. Sam snuggled deeper into Marshall's fleece, tugging the sleeves down over her wrists. It was warm, its shearling frayed on the inside, in the way that clothes are when they've been worn over and over for years.

"So, are you glad to finally be done with the royal tour?" Marshall asked.

Sam groaned. "You have no idea."

The greatest challenge with the tour had been the sheer monotony. It was always the same, no matter what city they were in. Samantha would arrive to a welcome speech from the mayor, and then a child would run up the steps with a bouquet—which was color-coordinated with Sam's outfit, thanks to the PR team's relentless planning. After a high school band played the national anthem, she would head to a reception at town hall, where Sam was instructed to weave through the crowds along a counterclockwise route, one quarter turn every fifteen minutes. "It's called 'the circular hour,'" her aide had explained. "Your great-grandmother patented this move."

Sam should have known what to expect from a royal tour. Her family had certainly done enough of them over the years. But those trips had been different, because her parents and Beatrice had shouldered most of the burden.

Back then, Sam had only been the spare.

Now she was the heir, taking her sister's place on what should have been a newlywed tour, and *Jeff* was the spare. A spare who would be serving as Regent while Beatrice was away at the conference.

As always, Sam wondered how different her and Jeff's lives would be if time had shifted by just four minutes—if her brother had been born first. Then *he* would be the one on tour, and she would be in Washington, cutting ribbons or going to college or . . .

Honestly, she didn't know. It was hard to imagine going back to her old "party princess" ways: dancing on tables, letting the media think she was spoiled and headstrong and undisciplined.

When she'd explained all of this, Marshall shook his head. "I didn't realize it was that bad. Every time I saw a photo of you and Nina, it seemed like you guys were having fun."

"We did, sometimes. But it's a royal tour. It's not meant to be fun."

"You sound like Beatrice."

"Is that so bad?"

The sun had set behind the hills, gilding the mist that hung over the vines so that they turned to gold, like some kind of temporary enchantment. If Sam had learned anything these past few months, it was that America had so much beauty in it, in its mountains and cities and everywhere in between.

Marshall reached an arm around her, tracing lazy circles over her shoulder. "Are you going to bring this up with Beatrice?"

"And make her regret asking for my help, the very first time I stood in for her?"

"That's the problem," Marshall insisted. "You were standing in for *her* instead of standing up there as yourself. All that pomp and ceremony? This tour was designed for Beatrice, to play to her strengths, when it should have been adapted for yours."

Sam pushed the porch swing back until the ropes creaked in protest. "And what are my strengths, exactly? Competitive sports and breaking the rules?"

"Your strength is connecting with people, Sam. Instead of asking you to stand there like a mannequin and listen to speeches, the palace should have planned things for *you*. Like being the guest commentator for a Little League game, or making a surprise appearance at a high school prom."

"I would *love* an excuse to rewear my old prom dress," Sam said wistfully. "It had feathers on the hem."

Marshall grinned. "Why am I not surprised."

She reached up to catch the hand that he'd looped around her shoulder, lacing her fingers with his. "What was your prom like? Did you have a date?"

Sam and Jeff had gone to their prom alone, because Sam had insisted on it, forcing Jeff to meet up with Daphne at the dance rather than invite her to share their limo. She felt vaguely guilty about that, now that she and Daphne knew each other better. Daphne had been surprisingly helpful earlier this year, when Sam was struggling with her new role as heir.

"I didn't go to prom, actually," Marshall admitted.

"Really? I would've thought you were elected prom king."

"That would require campaigning for votes, which requires *effort*. I was too busy surfing and bending the rules to really care."

"Of course, you're just a simple surfer bro at heart," Sam teased.

They leaned back, both increasingly aware of all the places their bodies were touching—Sam's head dipping onto Marshall's shoulder, the length of her leg pressed against his.

"I missed you this summer," Sam blurted out, and swallowed. "I just . . . Marshall, I . . ."

He stared at her for a moment, probably trying to figure out what she was asking. "I missed you, too, Sam."

"At least the League of Kings conference is here in Orange," she added, a little flustered. "I'll get to see you whenever I have time off."

"I'm excited about the opening ceremonies this weekend."

Marshall, along with five other young noblemen, had been named one of the lords attendant.

The wind picked up, loosening a few strands of hair from Sam's ponytail. Marshall brushed them gently aside. She looked up at him, and something so bright and buoyant filled her chest that it nearly stopped her breath.

Samantha, who'd spent years quietly building a wall around her heart, who'd dealt in flirtation and innuendo rather than real emotion, had finally let someone past her guard.

Before the truth could spill out of her, she pulled Marshall into a kiss.

He shifted on the bench, one of his hands tangling in her hair, another closing over her shoulder. Sam shut her eyes and let a single thought thrum through her, as insistent as her heartbeat.

She was in love with him.

3

DAPHNE

Daphne Deighton was in her element.

Tonight's event in the ballroom of the Waldemere Hotel was a benefit—the Youth Charity League's annual gala—so it wasn't quite as glittering or exclusive as an *actual* court function. Plenty of the guests were wealthy bankers or business-people who had only purchased a table because they knew Prince Jefferson was a patron of YCL. You could tell they were commoners from the nervous, giggling glances they kept shooting his way, as if they'd never been in the same room as royalty before. Probably they hadn't.

Still, Daphne warmed a little beneath the attention. It just felt so good, standing in a cocktail dress next to the Prince of America, accepting the adulation that was her due. This was what she did best: socialize, charm people, and, of course, look beautiful.

Jefferson plucked two flutes of champagne from a passing tray and handed one to Daphne. He looked so handsome in his tuxedo, the only outward sign of his rank an American flag pin on the lapel. But even in a room full of men in tuxes, there was no mistaking which of them was the prince. There was an indefinable air of royalty about him, something in his profile or the tilt of his head, and maybe a newfound hint of responsibility, now that he'd been officially named Regent.

The palace had just made the announcement yesterday:

that while Beatrice and Samantha were at the League of Kings conference, Jefferson would serve as the Crown's representative in the capital. He wouldn't actually *rule*, of course; Beatrice would keep up with the real work of government remotely. Jefferson just had to show up at a few formal dinners and ribbon-cuttings, smile for the cameras.

And Daphne would be there at his side.

Jefferson smiled, lifting his champagne. "Congratulations, Daph. You deserve this."

"I haven't won yet," she reminded him, though she still clinked their glasses in a toast. The champagne's bubbles danced merrily toward the surface, matching her mood.

Tonight the Youth Charity League would announce their Person of the Year, an award granted to the student who'd contributed most to the organization during their time in high school. There were a few other hopefuls milling about the ballroom, but they were really only here for appearances' sake. Everyone knew the award was Daphne's. She'd been the chair of her local chapter for three years running and had logged a record number of volunteer hours.

It was the type of thing that would look great in a coffee-table book.

Because that was what people expected from a princess, wasn't it? No one wanted to know Daphne's real story: how she'd set her sights on Prince Jefferson at age fourteen and never looked back. She'd made mistakes along the way—had hurt her friend Himari, and slept with Ethan Beckett, Jefferson's best friend—but that was all in the past. Daphne had no intention of letting anyone learn the truth behind her impeccable facade, because she couldn't show anyone her real self, not even Jefferson. *Especially* not Jefferson.

If he ever discovered the things she'd done, he would walk away from her without a backward glance.

As Daphne lowered the champagne from her lips, she saw

Lady Gabriella Madison weaving through the crowds toward them, and fought to keep her smile from slipping.

Gabriella and Daphne had met their freshman year of high school. They hadn't overlapped for long: Gabriella had moved away over the holidays, once her father was appointed ambassador to France. Yet it had only taken a single semester to establish the two of them as vicious rivals.

Daphne was irritated to see that Gabriella looked better than ever after her four years abroad. She was beautiful in that indefinable rich-person way, with the translucent skin and shiny chestnut hair that only money could buy. Daphne recognized her column gown as one that had just debuted at Paris Fashion Week. Its sheer, cap-sleeved overlay was embroidered with dozens of tiny crystals, though in Gabriella's case they might actually have been diamonds.

"Your Highness. I've missed you," Gabriella purred, and curtsied before Jefferson.

She sank low enough, but Daphne noticed that she never bowed her head as etiquette demanded, keeping her eyes on Jefferson the entire time. Something about the bold way she held his gaze suggested that, in Gabriella's mind, she was meeting someone of her own rank at last.

"Gabriella! It's great to see you," Jefferson said, reaching out a hand. Gabriella was still looking directly at him, ignoring Daphne's presence.

Clearly nothing had changed in the last four years.

Daphne remembered when she'd run into Gabriella in line at the cafeteria's salad bar. "Gabriella, right? We're in Honors English together," Daphne had ventured. "I'm Daphne."

The other girl hadn't moved her head a fraction of an inch. She'd just turned aside and started talking to the student on her left, as if she couldn't be bothered to acknowledge Daphne's existence with so much as a look.

Later, when Daphne recounted the exchange to Himari,

her friend had snorted in derision. "She's afraid of you," Himari declared, but Daphne knew better. Gabriella didn't see her as a threat, at least not back then. She was just so excruciatingly snobby that she refused to interact with anyone she considered beneath her. And since she was a Madison—her father, Ambrose, was the tenth Duke of Virginia—*everyone* was beneath her, except the other families in the Old Guard, the thirteen original dukedoms created after the Revolutionary War. Plus, of course, the Washingtons themselves.

Daphne's father, Lord Peter Deighton, was the second Baronet Margrave. Which meant that Daphne was too far down the aristocratic hierarchy for Gabriella to bother with.

"Welcome back, Gabriella." Daphne forced herself to smile pleasantly.

Gabriella looked over as if she'd just noticed her standing there. "Daphne. How lovely to see you." There was a syrupy insincerity to her words that grated on Daphne's nerves. Couldn't Jefferson hear it?

"How was France?" she asked.

Gabriella waved a hand dismissively. "You know how the French are. Oh, Jeff, I have *great* news." She turned back to the prince, looking up at him with thick-lashed eyes. "I'm starting at King's College with you next week! We'll be classmates again."

"That's awesome," Jefferson said warmly.

"How exciting that we'll all be reunited," Daphne cut in. She was starting at King's College this year, too. The timing worked out nicely: since Jefferson had taken a gap year, they would be entering in the same class.

"You're not living on campus, are you?" Gabriella asked the prince, as if Daphne hadn't spoken.

"Maybe later this year. Beatrice wants me at the palace as long as I'm her deputy in the capital."

"*Same.* The minute I saw the dorms, I told my parents I

would be staying at home. Communal showers?" Gabriella shuddered dramatically. "Whatever, by next year we'll be living in the frat and sorority houses anyway."

Daphne felt strangely uncomfortable, hearing her own thoughts voiced by Gabriella. She'd been relieved when Jefferson had told her that he wasn't living on campus, because it made her own decision seem a little more normal. There was no way she could room with a stranger or use a coed bathroom.

Not because she thought it was disgusting, as Gabriella clearly did, but because it was too risky. Daphne was a future princess; she couldn't afford to let anyone get close to her. What if they sold unflattering photos of her to the tabloids?

Though a small, unruly part of her wondered what it would be like to actually have a real college experience.

One of the waitstaff began to circle the room, ringing a chime that signaled the beginning of dinner. Daphne started toward the sign that read TABLE ONE, but Gabriella swept ahead of her.

"Oh, Jeff, look! We're at the same table." Gabriella slid into the seat next to Jefferson's as if this whole thing had come as a surprise, but Daphne wasn't fooled. She knew a calculated move when she saw one.

Throughout the dinner, Daphne's attempts to talk with Jefferson were consistently interrupted by Gabriella, who kept edging Daphne out of the conversation. Eventually Daphne gave up and chatted with Sandra Su, assistant director of the Youth Charity League. It was easy to half listen to Sandra's stories while keeping a cautious ear pricked toward Gabriella and Jefferson.

"By the way," Gabriella was saying, "I ran into Anne the last time I was in Vienna! You'll have to come with us the next time we do Oktoberfest. She has access to the most *exclusive* tents, the ones that serve champagne instead of just beer."

"Anne Devonshire was at Oktoberfest?" Jefferson asked, and Gabriella gave him a playful shove.

"Anne *Esterhazy*, of course!" Gabriella leaned forward. "Though I did see Anne Devonshire at Princess Maria's wedding. Everyone missed you *so* much. . . ."

It went on and on like that. Gabriella mentioned von Hohenbergs and Lamballes, Rochechouarts and Romanovs: families that had been noble since the Renaissance, since the *Crusades*. In the game of name-dropping, these were high stakes indeed.

Daphne, with her pitiful little two-generation baronetcy, could never hope to keep up.

Her spirits brightened when the waiters began serving dessert, and the chairman of YCL headed up to the podium. Daphne waited throughout the welcome and the obligatory slideshow demonstrating all the charity's good works, until finally it arrived. Her moment to shine.

"I'm so honored to be naming the Youth Charity League's Person of the Year." The chairman reached up to adjust his glasses, shifted his weight. "This year's recipient is a very special young woman. She continues to inspire us all with her dedication and overwhelming generosity. . . ."

Daphne discreetly tucked her feet to the side of the chair, nudging her gown to one side so that she wouldn't trip over it when she stood. She tilted her face upward, ensuring that the photographer in the corner would catch her most flattering angle—

"Gabriella Madison," the chairman finished.

An involuntary cry of surprise left Daphne's lips, though she quickly covered it with a breathless "Congratulations!" Hopefully, no one had heard beneath the applause.

Gabriella floated gracefully up to the microphone and lifted a hand to her chest, her eyes fluttering as if she were overcome with emotion. "Thank you. I'm so very honored."

Daphne watched, her face contorted into a smile, as the other girl accepted the recognition that should have been hers. It didn't make sense. Gabriella hadn't even been in the country; how could she have swooped in and stolen Daphne's award?

"I'm sorry." Sandra leaned in, her voice barely a whisper. "I'm not supposed to tell you this, but the Duke of Virginia made a large donation earlier today, with the understanding that, in exchange, his daughter would win this year's award."

"Of course," Daphne managed, and Sandra let out a relieved breath.

"Thank you, Daphne. I knew you would understand! Besides, it's about the charity, isn't it? This was never meant to be a competition."

What an utterly stupid thing to say. *It's not a competition* was something that losers told themselves after they lost.

As she watched Gabriella simpering up there onstage, Daphne reminded herself that it didn't matter. So what if Gabriella wanted to buy her way into the spotlight? She didn't have the one thing that really mattered—Prince Jefferson.

Daphne glanced down at the signet ring on her right hand, blazoned with the Washington family crest. It was so small, just a hunk of engraved metal, yet it was the most powerful thing she owned. This ring marked her as a member of the innermost circle of influence.

Of course it was a competition. Everything was a competition.

And right now, Daphne was winning.

4

NINA

"I can't believe you convinced me to live in the Chalet," Nina teased, propping open the door for her friend Rachel Greenbaum.

Technically their dorm was named Chalmondrey Hall, but it had always been known around campus as the Chalet. In a school full of Gothic buildings, of gabled ceilings and towering spires and gargoyles, Chalmondrey Hall was the most supremely Gothic of all. It had the iconic stone turret—the one featured in all the King's College brochures, and on the website—which actually housed three dorm rooms, one on each floor.

Rachel set down her bags and twirled around, arms outstretched. "We have a window seat! *And* a spiral staircase! Tell me this isn't your dream room."

"It does feel like something out of a fantasy novel. Like we're princesses in a tower—"

Nina broke off awkwardly, and Rachel pretended not to notice. It just didn't feel right, joking about being a princess when you'd once dated a prince.

"Although the bathroom situation is less than ideal," Nina went on in an upbeat tone. Their room occupied the third floor; the nearest ladies' room was three stories down, on the ground level. Apparently whoever built the turret hadn't installed indoor plumbing.

"Totally worth it," Rachel insisted. "Besides, think of how

fantastic you'll look in your jeans from going up and down the stairs so often."

Nina suppressed a smile. She didn't actually mind the stairs; she was just grateful to be living with her friends. After all the drama of last year, she could use a fresh start.

Rachel seemed to be thinking along the same lines, because she lowered her voice and asked, "So, have you talked to Ethan or Jeff yet?"

"You know Ethan's in Malaysia," Nina said quickly, ignoring the second half of Rachel's question.

She and Ethan hadn't spoken for most of the summer. When he'd finally reached out, Nina had felt a pleasant warmth at the sight of his incoming call—and that was it. Not the giddy rush of excitement she'd once felt at the prospect of talking to Ethan.

She may have forgiven him—she knew Ethan was a good person, despite what he'd done to her—but she didn't want to date him again.

Last year, Ethan had started flirting with Nina at *Daphne*'s request, to help keep Nina away from Jeff. Even though Ethan had begun to care about her for real, Nina couldn't get over the way it had all started. She expected such manipulative behavior from Daphne, but not from Ethan.

When Ethan had explained his plans to go abroad, Nina had told him she was glad for him. She hoped he got what he wanted out of this, whatever it was: adventure, perspective, a fresh start.

She and Rachel turned as the door swung open to admit their third roommate, Jayne Chu.

"Look what I found at the bookstore," Jayne announced, unrolling a poster for the new *Pride and Prejudice* remake. Nina laughed, but Rachel was vehemently shaking her head.

"No way. We can't have Mr. Darcy hanging in our common room!"

"What do you have against Darcy?" Jayne climbed onto the couch and held the poster against the wall, leaning back to check the placement.

Rachel reached for the edge of the poster and tugged at it. "When people come over here for parties, I want them to see something sophisticated. Like a black-and-white photo. Or something vintage! Not some random Victorian dude in tights."

"He's *Edwardian*, and they're *hose*, thank you very much."

Nina started rolling her suitcase into the larger of the bedrooms, the one that contained two twin beds, but Jayne interrupted. "Nina—Rachel and I talked about it, and we think you should take the single."

Nina glanced over in surprise. "Are you sure?"

Rachel let go of the Darcy poster and its edge furled up, so that only half of Darcy's waistcoat was visible. "Definitely. I'd get claustrophobia in a room that small. Why did they build it in the first place?"

"For the valet," Nina said, unthinking. When her friends both looked at her, she shrugged. "Back when King's College was for men only, aristocrats brought their menservants to school with them, to . . . I don't know, do their laundry and fasten their cuff links."

Rachel snorted. "By all means, if you feel like doing my laundry, go for it."

The three of them peered into the tiny second bedroom, which barely fit a twin bed and narrow set of shelving. There wasn't even a window.

"It's perfect," Nina declared.

"Great, it's all yours." Rachel grabbed Nina's bag from the common room and rolled it through the doorway. "Now can we please get lunch? I'm starving."

As they started outside, Nina caught sight of the enormous bronze lions at the front of Edwards Hall, which housed the university's main offices. Her steps slowed. "I need to drop something off at the registrar," she told her roommates. "I'll catch up with you inside."

"We'll save a spot for you," Jayne promised.

It was cool inside Edwards Hall, the walls lined with somber portraits of men in academic robes. Honestly, it felt a little like being in the palace. Nina started toward the registrar's office.

"Nina?"

She froze. This couldn't be happening.

"Jeff. Hi," she said clumsily.

Nina had known that Jefferson was starting at King's College now that his gap year was over, but she hadn't expected to run into him. After all, there were thousands of other students on this campus.

Apparently, she wasn't that lucky.

The prince shifted his weight. "Um, how have you—"

"I've been—"

Nina gestured for the prince to go ahead, and he swallowed. "It's been a while since I've seen you, Nina. How are things?"

"I'm good," she said carefully.

It was surreal, seeing Jeff after everything that had happened. Nina had known him since they were children, had spent years loving him in secret, then *dated* him in secret . . . only to date his best friend after she and Jeff broke up.

Now, finally, Nina was single again. And she intended to stay that way.

"I'm just dropping something off at the registrar," she went on, not sure why she was explaining herself, except to prove that she hadn't *followed* him here.

"Are you switching majors or something?" Jeff asked, and she shook her head.

"I need departmental approval for this seminar that I'm taking."

"Really? Why?"

Nina felt a bit sheepish as she replied, "It's a graduate course on Gothic literature."

The prince laughed. "Why am I not surprised."

"It meets in the basement of the library!" Nina hadn't even known there were classrooms down there, and she knew the library better than most.

"And you *want* to take a class that meets in the basement." There was a note of good-natured teasing in Jeff's voice that reminded her of how things used to be, back when they had simply been friends. It gave Nina the courage to keep their conversation going.

"What about you? What brought you to the registrar's office?"

Now it was Jeff's turn to look embarrassed. "I was meeting with my academic advisor."

That didn't make sense. There weren't any faculty offices in Edwards Hall, except . . . "Is *Dr. Hale* your advisor?"

He shifted self-consciously. "She insisted on it—she said that she's such a good family friend, she wouldn't feel comfortable off-loading me onto anyone else. . . ."

"I get it," Nina assured him, fighting to hide her amusement. Of *course* the university president had decided to personally oversee Jeff's academics. It was always like this with Jeff: he was so excruciatingly privileged that it should have been easy to resent him, except he somehow made that impossible. He was too good-natured, too guileless.

"Actually, Nina, I'm glad I bumped into you," Jeff told her. "Do you have a minute?"

She nodded, and he pushed open the nearest door, revealing an empty conference room. Had Jeff known it was empty, or had he just assumed that anyone in there would go away once he asked?

She pulled out a chair and sat, but Jeff remained on his feet. He wandered over to the window, pulled back the shade to peer out, then let it fall again.

"I'm sorry, Nina. The last time we talked, I said some unfair things."

Jeff had gotten angry with her for dating his best friend, especially for keeping it a secret from him. Not that it mattered anymore, anyway. Nina and Ethan were over, and by all accounts, Jeff was back with his ex-girlfriend Daphne. He'd apparently even given her his signet ring.

If Jeff wanted to date a backstabbing social climber, that was his problem.

"You and Ethan are two of my favorite people in the world," he went on. "Not that you need my approval, of course, but I'm happy for you. I should have said that from the beginning." He shifted awkwardly. "Maybe, if it's not too weird, we can all hang out someday? When Ethan is back, I mean."

The hopeful look on Jeff's face melted Nina's lingering resentment. She traced a circle on the surface of the conference table, avoiding his gaze.

"Thank you for saying that. But Ethan and I are just friends now."

"Oh. I wasn't sure," Jeff said clumsily. "I mean, Ethan didn't mention you when we talked, but I thought that was because . . ."

He trailed off before saying *because you and I used to date.* Nina flinched. Honestly, there should be some kind of law protecting you from having to discuss one ex-boyfriend with another.

"I'm sorry," Jeff said again. "Believe it or not, I really was rooting for you guys."

Since this conversation was already so uncomfortable that she had nothing to lose, Nina turned the focus back to Jeff. "I heard that you and Daphne are back together."

"We are." Jeff seemed visibly relieved at the mention of Daphne, as if the topic were a Band-Aid that had needed to be ripped off. "Things with Daphne are good. Great, actually."

Nina mumbled something that sounded vaguely like "Good for you."

It had been easy not to care about Jeff's love life when Nina was following along on the internet, same as the rest of America. It was harder to accept when he was right here, telling Nina how "great" his relationship was. He'd fallen for Daphne's act hook, line, and sinker.

Even if Nina wanted to intervene—which she didn't— there was nothing she could do to change his mind. She had tried to tell Jeff the truth about Daphne once before, and he hadn't believed her.

He sank down in the chair across the table. "I've been thinking," he went on. "Now that we're at the same school, and will probably keep running into each other, we should try again."

"Try again?" *But*—

"To be friends."

Right, of course. Jeff hadn't meant that they should try again *romantically*. Nina shifted in the stiff wooden chair, wondering why her mind had jumped there.

She looked across the conference table and had the disorienting sense of seeing all the different versions of him, layered one atop the other. There was Prince Jefferson George Alexander Augustus, the man who appeared on stages before a frenzied, screaming crowd, who was born to unimaginable wealth and titles. And then there was Jeff, the boy who'd once been Nina's friend.

She thought of all the years they'd spent together as children. Back then Jeff had been her partner in crime, her co-conspirator, the one who could talk Nina into whatever elaborate scheme Samantha had come up with, then talk all of them out of trouble. She was surprised how much she missed that version of him.

"Friends." The word felt natural on her lips, and she smiled. "I'd like that."

5

BEATRICE

The flurry of preparations this week had proven overwhelming, even for Beatrice, who had a lifetime of experience with stressful events.

All week the private airstrip up the coast had surged with activity as planes landed from Mumbai, Mexico City, Oslo. Bystanders lined the streets, cheering the fleet of private cars that whisked foreign royals onto a ferry or helicopter to Bellevue. Beatrice didn't know what she would've done without Sam and Teddy. It was especially sweet of Teddy to stay with her throughout the conference. Since he wasn't the monarch or her heir, he couldn't attend the actual sessions, but he was welcome at all the unofficial events and social gatherings. "I'm excited to work on my tan and go sailing," he'd jested, but Beatrice knew the real reason he was here: because she had asked.

When she'd said as much, Teddy's expression had grown serious. "Of course that's why I'm staying. I'd do anything for you, Bee."

And he had, hadn't he? He'd given up *everything* for her. In agreeing to marry her, Teddy had effectively promised to renounce his own title and succession rights. Now his brother Lewis would be Duke of Boston someday, while Teddy was a future king consort.

It was the same choice Beatrice's mother had made almost

thirty years ago, signing away her rights as a future duchess once she married George. One could not rule a duchy and be America's queen consort—or king consort—at the same time. That would involve a clear conflict of interest.

The orchestra at the front of the hall died down, jolting Beatrice back to the present. The opening ceremonies had arrived at last.

Samantha stood behind her, holding the end of Beatrice's purple train. Beatrice was supposed to enter the great hall, where all the foreign royals would be waiting. Yet her muscles seemed to have frozen.

"Bee?" Sam whispered. When her sister didn't answer, Sam dropped the cloak and took a few steps forward. "You okay?"

"I don't know."

When she walked down that central aisle, Beatrice wouldn't be appearing as herself. She would be standing on the world's stage as the representative of America.

Sam reached for her hands. Even though they were both wearing gloves, Beatrice felt the warmth of her sister's skin through the leather. "You've spent your whole life preparing for this moment, Bee. If Dad was here, he would remind you that you're ready."

The mention of their father strengthened Beatrice's resolve. She nodded to the nearby footman, who sprang forward to open the doors.

Beatrice was decked out in the full honors and regalia of her position—dressed for battle, as their dad used to say. The bodice of her pale blue gown gleamed with so many medals that it resembled the breastplate of a medieval knight. Dozens of pins dug into her scalp, anchoring the heavy Imperial State Crown atop her updo.

A carved throne normally sat in this reception hall. There

was a throne in each of the Washingtons' residences, even the ski house, in case the monarch ever needed to hold an unexpected audience or conference. But today the throne had been conspicuously removed, the room filled with rows of gilt chairs where the foreign royals were now seated. There were never thrones at the League of Kings. The whole point of a multinational organization was that no single nation could sit in precedence over the others.

Beatrice felt Samantha walking behind her, holding the train of the ermine-trimmed cloak with both hands. After Sam, the six ladies-in-waiting would process in a line, followed by the lords attendant, who would each hold an artifact on a velvet pillow: the Rod of Gold, the Orb of State, King Benjamin's sword. These were items normally on display in the Crown Jewels collection, which had been transported to Bellevue under armored guard.

At the front of the room, Beatrice turned, letting Samantha drop her cloak so that it curled dramatically around the hem of her gown. The ladies-in-waiting and lords attendant bowed and curtsied, one after the other in succession, then retreated.

"Your Majesties," Beatrice began. "It is my honor to inaugurate this twenty-fourth meeting of the League of Kings. I welcome you here in the spirit of international cooperation, and I pray that the blessing of Almighty God may fall upon our counsels."

From the back of the hall came the unmistakable clatter of horse's hooves. And then: "Hear ye, hear ye! All rise for the standard of the League of Kings!"

Lord Ambrose Madison, newly returned from his ambassadorship to France, trotted into the hall astride a white horse. His daughter Gabriella had been one of the ladies-in-waiting. Ambrose held the League of Kings flag in one hand, its pole wedged firmly in his right stirrup. Beatrice would have offered this position to Teddy, if only because she'd have liked to see him ride a horse inside a palace, but as head of the Madison family, Lord Ambrose was hereditary Queen's Champion. And protocol was protocol.

In this case, protocol was faintly ridiculous. Beatrice remembered how the horse at the last conference had left a trail of droppings in its wake. "Why do we present the flag on horseback?" she'd asked her father, who had laughed. "Beatrice, kings love pomp and circumstance. It's how they convince themselves that they're entitled to rule over mere mortals." King George had placed his hands on her shoulders, suddenly serious. "Never forget that our family doesn't rule because of these ceremonies. Our position is a privilege granted by the American people, and one that we must earn every day. When you start to believe all the myths about yourself . . . that's when monarchs make mistakes."

She watched as Lord Ambrose trotted to the front of the room, waving the League of Kings flag back and forth. At least he had a flair for showmanship.

The doors swung open once more, and a final figure made her way down the reception hall: Empress Mei Ling of China, who'd hosted the last League of Kings conference at her summer palace in Hainan. She was even more formidable than Beatrice remembered, her snow-white hair swept into a severe bun. In her hands she held a stone basin, about the size of a dinner plate.

This was the most sacred part of the entire ritual: the transfer of the Cauldron of Peace.

As the empress approached, Beatrice stared into the basin at the eternal flame. Its light curled and danced over the oil at the base of the cauldron. How humbling to think that this same fire had been burning for over a century, since her great-great-great-great-grandfather had been king.

The empress's voice was thin but unwavering. "Your Majesty. With the passing of this cauldron, I hand you the care and keeping of our great assembly."

"May the light of its eternal flame shine forth, as the light of our knowledge and goodwill lights the world," Beatrice recited.

She'd rehearsed this moment for weeks, using a porcelain vase in place of the cauldron. Beatrice swallowed and held out her hands.

Then the empress was passing her the cauldron, and Beatrice was trying not to stagger beneath its weight. Oh *god*. Forget training with a vase; she should have used a kettlebell. Why had she agreed to wear four-inch heels? Her grip was slipping, the cauldron was about to shatter on the floor—

She managed to loop an arm beneath its base and nearly fainted from relief. Except, she realized, something was very wrong.

The light had blown out.

"They're laughing at me." Beatrice had changed out of the Imperial State Crown and into the Winslow tiara, so her head felt pleasantly light again, except that it was currently pounding with mortification.

"No one's laughing at you," Teddy assured her, just as Samantha said, "So what if they are?"

Teddy and Sam exchanged a glance that Beatrice would have found amusing under different circumstances.

"Look, Bee. Laughing at me is practically the national pastime," Sam went on. "I can tell you from experience that people will lose interest and forget about it. There's no use worrying."

Beatrice wished it were that easy. She'd always envied

Sam's confidence in the face of defeat, her unapologetic bold-ness. But Beatrice just wasn't wired that way.

She sighed and leaned over the railing. The three of them had stepped out onto the balcony, ostensibly to get some air, but everyone in the ballroom had seen it for what it was: a strategic retreat.

Moonlight danced over the surface of the water. The crash of the surf was as steady as the exhalations of a sleeping giant. Perhaps that was why Beatrice always found the ocean so calming: the waves stopped for nothing, not even her first great failure as queen.

"I can't believe I did that. The eternal flame has been lit since the nineteenth century," she moaned, and Teddy shook his head.

"No way. It was definitely blown out a few times over the years."

"I'm sure the French spilled wine on it at some point and relit it with a cigarette lighter," Sam agreed.

Beatrice gave a strangled laugh. "Thank you," she told them both, then glanced regretfully back at the windows. "I guess we should head inside."

The ballroom of Bellevue felt like a medieval tapestry come to life. The mirrored arches along one wall matched the windows along the other, which overlooked the Pacific. Chan-deliers glittered like diamonds, casting everything in a golden light—all the opulent turbans and tiaras, precious gemstones pulled from Crown Jewels collections and museum display cases. Some of the older kings wore a painfully traditional form of court dress, complete with lace ruffles at their wrists and ceremonial swords buckled to their waists. The younger ones had opted for a less antiquated look, though their braided coats and epaulets were still worn with a sword.

How pointless, Beatrice thought. A room full of men armed with weapons that not a single one of them could actually wield. Unlike the women, who had nothing to defend themselves with but their wits.

She saw Empress Mei Ling a few yards away, her voice lowered conspiratorially as she said something to the Swedish queen. They both looked up at Beatrice's approach, then swiftly averted their eyes. Beatrice glanced frantically at King Frederick, but he too avoided looking in her direction. Beatrice felt as if she'd become a ghost at her own party.

Then a voice spoke behind her. "Ah, voilà! Here she is!"

Beatrice turned to greet Princess Louise of France, who was surrounded by a group of royals in their early to mid-twenties. There was Alexei, the tsarevich of Russia; his father, Dmitri, was one of the most intimidating and powerful people in this room. Beatrice had gone on a date with Alexei's brother Pieter once, only to leave when Pieter asked their waitress for her number.

There was Bharat, son of one of the maharajas of India, wearing a jaunty bow tie and a pair of square-framed glasses. He would have taken Beatrice on a date, too, like most every prince within a decade of her age, except that he'd come out at age twelve.

There was Princess Sirivannavari of Thailand, wearing a shockingly short skirt and pouting into her cocktail. She seemed more social-media celebrity than future ruler to Beatrice: she posted makeup tutorials, and videos of her *shoe collection*. Perhaps she was trying to be approachable, Beatrice thought generously. Though that was probably giving Siri too much credit.

And then there was Louise, Princess of France.

Beatrice would have died rather than admit it, but she'd always been intimidated by Louise. There was something proud and distinctly aloof about her, even now, as she surveyed the room with detached interest. They'd crossed paths a number of times over the years, yet Beatrice had always been too nervous to say much, though she and Louise had a lot in common. Both were the first female monarchs of their respective nations, and both had lost the guidance of their fathers far too young.

King Louis XXIII had fallen ill several years ago, leaving his daughter to rule as Regent in his stead. The French were notoriously tight-lipped about his health, though he must have suffered from something extreme, a mental illness or life-threatening injury. Beatrice had a feeling that if King Louis were in any condition to rule, even from his hospital bed, he would.

At the last League of Kings conference in Hainan, Princess Louise had been a stylish twenty-three-year-old, while Beatrice had just graduated from high school. Five years later, Louise was as glamorous as ever, with her dark mascara and languid voice. Her light blond hair had been pulled into a high ponytail, a bit like the way Sam usually wore it, except that Sam's ponytails always looked sporty, whereas Louise's projected a sort of regal insouciance.

Inevitably, the world had been comparing Beatrice and Louise ever since they were children. When Beatrice gave her first public address at age ten, the international media immediately played clips of it alongside Louise's. When Beatrice had briefly dated Prince Nikolaos of Greece, the tabloids all reminded her that he'd gone out with Louise first, so Beatrice was only getting her French counterpart's sloppy seconds. Most popular were the "Who Wore It Better?" features, where both women had on the same item of clothing: a red luncheon dress, a black one-shouldered gown. Louise always looked so slinky and chic that Beatrice seemed distinctly boring by comparison.

Their personas had only crystallized as they grew older. Louise's image was all art and culture and European sophistication—sponsoring a masked ball at the Louvre, skiing at St. Anton with her other royal friends—while Beatrice remained studious and thoughtful and *wholesome*.

Sometimes Beatrice couldn't help thinking that Louise's way of doing things looked a lot more fun.

"*Votre Altesse Royale,*" Beatrice said now, in answer to Louise's greeting.

"Please, we can speak English! We are in your home, Béatrice." Louise pronounced it like a French word, Bey-ah-*treece*, drawing out each syllable as if she relished the sound of her own voice.

It was a definite breach in protocol, using Beatrice's first name without being invited to, but for once Beatrice didn't mind.

There was an indefinable magnetism to Louise. Beatrice had *grown* into her position, in an ungainly and sometimes painful way, but she couldn't help thinking that Louise would have been a leader even if she hadn't been born a princess. When she turned her pale blue eyes on you, it felt like stepping into the glow of a spotlight.

"It's been so long. Since last year's Soirée Bleue, I think?" Beatrice ventured.

The other young royals were pretending not to listen, but Beatrice saw their eyes darting back and forth between her and Louise as if they were watching the volley and return of a tennis match.

"Ah, yes. The event celebrating the *Mona Lisa.*" Louise lifted an eyebrow, challenging and slightly teasing. "You didn't believe me when I said the woman in the portrait is hiding a secret."

Beatrice remembered standing with Louise before the *Mona Lisa*—which, after that night, had been on loan to America for nearly a year—as they discussed what the subject of the portrait was thinking about. Louise had insisted that the woman had a forbidden lover, which Beatrice had thought was a bit of a stretch.

But that was before Beatrice had fallen for Connor, then ended things with him after her father died. She didn't think Louise's theory was so unreasonable anymore, now that Beatrice had experienced her own forbidden love. And hidden her fair share of secrets.

There was no possible way she could say any of that aloud, so she smiled politely. "Thank you for lending it to us. I know that millions of Americans are grateful they got to see the *Mona Lisa* in person."

"Art should always be experienced in person. Great art should be experienced more than once," Louise said sagely. "After all, it changes each time you see it, because you bring something different to the artwork each time. Don't you agree?"

For a fleeting instant, Louise looked the way she had at the Soirée Bleue, wistful or even vulnerable. Beatrice recalled what Louise had told her that night—that as a future queen, she needed to always hold a piece of herself back from the world, or else the world would consume her whole.

"Louise . . ."

The princess looked at her expectantly, and Beatrice fumbled, not sure what she wanted to say. "It's good to see you again." She was repeating herself; she sounded drunk, though she hadn't even taken a sip of wine. "I hope you know that we're all still praying for your father's recovery."

"Thank you," Louise cut in stiffly, and Beatrice realized that somehow she had said the wrong thing.

It had been like this at Harvard, the few times she'd tried to attend parties. Everyone else seemed to behave naturally, at ease with their surroundings, while she had to second-guess her every move. And still she kept on failing.

At times like that, Beatrice would shoot panicked glances at Connor, her Revere Guard. He always knew when to rush over with a fake security alert and insist that she leave.

Connor was gone, Beatrice reminded herself. She had let go of him when she'd told him that he should stop loving her—that she didn't need rescuing anymore. She was strong enough now to rescue herself.

She just needed to make herself believe it.

6

SAMANTHA

Samantha leaned against Marshall and swayed contentedly to the music. They were nearly alone on the dance floor, but then, this wasn't exactly a dancing crowd. Kings and queens rarely danced in public unless it was for a national dance, like the French gavotte or Russian polka. Monarchs hated to appear foolish, especially around other monarchs.

People kept looking over at her and Marshall. Sam could feel the weight of their glances: some curious, a few judgmental. *Whatever,* she thought, *let them stare.* Sam couldn't care less what a bunch of foreign royals thought about her relationship.

"Thanks for coming. I know this isn't your ideal way to spend a Friday night," she murmured. As one of the lords attendant, Marshall was required to attend tonight's welcome reception and the farewell ball, as well as the photo shoot later this month. The ladies-in-waiting and lords attendant would return to Bellevue in a few weeks, for the official pictures that would be printed on postcards and in coffee table books for years to come.

"I'm happy anywhere with you, Sam." A wicked glint entered Marshall's eyes. "Besides, it's kind of nice being the lowest-ranking person in the room for once. With all these kings and emperors around, I doubt anyone will notice if I misbehave."

Sam lifted an eyebrow. "What kind of misbehaving do you mean, exactly?"

"Red-wine pong, of course. What else would I have meant?" Marshall asked, all innocence.

"Of course. We should re-create your high school glory days." Sam nodded to the King of Serbia, or maybe it was Croatia, who'd stationed himself firmly at the door to the kitchens. Each time the butlers emerged with a new tray of hors d'oeuvres, the king grabbed an entire fistful. "We could recruit that guy. He seems like a red-wine pong dude for *sure*."

Marshall chuckled appreciatively, pulling Sam closer. A golden pin shaped like a grizzly bear, the emblem of the Dukes of Orange, gleamed on his chest.

"By the way, Aunt Margaret's latest movie is premiering next week," Sam went on. "Beatrice can't get away from the conference, so she asked me to go. Will you come with me?"

Sam's aunt Margaret had always delighted in breaking the rules and stirring up trouble. She'd moved to Orange years ago, married a relatively unknown actor ten years her junior, and started producing and financing movies—usually starring her husband.

"You know I'd never miss a chance to see an Aunt Margaret movie." Marshall grinned. "Let me guess, it's a bodice-ripping epic starring your uncle Nate as the swashbuckling hero?"

Aunt Margaret's movies were usually based on books, and since the only books she read were steamy historical romances, Sam's uncle Nate had been cast as more soldiers, cowboys, roguish dukes, and kilt-wearing Scotsmen than anyone could keep track of.

Sam rolled her eyes. "I assume so. It's called *Stowaway*."

"Wait, I've seen the posters for this! It's a pirate movie. I'll wear my Hawaiian shirt to the premiere," Marshall exclaimed, delighted.

"If I'm forced to wear a cocktail dress, the least you can do is put on a button-down in solidarity."

"Sorry, you get one night of formal Marshall per week." He winked. "The rest of the time, you're stuck with regular old Hawaiian-shirt-wearing Marshall."

Sam tried to sound offended, but she couldn't keep the laughter from her voice. "Sometimes I think you're being difficult just to provoke me."

"Of course I am. But I make up for it with my devastating good looks and quick wit."

"And your humility," Sam teased.

Marshall swept an arm toward the rest of the room. "Just think, you could've had one of these nice, bland, well-behaved princes instead. Like that guy," he said, nodding at the Crown Prince of Japan. "Or that guy," he added, indicating Prince James of Canada.

Seeing the gesture, Jamie caught Sam's gaze and grinned devilishly. She rolled her eyes, then turned back to Marshall. "You're right. None of those princes would argue with me the way you do, or wear ugly Hawaiian shirts in public, or drunkenly sing the wrong words to 'Beer for My Horses'—"

"My words are *so* much better than the original," Marshall interjected.

"And yet here I am," Sam finished in a softer tone. "I'm not going anywhere, Marshall."

She'd never belonged with one of those guys: the type who would have nodded and agreed with anything she said, because she was a princess and they hated controversy. She *liked* that Marshall pushed her buttons. He challenged her and teased her and made her a better version of herself.

Marshall's eyes met hers. "Glad to hear it, my gordita."

"Your what?" Sam blinked. Surely her boyfriend hadn't just called her fat.

"Gordita! I like you more than a Cheesy Gordita Crunch."

At her expression, he clarified his remark. "Please tell me you've eaten Taco Bell. If not, I'm stealing one of the palace cars and taking you on a field trip this minute."

I like you more than a Cheesy Gordita Crunch. That was far less of a statement than the three words that kept fluttering insistently in Sam's chest.

Before she could reply, Marshall took a step back and pulled his phone from his pocket. He scanned the screen, cursing softly under his breath, then lifted his eyes to hers.

"I'm so sorry. I knew Kelsey was a loose cannon, but I didn't think . . ."

People were staring, and whatever was going on, Sam had a feeling that it shouldn't be overheard. She grabbed Marshall's elbow and led him out the double doors along the side of the ballroom.

A few stray royals were gathered out on the terrace; they took one look at Sam's expression and skittered inside. Sam stalked over to the iron balcony with a sigh. To her right she could see the stone roofs of the guest cottages, which were scattered below like toy houses in a game of Monopoly. Each of them had a name: Two Step, Summer Camp, or Sam's favorite, called simply the White House.

She turned back to Marshall, who'd come to stand next to her, his expression somewhere between angry and regretful. "What's going on?"

"Kelsey gave an exclusive interview to some tabloid," he explained. "Normally I get a warning about stuff like this, but apparently the magazine kept it under wraps."

"Your ex-girlfriend Kelsey?"

Wordlessly, Marshall handed Sam his phone. The headline read KELSEY BROOKE'S WILD REVELATIONS ABOUT LORD MARSHALL DAVIS AND PRINCESS SAMANTHA!

At first, Sam didn't even scroll down to read these so-called wild revelations. She was too busy staring at the photo of Kelsey, who was just so unfairly gorgeous. *All* of Marshall's exes were gorgeous. Until Sam he'd only ever dated models and starlets, each a size zero, with long shiny hair and big doe eyes. Samantha was many things, but conventionally beautiful wasn't one of them.

It was hard not to feel insecure about that sometimes.

When Sam scrolled down and began reading, her eyes widened. "Kelsey really hates us, doesn't she?"

"She hates *me*. I'm afraid you're just collateral damage," Marshall apologized. "She's desperate to be famous, and she used to date the princess's boyfriend. Of course she was going to make up a bunch of garbage for some stupid interview."

Kelsey certainly hadn't held anything back. She called Samantha and Marshall "the most spoiled, self-obsessed people I've ever met." *You hardly met me at all,* Sam wanted to cry out. *We spoke for two minutes in a bathroom!* But it was Kelsey's next accusation that made her blood run cold.

She claimed that Marshall and Samantha weren't in a relationship at all; they were just pretending to date because they craved the spotlight. According to Kelsey, Samantha was jealous of her older sister and wanted to "steal attention from Beatrice." Marshall, too, apparently just wanted the fame that came with dating a princess.

It sickened Sam, mostly because there was a kernel of truth beneath all the invective and lies.

"How did Kelsey know that when we started dating, it was all for show?"

"She doesn't know anything. She's just firing shots at random, trying to see what gets a reaction out of people. I'm sorry," Marshall said again, typing furiously on his phone. "I'm getting my family's lawyer to sue her for slander."

"Don't." Sam held out her hand, forcing him to fall still.

"She's a liar!"

Marshall shoved his phone back into his pocket and leaned forward, staring out at the vast expanse of ocean. It made Sam think back to the night they'd met: at the G&A Museum, when they had been out on the balcony, both avoiding the party. So much had happened since then. So much had *changed*.

"Kelsey is a minor TV actress on a show that wasn't even renewed for next season. No one cares what she thinks," Sam assured him. "Let it go."

"That's easier for you than for me," he said softly.

Sam hated how much pain was wrapped up in that statement. She hated that Marshall was judged more harshly, simply because of the color of his skin—that people like Kelsey Brooke could accuse Sam and Marshall of dating to "shock" people. The implication being, of course, that dating Marshall was provocative because he was Black.

Most of all, she hated that America had proven Kelsey right.

Marshall had gotten far more attention than any of Sam's former romantic entanglements, more attention even than Daphne and Jeff. Some of it came from his reputation— his famous ex-girlfriends, his snarky humor, the fact that he was wealthy and titled and unbearably handsome—but race played a part in it, too. The nation wouldn't have reacted so vociferously if her sarcastic playboy boyfriend were *white*.

Sam attempted to lighten the mood. "You know this is all worthless clickbait. I mean, there have been so many ridiculous headlines about me. That I'm allergic to water—"

To her relief, Marshall cracked a smile. "That can't be a thing."

"That I have calf implants—"

"You do have excellent calves," he agreed, bending over as if he meant to lift the hem of her gown. She swatted him away.

"But hey," Sam added, now grinning mischievously, "if you're worried that people think we're fake dating, we can always make a sex tape."

"Somehow I doubt a sex tape would repair either of our reputations."

Sam shrugged. "I never said we have to release it."

Marshall laughed at that. "You're too much, Sam."

"Let's blow off the rest of this party. It's getting late anyway." She reached for his hand and pulled him back toward the door. "Have you seen the pool downstairs?"

"This house has an *indoor* pool too?" Marshall asked, momentarily distracted.

"It's Olympic-sized, and heated."

"I didn't bring a suit, though."

"Somehow I don't foresee that being a problem."

Marshall nodded. "Good point. I'm more hydrodynamic without swim trunks anyway. That's how the professional athletes train when they're racing at the Olympic Club."

"Racing? Is that what they call it these days?"

He laughed again, pulling her closer and dropping a quick kiss on her lips.

Samantha had never felt this way about anyone before—like she was grateful to the world simply because Marshall was in it, and at the same time like she wanted to make the world *better* because Marshall was in it.

She loved him. It was as simple as that. And Sam would do anything, would confront all the false accusations and prejudices in the world, to protect that love.

7

DAPHNE

Daphne stood before her full-length mirror, turning back and forth as she assessed her navy dress and cropped blazer. Would people think she was overdressed for freshman orientation? Maybe she should switch to jeans. Her mother always complained when Daphne wore denim—"Beatrice doesn't wear jeans in public," she would sniff—but the other students would probably look like they'd just rolled out of bed.

Daphne hated this sense of uncertainty. By now she knew how to dress and what to expect from all the myriad types of royal events, but college was entirely new territory, with a new group of people to win over. Some of her classmates might even become her friends, or at least as close to *friends* as Daphne could allow. Friendship required trust, which required showing someone who you really were.

Daphne couldn't afford to do that with anyone.

She started down the stairs, moving with slow, graceful steps. When she was a child Daphne used to take the stairs as fast as she could, until her mother had snapped: "Stop it! You clatter down the stairs like a thousand-pound elephant." Rebecca had promptly enrolled Daphne in an intensive ballet program, the kind meant for future professionals, taught by an old woman who screamed at them in Russian and whacked their legs with a cane if their form wobbled.

Daphne now walked down staircases like a queen, danced

53

as gracefully as a prima ballerina, and curtsied more beautifully than anyone at court.

"Daphne?"

Her mother sat in the living room, scrolling through something on her phone, probably the royal family's recent media coverage. Between Kelsey Brooke's tell-all about Samantha and Marshall and Beatrice's debacle with the eternal flame, the Washingtons weren't having a great week.

Daphne hadn't been all that surprised by the article about Samantha; Jefferson's twin was always embroiled in some scandal or another, even if most of them were made up. Samantha was just too controversial for the tabloids to resist.

But Beatrice's slipup had caught her off guard. It was like a highway accident that Daphne couldn't look away from; she kept tracking the latest hashtags and comments on social media. By now the image of Beatrice—standing there with an empty basin, looking utterly stricken—had been used in dozens of memes, everything from *When my date shows up and looks *nothing* like his profile picture* to *How I felt when I got stranded at the airport overnight.*

The blue light of the screen illuminated her mother's face from below, distorting her beautiful features into something eerie. Rebecca looked like her daughter in so many ways, with the same upturned nose and vivid green eyes, though her hair was blond instead of Daphne's rich red-gold. Sometimes when Daphne looked at her mother, she had the sense that she was staring through a fun-house mirror into the future, seeing herself thirty years from now. She didn't always like what she saw.

Daphne hesitated in the doorway. "I'm on my way to orientation. Can we talk later?"

"You're not going to orientation," her mother replied. "Sit down."

There was a flinty resolve in her tone that Daphne didn't dare contradict. She walked to the opposite armchair and perched on its cushion, tucking one ankle behind the other as if she were at a tea party rather than in her own home. The habits of protocol were deeply ingrained in her by this point. And it was impossible to relax around her mother.

"Our family is in trouble," Rebecca said without preamble.

"Financial trouble?"

There never seemed to be enough money in the Deighton household; they were always a mere breath ahead of their creditors, always outspending their means. Unlike the other girls at St. Ursula's—who could snap up a dozen couture gowns like they were a sleeve of macarons—Daphne cobbled together her wardrobe on a shoestring budget, through aggressive online shopping and monitoring of the sale rack. Once when Jefferson had given her an expensive handbag, Daphne bought a knockoff version of the same purse from a street vendor, then sold the real one to a resale shop. Jefferson would never know the difference, and she'd gotten three new cocktail dresses from the proceeds of that bag.

"Yes, we're in financial trouble, but that's the least of our worries," Rebecca said impatiently. "The real problem is that we might lose our title."

Everything went silent. There was no noise, no cars passing or wind whistling through the trees. It felt like the rest of the world had dissolved, like there was nothing and no one except the two of them, alone, in this house.

"Lose our title?" Daphne whispered.

"The Conferrals and Forfeiture Committee will review your father's case next month. If they find him guilty of ungentlemanly behavior, they'll strip him of his baronetcy."

"What did he *do?*"

Her mother sighed. "He gambled, Daphne. On you."

Daphne listened, stunned. Apparently, when she and Jefferson were broken up last year, the Vegas odds on a Daphne-Jefferson wedding had dropped from one in three to one in twenty. Peter Deighton couldn't resist those numbers.

"He placed the bet under a fake name. And he almost got away with it, until *People* did that feature on you last month and included a photo of our family. One of the bookies saw the picture and recognized him. He reported Peter's behavior to the gambling commission, which then reported it to the Duke of Virginia," her mother said wearily.

"Lord Ambrose Madison?" What did Gabriella's father have to do with this?

"He's chairman of the Conferrals and Forfeiture Committee." Rebecca drummed her red-painted nails against the side of the armchair. "Ambrose could have let it go, the way he would've done for one of his cronies. Those men always cover each other's backs, help each other hide things that are far worse than a bit of gambling," her mother said bitterly. "Instead, Ambrose submitted your father's title for formal review."

"Because he's as snobby and cruel as his daughter?"

"Because he and Peter have hated each other for years. You didn't know?" her mother asked, at Daphne's surprised look. "Why do you think Gabriella goes out of her way to attack you? Their family has always despised ours."

"I thought it was because we're . . ."

"Newly noble, yes," her mother finished for her. "Ambrose never forgave your father for daring to outshine him. He'd grown up as a future duke, praised since childhood for talent and brilliance that he didn't possess, and then Peter Deighton came along—a second-generation baronet, the lowliest title on the rung—and refused to suck up to Ambrose like everyone else did. If anything, I think your father poked fun at him for being awkward and ungainly." Rebecca lifted one shoulder in a shrug. "Obviously, Ambrose couldn't allow that."

Daphne pictured the Duke of Virginia as a teenager: the sort of self-important, red-faced boy who bragged loudly about his family's connections. She felt an unexpected pride in her father for refusing to kowtow to him.

"When you started dating Jefferson, it just about killed the Madisons," her mother went on. "The duke and duchess clearly assumed that Gabriella would be the one to become a princess."

Daphne's stomach turned. If she went from being the daughter of a baronet to an utter nobody, it would be much harder to marry into the royal family. No commoner had ever done it.

"Are you saying that the duke wants to revoke Father's baronetcy because of *me*? Because he wants to clear the way for Gabriella to make a move on Jefferson?"

"Revenge, spite, jealousy—why else does anyone do anything in politics?" her mother asked bluntly. "The Madisons think we've overreached, that you should never have presumed to date a Washington in the first place. Lord Ambrose wants to take us all down a peg."

Daphne gripped the edges of her chair until her knuckles turned white. "Gambling isn't illegal," she pointed out, and her mother gave a mirthless laugh.

"The committee isn't ruling on whether Peter's behavior was illegal, just whether it was ungentlemanly. In poor taste."

Daphne knew enough to be frightened. The Conferrals and Forfeiture Committee focused more on the conferrals part of their job—recommending candidates for knighthood to the sovereign—than on the forfeiture part. Still, they had stripped plenty of titles over the years. In the nineteenth century it had been for dramatic reasons: adultery, treason, even murder. These days the cause was usually embezzlement or tax evasion.

Or, apparently, gambling on your daughter's chances of becoming a princess.

"We have to stop this," Daphne thought aloud. "I can talk to Jefferson after class tomorrow, see if he can help."

"Absolutely not! You cannot mention this to anyone," Rebecca breathed. "We aren't even supposed to know that your father's nobility is up for review. The committee's deliberations are top secret."

Daphne decided not to ask how her mother had found out.

Rebecca leaned forward. "And you're not going to orientation, because you'll be withdrawing from King's College in a press conference tomorrow morning. Given all these recent developments, we can't afford the tuition."

"If we can't pay for college, I'll apply for financial aid," Daphne began, but her mother spoke over her.

"Don't be a fool, Daphne! If you apply for financial aid, people might learn how dire our position is. You *cannot* seem desperate. What if the press claims that you're dating Jefferson for the wrong reasons?"

They stared at each other for a long moment, both well aware of the reasons Daphne had started dating Jefferson.

"I don't understand. What happened to my college fund?" Daphne asked, and her mother's eyes narrowed.

"We spent it already—on *you*. Come on, Daphne, you must realize that you are the most expensive asset in our family's portfolio. We've been investing in you for years: your expensive private school; your clothes and salon treatments and orthodontia; the tickets to every charity gala you had to attend with the prince."

And we're ready to see a return on our investment, her mother didn't need to add.

Daphne was surprised to feel a stinging in her eyes, but she blinked it away; she knew better than to let herself cry in front of anyone. Least of all her mother.

"If you won't let me go to college, what am I supposed to do all year?"

Rebecca frowned at the question. "You'll keep doing exactly what you were doing before: dating the prince. Tell the reporters that you're taking a gap year to focus on charity work, if you think it sounds better."

Daphne strove to remain calm. "It's the twenty-first century. I doubt anyone will applaud me for just sitting around, waiting for Jefferson to propose."

"You've graduated from high school—which, by the way, is far more of an education than I ever got! Be realistic, Daphne. What were you planning to do with a college degree anyway? Cure cancer? Rebalance the national debt?" Her mother gave a dismissive laugh. "No one wants a nerd for their princess. They want a *lady*."

A *lady*. Like Lady Gabriella Madison. Someone who'd been born to all the titles and gowns.

Unlike Daphne, who'd plotted and schemed for everything she had, who'd gotten this far by relying on her wits.

Except . . . Daphne had been looking forward to college. Not just because it would keep her close to Jefferson, but for its own sake. Yesterday she had actually pulled out the course catalog and slapped pink Post-it notes on all the classes that interested her—a politics seminar on diplomatic strategy, a psychology class called Obsessions and Delusions. She'd imagined walking across campus, a tote bag of books slung over her shoulder, a cappuccino in hand.

She weighed that daydream against the image she'd been working toward all these years: herself wearing a tiara at last.

The tiara won out.

She'd come too far, sacrificed too much, to stop now. Even if it meant giving up on her chance to go to King's College.

This was Gabriella's fault, Daphne thought angrily. Lord Ambrose could so easily have looked the other way, given her father a freebie the way those aristocratic men all did for each other. They cheated on their spouses and committed insider trading, and then they all closed ranks and guarded each other's backs. Yet they wanted to attack her father for a bit of gambling that hadn't hurt anyone?

She would show them—Gabriella, Lord Ambrose, *all* of them—just how wrong they had been to underestimate Daphne Deighton.

8

NINA

Nina couldn't believe that she and Prince Jefferson were texting again.

It had started small. A few days ago, Jeff had sent a furtive photo of Professor Urquhart at the front of the lecture hall: *Doesn't he look like that guy from* A Christmas Carol?

Ebenezer Scrooge? When they were kids, Nina and the twins saw the play every year: His Majesty's Players performed it each Christmas, and Sam always asked Nina to watch it with her from the royal box.

No. This guy, Jeff had replied, and screenshotted the Ghost of Christmas Past: the one from the animated movie, with a long red beard and pointed nightcap. Nina had choked out a laugh. Come to think of it, there *was* a resemblance.

Then, after a long evening reorganizing the library's Royal Records Room, Nina had texted, *Your ancestors wrote too many diaries. It's exhausting.*

This is why I don't keep a journal, Jeff had replied, barely a minute later. *I don't want future generations of librarians sorting through my thoughts.*

They don't need journals. They'll have all your text messages and emails.

So, a lot of bad inside jokes and GIFs from Sam. Good luck to whoever has to archive all of that.

It was weird, picking up the thread of their friendship as if the events of the past year hadn't happened—weird, but not impossible. Nina had mentioned it to Sam the last time they'd talked, and Sam had nearly shrieked over the phone. "Thank god," she'd exclaimed. "Now we can quit being awkward and all hang out together, just like old times!"

Nina smiled at the memory, holding out her student ID to buzz herself into the Chalet. As she started inside, her phone rang. She felt a cautious glow of surprise when she saw the prince's name on her screen.

"Jeff. Hey," she said uncertainly.

"Nina!" he exclaimed, as if it wasn't unusual to be calling her. "I was wondering, do you know how to get to Clyburn Hall?"

"The dining hall?" She paused in the hallway, propping her phone against her shoulder. Had Jeff not eaten on campus yet?

"Yes, exactly. Want to grab dinner?"

Someone who didn't know Jeff might have assumed he was just being friendly and outgoing, but Nina heard the hesitancy beneath his casual tone. Prince Jefferson, the most famous and beloved young man in America, was *nervous*. He didn't want to show up at the dining hall and have to sit alone.

"Meet me in half an hour," she told him.

♕

Jeff's eyes widened as Nina led him into the massive dining hall. His protection officer Matt—who was only a few years older, and dressed in a King's College sweatshirt and jeans—lingered unobtrusively in the corner, watching the prince's movements. Nina smiled at him in greeting, then did her best to ignore him.

"You have lots of options," she began, feeling like one of the campus tour guides waving a cheerful blue flag. "The grill always has burgers and sandwiches, and there's a salad bar, and the hot-food line has tonight's special." She gestured to one of the food stations, where industrial-sized pots held steaming green curry and saag paneer.

Jeff clutched his plastic tray with both hands, as if he wasn't quite sure how to hold it. "And I can get whatever I want?"

"Have you seriously never been in a cafeteria before? Not everything is a full-restaurant buyout, Jeff." Nina was thinking of the first date he'd taken her on, when he'd rented out Matsuhara so that they could have a Michelin-starred sushi dinner alone. "You've got to face your subjects sometime," she added, only half teasing.

Jeff met her gaze. "First of all, these aren't my subjects; they're Beatrice's. And I don't do restaurant buyouts because I'm scared of seeing people."

You do it because your girlfriend is a snob, Nina thought.

"When I rent out an entire restaurant, it's only because it seems unfair to all the other guests when I show up," he went on. "They've gone out to celebrate something—a birthday, a friend moving to town, maybe just the fact that it's Friday— and then I appear, and the spotlight shifts from them to me. It feels selfish to steal everyone's night like that."

"Oh," Nina breathed, a little chastened.

There were some whispered comments and curious glances as they headed from one food station to another, but Jeff seemed oblivious, or perhaps he didn't care. He was probably numb to it by now.

They hesitated at the entrance to the seating area, and then Nina saw a table of her friends. She beelined toward it, re- lieved.

"Hey, everyone. This is Jeff," she announced, though he needed no introduction. "Jeff, this is Logan, Jayne, and—"

"Rachel," Jeff remembered, scooting next to Rachel on the

wooden bench. They had met last spring, when Jeff and Nina were dating. "Good to see you again."

Rachel beamed at him. Nina eyed his plate, which was heaped with foods that didn't seem to belong together: a burger and Indian food and mashed sweet potato. "Jeff. I know they have a lot of options, but it doesn't mean you're obligated to try everything."

"You're just jealous you didn't think of this first." He placed a hamburger patty between two slices of garlic naan and took an enormous bite.

"That's genius," declared Rachel's on-again, off-again boyfriend, Logan, with something like awe.

"So . . . Jeff." Rachel clearly loved using his first name. "Where are you living?"

"I'm actually at home for now, since my sister is at the League of Kings conference. Maybe in the spring I'll get to transfer to the dorms," he said hopefully. "I don't know. It was such a hassle when Beatrice lived at Harvard."

Apparently no other students had been able to live on Beatrice's hall. The school had installed biosecurity outside her door, posted video cameras in the hallways, and replaced her windows with bulletproof glass. None of it had been very popular with the other students.

On the bright side, Nina thought, there was no risk of running into Jeff on her way to the showers, wearing a towel.

The prince looked around the table and grinned. "I don't want to miss out on anything, though. You'll give me a heads-up when there's a party, right?"

The table dissolved into easy conversation as everyone discussed classes, the school football game this weekend, the perennial rumor that the university would start breaking up on-campus parties, which were usually ignored. Nina sat back, content to listen as Jeff charmed her friends. It was funny—at times like this he seemed almost like another ordinary student hanging out at dinner.

Eventually they headed toward the ice cream bar at the back of the dining hall, Nina joking about how many scoops Jeff would get. "At least three, depending on whether they have mint chocolate chip today," she teased.

"Jeff?"

A young woman stepped into their path, tossing her chestnut hair over one shoulder as she bobbed a quick curtsy. Nina didn't recognize her, but then, she didn't exactly look like the type of person Nina would have met: her pink dress had dramatic poufed sleeves that covered her pale shoulders, and she held one of those tiny leather purses that barely fit a cell phone.

"Gabriella, hey. This is my friend Nina," Jeff offered.

The girl's eyes flicked contemptuously over Nina, dismissing her faded paisley dress and denim jacket, but then they drifted back up to her face, and Nina saw the moment of recognition. Gabriella knew she was Jeff's former girlfriend.

"Lady Gabriella Madison," she said coolly. So, she was one of those nobles who made a point of using her title.

Gabriella held out a limp hand, palm down. It almost looked like she expected Nina to kneel and kiss her ring, as if she were a queen deigning to meet some commoner.

Nina took Gabriella's hand and gave it a hearty shake, secretly enjoying the other girl's look of dismay. "Gabriella," she said, deliberately leaving off the *Lady*. "It's great to meet you. How do you know Jeff?"

"We go *way* back. There are photos of us in the *bathtub* together as babies!" Gabriella gave a funny little laugh and tugged her hand away, looking as though she wanted to wipe her palm against the side of her dress. She turned back to the prince. "Jeff, I didn't know you were allowed to eat in the dining hall. Next time, you'll have to text me and Bradley so we can come sit with you."

"Nina and her friends took great care of me," Jeff said easily. "We're actually about to get some ice cream, if you want to join us."

Gabriella shook her head. "I'm fine, thanks. But I'll see you at the tailgate on Saturday?"

"Sure. You in, Nina?" Jeff added, glancing over.

Before Nina could reply, Gabriella rushed to interrupt. "Nina probably has other plans for the game."

The casual disdain in her words made Nina stand up a little straighter. "A tailgate sounds fun. I'd love to come."

Gabriella held Nina's gaze, unblinking. It reminded Nina of the staring contest she'd had with Stuart Randall in second grade, when the entire playground had gathered around to watch.

"It's hosted by Tri Alpha. You probably won't know anyone," Gabriella challenged.

"I'll know Jeff."

Nina had met plenty of Gabriellas in her life—spoiled, selfish people who thought they mattered more than the rest of the world simply because of their rank. The type of people who stared straight through Nina at court functions, only to realize she was Princess Samantha's best friend and make a halfhearted attempt to *use* her.

She couldn't let someone like that win.

"Count me in," Nina declared, forcing a smile. "I can't wait."

BEATRICE

Beatrice missed her father most in the mornings. Or, at least, she *hurt* most acutely in the mornings. Once the day began and she was pulled in a million different directions, rushing to events and reading legislation, the pain of missing him subsided to a dull ache. It would still pop up occasionally, little pockets of grief working their way to the surface, but she could manage it.

In the mornings, though, the loss seemed to hit her anew. Which was why Beatrice had gotten in the habit of taking Franklin on a walk—or run—herself, instead of sending him with one of the footmen.

Her father had gone on a run nearly every morning of his reign. Often Beatrice had joined him: the two of them, flanked by their Revere Guards, jogging through the streets of the capital.

Now Beatrice stood on the back terrace of Bellevue, pulling one leg behind her in a quad stretch. Franklin looked hopefully toward the ocean, his tail wagging frantically. Dawn had just begun to streak the purple sky with hints of rose and aubergine.

"Ready, Franklin?" she murmured, only to pause at the sight of a figure coming up the path from the guest cottages.

Even in the morning, in workout clothes, Princess Louise looked painfully chic. Her black leggings had mesh cutouts, revealing triangles of skin along her calves. They were practically *sexy*, unlike Beatrice's faded sweatpants with elastic at the waist and ankles.

"Hello, Béatrice. I was heading to the gym." Louise laughed: a hoarse, throaty sound. "Though I'm not sure it will be pleasant, given how late I was up."

Beatrice ached to know what Louise and her friends had done last night. She'd noticed them skipping out on the conference's official programming—there was always something scheduled in the evenings, a reception or a guest lecturer or even a tai chi class on the lawn. But whatever Louise and her friends were doing, they kept it to themselves.

"Franklin and I were about to run on the beach, if you'd like to join us," Beatrice heard herself say.

Louise glanced down at the golden Labrador, no longer a puppy but still so exuberant and playful. "I like to run fast," she warned.

"So do I," Beatrice declared.

What had gotten into her? She was acting like Samantha—issuing challenges, daring people to accept them.

"By all means, then. Let's run." Louise smiled in a way that was somehow amused and skeptical at once, nodding at Beatrice to go ahead.

Neither of them commented when Beatrice picked up the pace, running at a far greater clip than her usual jog. Louise gritted her teeth but kept up. Franklin, for one, seemed delighted by the speed, straining at the end of his leash as he loped ahead. His paws left imprints in the sand, still damp from the receding tide.

Finally they turned the last curve around the island, and Bellevue rose up before them, its white stones gleaming against the gold-streaked sky.

Beatrice began to sprint. Her entire body screamed in

protest, the air sharp in her lungs, but still she ran faster. Louise matched her step for step, though her breath came in ragged, wheezing gasps. Beatrice wondered how immature they looked: a pair of queens racing like children on the playground.

Still, Beatrice couldn't bring herself to slow down. She refused to let Louise beat her.

They reached Bellevue neck and neck, both stumbling the last few steps. Louise leaned forward, bracing her hands on her legs. Her nose and cheeks were flushed a bright red.

Then, to Beatrice's surprise, Louise bent down and ruffled Franklin's ears. "You did well, Monsieur Franklin."

"It's *Monseigneur* Franklin, actually," Beatrice said, testing a joke. *Lord Franklin*, not *Mr. Franklin*.

"But of course, I should have known. It says right here that he is royalty." Louise reached for the gold tag on Franklin's collar, which was engraved with *BR* for *Beatrice Regina*. "My Geneviève wears something like this. But with an *L*, of course."

"You have a dog?"

"A cat," Louise corrected. "Geneviève thinks that *she* is the Acting Queen of France, not me."

Beatrice smiled. "Franklin just thinks everything is a game."

"He certainly did well at this game. If it had been a race, Franklin would have beaten us both. You must run that loop often," Louise added.

"I used to run here with my father, whenever we came to this house."

"Ahh." Louise said nothing else—no *I'm sorry* or other expression of sympathy, the way most people would have. She just nodded, her blue eyes darkening in understanding.

A few yards away stood the fountain at the entrance to the

gardens. A trio of carved cherubs perched at its top, water spilling from the tips of their arrows into the stone basin below. Before Beatrice realized what she was doing, Louise marched over to it and leaned down like a child at a water fountain in the school hallway, lowering her mouth to the water.

"Don't do that!" Beatrice cried out, but Louise had already stumbled back, coughing furiously.

"Well. If that sprint hadn't cured my hangover, this would." Louise choked out a strangled laugh. "I certainly didn't expect salt water."

Beatrice flushed. "I'm sorry. We pump it up from the ocean—"

"You shouldn't do that," Louise interrupted.

"It's more environmentally friendly this way," Beatrice explained, puzzled.

"No, you shouldn't *apologize*." Louise flicked her ponytail over one shoulder. Sunshine shot through her blond hair, highlighting its platinum streaks. "You just told me that you're sorry. Never use those words."

Beatrice hesitated. "What if I really am sorry?"

"It doesn't matter. *I'm sorry* means that you made a mistake, and you cannot admit to that. The world will forgive a man, but rarely a woman. Certainly not a woman in power."

No one had ever spoken to Beatrice like this before. It was exhilarating.

"You're right," she agreed, nodding. "That makes sense."

"Of course I'm right. I'm always right," Louise said breezily.

They started up the lawn toward the terrace. A footman must have seen them through the windows, because he hurried forward with a pair of chilled water bottles. Beatrice took a grateful sip. Franklin whined softly until the footman returned with a bowl of water.

"I noticed that you don't run with headphones." Louise

shot her a curious glance. "I assumed you were the type to listen to a podcast, or at least music."

"You didn't run with headphones either," Beatrice pointed out.

Louise shrugged. "I prefer silence."

"Exactly. I want to turn my brain off, for a little while at least."

When her feet were pounding against the pavement, Beatrice could temporarily silence the anxieties and fears that flitted around in her head like birds in a cage. If she ran fast enough, she could wipe her mind clear.

"I know the feeling. I'm trying to outrun some things too," Louise said softly.

Beatrice blinked, surprised by that level of vulnerability from magnetic, enigmatic Louise. Before she could formulate a reply, the bells in the clock tower chimed.

"We should get going," she said reluctantly.

Louise nodded. "See you later, Béatrice." She started back toward the cottages, moving as if she were weighted down by a tiara and the full regalia of state, rather than sweat-drenched workout clothes.

Beatrice had long ago accepted that no one could ever really relate to her. Her position was too unique, too specific and strange. But . . . Louise was the first female ruler of her nation, too.

If anyone could understand, it was Louise.

Beatrice reached out a hand, and Franklin nuzzled into it, whining when he realized that she wasn't giving him a treat.

"You know what, Franklin?" she murmured, smiling a little. "You and I might have just made friends with a cat lady."

10

SAMANTHA

Samantha had walked down plenty of red carpets in her day, but they were East Coast red carpets, rolled out before a charity gala so that wealthy donors could stand before the flashbulbs and feel momentarily famous.

Sam's mother—and her grandmother, and even Beatrice, for that matter—always resented being asked to walk down a red carpet. *Don't linger before the cameras a second longer than necessary,* her mother would say. *You pause once, smile, then move along. You're a princess, not a pinup girl.* Queen Adelaide believed that the royal family wasn't there to be celebrities; they were meant to govern and to do good in the world. She saw their fame as an unfortunate but requisite part of their position.

Everything was different in Hollywood. Instead of bored, wealthy businesspeople and gossiping heiresses moving slowly past the photographers, this red carpet seethed with frantic celebrities. Even the *carpet* looked better, a crisp crimson instead of the tattered felt rugs that museums rented. Everyone was shouting, laughing, sucking in their stomachs, blowing kisses to the crowds in a shameless bid for attention. A wild, thrilling energy pulsed through it all.

When Marshall got out of the car, then extended a hand to help Sam onto the steps, the roar escalated into complete frenzy.

For a moment, everyone at the premiere looked her way.

The director—an Oscar winner who'd recently gone over budget on a space epic and somehow got talked into Aunt Margaret's pirate movie—was so stunned that his jaw fell open. The lead actress jabbed an elbow into her date's ribs; a pop singer tripped on her heels. They were all stars in their own right, yet they stared unabashedly at Sam, the most famous of them all.

It wasn't the date night Sam would have picked, but at least she got to be there with Marshall.

The two of them had seen each other nearly every day that week. At first they'd tried to go out: to drive along the coast, eat oysters at the famous food truck overlooking the water, stroll up the boardwalk and watch the sunset. But they'd quickly realized it was easier if they just hung out at Bellevue or at Marshall's apartment in LA. Their relationship was so famous, so incendiary, that everywhere they went, people seemed to want a piece of them.

Sam laced her hand in Marshall's and they started up the steps together, smiling into the blinding explosion of flashbulbs. Paparazzi lobbed questions at them. Unlike the journalists in Washington, who at least wore a veneer of professionalism as they pried into her life, these reporters seemed out for blood.

"Sam, do you really think you and Marshall make more of an 'it couple' than your sister and Teddy?"

"What do you have to say to Kelsey Brooke?"

"Marshall, how does it feel being ranked *lower* than your girlfriend? Does she wear the pants in the relationship?"

She expected Marshall to make a snarky reply to that one, maybe joke that rank didn't matter or that only weak men were intimidated by women in power. But he just squeezed Sam's hand, his jaw set.

Finally they emerged into the theater lobby, which was mercifully free of photographers but crowded with guests.

Stowaway's promotional poster—which featured a half-naked couple in a very suggestive embrace, a ship's sails billowing in a way that strategically covered all necessary body parts—had been blown up in the corner, and the cast and crew were all signing it.

Then Aunt Margaret herself was rushing toward them, a gauzy white caftan floating around her legs. How typically capricious of her, to wear a resort dress in September.

"Samantha! I'm so delighted you could make it." Margaret pulled her into a hug. "I've been missing my favorite niece. Don't tell Beatrice I said that," she warned, and Sam laughed. Aunt Margaret had always had a soft spot for her, probably because she saw so much of herself in Sam. They both chafed at the constraints of the family they'd been born into, both grappled with what it meant to be a spare royal sibling.

"I miss you, too. Hopefully I'll be out on the West Coast more often," Sam told her.

"Of course! Now that you're dating our favorite future duke, I expect to see a lot more of you." Margaret turned to Marshall, who bowed at the waist. He hadn't worn the Hawaiian shirt after all, but was in a simple navy suit without a tie, his dress shirt unbuttoned at the neck.

Her aunt smiled at him, looping an arm through Sam's. "Tell your mother I said hello, will you? Now, if you'll excuse me, I need to show off my fabulous niece."

When she'd led Sam a few yards away, Aunt Margaret lowered her voice. "Dare I ask how you're doing?"

"You mean now that my relationship is more under the microscope than ever, thanks to Kelsey Brooke?"

"Your relationship was always going to be under the microscope, given who you and Marshall are. But Kelsey Brooke didn't help things. I would have cut her from this premiere, the lying little snake, except she wasn't important enough to be on the invite list to begin with." Margaret sniffed. "Good luck to her, trying to get a role after *that* stunt. I'm telling every director in town to cut her from future auditions."

Sam smiled. It was nice having Aunt Margaret in your corner.

A talk-show host veered determinedly in their direction. He clearly wanted to say something, ask a question about Marshall or offer Sam the chance to come on his morning show—but before he reached them, Aunt Margaret skewered him with a vicious stare. The host swallowed and turned away.

"Aside from that absurd interview, though, things with Marshall are good?"

"They are," Sam replied, and her aunt smiled.

"I'm glad. You deserve a good fling, and Marshall certainly is gorgeous," Margaret said appreciatively. "Promise me you'll enjoy it, for as long as it lasts."

A *fling?* "I really like Marshall," Sam started to say.

"Of course you do." There was something troubling about the dismissive way Aunt Margaret said it, as if she hadn't even considered that their feelings might actually run deep.

As if their relationship were implausible or, worse, impossible.

♛

The after-party at Margaret and Nate's beach house in Malibu felt like an extension of the movie. The enormous yard was hung with netting and sailcloth, and the waitstaff all looked like extras in their vests or corsets. There were even cocktails colored the same deep blue as the pool, which—as far as Sam could tell—had real fish in it.

Sam had gotten separated from Marshall practically the moment they arrived. By now she'd talked with the new James Bond and the old James Bond, with the teenage pop star who'd been discovered through her viral videos, and with the heads of two rival studios, who made a point of ignoring each other. She had to hand it to Aunt Margaret: the Hollywood power players had all turned up for her premiere, even if the movie was as delightfully cliché as Sam had expected.

She wandered over to the railing at the edge of the terrace, which looked out over the ocean. The water sparkled in the sunlight, a few surfers dotted among the waves.

"Brought you something," she heard Marshall say behind her.

He was holding a paper plate with two slices of pepperoni pizza. Real thick-crust pizza, the kind that left grease spots on napkins, not some gluten-free LA flatbread masquerading as pizza.

"I've never been so grateful to see cheese-soaked carbs," she said eagerly. The appetizers at this party were total rabbit food, things like tuna tartare and cucumber slices with feta. "Where did you get this?"

"The valets ordered it. I bribed them to share a couple slices." Marshall finished one and automatically passed Sam the crust.

"I can't believe you don't eat the crusts. They're the best part of the pizza."

"They're really not," Marshall said emphatically. "They're just *your* favorite part, you weirdo."

"They're even better when you dip them in ranch dressing."

He snorted. "You know, most Americans think you sit around eating foie gras. If they had any idea how delightfully simple your tastes are, they would love you for it."

He'd said the word *love*, even if it wasn't in the context of *I love you*. Sam couldn't stop the smile that spread over her face.

"By the way," he went on, "can you come to dinner at my

grandparents' house next week, or are you busy with the conference?"

Marshall's parents had been at the Napa house when she visited, and Sam had met Marshall's grandfather years ago: as Duke of Orange, he was often in the capital on official business. But she'd only been to the Orange ducal mansion once before, at the Accession Day party earlier this spring. That was the night she'd realized her feelings for Marshall.

"I'd love to," she told him.

Marshall grinned. "My grandmother is cooking—she insists on making everything herself for our family dinners—so you should eat before. Her food is always burned or oversalted. Or both."

"I'm sure it's not that bad."

"It's completely inedible," he said happily. "But I'm glad you're coming, Sam. This will be fun."

Sam grinned as she started to reach for the pizza again, then paused. A young woman with dark hair was edging stealthily toward them. When she saw Sam looking at her, the girl squeaked, holding a hand to her chest.

"Oh my god, Your Royal Majesty! It's such an honor!" She sank into the lowest curtsy Sam had ever seen, so deep that it was practically a yoga move. Sam tried not to laugh at how terribly the girl had bungled her title. These Hollywood types were so over-the-top.

"Hi, it's nice to meet you . . ." Sam trailed off expectantly, and the girl jumped to provide her name.

"Ashley," she chirped. "Sorry, I know you two are, like, having a moment"—she nodded at the plate of half-eaten pizza, and Sam felt Marshall chuckling quietly next to her—"but I wanted to introduce myself, since I'll be playing you."

Sam stared, bewildered, as Ashley gestured toward a young man who'd come to stand next to her. He was unquestionably gorgeous, with deep brown skin and the hint of a beard. "R.J. will be playing you, of course, Your Grace," Ashley added, turning to Marshall. "Isn't he well cast?"

That was when Sam realized that Ashley looked a lot like *her*—just thinner and prettier, her hair a little longer and glossier, her arms a little more toned.

Ashley and R.J. were the Hollywood versions of Sam and Marshall.

Sam exchanged a glance with Marshall, who looked equally perplexed. "What's the movie?"

"A made-for-TV romance about you two, called *Queen of Hearts.*"

"I'm not the queen. My sister is," Sam said automatically.

"Oh my god, right? I told the producer it was a cheesy title, but she ignored me!" Ashley beamed as if she and Sam had suddenly become best friends. "You are, like, even more awesome than I imagined. Both of you!" she added, glancing from Sam to Marshall and back again. "You should know that I've *totally* been shipping you two. Like, since the very beginning."

Marshall smiled, but there was a shadow behind his eyes. "It was nice to meet you both. Good luck with the movie."

The actors clearly picked up on the note of finality in Marshall's tone, because they murmured their goodbyes and drifted off to rejoin the party. Sam looked from the pizza, which had gone soggy and cold on its paper plate, to Marshall's face.

"I'm sorry about the movie. Unfortunately, I know from experience that we can't get this kind of thing shut down." The royal family's lives were in the public domain, which made them fair game for adaptation by directors, artists, even fan-fiction writers. "I can try to find out more about it if you want," she added. "Maybe it'll be a good thing, get more people on our side?"

"I wish we didn't have to be a *side* at all," Marshall said, frustrated.

Sam knew he wasn't comfortable with how public their relationship had become. Marshall had been notorious for years: aside from dating starlets and models, he was a Black future duke, and there weren't many of those. But now that he was dating Samantha, his fame had skyrocketed. He wasn't just famous enough to appear *inside* a tabloid; now he was on its cover. His name was a joke on late-night talk shows, bandied about in conversations and debates all over the globe. Now an actor was playing him in a movie, reciting dialogue that some screenwriter had written, and half the people who saw it would think that those were things Marshall had actually said, that he actually believed.

Sam had grown up with that stratospheric level of fame; she'd long since gotten used to it. But it was new to Marshall.

"Hey. Talk to me." She nudged him with her hip. When he didn't answer, Sam let out a breath. "That's it. I'm going after this stupid movie."

"It's not just the movie, Sam." Marshall opened his mouth—then let out a defeated breath, as if he'd been about to tell her something, only to change his mind. "Just forget about it, okay?"

No, she wanted to say, *it's clearly not okay!* She felt so helpless at moments like this, knowing that there were whole pieces of her relationship that existed outside her control. That it wasn't about just her and Marshall, but the entire world.

Yet Sam didn't dare press the issue. She felt suddenly terrified that if she pushed on this sensitive spot, she and Marshall would never come back from it.

So she turned and smiled, trying to ignore the tension that had grown between them like a thin layer of scar tissue. "Should we get going?" she asked.

On their way out of the party, Sam noticed Ashley and R.J. sneaking into an empty room, giggling like a pair of misbehaving schoolchildren.

Well, at least fake Marshall and fake Samantha would have chemistry on-screen.

For a piercing moment, Sam felt jealous of them—that they could slip into a room at a party and make out, simply because they couldn't bear to keep their hands off each other. That their relationship was uncomplicated and straightforward, free from public scrutiny, without duchies and monarchies and successions at stake.

Sam wondered what she and Marshall would be like in a world where they only had to worry about each other, where their relationship belonged to them alone.

11

NINA

The second she walked onto the tailgate field, Nina had the sinking feeling that she shouldn't have come.

This was nothing like the tailgates she and her friends had thrown last year, when they'd popped open the trunk of someone's car and shared a platter of bagels or a bag of potato chips. This was another side of King's College entirely, populated by students who apparently had unlimited party-planning budgets. This was what the wealthy, titled kids had all been doing while Nina's crew put on face paint and cheered from the nosebleed section of the stadium.

This was the version of King's College that Jeff belonged in. Or at least, where everyone assumed he belonged.

Near the duck pond across from the stadium stood a row of white tents: the professional kind with enormous metal supports, enclosing a space bigger than the Gonzalezes' living room. Nina passed tents labeled things like CLASS OF 2008 ALUMNI, FRIENDS OF VARSITY ATHLETICS, TFI, and UCC, until she found the one labeled AAA in gold letters. Snacks had been arranged with painstaking precision on the tables: iced cookies and a cheese platter and mason jars filled with blue and white M&M's. A table in one corner held bottles of champagne and carafes of orange juice in sweating ice buckets. Outside the tent, a boy in a polka-dotted bow tie was flipping hamburgers.

Everyone here looked like they'd dressed for a garden party rather than a college tailgate. The sorority girls were in dresses and designer sunglasses, the boys in button-downs and khakis and, in some cases, blazers. Nina shifted, feeling self-conscious in her wide-leg jeans with their ratty, frayed hem. She could still leave; Jeff hadn't even seen her yet.

But that would just prove Gabriella had been right when she'd declared that Nina didn't belong at a party like this.

At least Daphne wasn't here. Apparently she had deferred her acceptance at King's College to spend the year "focusing on her charities," as if her charities actually mattered to her.

"Nina! You made it!" Jeff headed toward her, looking outlandishly preppy in a white Oxford shirt and blue sweater. "Are you hungry? We've got burgers."

She was about to say no, but then she noticed that a couple of sorority girls were looking over—and that none of them were eating, not even a single M&M, though they all clutched red plastic cups in their hands.

"You know what? A burger sounds fantastic," she said.

Jeff led her over to the grill, where the guy in the bow tie threw a patty and a bun onto the grill's surface.

"So, how's everything going?" Jeff asked.

"We had a minor drama in the Chalet last night. Rachel nearly set fire to the downstairs lounge," Nina recounted.

Jeff's eyes widened. "Is everyone okay?"

"Yeah, it's all fine—except the slice-and-bake cookies Rachel was baking. Those didn't survive."

"Slice-and-bake?"

It was so easy to forget how detached Jeff was from reality. He lived in a world where cookies appeared at the push of a button, literally. All he had to do was dial KITCHENS from the phone in his room—the direct line was right there between PRESS OFFICE and STABLES—and make a request of the chef, and twenty minutes later a footman would knock at his door with a tray of fresh-baked cookies.

"Slice-and-bake is exactly what it sounds like." She rolled her eyes affectionately. "It's a roll of cookie dough that you cut into cookies and bake."

The boy behind the grill handed over her burger, its bun toasted to a golden brown. Nina added onions and condiments from the nearby table, feeling the stares of all the girls in their tight sundresses, and took a huge bite. It was delicious.

"What about you? How's everything going?" she asked Jeff, wiping ketchup off her chin.

"Pretty good, except Urquhart's class. It's so boring that I keep wanting to ditch it and stay in bed," he admitted.

"Don't do that! Urquhart pulls most of his exam questions from the lecture slides, so you need to write down every word of his PowerPoint, just to be safe." When she saw Jeff's sheepish expression, Nina added, "Don't tell me you've already skipped class."

Jeff hurried to shake his head. "I haven't skipped—but I did fall asleep yesterday. It's a really early lecture!" he protested.

"Ten a.m. probably does feel early when you're out late," Nina joked.

A mischievous expression stole over Jeff's face. He looked the way he used to when he and Sam were trying to talk Nina into something illicit: breaking into the armory to steal one of the old swords, or hiding behind a curtain to make spooky ghost noises as a tour group walked past.

"If only I knew someone who took perfect notes. Someone who undoubtedly got an A in this class last year," he said leadingly.

Nina scoffed. "I might consider lending you my notes, but it would cost you."

"Excellent, I'm open to bribery." Jeff grinned. "What's your price?"

Suddenly, their conversation felt like it was verging on dangerous territory—like it was too close to flirtation. Nina took one last bite of her burger and threw the remaining half in the trash.

"I need a drink," she blurted out. "Can I get you something?"

"Another beer would be great," Jeff said, a little confused by her abrupt departure.

This time, as Nina headed into the tent, she felt certain that the other girls were looking at her. Where before they'd glanced at her with bored curiosity, now they stared at her with a simmering resentment, as if she were an interloper, a thief who'd stolen into their closed-off world and tried to make off with the greatest prize of all: the prince himself. *But of course it didn't work*, they would reassure each other in relieved whispers. *Because she's a nobody.*

Ignoring the orange juice and champagne that the other girls all seemed to be drinking, Nina grabbed a pair of beers from the cooler. As she popped the cans and poured the beer into cups, a strident voice rose over the rest of the noise.

"I'm just *so* proud of Nigel. Did you know the gown he made for my court presentation at Versailles is on display at the Louvre? They asked to borrow it, and *of course* I lent it to them. I mean, it's a work of art."

Surprise, surprise: Gabriella Madison was here. She stood at the center of a group, wearing a color-blocked dress with a cutout that revealed a sliver of her pale midriff. An amethyst velvet headband and towering wedges completed the look. Even her toenails had been painted the exact same shade of purple, Nina realized.

She wondered what kind of person had enough time and money to get a mani-pedi that matched her outfit for a *tailgate*.

Then again, Gabriella's family probably had a nail technician on staff.

"I can't believe you're friends with Nigel. You're so lucky," breathed another of the girls. "Is it true he asked you to model in his runway show?"

"He did," Gabriella simpered. "Though of course Daddy would never allow me to do something so public! And I'd have to lose five pounds."

She tilted her head, waiting, and the other girls rushed to chime in.

"Omigod, Gabriella, you don't have five pounds to lose!"

"You're way skinnier than all those runway models!"

Gabriella shrugged, accepting the praise complacently. "Just wait until you see the dress Nigel designed for my birthday party. It's *stunning*. And of course you know there's a surprise guest performer. . . ."

Nina didn't bother hiding her eye roll as she turned back toward Jeff, a cup of beer in each hand. But apparently luck wasn't with her today, because Gabriella's voice stopped her in her tracks.

"Excuse me? Hi."

Nina looked up and saw that Gabriella was staring daggers in her direction. "Yes, *you*," Gabriella said impatiently. "Are you lost?"

Was this some kind of intimidation technique? "I'm Nina Gonzalez," Nina said, though Gabriella was clearly well aware who she was. "We met in the cafeteria the other day."

Upon hearing her name, one of the other girls gasped in recognition. "You're that friend of Samantha's, aren't you? The one Jeff—"

Gabriella elbowed the girl, who let out a muffled squeak and fell silent. Her eyes still boring into Nina's, Gabriella said, "You're not a Tri Alpha. You really shouldn't be here."

"Jeff invited me. This is a fraternity party too, isn't it?"

Gabriella shrugged. "Technically, yes. But it's really more our thing. We set up, decorate the tent, and buy all the food and drinks. The boys just work the grill."

"Wow. That's pretty regressive and sexist," Nina said drily. "Maybe you should make the boys pull their weight. Not that it's any of my business," she added, "since, as you so kindly pointed out, I'm not a Tri Alpha."

"As if you could ever make the cut," Gabriella muttered under her breath.

Nina forced herself to hold her head high and walk away. It wasn't worth bickering with someone as petty and small-minded as Gabriella.

She headed back toward Jeff—who, of course, was surrounded by a semicircle of guys all jostling for his attention. But before she could reach him, someone blew a whistle.

"Listen up!" An upperclassman climbed atop a car, bellowing into a megaphone. "Pledge football will begin in five minutes! Each fraternity must send one pledge to compete on their behalf."

A murmur of excitement rippled through the crowd. More than one guy glanced at Jeff, who clearly sensed what was expected of him, because he shouted, "I'm in!"

The guy with the megaphone seemed uncertain. "You sure?"

Jeff hooted in excitement, letting the tide of the gathered crowd carry him along, then glanced back over his shoulder. "Matt, can you handle photos?"

Nina hadn't even noticed that Jeff's Revere Guard was here; he'd been standing to one side of the party, wearing a preppy button-down like all the fraternity brothers. He grabbed a trash bag from beneath a folding table and began circulating through the tailgate, commanding each student to drop their phone into the bag. A few people bristled, but between Matt's assurances that their phones would be returned and his burly, intimidating muscles, they soon fell silent.

When Matt reached Nina, she handed over her phone without arguing. "Thanks, Nina," he told her with a knowing wink.

Nina was gratified to see Gabriella's face turn a mottled shade of red. She clearly didn't like that the prince's Revere Guard was on first-name terms with Nina.

Everyone cheered as the contestants from six different fraternities lined up along the edge of the duck pond. The pledges stretched their arms, warming up as if they were about to hold some kind of competition—a race, maybe?—and then, as the cheers intensified, they began stripping down to their boxers.

Now Nina understood why Jeff couldn't allow photographic evidence.

She didn't *mean* to look at him. Really, she didn't. But her gaze, along with practically everyone's, was drawn to him as he pulled his sweater and collared shirt up over his head, then shimmied eagerly out of his pants. He was wearing pale blue boxers—a long pair that looked like swim trunks, at least, instead of tighty-whities.

Afternoon sunlight fell over the lines of his body, his carved shoulders, the hollow at the base of his throat. His torso was taut, a smattering of dark hair trailing over his chest and down his carved abs.

Nina watched, shocked into utter stillness, as the pledges all bent down like runners at a starting block. Their legs tensed—

A whistle blew, and someone threw a plastic football out over the pond. Ducks made angry sounds of protest and fluttered away. The boys sprinted into the water, half splashing and half swimming as it grew deeper. Nina could practically see their skin prickling with cold; that water did not look pleasant.

"This is torture," she muttered.

"Isn't this hilarious?" Gabriella asked loudly, to directly contradict Nina. "It's like watching a bunch of puppies play fetch."

The other girls all laughed obediently, and Gabriella kept going, really warming to her theme.

"Honestly, Jefferson is like a puppy sometimes. Overeager and excitable, sniffing around things that turn out to be a stinking pile of poo."

Way to be unsubtle, Nina thought, almost amused.

"And he's kind of stupid like a puppy is, you know?" Gabriella pursed her coral-painted lips. "Good thing he's so rich and good-looking, because it's not as if he could make it through the world otherwise."

Something in Nina snapped. She had no more tolerance for people like this—selfish, entitled people who did nothing but spread rumors and stir up drama. She'd had more than enough of that last year, with Daphne.

She marched over and stood right next to Gabriella, an eyebrow raised in challenge. "I thought you and Jeff were friends."

"His Highness and I have been friends since we were babies," Gabriella said stiffly. As if by employing Jeff's proper title, she could shove Nina down a peg.

"Then I don't want to know how you talk about your enemies." Nina shook her head. "That was rude, and unnecessarily cruel."

Gabriella gave a brittle laugh. "No one cares what you think. No one even knows who you *are*! You're just Jeff's pity invite, some nobody with no class."

In the duck pond, the pledges were now wrestling over the football, but Nina kept her eyes on Gabriella. Their confrontation had drawn a bit of a crowd.

"Look, Gabriella, I couldn't care less what you say about me. But I do care what you say about Jeff. You act like a friend to his face, then call him stupid behind his back?" Nina drew in a breath. "*That* is the behavior of somebody with no class."

Gabriella recoiled as if slapped. Her eyes narrowed. "Do you have any idea who I am?"

"I know *exactly* who you are," Nina told her. "Spoiled and completely self-centered. You steamroll through life doing whatever you want, and everyone in your world is too intimidated to argue with you. Well, I'm not *in* your world, as you so rudely pointed out. So, unlike your little fan club"—Nina gestured at the posse of sorority girls—"I'm not afraid to tell you the truth."

"How dare you." Gabriella's cheeks were flush with color.

"No, how dare *you*! Jeff isn't stupid. He's earnest and trusting, not that I would expect someone like you to understand."

Gabriella took a step closer, her chin tipped up. "You're going to regret this."

"I already regret wasting my breath on you."

Nina didn't wait for Gabriella to reply. She turned and marched away from the tailgate field. Her pulse was pounding, adrenaline rushing through her veins as if she'd just sprinted a mile.

For a moment she wondered if she'd gone too far, if she'd unloaded all her pent-up frustrations about Daphne onto Gabriella. Well, so what if she had? Gabriella deserved it.

It felt good, telling people what she really thought of them. Honestly, Nina should do it more often.

12

BEATRICE

Mealtimes were one of the strangest parts of the League of Kings conference. At least twice a week, dinner was a formal state affair, where everyone sat at banquet tables and wore full decorations. It must have been a nightmare for the valets, keeping hundreds of tiaras and medals of honor polished to their greatest sparkle.

At breakfast and lunch, though, the monarchs would drop by as their schedules allowed, grabbing a plate when they were in a hurry. In a corner of the banquet hall stood platters of fruit, bowls of salad, and trays of gourmet sandwiches, everything from turkey-and-pesto panini to Vietnamese banh mi. Often the royals wandered through the double doors to sit at the picnic tables out on the grounds. Just yesterday Beatrice had caught the King of Ghana playing fetch with Franklin, tossing a Frisbee out into the surf and letting Franklin sprint after it.

Today, however, rain streamed in fat droplets along the windows. Everyone shot longing glances outside, as if the universe had played some kind of cosmic trick on them. They had all clearly bought into the myth that life in Orange was nothing but endless sunshine and cloudless skies.

Beatrice didn't really mind the rain. She loved how the slanted gray light made everything feel muted and soft, loved the drowsy patter of raindrops against the windowpanes. Or maybe she liked the rain because it reminded her of Teddy.

It had rained the night before they were supposed to get married, the night they first said *I love you*.

She paused at the entrance to the banquet hall, scanning the tables for Samantha, but she didn't see her sister anywhere. Maybe Sam was stuck in a small-group session, or on the phone with Marshall.

Beatrice shifted her weight, uncertain. King Frederick and a few other monarchs lounged near the windows, lingering over their glasses of Sancerre—Beatrice had tried, at first, not to serve wine at lunch, but the Europeans nearly revolted in protest. Nearby, Tsar Dmitri sat with his friends; they usually gathered outside so that they could smoke their cigars without being glared at. A few tables away, the Queen of England and the Prince of Wales read on their tablets in placid silence.

Beatrice's eyes lit on Queen Irene of Slovenia, who was sitting at a table along one wall. With her wild cloud of gray hair and her mismatched assortment of shawls, she rather unfortunately resembled a fortune-teller at a carnival. She looked up, meeting Beatrice's gaze, and lifted her arm in an overeager wave.

Well, it was better than eating alone.

Beatrice had just started forward when Louise appeared next to her. "Béatrice. Hello," she said in that low, throaty voice of hers.

Louise's eyes were rimmed by whorls of black eyeliner, and her hair was pulled into a casual knot. The edge of a bra strap peeked out from the collar of her button-down, which had such a boxy and loose fit that Beatrice suspected it was a men's shirt. Louise had paired it with a short skirt and tall black boots, giving the whole outfit an artfully disheveled look.

Beatrice tried not to feel self-conscious about her own dress, which was printed with yellow lemons. She'd thought it seemed cheerful, but now the pattern struck her as silly and girlish.

The past couple of mornings, Beatrice had lingered over her warm-up stretches, finally taking Franklin out when it was clear that Louise wasn't coming. They hadn't spoken again, though she kept seeing Louise around the conference.

Really, it was impossible *not* to see Louise. She flitted about like a butterfly, vivid and electric. Half the time she arrived late to the monarchs' sessions, casually sipping a coffee. She would settle into her seat, swish her long hair over one shoulder, and lift her hand to ask a pert question of whoever was presenting. No one chastised Louise for her behavior. If anything, the other monarchs seemed slightly in awe of her, as if Louise behaved the way they all wished they could.

"Come sit with us," Louise said. It should have been a question, though it came out more like a command.

"Really?" Beatrice blinked, wishing she hadn't just said that. "I mean, yes. I would love to."

She tried not to bounce with excitement as she followed Louise to the back of the banquet hall, where Louise's friends—Alexei, Sirivannavari, and Bharat—were already gathered. The seat in the corner was empty, clearly reserved for their ringleader. Beatrice assumed that Louise wanted to sit there because it had the best view over the rest of the room, but as they sat down, Beatrice realized that Louise wasn't actually looking at the rest of the room.

Louise sat in the corner chair because she wanted everyone else to look at *her.*

Beatrice shifted in her seat, glancing nervously around the table. "Um . . . hi, everyone."

No one spoke for a long moment. She had a panicked impulse to make a comment about something, anything—the conference, the rainstorm—but swallowed back her words. There was nothing more painfully desperate than talking about the *weather.*

Princess Sirivannavari glanced up from her phone, breaking the silence. "I've been thinking about getting a pixie cut. Can I pull it off, yes or no?"

Bharat looked at the Thai princess with intense concentration. "How pixie are we talking, exactly? Sleek or shaggy? Punk rocker or Old Hollywood screen siren?"

Beatrice didn't understand half of what he'd said, but Sirivannavari answered right away. "Sleek, of course. Like, the short-hair-but-big-earrings look. Very Queen Geraldine in the sixties."

Bharat nodded sagely. He and Sirivannavari both looked to Louise, awaiting her verdict.

Louise took a delicate bite of her salad, then wiped her mouth on her napkin. The crimson of her lipstick left a smear on the white fabric. "I don't know," she said. And to everyone's surprise, she turned to Beatrice. "What do you think, Béatrice?"

Beatrice was so caught off guard that she blurted out the truth. "Pixie cuts always remind me of my high school math teacher, at St. Ursula's. She rode a motorcycle to school every day. We were all a bit terrified of her."

Oh my god, she thought as the rest of the table stared. Why had she brought up Ms. Linfield?

Then Louise burst into laughter. "Béatrice is right. Siri, you *cannot* risk looking like a high school math teacher. I forbid it."

Beatrice feared she might have hurt Sirivannavari's feelings, but Siri didn't seem offended. She just shrugged and looked back at her phone, clearly relieved that the decision had been made.

Bharat sighed, leaning his elbow on the table and cupping his chin in his palm. "I would have made a great math teacher or professor. All those tweed vests and plaid scarves!"

"If you want to dress like that, you should do it." Louise smiled. "You know what, we should *all* do it! We'll call it academic chic."

"It would be a fun experiment," Bharat agreed, and Louise laughed.

"Experiment? Academic chic is going to be the hot new thing," she said firmly. "If we start dressing in plaids and vests, the fashion magazines will take notice, and then the internet bloggers. We'll have started a global fashion movement within the month—because we *decided* to, right here at this table."

Sirivannavari tilted her head. "You really think so?"

"I *know* so," Louise said emphatically. "The five of us can make anything happen."

The five of us. She had included Beatrice in their number. And maybe they were just talking about fashion, but Beatrice still felt swept along by the intensity of Louise's conviction.

What did it feel like to be that confident, to know that you were strong enough to shape the world to your will? Beatrice had spent so long shaping *herself* according to the world's expectations—trying to be the princess, and then queen, she thought America wanted.

Maybe it was time she acted a bit more like Louise.

The rest of the lunch passed all too quickly. Beatrice knew she should get going; she'd planned on reading the Financial Committee's report before they presented it this afternoon. But it was so much more fun here, listening to the rapid back-and-forth of conversation.

Louise and her friends had an extensive shared history. They had all gone to school together in Switzerland, referenced birthday parties and trips to Verbier and classmates they'd lost track of. They teased mercilessly: *Remember when you stepped on a sea urchin at Livadia, and we had to use a fake name at the emergency room?* or *Whatever happened to your mom's* old assistant, *the one who wore the creepy hats?* It would have seemed off-putting and exclusive, except that Louise always paused to explain the inside joke, drawing Beatrice into the circle of their shared intimacy.

After a while she noticed that Louise was multitasking, swiping nonchalantly at her phone even as she chatted with the others. When Louise saw her looking over, she edged the phone toward Beatrice.

"What do you think, is he attractive?"

Princess Louise was on a *dating app?* "You're not seriously going to meet up with this guy, are you?" Beatrice blurted out.

"Why not? This conference is boring. And I doubt anyone would recognize me. Your people only care about their *own* royals. Which makes sense, since you've got enough drama for at least five families." The way she spoke, it sounded oddly like a compliment.

"As if you'd really go out with a stranger." Alexei turned to Beatrice. "Louise just likes to get on the apps for fun."

"It's not my fault they make the whole thing feel like a game!" Louise protested. Bharat reached eagerly for the phone so that he and Sirivannavari could study the screen.

"Ooh, I like him," Siri said approvingly. "He's got a total brooding-and-sensitive thing going on."

Alexei shook his head. "If you're bored, Louise, we should throw a party."

She visibly perked up. "Good thinking—we should throw a party! After the next state dinner, at my place?" Louise offered, as if the guest cottage really did belong to her. She quickly began doling out orders to her friends. "Alexei, you can handle drinks, can't you? Siri, you're in charge of getting the word out."

Sirivannavari nodded as solemnly as if she'd just been entrusted with the nuclear launch codes. "On it."

"Bharat, you're in charge of music. Whatever happened to that DJ we heard in Ibiza back in March? That was a *fantastic* night," she added wistfully, and Alexei made a funny noise in the back of his throat.

"I'll see if we can fly him here by then," Bharat said, as if it was no big deal.

Beatrice stared down at the remains of her turkey sandwich, willing herself to look normal, but then Louise's gaze landed on her. "You're coming, aren't you, Béatrice?"

The pinch of loneliness in her chest melted away. "I'd love to."

"Perfect. Bring your fiancé. And your sister and her boyfriend! Marshall, right?"

Beatrice nodded. "We'll be there."

Louise flashed her a smile. Beatrice wondered, suddenly, if this lunch had been some sort of test—if Louise had wanted to see how Beatrice fit in with her group of friends.

If it was, then Beatrice had passed.

♛

That evening, as she was getting dressed, Beatrice heard movement in Teddy's room and hurried to open the connecting door. They still didn't technically share a room, for propriety's sake.

"Teddy! How was your day?"

"I was going to take the boat out." He gestured to the windows, where the rain still pattered gently. "I ended up reading instead. There are a ton of old mystery novels in the library; did you know that?"

Teddy had taken the boat out every afternoon of the past week, so that now his fair skin had turned a golden tan from the sun. He had also started swimming laps in the downstairs pool, watched an entire TV series about Lord Alexander

Hamilton, and started cooking—or at least he'd started making peanut-butter-and-banana smoothies every morning when Beatrice came back from her run. They were heavy on the peanut butter, which made them taste more like dessert than breakfast, but Beatrice wasn't complaining.

Yet as much as he professed to enjoy his forced time off, Teddy was clearly growing restless. He was too smart to enjoy sitting around without stimulation, without any kind of *purpose.*

Things would get better once the League of Kings conference was over, Beatrice reminded herself. They would carve out a clear role for Teddy.

She took a step forward, trailing a hand over the doorframe. "I had lunch with Princess Louise and her friends today. You know, Bharat, Alexei, and Siri." Beatrice felt a little silly using Sirivannavari's nickname, but the rest of them all had.

Teddy gave her an encouraging smile. "That's great, Bee. How was it?"

"I really liked them. Even though they're all best friends, they made me feel included."

"How did they become best friends when their countries are so far apart?"

"They all went to that boarding school in Switzerland, the one with a summer campus and a winter campus." Beatrice, meanwhile, had been in the capital, at the same all-girls private school that generations of Washingtons had attended before her.

You don't need to be at school with other royals; you should surround yourself with your future subjects, her father had said when Beatrice brought it up at her first League of Kings conference. *You may be an American princess, but you're an American first, and a princess second.*

"It seems like they've all been close since they were kids,"

Beatrice went on. "And they jet-set all over the place, to Louise's family's house on the Riviera, or skiing in Verbier."

Teddy grinned. "Verbier, huh? I've never skied the Alps. If your new friends want to invite us this year, I'm willing to make the trip."

Beatrice stepped forward, lacing her hands in his. "Oh, are you?"

"I promise to win them all over with my triple-cheese nachos and my chairlift banter. I'm an excellent chairlift buddy," Teddy assured her. "I have great jokes."

"You have *dad* jokes." Beatrice laughed, shaking her head. "Actually, you'll get to spend more time with everyone this weekend. Louise is throwing a party and she wants us to—" At the look on Teddy's face, she broke off. "What is it?"

"I was going to tell you—I want to head back to Boston. I'll stay for Louise's party," he said hastily, "but after that, I need to head home. I have to deal with a few things."

"Is everything okay?"

"Just some stuff related to the duchy."

Beatrice felt a pang of guilt. Several months ago, the Eatons had begun training Teddy's younger brother Lewis as the future Duke of Boston, since Teddy would be forced to relinquish the title. Unlike Teddy, who'd been studying the ducal responsibilities and finances practically since birth, Lewis had grown up like Samantha or Jeff: assuming he would never have to carry the burden.

"It sounds like Lewis needs me," Teddy added. *And you don't,* Beatrice silently finished for him.

"Of course you should go," she assured him.

The grandfather clock in her bedroom chimed, making them both jump a little. "I should finish getting ready," Beatrice murmured.

"Here, I'll help." Teddy followed her through her bedroom and into her massive walk-in closet.

"If you insist," Beatrice teased. She untied her robe, letting it fall in a fluffy heap to the floor, and nudged it to one side with her bare foot. Underneath she was wearing nothing but whisper-thin underwear; her gown tonight was strapless, and too tight to need a bra.

Teddy met her gaze in the floor-to-ceiling mirror. His eyes darkened, turning from cornflower blue to a deeper, burning sapphire. Heat pooled low in Beatrice's belly.

"How much time do we have before dinner?" Beatrice murmured.

Teddy's answer was hoarse. "Not nearly enough."

"Then you'll have to find me afterward," she managed. "Especially if you're leaving soon."

Her gown—a delicate tulle one with floral lace appliqué down the skirt—hung on a hook inside the closet. Beatrice lifted it off the hanger and stepped inside.

Wordlessly, Teddy walked around to help with the silk-covered buttons that trailed up the back. Beatrice watched his reflection, holding her breath. He fastened the buttons slowly, one at a time, dropping a kiss on her neck with each one. *Kiss*, button, *kiss*, button. Beatrice felt like her body had surely reached melting point.

"I love you," she told him, her breath catching.

"I love you," he answered, fastening the last button.

Their eyes met in the mirror, and for a moment Beatrice was nothing more than a girl in a pretty dress, standing with the boy she loved.

When he was done, they backed away, breaking the spell that had woven itself between them. Teddy smiled and held out an arm so that Beatrice could place a hand on his elbow.

She stole one last glance at their reflections, then let her fiancé lead her downstairs to dinner.

13

NINA

"I can't believe I'm going to a royal event without you." Nina propped her phone against her shoulder and bent down to adjust a strap on her chunky red heels.

"It's a *library* event. This is the exception that proves the rule," Samantha pointed out. A horn blared a few feet from Nina, and on the other end of the line, Sam sighed. "Please tell me you didn't take the metro in a cocktail dress."

"Of course not." Nina's outfit wasn't actually a cocktail dress, but she didn't bother correcting Sam. "I walked."

"That's even worse!"

"Why? It's nice out, and it was only a quarter mile."

"That's not the point! You'll show up at the event with sweat stains," Sam spluttered. "And messy hair!"

"Like you just said, it's a library event. No one will care what I look like. I'm just here to get Makayla's signature and pig out on hors d'oeuvres." *And see Jeff,* Nina didn't say aloud.

Samantha groaned. "You brought books with you, didn't you?"

"Only one book!" Nina said defensively. "What else was I supposed to do? I'm not going to be one of those weird fans who ask an author to sign a body part."

Sam chuckled. "Nina—I hate to cut this short, but I actually need to go get ready. I'm having dinner with Marshall's family tonight."

"That's great!" Nina was excited for Sam and Marshall; their relationship was clearly getting more serious.

"Anyway, have fun nerding out! Love you," Sam told her before hanging up.

When Nina reached the library's front steps, she paused. The building felt different than usual tonight, its iconic stone columns bathed in the glow of the party lights, making it all seem like a mirage. Inside, she heard the raised voices and laughter of the usual gala crowd—glamorous young people, all vying to outshine and outtalk and outmaneuver one another.

She'd been surprised when Jeff invited her to tonight's event. He'd brought it up yesterday, over lunch in the dining hall. Nina had resolved not to mention the tailgate, but Jeff had asked about it right away.

"You left before I could say goodbye," he'd ventured, casting her a curious glance. "Did you have fun?"

Nina wondered why no one had told him about her confrontation with Gabriella. Maybe Gabriella was embarrassed to admit she'd caused a scene.

"I had fun. Thanks for inviting me," Nina told him. Jeff nodded, though she could tell he didn't quite believe her.

Nina often couldn't help feeling like they were enrolled at completely different schools. Jeff belonged to another side of King's College, populated by the same people he'd known at his all-boys high school, and at court, and in every other corner of his wealthy, royal life. Nina didn't have much in common with those people.

At least she could be certain that her friends liked her for her own sake, not because of what she could *do* for them.

"I have this event coming up for the Young Patrons of the Public Library," Jeff had explained, setting down his fork. "I have to go on Beatrice's behalf. Do you want to come?"

"That's okay." Nina had attended enough of these parties

with Sam to know that the Young Patrons—of every organization, whether it was the ballet or the museum or the wildlife conservation fund—were people who wanted to *see and be seen.* They rarely cared all that much about their so-called cause.

"Are you sure? The guest of honor is Makayla Oyeney."

"What?" Nina's voice came out as a barely audible squeak. Makayla was the author of the Kingmaker series, a fantasy epic that had just been adapted into a hit TV show. Now the world was anxiously awaiting the sixth and final book.

"So you'll come?" Jeff had asked.

"For the record, this is shameless bribery. But yes, absolutely."

Now, as Nina glanced around the entrance hall, she felt acutely aware that she didn't know anyone here. Women in couture dresses clutched champagne in thin-stemmed flutes; men in tailored suits laughed as they snatched Gruyère tartlets from passing trays. Nina's flowy skirt and top felt too casual; she thought of Sam's admonishment and resisted the urge to check her armpits for sweat stains.

She pulled out her phone, if only to look busy, and saw a notification bubble alerting her to a new email. Reflexively Nina clicked over to the message. As she read, her stomach seized in panic.

Ms. Gonzalez:

We regret to inform you that we are terminating your status as a recipient of financial aid for the upcoming quarter. This year, King's College saw a tremendous increase in the number of students receiving economic assistance, which forced us to reexamine the qualifications of our current financial aid students. Upon review of your family's tax records, we have determined that your Expected Family Contribution does not qualify you to receive funding. . . .

Surely this was a mistake. The school *couldn't* be withdrawing her financial aid. Yes, Nina's mamá worked for the government, but her perks came in the form of free housing—they lived in a grace-and-favor house, owned by the royal family— rather than a high salary. Nina wasn't sure what her parents would do if asked to pay her tuition in full.

Numbly, she glanced back at the email. The message was signed *The King's College Board of Trustees*, followed by a list of eight names: Lady Ottoline Hereford, Guarav Mehta, Dr. Bernard Fjeld, and so on.

The final name on the list: His Grace, the Duke of Virginia. That is, Ambrose Madison.

Gabriella's words echoed in Nina's head. *You're going to regret this.*

No, Nina thought wildly. Gabriella might be selfish and awful, but surely she hadn't asked her father to pull Nina's financial aid because Nina had stood up to her. Surely she wasn't petty enough to try to get Nina kicked out of *school*. It was nowhere near a proportional response to their fight at the tailgate.

Except that people like Gabriella had no sense of proportion, since they didn't live in the real world. Nina had seen it herself, in all her interactions with Daphne.

"Nina!" Jefferson wove through the crowds toward her. His grin faded when he saw the look on her face. "Is everything okay?"

It *wasn't* okay, not by a long shot, but this wasn't the time or place to lecture Jeff about his choice in friends. Or to tell him that she might be forced out of King's College. So Nina smiled and slid her phone back into her bag. "All good."

"I was just talking with Makayla. Want me to introduce you?"

"*Hell* yes." Nina didn't want to face that email right now. She wanted to meet her literary icon and think about fantasy, not reality.

Brimming with questions, she followed Jeff toward the center of the atrium—only to freeze when she saw that Makayla was deep in conversation with none other than Daphne.

"You didn't tell me Daphne was coming." Normally Nina wouldn't have spoken that thought aloud, but her patience for spoiled aristocrats was at an all-time low right now.

A sheepish expression darted over Jeff's face. "I know it's uncomfortable between the two of you, since you and I—I mean—because of our history," he got out. Nina imagined that this must be as awkward for him as it was for her. "But I meant it when I said that I hope we can all hang out. Can you try to get along with her? Please?"

It was the *please* that got her. Nina's relationship with Jeff had been through so many ups and downs; she couldn't risk damaging it, now that they were finally, tentatively, friends again. Daphne wasn't worth that.

Makayla smiled as they approached. "Your Highness, Daphne was just telling me that the proceeds from tonight's event will be spent redoing the children's wing."

Nina gave an involuntary gasp of outrage. "The children's wing? You can't get rid of the tree house!" The artificial tree, complete with plastic roots that curled over the green carpet and a wooden platform perched up in the branches, was an iconic part of the library.

"Makayla, I'd like you to meet my friend Nina," Jeff interjected. "She's the one I was telling you about."

Nina waited for Daphne to excuse herself—surely she wanted to work the room, filled as it was with the wealthy and titled—but for some reason Daphne stayed put. Fine, then. Nina would just ignore her.

"Ms. Oyeney, I'm such a fan of yours." A million questions vied in her head, and she blurted one out. "I have a theory that Luke is really Nymia's son. Am I right?"

Makayla smiled. "If you're as voracious a reader as

Jefferson says you are, then you'll know I can't reveal any plot secrets. Not when I have another book to write."

One of the librarians bustled over. "Ms. Oyeney, the photographer was hoping to get a photo of you and His Highness with the library's chairwoman. Are you free?"

"Please, before you go—can you sign my book?" Nina was too eager to be embarrassed as she opened her tote bag and pulled out the third Kingmaker book, *Of Sea and Sky*.

Makayla unearthed a Sharpie from her pocket and scrawled *To Nina* on the title page. "It was lovely to meet you. Have a wonderful rest of your evening."

Once the author and Jeff had left, Nina started to turn aside. She refused to acknowledge Daphne with even a single syllable.

"You're wrong about Luke, you know." Daphne was still staring pointedly down into her champagne. But she had to be talking to Nina; Jeff and Makayla were already halfway across the room.

Nina stared at her. "Excuse me?"

"Luke can't be Nymia's child; his mother is clearly the Lady of the Rivers," Daphne said impatiently.

Nina couldn't tell what surprised her more: the fact that Daphne had spoken to her, or that Daphne knew anything about the Kingmaker series. "The Lady of the Rivers?" Nina said slowly. "How would Luke have gotten earth magic if his mother is a water nymph?"

"But is it *really* earth magic?" Daphne glanced up, her eyes glinting in challenge. "He can transfigure. No one knows where that power comes from. And it fits the words of the prophecy."

Nina listened, dumbfounded, as Daphne recited the prophecy from the first book. "Wow," she said at last. "I never pegged you as someone who reads Kingmaker."

"We all need a little escapism, don't we?"

It bothered Nina, knowing that she and Daphne were fans of the same series. "I just figured that you're too busy painting your nails and planting stories in the press to bother with books. Aside from Machiavelli, of course."

Daphne didn't flinch. "Really? I'm shocked that *you* like the Kingmaker books. They're about a cunning, devious princess who plots and kills people in order to get back her throne."

When Daphne's words sank in, Nina barked out a disbelieving laugh. "The books aren't about Alina. She's a cold-hearted, scheming manipulator. She's the villain!"

Daphne shrugged. "Villain, hero—isn't it just a matter of perspective?"

Nina felt herself getting increasingly angry, at Daphne and Gabriella, and—irrationally, ridiculously—at Alina, though she was a fictional character. They all just steamrolled through the world, taking what they wanted, tossing aside anyone they couldn't use. Letting their whims dictate their actions.

"You're wrong," she said hotly.

Daphne smirked. "Nina, I can't be wrong about my favorite character. That's a matter of personal opinion, definitionally."

"It's still wrong of you to like her! But you don't see her as evil, do you? Anything is acceptable in pursuit of a crown, is that right?"

Nina's blood was pounding, the rest of the room receding to a blur as she stared at Daphne. And yet . . . there was something oddly refreshing about talking to Daphne like this. With Daphne she could say exactly what she thought, no matter how viciously unfiltered. The only other person she could talk to with such brutal honesty was Sam.

"I respect that Alina is clearheaded in going after what she wants," Daphne countered. "And I still don't understand why you insist on calling her evil. Luke has killed people over the course of the series too. A lot of people. Yet he is brave and she is evil?"

"Because Luke was defending his throne!" Nina burst out.

"Alina thinks it's *her* throne," Daphne said quietly. "They can't both have it."

She wasn't talking about Kingmaker anymore, was she? This was about the two of them, and Jeff.

"Jeff and I are friends again, okay? That clearly bothers you, but guess what? I don't care."

Daphne's voice was low and significant. "That's all you want with Jefferson? To be *friends?*"

"I know this won't make any sense to you, given the way your mind works," Nina scoffed, "but some of us actually hang around Jeff because we *like* him. Not because we want to be a princess."

It was probably time to head home; Nina had already gotten her moment with Makayla. But Rachel had looked up the tickets to this benefit online, so Nina knew that they'd cost six hundred dollars apiece. For that much money, she should at least try one of the cheese tartlets that were being passed around. And whatever expensive beer they served at events like this.

Nina started to turn, but Daphne's voice chased her. "Where do you think you're going?" She sounded outraged that Nina had dared to walk away mid-conversation. As if Nina owed Daphne anything.

"To the bar," Nina snapped.

Daphne elbowed past her. "Not if I get there first."

14

DAPHNE

Daphne stormed ahead, her heels making satisfying clicks against the stone floor. She had no idea why she was blazing past Nina like this, or really why she was talking to Nina at all, except that something about it was curiously refreshing.

Lately it had felt like Daphne did nothing but pretend. She pretended with the press, with the world, with Jefferson, saying over and over how "excited" she was to take a year off school. Daphne was a master of artifice, but this lie kept turning sour in her mouth—because her heart wasn't in it.

Talking to Nina, Daphne could drop the picture-perfect act and say how she actually felt for once. After all, that was how she and Nina had always been: each of them hurling barbed truths at the other with the intention to kill.

They reached the bar on one side of the atrium. To their right, a set of doors led to the public reading room, its walls lined with stained-glass windows. The setting sun slanted through the panes, casting dancing patches of red and blue and gold over the floor, like a living carpet.

Daphne watched Nina shove her way to the bar, waving enthusiastically to get the bartender's attention. "Excuse me. Can I get a beer? And a specialty cocktail for her," she added, with a dismissive wave in Daphne's direction. "If you could find a paper umbrella, too, that would be great."

Daphne cut in. "I don't need the cocktail, thanks. A white wine would be perfect."

"You don't want the . . ." Nina paused to read one of the hand-lettered signs near the bar, then winced. "'Rye and Prejudice'?"

"Whiskey and cherry juice? No thanks." Daphne shuddered. "Besides, a Jane Austen drink should never be pink."

"That might be the first thing you and I have ever agreed upon." Nina sounded annoyed to have been deprived of another reason to hate Daphne. But then, she had more than enough reasons as it was.

"Second, if you count our love of Kingmaker," Daphne pointed out, only somewhat sarcastically.

"I refuse to count that, given how misguided your opinions are."

The bartender returned with their drinks. Daphne took a sip of wine, her eyes automatically flicking around the room to study the crowds. Lord Philip Rattray stood in the corner; he always had the irritated, slightly impatient look of someone who thought he had better places to be. And there was the Countess of Claremont, deep in conversation with Madeleine Barrett—who was only five years older than Daphne but already had three broken engagements to her name.

Unlike Nina, whose discomfort in this crowd was evident, Daphne belonged with these people. She should be circulating through the party, trading favors and gossip, instead of standing here with a nobody who had nothing to offer.

Yet she didn't move, and neither did Nina.

"So. You used to spend time in the tree house?" Daphne meant it as an innocuous question, but habit won out and it sounded more like criticism.

Nina's reply was equally biting. "I did. This may shock you, but I came to a charity event at the library because I actually care about the library."

"You have no idea what I do or do not care about. For your information, the library matters to me, too." Daphne let out a breath. "I also love that tree house. I used to climb up there and read whenever I couldn't bear to be at home. Which was often."

Nina seemed startled by that admission. Daphne gave a breezy laugh, trying to recover. "If I have to do charity work during this joke of a gap year, then the charity work should at least *matter* to me."

"What do you mean?" Nina asked, angling away from the rest of the room. "You don't want to take a gap year?"

Daphne hesitated. She hadn't meant to let that slip, especially to Nina. She'd done such a good job convincing the world that this was her choice.

What hurt was how deeply unsurprised everyone had seemed by her decision. They probably all agreed with Daphne's mother, and assumed she was just waiting around for her royal boyfriend to propose.

Jefferson was the only one who'd really questioned her. "Are you sure?" he'd asked when she broke the news. "I thought we wanted to start King's College together."

"We'll still be there together! Just a year later than we planned," Daphne had exclaimed, her voice falsely bright.

The prince had dropped a kiss on her brow. "Okay. As long as it's what you want."

"It is," Daphne had assured him. Pretending, pretending, the way she always did, as if her life were nothing but one great performance.

But there was no need to pretend anything right now. She'd shown Nina her true colors long ago.

"It's complicated," she said, and sighed. "Let's just say that my family can't afford to send me to college anymore."

"I thought your family was rich," Nina argued.

"We're titled, but that definitely doesn't mean we're rich. Money has always been tight." Daphne leaned her elbows on the bar, then tucked one stiletto behind the other. "Whatever money we did have, my parents spent long ago. Or my dad gambled it away."

"I'm sorry." Nina sounded like she actually meant it. "If it makes you feel any better, I'm in a similar situation. The school's board of trustees has pulled my financial aid."

"What? That's awful," Daphne was shocked into replying.

"I know. I actually just found out," Nina said flatly.

"Are they *allowed* to do that? Did they say why?" Daphne seriously doubted that Nina was failing any of her classes. She felt surprisingly outraged on the other girl's behalf.

"They didn't say, but I know why. Gabriella Madison."

"*Gabriella?*" Daphne was so startled that she blurted out the name. She winced and lowered her voice. "How is she involved in any of this?"

Nina's face hardened. "I should have known she's your friend."

"Absolutely not. I hate her." It was such a relief to admit that aloud. "But what did she do to you?"

Nina launched into a story about how she'd insulted Gabriella at a tailgate for being rude to Jefferson behind his back. "She threatened that she'd make me regret it, and it turns out that she was right," Nina said bitterly. "Honestly, I just can't believe she got her father to have the board of trustees pull my financial aid. Who does that?"

"Gabriella doesn't have a conscience."

"As if you do."

There was something different about Nina this year. A new spiciness to her comebacks, a brazen *I don't care* attitude that Daphne curiously admired. Ever since Ethan had gone

111

abroad, there was no one for Daphne to contradict, to *push* against.

Sparring with Nina, she felt more like herself than she had in months.

"Well, look at that. It seems we found one more thing to agree on: our dislike of Gabriella Madison." At Nina's bemused look, Daphne explained. "She's the source of all my problems, too."

"She's the reason you're not in school?" Nina asked.

"She's trying to get my family stripped of our title. Her father will be putting my father's baronetcy under review at the next Conferrals and Forfeiture Committee meeting. I know Gabriella is really the one behind it." Daphne shot Nina a glance. "And before you say something about how titles shouldn't matter, that they're a stupid holdover from a bygone era, just know that they matter to me."

Nina got a strange look on her face. It was clear that she'd been about to say exactly that.

"Losing our status would be humiliating, and awful. It would make me feel utterly helpless. Kind of like being a student and having someone take away your financial aid just because you refused to suck up to her like everyone else does," Daphne added pointedly.

To her surprise, Nina nodded in understanding. "What are you going to do?"

"I don't know. The committee will review my father's case later this month." Daphne looked over at Nina. "What are you going to do about your scholarship?"

"I'll start by appealing my case to the financial aid office."

"That won't accomplish anything, if Gabriella's father was personally involved."

"Then I'll look for another job, ask my parents what we

can do to pay. I'm not dropping out of school, no matter what it takes," Nina said vehemently.

Daphne wished she'd had that option.

"Daphne—Nina." Jefferson came to stand between them, the crowds parting before him like the Red Sea, the way they always did. He seemed pleased to see them together. "What are you two talking about?"

"Just girl stuff," Daphne said evasively.

But to her shock, Nina chimed in. "You know, gossiping about people we don't like."

Jefferson seemed puzzled, but then he shrugged. He had no interest in the rumor mill, unlike practically everyone else at this party.

If she didn't know better, Daphne might have said that she and Nina shared an amused, almost complicit look at his expression. She quickly broke eye contact and looped an arm proprietarily through Jefferson's, nestling closer to him.

She had no business finding any sort of common ground with Nina. It was too dangerous, relating to an enemy.

Even if the thing you had in common was another enemy.

♛

Jefferson shifted on his sectional so that his legs stretched out, bare feet crossed one over the other. He'd tossed his blazer over a nearby chair and unbuttoned the collar of his white button-down, revealing a tanned triangle of chest. It was a sight millions of women would have killed for.

"You were amazing tonight, Daphne," he told her. "I don't know how I could manage those things without you."

"Luckily for you, you'll never have to find out," she said lightly.

They were in his sitting room upstairs, sprawled out before

113

the TV, which they'd flipped to an old action movie. Daphne didn't always return to the palace with him after these events, but when the library party had ended and Jefferson had asked if she wanted to come over, she'd realized that she did want to, very much. There was a hollow ache in her chest that she refused to diagnose, though deep down she recognized it as loneliness.

"By the way, thank you for making an effort with Nina. I know she's Sam's best friend, but she was my friend too, before . . ."

Before you ruined the friendship by dating, Daphne thought. She wondered briefly if that was what had happened with her and Ethan. Maybe they should have been friends all along, and she'd let sex muddle everything between them.

"I'm glad you and Nina are friends again. Really," Daphne lied.

Jefferson smiled, relieved. "Thanks, Daph. It's just nice having Nina at school, you know? I wish you were there too, of course."

It was endearing how nervous he was to discuss Nina with Daphne. He was so solicitous of her feelings that it made Daphne oddly self-conscious of how little she returned the favor. She so rarely put anyone else's desires before her own.

"Don't worry, I'll be at school next year. And in the meantime, you're getting the lay of the land for me. It's perfect."

Daphne must have delivered her line with a little too much enthusiasm, because Jefferson looked at her curiously. "Do you still feel like you made the right choice, taking a gap year?"

She readied herself to deliver her usual canned answer, the one she'd been giving to courtiers and reporters who asked about her time off: *Between all my junior board positions and charities, I don't even have time for class right now!*

But Jefferson was looking at her with bright, earnest eyes, and now that Daphne had told the truth—to Nina, of all people—she found that the lie just wouldn't come.

"Honestly, I'm not sure," she confessed. "I guess I thought I would have more to do."

"In that case, I was wondering if you would help with some of the events I have to carry out as Regent. Will you cohost the military banquet in a few weeks?"

Daphne tried not to let her excitement show. Did Jefferson realize the full import of what he was asking? Hosting an event, particularly something as rigidly protocol-driven as a military banquet, was a task that could only be performed by a senior member of the royal family. She was pretty sure Jefferson had broken an unwritten rule by asking her to take this on. But no way was she going to point that out.

She'd attended more events with Jefferson over the years than she could count, but always as his date, as a *guest*. Being the *hostess* of an event at the palace was something else entirely.

"Thank you. I'd be honored," she told him, and he smiled.

"Of course. I just want to make you happy, Daph."

The warmth of his eyes was so disarming, she almost— *almost*—told him everything. About Gabriella, and her family's demise, and how truly desperate she felt.

Yet she couldn't risk tugging even a single thread of the image she had woven around herself. If Jefferson learned about her family's title, everything else might begin to unspool— what she and Ethan had done, and what she'd done to Himari.

Jefferson wouldn't want the *real* her.

No one would.

The Daphne he thought he knew was a myth. That girl had never existed; Daphne had invented her, over years of painstakingly doing or saying exactly what she thought Jefferson wanted. That Daphne was utterly separate from her, a persona she took off at the end of the day, like the Korean sheet masks she used.

Jefferson snaked an arm around her, pulling her closer. There was something so reassuring about the rise and fall of his chest. "I love you," he said softly.

He spoke the words so easily, with his whole heart. And for the first time in all their years together, Daphne wondered if she might love him, too. Not in the way he thought she loved him—the passionate, romance-novel, heart-stopping way—but something softer and more tranquil.

She might not be *in* love with Jefferson, but she did love him. There were many kinds of love, weren't there? Who was to say that one was any more valid than another?

She shifted around to stare at him: his thick lashes, the even slope of his nose, the hint of stubble along his jawline. After all this time, his features were as familiar to Daphne as her own reflection.

Her relationship with Ethan had been turbulent and painful. They were both too sharp, too aggressive, and far too ruthless. Daphne had spent years peeling away his layers, searching for the real Ethan beneath all the bravado and wit.

There were no layers to Jefferson. He was sweet and uncomplicated all the way to his core, which was more than Daphne could say for herself.

Jefferson caught her glance and smiled. "What are you thinking about?" he asked, and for the second time that night, Daphne answered honestly.

"About us."

She was suddenly aware that they were alone in the palace. Jefferson's sisters were both at the League of Kings conference, and Queen Adelaide was out of town. For once, there was no one to walk in on them.

Daphne knew that most of America assumed she and Jefferson had been sleeping together for years. But they never had.

If Jefferson had pressured her even once, Daphne might have changed her mind, but he seemed content to let her set the pattern of their relationship. Which only confirmed Daphne's faith in her strategy. She wasn't some casual hookup; she was a princess-to-be, and she'd behave accordingly.

That was the reason she and Jefferson had waited, Daphne told herself. It had nothing to do with the fact that she'd been in love with Ethan all those years.

Well, Ethan was in the past now. She was done with him and recommitted to Jefferson. What was she waiting for anymore?

Daphne tipped her face up to Jefferson's and kissed him.

He returned the kiss easily, tracing circles on her back, and Daphne skimmed her hands up his arms and around his shoulders, deepening the kiss.

One by one, she undid the buttons of his shirt, then slid it off. Jefferson sucked in a breath as she reached around her back to pull at her zipper. Her cocktail dress loosened, falling in a delicate pink spill around her waist and frothing up around her legs.

"Daph." Jefferson's heart was pounding beneath her palm. "Are you—"

"Shhh." She silenced his question with a kiss. Then, her meaning unmistakable, she reached for the waistband of his trousers. His skin felt hot to the touch.

Still, Jefferson pulled away and caught her hands in his. "Daphne," he asked hoarsely. "Are you sure? I thought . . . I mean . . ."

"I'm sure," she told him.

Jefferson studied her expression for a moment, as if trying

to figure out what had changed her mind. Then he smiled. "All right."

He stood in a single movement, swept Daphne into his arms as easily as if she weighed nothing at all, and carried her through the doorway to his bedroom.

15

SAMANTHA

"Marshall, please!" Sam whacked her boyfriend lightly on the shoulder. "We're almost at your grandparents' house, and you haven't told me which of these I should bring as a thank-you gift for dinner. What will they like more, the chocolate truffles"—she pulled each item out of an oversized shopping bag as she narrated—"the aromatherapy diffuser, the coffee beans, or the linen hand towels? Beatrice says if you give hand towels, they have to be monogrammed, but I didn't have time for that."

He began sorting through her various gifts. "You don't have any wine in this Mary Poppins bag of yours?"

Sam flushed. "I worried it might seem rude, bringing wine to people who own a vineyard. If you give them any other wine, then you're implying theirs isn't the best, but it would be weird to bring them a bottle of their *own* wine, right?" Flustered, she called out to the driver. "Sorry, is there a liquor store on the way? We need to make a stop—"

"Sam, I was kidding." Marshall put a hand over hers. "This is just dinner, okay? It's not a big deal."

She knew he was trying to reassure her, but for once, she wished he were less flippant, less irreverent. "It's a big deal to me," she said quietly.

Their car slowed to a halt, and Sam looked up at the soaring white pillars of the ducal mansion. "You know what? I'll just bring everything," she decided, gathering the various boxes into her arms as the driver came around to open the door. She had to jostle all the gifts in her arms to keep from dropping any of them to the ground.

"I can carry some of that for you, if you want," Marshall offered, trotting alongside her.

"Fat chance. They're *my* presents."

"Wait a second. *What* are you wearing?" he asked, as if just now noticing her cowl-necked sweater dress and black heels.

Sam must have tried on two dozen outfits before finally admitting defeat and asking for her sister's help. Getting old people to like her was one of Beatrice's strong suits.

"I got dressed up," she told him, and Marshall barked out a laugh.

"For a job interview to sell life insurance in Ohio?"

Before Sam could answer, Marshall's grandmother—Lady Joanna Davis, Duchess of Orange—opened the door.

"Your Royal Highness," she said warmly, lowering herself into a curtsy before Sam.

"Oh, please don't call me that! It makes me sound a hundred years old!"

The moment she said it, Sam cringed; that probably wasn't the right thing to say to Marshall's eighty-two-year-old grandmother. But the duchess just smiled, her eyes crinkling pleasantly around the corners.

"What I meant was, please call me Sam." She tried unsuccessfully to hand over the gifts, but the diffuser almost shattered on the floor, and Marshall stepped forward to help. "Um—these are for you, Your Grace. Thank you for inviting me into your lovely home."

"It's our pleasure, Sam. And please, call me Jojo, like Marshie here does." The duchess turned and pulled her grandson in for a hug. Sam nearly hooted with delight.

"Marshie!" she whispered as they followed his grandmother into the cavernous entry hall. "I can't believe I didn't think of that one. Best. Nickname. Yet."

"I already regret bringing you here," he replied.

"Sam!" Rory, Marshall's sister, stepped forward to help Sam deposit the rest of her boxes on a side table. "You came prepared," she added, opening the box of truffles and popping a coconut one into her mouth.

"How's school?" Sam asked.

Rory brightened. She was a junior in college, studying computer science. "I'm in this amazing class on robotics right now. I programmed a toy car to drive itself around the room!"

"Rory's on track to graduate with honors," Marshall's grandfather announced, joining their conversation. His eyes cut to Marshall, and Sam felt the silent reproach beneath his words—the disappointment that Rory was succeeding where Marshall had barely squeaked by with passing grades.

Sam didn't understand the Davises' attitude toward Marshall's dyslexia. He had a learning difficulty, but so what? He was still one of the smartest people she knew; his intelligence just manifested in different ways. He was perceptive and quick-witted and empathetic and thoughtful, instead of book smart. Yet his family acted like his dyslexia was something to hide, as shameful as if he'd committed a felony.

She fought back the urge to rush to Marshall's defense and instead turned respectfully to his grandfather. "Thank you for having me, Your Grace."

Stephen Davis bowed stiffly, his back ramrod-straight. "It's an honor, Your Royal Highness."

He didn't ask her to call him by a grandparent name, and Sam knew better than to suggest he call her Sam.

Marshall's parents greeted her a bit more warmly, but Sam told herself that was because they knew her better, not because Marshall's grandfather disapproved of her.

When they all sat down to dinner, Sam was disappointed to see that she'd been seated as far from Marshall as possible. At least she was next to Rory. They began passing dishes around the table: biscuits and butter, green beans, and an enormous Pyrex filled with something vaguely beige and sloppy-looking. No one said what it was. As Sam scooped some onto her plate, she felt Marshall's grandmother watching her.

"This looks delicious. I love chicken," Sam said, trying to sound enthusiastic.

Next to her, she felt Rory swallowing silent laughter.

"This isn't chicken casserole; it's grouse," the duchess explained. "Stephen and I hunt these ourselves, when we go shooting up in the valley. The grouse are becoming a real problem up there, overbreeding, forcing out the natural wildlife."

"Well, I can't wait to try it." Sam forced herself to take a bite of the casserole, though it looked alarmingly like dog food. Somehow it managed to be too salty and bland at the same time.

"Be careful how you bite into it. There might still be some shot in there," the duchess added placidly. "I wouldn't want you breaking a tooth."

As Sam was still grappling with this alarming possibility, the duke turned to her. "Samantha, how is the League of Kings conference going so far?"

Marshall's parents, who'd been asking Rory about her professors, fell silent. An expectant hush extended over the table as everyone glanced at Sam.

She didn't want to admit that the conference had been something of a letdown—that the heirs probably didn't need to be there at all. Their presence was purely ceremonial, their lectures designed to keep them busy, with topics like "Financial Markets in an International Context" and "Labor and Infrastructure: A Symbiotic Relationship." Sam had already dozed off on two occasions.

"It's been informative," she said diplomatically. "Mainly I'm grateful that I get to be in Orange for a whole month and spend time with Marshall. I don't know if any of you watched, but he did a fantastic job at the opening ceremonies," she added. "It's no easy feat, keeping the Orb of State balanced on a velvet pillow, but Marshall managed it."

Marshall shrugged. "At least I looked better than the Duke of Virginia, galloping down the great hall."

"He didn't *gallop*," Sam admonished, a smile tugging at her mouth. Ambrose Madison *had* seemed a little ridiculous, especially since he was such a heavy man and on such a heavy horse.

"If he'd galloped, the whole thing would have been even better." Marshall's eyes danced. "Can I trade roles with him? I'd rather be the guy on horseback than the guy with the Orb of State."

"Marshall," his grandfather cut in, "I hope you're not distracting the princess from her duties."

Sam hurried to answer. "Of course not, Your Grace. If anything, Marshall is making things easier on me."

"Still, perhaps it's best that he give you a bit of distance. I know how important your presence at the conference is. After all, the whole purpose is to forge connections with your fellow monarchs and heirs."

Sam bristled. Was the duke implying that she'd been playing hooky in order to skip around town with his grandson?

"I've spent a lot of time with Princess Louise, actually," Sam fibbed. "She's hosting a reception soon, and Marshall and I are going."

Really, Sam had only spoken to Louise in passing—and from what Beatrice had said, it sounded like Louise was throwing more of a house party than a networking event— but Sam figured a bit of exaggeration wouldn't hurt anyone.

The table dissolved into several conversations at once.

Marshall and his grandfather debated how bad this year's drought would be, Sam asked Rory in more detail about her classes, and Marshall's mother and grandmother wondered if they could get someone they disliked kicked out of their church choir.

"Monica just doesn't have any *range*," Marshall's mother was saying. "I mean, even Marshall or Rory could sing better than she does."

"You can sing?" Sam asked Rory, who laughed.

"No, that's the point: neither of us has a shred of musical talent. Marshall was so bad he actually got cut from an elementary-school skit."

"I wasn't cut!" Marshall protested, jumping into their discussion. "I was just demoted from the chorus, since I was so woefully off-key. I played a tree."

"A tree," Sam repeated, fighting very hard not to laugh.

"I had to wear green and stand there with my arms lifted."

"And he couldn't even manage that! He let his arms fall partway through," Rory exclaimed.

"I got tired, okay?"

"The skit was three minutes! It was *one* song!"

The entire table erupted in good-natured laughter.

Finally, when her chuckling had subsided, Sam spoke up. "Marshall may not be able to carry a tune, but he's definitely creative. I can't wait to have him on our charades team at New Year's. Jeff and I lose every year." Sam felt a pang at the thought of that game; their dad used to play with the twins, against Beatrice and their mom.

Marshall's grandfather lifted an eyebrow. "New Year's?"

Sam glanced at Marshall, who was staring at his plate. She hadn't meant to offend anyone or imply that she was pulling rank. "Sorry," she said haltingly. "I didn't mean to steal Marshall away. I just hoped he could come with us to Telluride."

"That sounds lovely, but I'm afraid he won't be able to

make it. He's got a lot of obligations at home," his grandfather said smoothly.

Obligations? When she and Marshall had talked about it, he'd made it sound like his family was rarely together on New Year's Eve, that there wasn't even an official event for the duchy. He usually just went to a friend's party in Malibu.

"I understand." Sam tried to sound upbeat. "We can talk about it in a few months and see if your plans have changed. Marshall, maybe you can come for just a day or two—"

"Marshall's plans aren't changing." Any trace of warmth was gone from his grandfather's tone. "He's the future duke, and he needs to be here. This isn't up for discussion."

Sam didn't dare say more. Marshall still wasn't looking at her, instead staring vaguely down at the table.

When Rory stood to go to the bathroom, she looked at Sam in a way that made Sam rise to her feet and join her.

"I, for one, am still hungry," Rory whispered, when they'd left the dining room. "Want an ice cream sandwich?"

"Absolutely."

Sam followed Rory to a mudroom off the garage, which held a jumble of gardening tools and old shoes. A refrigerator hummed against one wall. Rory opened the freezer door at the top and reached behind bags of frozen vegetables to pull out a box of ice cream sandwiches. She handed one to Sam.

"Grandpa keeps these here so Jojo won't catch him," Rory explained. "She thinks he needs to cut back on desserts."

As Sam bit into the ice cream, she stepped closer to the refrigerator. It was covered in photos held up by magnets— nothing like the formal portraits that were framed in the living room, but casual family snapshots, messy and chaotic and full of love.

Sam recognized three-year-old Marshall in a photo at the beach: peeking out from behind his mother's legs, wearing the mischievous expression that Sam knew so well. Marshall at age five, sitting on a horse that was a thousand times bigger than he was. Marshall at his high school graduation, Marshall playing water polo, Marshall with his grandmother up in the mountains.

There were other photos—some of Rory, and some of what Sam assumed were Marshall's cousins—but Marshall certainly took the lion's share.

"From these photos, it looks like your grandparents really love Marshall. But they're so hard on him. On all of you," Sam added clumsily.

"No, you're right—they're stricter with Marshall, since he's the future duke. Grandpa always says that he can't cut Marshall any slack, because the world never will. That in politics, no matter what good you do, you'll always face criticism."

Sam swallowed her bite of ice cream. "That's why governing is so hard, isn't it? You have to balance all these different viewpoints, try to understand where everyone is coming from, and then decide the right path forward."

"Sounds like you've been thinking about this," Rory observed.

"I had a lot of time to think on tour this summer." Sam reached up to straighten one of the photos that had gone askew. "We don't get to choose whether we rule. It's chosen for us, because the best rulers are the reluctant ones. People who *want* to lead, people who are in it for the fame and power—those people will never put the country first."

"You've been reading Socrates," Rory said appreciatively, and Sam smiled.

"I thought you were a computer science major."

"I like to think of myself as a Renaissance woman," Rory quipped.

Sam crinkled her ice cream wrapper into a little ball, then tossed it into the trash can. Still just as good as she was in elementary school. "Okay, now I really do need to use the bathroom," she confessed, and headed inside.

On her way back, she saw that the rest of the group was still in the dining room. Sam wasn't trying to eavesdrop, but when she overheard her own name, she stopped in her tracks.

"You and Samantha seem to be spending a great deal of time together," the duke was saying.

Marshall's mother interjected. "Of course he's spending time with her! She's the princess, and she's here in Orange for the month. What would you suggest he do, ignore her?"

Sam held her breath. Light spilled out of the doorway a few feet ahead of her.

"The newspapers are paying more and more attention to you both."

Finally she heard Marshall's voice. "Isn't that what you wanted, Grandpa? *You're* the one who encouraged me to date her in the first place, because you thought it would be good for Orange."

"I encouraged you to *be her date* to her sister's wedding, which didn't even happen! And because she was a nice change from those starlets you used to run around town with." The duke snorted. "They were an embarrassment."

"I'm aware," Marshall said impatiently.

Sam's stomach twisted. She knew that Marshall's grand-father had encouraged their relationship, back when they were only pretending to date. But it still hurt, knowing that he'd only ever thought of her in terms of what she could do for his family—for their image.

The duke sighed. "When I encouraged you to go out with Samantha, I assumed you would move on after a few months, the way you always do. I certainly didn't expect it to get serious."

"It's not serious," Marshall assured him.

Sam sucked in a breath. She must have misunderstood, or misheard, or . . .

"Of course it's not serious!" Marshall's mother chimed in. "He knows better, don't you, Marshall?"

"I hope so. You could never actually have any kind of future with a Washington."

There was so much anger packed into the way the duke said *Washington* that Sam wondered if he hated her family for ruling over his. The Davises were former kings, after all—maybe Stephen thought that the Davises should never have given up Orange's independence to join the union.

Maybe the transfer of power from Marshall's family to hers, over a hundred years ago, hadn't been as amicable and easy as the history books made it seem.

"Trust me, you have nothing to worry about," Marshall told his grandfather. "Sam and I certainly haven't discussed the future."

Sam's eyes stung. She retreated back down the hallway, trying to rearrange her face into something like normal. She could do that, because it was what being a princess had trained her to do—to pretend that everything was fine, even when her heart was breaking.

16

DAPHNE

Daphne breezed through the revolving door to the King's College library, where students were busy typing at their laptops or flipping through books. She wasn't particularly worried about being seen; anyone who recognized her would assume she was on campus to visit Jefferson.

The guy behind the reference desk looked up at her approach. From his blank expression, it was clear that he had no idea who Daphne was. "Can I help you find something?"

"I'm looking for Nina," Daphne said brightly. "She's still on her shift, right?"

"She's here," he started to say just as Nina emerged from the back room. Her eyes widened when she saw Daphne at the desk.

"I've got this one, Greg." Nina's voice was deadly quiet.

Greg shrugged and vanished into the back. The moment he was gone, Nina whirled on her. "Seriously, Daphne? You're stalking me now?"

Daphne held her gaze. "I tried calling you, but you never answered."

"Because I have no desire to talk to you!" Nina spluttered. "How did you even get my number? Did you hack my phone?"

"Don't be so dramatic. I asked Jefferson for your info." At the mention of the prince, Nina hesitated, and Daphne hurried to keep talking. "I told him that we bonded at the library event, and said I wanted your number, since we're friends now."

"You and I are *not* friends," Nina snapped.

Daphne gave a cool smile. "Of course not. But I want to talk. I have a proposition for you."

"I'm not interested."

"Just hear me out, okay?"

Daphne wasn't used to working this hard for attention. Her words were falling on deaf ears; Nina grabbed a cart laden with books and began pushing it toward a freight elevator. "I have to shelve these."

"I'll come with you, then."

Nina rolled her eyes but didn't argue as Daphne followed her into the elevator. She leaned over the cart and pressed the lowest button, presumably taking them all the way to the basement.

"We're going somewhere quiet, right?" Daphne wished they weren't having this conversation in a public place.

"You don't want anyone to overhear your dark, twisted plots?" Nina asked sarcastically.

"Not really. I'd prefer the dark and twisted stay between us."

Nina made a *hmph* sound, though Daphne detected a note of amusement beneath the annoyance.

When the doors opened onto the C floor, Nina pushed her cart out into the deserted stacks. The lights of each section flickered on at her approach, only to dim again when she'd passed. Daphne trailed along in her wake, footsteps echoing in the stillness.

It should have been creepy down here, but Daphne didn't really mind. There was something oddly comforting about being surrounded by thousands of books.

"I've been thinking a lot about our respective problems," she began, "and I realized that we can work together."

Nina removed a cloth-bound volume labeled *Theodore: The Boy King* and knelt down, tracing the spines until she found whatever call number she was looking for. She wedged the book into its spot on the bottom shelf, then stood. "I'm not interested. Find someone else to be the pawn in your scheme."

"Even if the scheme is to take down Gabriella?" Daphne replied, and Nina fell still.

This was an outrageous, outlandish proposal. A week ago, the thought of asking Nina for help with anything would have made Daphne burst into laughter. Yet she'd been toying with this idea for a few days now, and the more she thought about it, the more appealing it seemed.

"I don't like this any more than you do, but it makes a weird kind of sense. We both want to get out from under Gabriella's thumb," Daphne hurried to explain. "We just need to find something on her—"

"Find something on her? What does that mean?"

"Something incriminating. That way we can hold it over Gabriella's head: threaten to use it against her unless she gives back your scholarship and lets my family keep our title."

A flurry of emotions darted over Nina's face, stunned shock giving way to incredulity. "Is this seriously how your mind works? You went straight to *blackmail?*"

"You're right," Daphne said crisply. "We should just walk up to Gabriella and ask her to pretty-please stop bullying us."

Nina grabbed the cart with both hands and began pushing it again. "Even if that's true, there's no way I could work with you."

Daphne trotted to keep up. "You don't have to *like* me, Nina. You just have to team up with me against the person who's ruining both our lives."

"Why are you so desperate for my help?"

"This is a two-person job," Daphne began, but Nina's eyes narrowed in sudden suspicion.

"You're setting me up to take the fall, aren't you? If you get caught, I'm the one who'll go down for it, not you!" Nina shook her head. "I'm not going to be your scapegoat."

"See, this is why I need you—because you're smart!"

"Did you actually just compliment me?"

"I was stating a fact. You *are* smart. Smart enough to second-guess me, and I respect that." Daphne met Nina's gaze. "But I swear I'm not going to sell you out."

"Maybe *I'll* sell *you* out," Nina warned.

"Maybe," Daphne agreed, "but I don't think you will. You're too honorable to betray someone like that. Even someone you hate," she added, in a softer tone.

Nina said nothing for a long time, but she didn't tell Daphne to leave, so Daphne stayed. She trailed alongside the cart as Nina reshelved books throughout the biographies section. The silence between them was heavy, but not uncomfortable, probably because neither of them expected the other to fill it. It was a simple, undemanding silence, the kind of silence that falls between two very good friends—or between two people who don't care about each other at all.

Daphne watched, a bit curious, as Nina led them to a door along one wall marked OVERSIZED. She flicked on the lights, revealing a storage room filled with various items that wouldn't fit on the shelves: atlases with poster-sized pages, scrolls rolled up in cylindrical tubes. Nina pulled an oversized book of maps from the cart and shelved it. Finally she cleared her throat.

"If we were going to do this—and that's a very hypothetical *if*—what would our plan be?"

Daphne tried, and failed, to hide a smile. "Gabriella is having a birthday party at her family's house this weekend. You and I will both be there."

"She won't let me in the door. I insulted her in front of all her friends," Nina reminded her.

"She can't turn you away if you come with Jefferson. Even Gabriella wouldn't dare tell him no."

Nina frowned. "And then what?"

"We snoop through Gabriella's room, look for something incriminating. Or, *I* do the snooping while you stand guard."

"What do you expect to find?"

"*Anything!* Prescription drugs that were prescribed to someone else. Love letters. Sexy photos. A diary would be best, though I doubt we'll get that lucky."

Nina sounded dubious. "What if we snoop through her room and don't find anything?"

"We'll find something," Daphne assured her. "Everyone has made a mistake. Everyone is hiding some kind of secret."

Nina met her gaze, and Daphne wondered if she was thinking of the various secrets she'd buried. Or maybe Nina was so genuinely open and honest that she *had* no secrets, and was really just remembering all of Daphne's. There were certainly plenty of them.

"Okay. Let's do it," Nina said at last. "Just to be clear, though, I still hate you."

"That makes sense, because I still hate you," Daphne said pleasantly. "I just happen to hate Gabriella more."

♛

That night, after Daphne had met Jefferson at the palace for dinner—and stayed a few more hours, intertwined with him in bed—she took the palace car service home. She was grateful that Jefferson always insisted upon it, since her parents had sold her car a few weeks ago. But as the sedan pulled up her family's driveway, Daphne noticed a strange van parked out front.

"Thank you," she said quickly, throwing open the door before the chauffeur could do it for her. Whatever was going on, she probably didn't want the palace to know.

The driver nodded and pulled away. The Deightons' house was as dark as the night sky, the only light coming from a pair of windows on the second floor and the lemon wedge of moon overhead. Daphne started up the driveway just as a pair of men emerged from the front door. They were carrying something bulky beneath a white dust cloth.

"Careful with that one. It's a real Louis XVI," Daphne's mother hissed as she trailed after them. She was all angles and sharp edges: her brows drawn together, her shoulders hunched beneath a puffy coat.

"It's a little late to have movers here," Daphne ventured, and her mother sniffed.

"I had them come at night so that the neighbors wouldn't see. What if they sold photos to the paparazzi? I can see the headlines now: 'Prince's Girlfriend Strapped for Cash, Sells Off Family Heirlooms.'"

They're not heirlooms, Daphne thought, but kept it to herself. Aloud she said, "Are things really that bad?"

"Your father hired a lawyer to advise him on this whole . . . *situation,*" her mother snapped. "The legal fees are astronomical."

The two of them headed inside, pausing at the entrance to the living room, or what used to be the living room—the only part of the Deightons' house with expensive furniture, since it was where they received all their guests. Upstairs, everything was from mail-order catalogs or secondhand.

Where the plush green sofa used to stand, there was now a yawning blank space. The pair of carved wooden tables that used to sit against the far wall, gone. The tasseled ottoman that Jefferson always propped his feet on, gone.

Daphne could practically feel her mother's frustration

emanating from her in waves, like heat. Rebecca had spent years collecting these pieces, painstakingly scouring estate sales and resale shops, crafting an illusion of generational wealth that fooled no one.

Neither of them spoke as the movers removed the full-length portrait of the old lady in black from its spot above the mantel. The painting, and its placement, implied that she was an illustrious Deighton ancestor, but the truth was that no one knew who she was. When Daphne was little, she used to secretly imagine that the woman was related to her—though she didn't look especially grandmotherly, with her widow's garb and stern, unsmiling expression.

Holding the portrait by its wooden frame, the movers carried it unceremoniously outside.

"I'll buy a couple of reproduction pieces for the living room so that it's not completely empty. Just don't invite Jefferson over," Rebecca said into the silence.

"I won't," Daphne assured her, and started up the stairs. "Good night, Mother."

Well, there clearly wouldn't be money for college tuition anytime soon.

Daphne got ready for bed, but even with a gel mask under her eyes, she felt too agitated to sleep. Everything was roiling wildly in her brain—her parents' desperation, her own fear, and this strange new alliance with Nina Gonzalez.

Already their conversation in the library had acquired the sticky, distorted feeling of a dream. It seemed impossible that she and Nina might actually set aside their resentment long enough to take down a mutual enemy.

Yet it did make a strange kind of sense. For a job like this it was almost *better* that she and Nina didn't like each other. It would keep things unemotional.

Restless, Daphne threw off her bedcovers and padded over to her closet, where she began sliding hangers over the rod. What could she wear to Gabriella's birthday? A navy romper that tied with a white sash: too summery. A silk dress in a bold floral print: too distinctive—everyone had seen it a dozen times. Everything in her closet felt tired, and Daphne couldn't bear the thought of showing up at the Madisons' sprawling mansion in a rewear.

If only there were a way for her to make money without anyone finding out.

Her eyes drifted to her bedside table, where she'd framed an old photo of her and Jefferson, from the very first time she'd been invited to Telluride. She thought of what her mother had said just a few minutes ago. *What if our neighbors sold photos of this to the paparazzi?*

Daphne glanced back at the photo. It was a rare spontaneous shot; these days Daphne was careful to pose, sucking in her stomach and turning to the most flattering angle. In the photo, she and Jefferson were both laughing, their eyes bright. They looked young, and happy, and innocent.

As if Daphne had ever been innocent a day in her life.

It was the work of a few minutes to create a dummy email address—she couldn't afford to contact anyone as herself— and email Natasha, an editor at the *Daily News*.

I have a never-before-seen picture of Prince Jefferson and Daphne Deighton for sale.

Natasha's reply came in seconds later; she was always on her phone.

We offer a standard fee of $1,000 per image. Unless it features tears or nudity, in which case we can negotiate a higher price.

Shoving aside her lingering feelings of regret, Daphne pulled the picture from her photo stream and sent it over.

This wasn't that different from what she usually did, was it? She'd slipped gossip to Natasha countless times. They had a silent understanding that in exchange, Natasha would ensure that Daphne's coverage in the *Daily News* was always flattering, photos glowing and headlines full of praise.

Selling an image of herself for *cash*, though, made Daphne feel like a paparazzo—intrusive, and kind of tacky.

Desperate times called for desperate measures, she reminded herself, and hit Send.

17

NINA

Later that week, Nina smiled at Kenny, the security guard stationed at the back entrance to Washington Palace.

"Hey, Nina," he said pleasantly, not bothering to check her ID; Nina had been on the palace's approved-entry list since she was seven. "You here to see Prince Jeff?"

"Oh—is he home?" Nina felt a funny little flutter of anticipation; she'd thought Jeff might still be on campus. "I'm actually here to borrow something of Samantha's, if that's okay," Nina explained, and Kenny waved her through.

She and Sam had talked on the phone for over an hour last night, Sam recounting what had happened at dinner with Marshall's family. Nina wished she were more surprised. She'd always liked Marshall, primarily because of how happy he made Sam, but she had also worried that their relationship might not last.

She knew firsthand how hard it was to be an outsider, and a person of color, dating a member of the royal family.

"Let's talk about something else," Sam had finally said. "Are you doing anything fun this weekend?" At which point Nina had let slip that she was going to Gabriella Madison's birthday party. Sam had seemed perplexed by the news. "Oh, that should be fun! I've never liked Gabriella, but there's no denying that the Madisons throw a great party. I remember in sixth grade she had a pink-themed birthday." Sam snorted.

"She rented *flamingos* from the zoo as part of the decorations. I think one of them escaped her backyard and still lives out on the river."

"That's pretty excessive for a middle schooler," Nina had said, distracted. She wanted so desperately to tell Sam about Gabriella and her financial aid, but the words kept sticking in her throat. It might be stupid and stubborn of her, but she hated talking about money with Sam—or Jeff. No matter how well intentioned they were, they couldn't relate to Nina's situation in the slightest.

Daphne might be a conniving manipulator, but Nina would say this for her: she understood how it felt to be powerless. And she knew how to fight to reclaim that power.

"Sam," Nina had asked, "would you mind if I borrowed something for the party?" For once, Nina didn't want to show up in one of her cheap fast-fashion dresses and look out of place around all the girls in sequined couture.

"Will Jeff be at this party?" Sam had replied, which seemed irrelevant to Nina.

"Um, yeah. I'm actually going with Jeff and Daphne."

"Ahh," Sam had said meaningfully, then cleared her throat. "Yes, Nina. Obviously you can borrow whatever you want. Maybe that off-the-shoulder pink dress you look so great in?"

Now, as Nina turned onto the upstairs hallway, she saw Jeff emerging from his room. "Nina, hey!" he exclaimed. "You didn't tell me you were coming by."

"I'm here to borrow a dress of Sam's," Nina explained as he fell into step alongside her. "She knows I'm coming— I mean, she said I could wear it," she added, just so he wouldn't think she regularly raided Sam's closet.

"You've talked to Sam recently? How's she doing?" Jeff asked, concerned.

"She's been better, I think." Nina decided to change the subject. She had no desire to get into all the complications of Sam and Marshall's relationship, not with Jeff. It hit too close to home. "You've been busy. I saw you had another few events this week." Jeff had been all over the papers lately, playing catch with the students at an elementary school, unveiling a new statue in John Jay Park.

He shrugged. "I'm just glad to be useful to the monarchy for once."

Nina's chest ached at those words, and she paused in the doorway to Sam's sitting room. "Jeff, you have always been useful to the monarchy."

"Sure, as comic relief," he said easily. "When my family needed someone to go to a dive bar and play darts with the locals, or hand out the trophy on the PGA tour, or salsa dance with the Princess of Mexico, I was the one they called in."

"You *are* a good dancer. Remember that time at the beach house when you danced so hard, you literally danced yourself into the pool?" Nina reminded him, striving for levity.

He chuckled. "I'm lucky none of you got that on camera. Otherwise it would have become a GIF I could never escape."

"It would top all those 'Ten Reasons We're in Love with Prince Jefferson' lists." Nina instantly felt weird; why had she said *love* to Jeff? Luckily, he didn't seem to notice.

"Anyway, I recently met with a few military aides about an upcoming event, and it made me wonder if I should get more involved," he went on.

"As a military liaison?"

"I was thinking more like active service."

Nina blinked. Jeff was still talking, saying how the men in his family had traditionally served in the armed forces, that he would probably enter training after he graduated.

"Jeff. That sounds dangerous," she squeaked. "You could be hurt!"

"So could everyone who enlists in the army. It's a risk I'm willing to sign on for."

Nina was startled by the seriousness in his voice. It was a tone she'd never heard from Jeff before.

She looked up at him—and while she still saw echoes of the boy he'd been, mischievous and playful and spontaneous and warm, she also saw the man he was becoming.

"Anyway, it wouldn't be for another few years. These things always take time," he explained.

Nina's throat closed up. She should tell him how proud she was, and afraid—that she cared about him too much to let him step into harm's way. But before she could articulate any of that, he smiled.

"Sorry, I didn't mean to unload on you. I just . . ." He hesitated. "There aren't many people I can talk about this kind of thing with."

Of course. People were always flocking to Jeff, but they didn't actually want a real conversation. They had no interest in his worries or fears or plans for the future. They wanted a breezy, three-minute exchange—wanted him to crack a joke, chat about sports or a party—and then they wanted to move on, so they could tell everyone for the rest of their lives that they'd met a prince. They wanted a piece of him. They had no desire to get to *know* him.

He was constantly surrounded by people, yet it had to be lonely.

"I'm always here if you need to talk," she promised.

"I know you are."

Nina wasn't sure how to reply to that, so she didn't. She and Jeff seemed to linger in the silence, to dwell in it, as if it were drawing them closer to each other.

"Anyway," he said at last, "tell me about this party that's so formal you need to borrow a dress of Sam's. Why am I not going?"

"You are going. It's Gabriella's birthday party." Nina disappeared into Sam's closet, emerging a moment later with the dress Sam had mentioned, a short fuchsia thing with lace that spilled over its off-the-shoulder neckline.

"Oh good, I'm glad you'll be there," Jeff said excitedly. "Though I have to admit, I didn't know that you and Gabriella are friends."

Nina quickly shook her head. "We're not. Daphne invited me, actually." She tried to sound offhand, but her voice betrayed her.

Jeff beamed. "That's awesome! I was so glad when Daphne asked for your number; I've always thought the two of you would get along. You're actually more like Daphne than like Sam."

"I don't think so," Nina said faintly.

"You're both so smart, and organized, and independent. Sam . . ." He shook his head. "She's way more a fly-by-the-seat-of-your-pants type than a plan-ahead type."

Nina forced herself to smile. "Maybe you're right. Daphne and I really bonded at the library event." *Over our mutual hatred of Gabriella.*

They headed downstairs; Jeff was still at her side, clearly determined to walk Nina back to her car. When they passed one of the sitting rooms, he paused. "Remember when we used to come in here to duel?"

"Of course I remember. We pretended that we were pirates."

"Or revolutionaries fighting George III, or King Benjamin at war with the Spanish."

Jeff walked over to the wall, where rows of épées, their points dulled with rubber tips for safety, hung on wooden plaques. He grabbed two and handed one to Nina. "Let's see if you've still got it."

"Right now?"

"Scared you've lost your touch?"

"Not a chance."

Nina hung Sam's dress over the back of a couch, then turned to face Jeff. It had been years since she'd done this, yet her body slid instinctively into fencing position: her left hand tucked behind her waist, her right foot forward.

Jeff lunged forward. "Take that, you British scoundrel!" he cried out, just as he used to when they were kids.

Their blades met with a resounding crack as Nina parried his blow. "Why am I the British in this scenario?"

"I figured you'd rather be British than a pirate," Jeff breathed, whirling aside.

"You thought wrong!" Nina clambered onto an ottoman, then jumped off when it creaked dangerously beneath her weight. She and Jeff were still slashing at each other with unabashed enthusiasm. "I'll show you, you plague sore, you moldy rogue!"

He stumbled at that. "Moldy what?"

"I'm in a class on Shakespearean dramas right now. No one knew how to insult like Shakespeare."

She sliced her sword through the air, and Jeff lifted his to block it. "Can you blame me for assuming you wanted to be the British?"

Their steps grew faster as they danced around each other, jumping over the antique furniture. They advanced and retreated, twisted and sidestepped, laughing as their insults grew more and more ridiculous.

Suddenly, Nina fell back onto an armchair, the prince's sword poised over the center of her chest. "Surrender or die!" he proclaimed in an overblown stage voice.

Nina laughed. "I concede!"

Jeff was laughing, too, as he reached out and pulled Nina to her feet.

She stumbled forward and fell still. The feel of his skin

had kindled something within her, something that Nina had thought was long since evaporated.

She tipped her face up and saw that Jeff was blinking down at her, his eyes wide with a confusion that matched her own. Surely he felt the longing that pulsed through her.

Nina gave a tug, and Jeff released her hand as if coming to his senses. Her heart thudded a frantic rhythm in her chest, but somehow her voice came out normal.

"I have to go. I'll see you later." In a fluid motion she grabbed Sam's dress and started toward the front driveway.

It was nothing, she told herself, just a weird moment between old friends. They'd been *fencing*, after all. It was practically the least romantic activity of all time.

It meant nothing, and it *was* nothing, and Nina wouldn't think about it again.

18

BEATRICE

"Thanks for coming with me," Beatrice told Teddy and Sam as they walked up the steps of Louise's guest cottage. Her palms felt clammy, and she curled her hands into fists, wishing she didn't always feel so nervous arriving at a party.

"Are you kidding? I'm *so* ready for a night off," Sam announced, pushing open the door.

A crowd of at least fifty royals spilled through the living room and onto Louise's back terrace. They all wore jeans and silk tops, studded denim jackets or skintight leather pants, when just an hour ago they'd been decked out in full state attire. Music pulsed from the speakers. On a sideboard by the kitchen were platters of cheese and charcuterie, half-empty bottles of champagne on ice, and rows of red plastic cups, the kind Beatrice had seen at parties in college basements.

"Is Marshall coming?" she asked.

Sam shrugged as if she didn't care, but Beatrice could tell from the set of Sam's shoulders that she did care, very much. "I'm not sure."

"I'll get some drinks." Teddy retreated, clearly sensing that he wasn't needed, and Beatrice turned back to her sister.

"Is everything okay?"

"Not really." Sam bit her lip, then admitted, "Marshall isn't as serious about our relationship as I am."

"What makes you say that?" Beatrice asked. Honestly,

though, she hadn't quite realized that Sam was serious about Marshall, either.

"I heard him say so to his grandparents! He told them that it isn't a big deal and they don't need to worry about me. What does that *mean*? Why are they opposed to me dating their grandson?"

"I'm sure they're just concerned that Marshall has a lot on his plate, being the future duke." *And you're the princess.*

Beatrice understood where Marshall's family was coming from, if they were opposed to his dating someone higher-ranking—someone whose title and needs would come first. She just wished she had a kernel of wisdom to share. The only thing worse than grappling with a fundamental issue in your own relationship was watching that very same issue plague the people you loved.

As much as Beatrice hated to admit it, maybe the Duke and Duchess of Orange had a point. What were Sam and Marshall going to do if they ever got truly serious?

Things were hard enough for Beatrice and Teddy, and she was the *queen*.

"Béatrice, Samantha! There you are." Louise flitted over, dropping a European double kiss on their cheeks. In tight black leggings and a black top, Louise almost looked like she was ready for another run along the beach, except that she was still wearing her earrings and tiara from the state dinner. There was something blithely discordant about the contrast between her deliberately casual outfit and the near-priceless diamonds.

"How do you like our cups?" Louise asked, lifting one of the Solo cups. Beatrice saw that it was filled with red wine—probably a very expensive red wine. "Bharat ordered them for next-day delivery! Aren't they fun? It's like a *real* American party!"

"Yes! It reminds me of college." Beatrice looked over, expecting Sam to chime in, but her sister was typing into her phone.

"Come join us outside, both of you?" Louise asked, positively crackling with energy.

Samantha slipped her phone back into her clutch. "I'll wait here. My boyfriend is on the way."

"Oh yes, Marshall!" Louise declared. "Come find us when he arrives. We'll be out by the firepit."

"Sure," Sam replied, distracted. Louise started back toward the main crush of the party, but Beatrice hesitated.

"I can wait with you . . ."

"Go," Sam insisted. "You don't have to babysit me, I promise. I'll be fine."

Beatrice nodded, then hurried to catch up with Louise. She caught sight of Teddy near the fireplace with Rudolph and Rupert, the Austrian and Hungarian crown princes. He looked up, meeting her gaze, and waved jauntily. From the snatch of conversation she overheard, it sounded like they were talking about the World Cup.

She headed out onto the terrace; the pool lights made the surface seem to shimmer with gold flecks, as if someone had dropped a bucket of glitter onto it. Beatrice watched Prince Juan Pablo of Spain holler, then cannonball into the deep end fully clothed.

"It's getting a little too rowdy out here." Louise put a hand on Beatrice's shoulder, steering her toward a firepit tucked around the side of the cottage, with a circle of wooden folding chairs ranged around it. "Welcome to the *real* party," she added with a wink.

"Beatrice! We wanted to wait for you before we got started." Bharat had a bottle of wine in his hand, which he lifted to his lips, drinking straight from the bottle.

"Before you started what?" Beatrice asked.

"Our game," Louise said, as if it were obvious.

For a moment, Beatrice wondered why they'd gone to the trouble of planning a party if they were just going to spend that party hiding from everyone, playing a game in their own exclusive circle. Maybe they liked the notoriety that the party brought them. Whatever their reasons, Beatrice didn't really care—not now that she was part of that inner circle.

"Truth-or-dare?" Sirivannavari suggested.

"I'm not really in the mood for dares." Louise made eye contact with Bharat and, understanding, he passed her the wine.

"God Save the Queen?" Alexei suggested. Beatrice had never heard of that game; was it British?

"No, I was thinking something a little more intimate. Like . . . kiss-marry-kill." Louise hesitated a beat before *kiss*, and Beatrice suspected that she'd been about to use a more profane word, then changed it at the last minute.

"What are our choices?" Sirivannavari asked.

Louise shook her head. "We aren't playing the ordinary way, where I come up with three names and you sort them. Tonight we're playing a version where you have to do it all yourselves. It's more personal that way," Louise declared. "So, each of you needs to choose three people. One you would kill—not actually, of course," she added. "Just someone you dislike. One you would marry. And one you would kiss."

"Or more than kiss," Sirivannavari corrected, and they all laughed.

This wasn't so bad, Beatrice thought. She'd obviously like to marry Teddy, she hated Robert Standish, and . . .

"But you can't pick just anyone. It has to be someone we all know; otherwise it's no fun," Louise clarified. "So, monarchs and heirs only."

"League of Kings edition. I like it," Alexei growled.

Louise tipped her head, and her tiara glittered magnificently in the light of the flames. "Here, I'll go first. I would kill Princess Maria, because she wore the same dress as me to the opening day of Paris Fashion Week!" Louise said it lightly, with just enough self-mockery. "And I'd kiss Prince James. I've heard all *kinds* of stories about him."

"Jamie?" Beatrice blurted out, surprised. The Prince of Canada was a little young for Louise—closer to the twins' age.

"You know him well?" Louise asked, then answered her own question. "But of course you do! Your countries are neighbors!"

"It's been a long time," Beatrice demurred. Years ago, Jamie used to accompany his parents on their annual state visits to Washington. He and Jeff had been inseparable, a pair of dangerously charming troublemakers dreaming up pranks—until one year, when they stopped speaking. Beatrice had asked what had caused their rift, but Jeff never told her.

"Prince James is a dreamboat," Bharat agreed. "Have you *seen* the clips of him speaking French? Mmm."

"I invited him to our party tonight, but he didn't show! I wonder why." Louise sighed. "As for marriage—I'd marry no one. I refuse to be tied down."

It was a cop-out answer, but everyone let her get away with it, because she was Louise. She glanced across the firepit. "Bharat, my darling, you're up."

"Easy. I'd kill the Prince of Wales because, you know, he's the absolute worst." Everyone murmured in agreement. "I'd kiss you, Louise."

"Anytime," the French princess cooed, leaning across the firepit to peck him on the cheek.

And so the game went on, interspersed with fits of light, fizzy laughter. Beatrice noticed that the friends named one another for various categories—Alexei said he'd marry Louise, who replied breezily that she could never live somewhere so cold; Princess Siri said she'd kill Bharat, because he stole that hot reporter from her at the Cannes Film Festival, at which Bharat pointed out that the reporter wouldn't have been interested in her anyway.

Finally, they were all gazing expectantly at Beatrice. She felt her mouth go dry.

"Um, well. I guess I would kiss . . ."

"Nikolaos?" Sirivannavari guessed, naming the Prince of Greece. "Didn't you used to date him?"

"Ugh. Nikolaos was a terrible kisser."

Beatrice felt ashamed the moment she said it. She and Nikolaos had only kissed once, a brief, awkward moment in the back of a moving car. But her remorse dissipated as everyone laughed uproariously at her words.

"Come on, Siri, you know Nikolaos doesn't count. He's a younger son, not an heir," Louise admonished, though she was smiling broadly. She glanced at Beatrice, lowering her voice to a whisper. "You probably know that I went out with Nikolaos a few times, too. I agree, he was disappointing. Anyway," Louise went on, "you still need to pick someone. Who would you kiss?"

By now Beatrice had a safe answer. "Prince Ugyen."

"Of Bhutan!" Alexei protested, spluttering. "He's only seven months old! He's not even here!"

"Louise said that we were playing monarchs and heirs. She never specified that they had to actually be at the conference."

Louise chuckled, delighted by Beatrice's loophole. "Prince Ugyen is adorable. I just want to pinch those chubby baby legs."

"And I wouldn't marry anyone, either," Beatrice added, emboldened.

"Good choice." Louise met her gaze and winked. "What's the point of a king consort, anyway?"

Those words struck a momentary pang in Beatrice. Before she could rush to Teddy's defense, Sirivannavari cut in. "You forgot to say who you would kill."

Beatrice hesitated. Perhaps she could name Alexei or Bharat; most of them had named each other, except she didn't know any of them well enough for the joke to land. . . .

"What about King Frederick?" Louise suggested.

"Frederick?"

"Or King Takudzwa, or Emperor Akito. They've all interrupted you during our plenary sessions."

Beatrice hadn't given it much thought, but it was true. At some point each of those kings had stood and talked over Beatrice, as if she were an unruly toddler, not a queen who had the floor.

"You're right," she said.

Louise rolled her eyes. "Frederick and his clique are a holdover from a bygone era. They think women, especially young women, should be seen and not heard."

Beatrice's mind snagged on Louise's choice of words. "What do you mean, Frederick's *clique*?"

"You know: Akito, Juan Pablo, Gustav. That whole gang."

Clique, gang—Louise was speaking like a seventeen-year-old. "You make them sound like high schoolers competing for prom king."

"Is it really all that different? High school politics or international politics, the dynamics are the same. People don't actually change, no matter how old they are."

There was an element of truth in Louise's statement. No one ever fully shed their teenage selves, did they? No matter how much you grew up, your old anxieties and insecurities would always be there, knitted into the fabric of your being.

"Perhaps I should find a less juvenile term," Louise mused. "But to me, a clique is a group of people who have each other's backs. Who stand up for each other, help each

151

other navigate all the drama and petty gossip out in the world. By that definition, we are a clique, aren't we?"

Something about that *we* made Beatrice feel warm inside. It made her want to live up to whatever Louise saw in her.

The game had reached a natural close; Alexei headed off in search of more wine, and Siri glanced down at her phone.

Bharat leaned toward Beatrice. "I know what it's like to have people trying to silence you," he said softly. "I've certainly gotten plenty of opposition as a gay future ruler."

Beatrice nodded, letting him continue.

"It's hard enough dealing with criticism in my own country, but then to come here and have all the kings dismiss me, call me unfit to rule, question my line of succession . . ." Bharat broke off in disappointment and sighed.

"I'm so sorry. That's terrible." No one should be precluded from doing their job because of who they were or who they loved.

Bharat shrugged. "Change happens one generation at a time. If I go through hardship, hopefully it means future generations won't have to."

That, Beatrice understood. Whenever the press was especially hard on her, whenever it felt like the road ahead was too steep, she reminded herself that she was doing this for a future queen. She didn't know if it would be her own daughter, or her granddaughter—but the next Queen of America would have an easier time of it because Beatrice had been first to forge the path.

"Anyway. I'm going to tell my father to vote for your climate accord," Bharat promised, and Beatrice looked up.

"Thank you. That means so much."

"Of course. I can tell you really believe in it."

"Excellent!" Louise exclaimed, having clearly overheard. She held out the bottle of wine with a questioning expression, and to her own surprise, Beatrice took it. She lifted it to her lips, drinking straight from the bottle—and immediately burst out coughing. It had gone down the wrong pipe.

Beatrice would have felt sheepish, except Louise was laughing in an affectionate, delighted way.

"Oh, Béatrice." Louise slapped her on the back a few times. "You can't even drink properly? I have so much to teach you. But don't worry," she added gleefully. "The fun is just beginning."

SAMANTHA

Samantha prowled from the living room to the terrace and back again, snatches of conversation drifting around her.

"At least your legislature stays in line. God only knows what mine has been up to in my absence. When the cat's away, the mice will play. . . ."

"She's so dumb, she spelled *per se* as '*per s-a-y.*' I'm telling you, these assistants always claim to be fluent in English, but they disappoint every time. . . ."

"God, this conference is boring. Makes me want to go full-on Prince Franz and sail off to Hawaii. . . ."

Prince Franz? Sam wondered who he was; she didn't think she'd met him so far. Then her phone buzzed, and she fumbled for it so frantically that she nearly dropped it in the pool, only to see that it was just Nina.

Sam had been avoiding Marshall the past couple of days, ignoring his calls and sending vague replies to his messages. But she knew she couldn't dodge this conversation any longer.

When Marshall finally texted that he'd arrived, Sam made her way to the front of Louise's cottage. He broke into a smile at the sight of her.

"Sorry I got delayed. This party looks amazing." Marshall stepped forward to hug her, then clearly sensed her mood, his arms falling listlessly to his sides.

"Sam—is everything okay?"

A narrow path wound between the guest cottages and out onto the sand. Sam nodded toward it. "Walk with me?"

They kicked off their shoes and headed along the beach, staying near the edge of the surf. If this were a different night, Sam would have danced in and out of the waves, laughing when the water reached her bare knees. There was nothing playful about the conversation they were about to have.

"I feel like you're upset with me. Whatever I did wrong, I'm sorry," Marshall said hesitantly.

"Why would you care?" Sam's voice came out sharp. "We don't do emotions, right? We're just hooking up, messing around—"

"What are you talking about?"

"You're not serious about me. We haven't *discussed the future*. Right?"

They had drawn to a halt. Sam crossed her arms, staring accusatorily at Marshall, who winced.

"You heard us at dinner last week."

"I didn't mean to, but I walked past and realized you were all talking about me." She shook her head and started walking again. "Look, we never really defined what this is. If we're just physical—if that's all you feel—then it's fine."

It wasn't fine, but Sam was determined to hang on to a shred of pride.

Marshall caught her wrist, pulling her to a stop. "I'm sorry. But if you overheard that conversation, then you must have realized how adamantly my family wanted me to say that."

She sighed. "Why does your grandfather hate me?"

"It's not about who you are, but what you are. You're the princess, which makes things . . . complicated."

"If it's complicated, then let's figure it out. Together."

"It's a lot bigger than you and me," Marshall said heavily. "Look, I really didn't mean for you to hear all that—"

"But you should never have said it in the first place! You

should have *fought* for us, because that's what you do when you *love* someone!"

Now she'd done it. She'd spoken the words she had both longed and feared to say.

Well, she couldn't unsay them.

Marshall met her gaze and swallowed. "I love you, too, Sam. Surely you know that."

Nothing followed his words but silence, underscored by the gentle sounds of night: a bird trilling, the low rumble of conversation from inside, waves crashing against the shore. Sam's heart swelled.

Marshall loved her. Everything would be all right.

Except . . . if they'd just said *I love you*, why wasn't he smiling? He was staring at her with such a stricken expression.

"My grandfather never expected us to get serious," Marshall said softly. "And if I'm being honest, *I* never expected us to get serious. Not at the beginning."

It was part of the reason their original fake-dating scheme had worked so well, because they were both notorious for their inability to commit. The press had loved it.

"That's not the point," she reminded him. "We're serious now. We love each other!"

"Which means we should probably face the fact that we can't really have a future."

"I'm not asking you to *marry* me, Marshall. But don't you think we owe it to ourselves to see where this goes?"

"That's just the thing—it *can't* go anywhere! Sam, if we ever did want to get married, I would have to renounce my succession rights!" he burst out. Her eyes widened, and his next words came out softer. "You know that a member of the royal family cannot also govern one of the duchies; it's a conflict of interest. If we got married, I would have to step down as the future Duke of Orange, and just be . . ." Marshall faltered. "Mr. Samantha Washington, I guess."

On some level, Sam had known this, but she'd never really confronted the truth of it. She'd never let herself imagine their relationship going all the way to the altar.

A cold, hard realization was beginning to dawn on Sam, but she fought it; she pushed it away with every ounce of strength. "There has to be another solution."

"Me giving up my title *is* the solution."

There was a raw, rough emotion beneath Marshall's words; he looked almost like he was blinking back tears. Sam felt a stinging heat behind her own eyelids.

"I wish I could give up Orange for you, Sam. But there's so much at stake." He sighed. "It's not the same for me as it is for Teddy. Do you know how many Black families there are in the nobility?"

Sam nodded. She knew that things were different for Marshall, and always had been.

"My grandfather is one of the only Black dukes in America. There is an unbelievable amount of pressure on me. What kind of message does it send, if I renounce my position and title for you? I hate to say it, but Grandpa is probably right," Marshall concluded. "The smart thing to do is to just . . . stop."

"You don't mean that," she protested, voice quavering. "It's not fair. You're supposed to give up on our relationship because you're some kind of symbol?"

"I'm a symbol because I was born to be. We both were."

Sam shook her head vehemently. "This can't be it. We'll find another way out, we'll change things—"

"Change what?" Marshall asked wearily. "Change my family? Change the laws of succession?"

"*Everything,* if we have to! We'll change the *world,* okay?"

Marshall smiled, but there was no joy in it. "That right there is one of the many reasons I love you. You refuse to accept defeat, even when it's staring you in the face."

Sam's hands were clenched at her sides. Marshall reached for her fist, gently unfurled her fingers, and laced them in his.

She squeezed his hand tight, silently pleading with him not to leave her.

"Sam, no matter how much I love you, I won't walk away from the dukedom. I can't do that to my family, or to Orange. Not even for you."

"I wouldn't want you to," she whispered.

Marshall had spent his whole life training to be the Duke of Orange. It was the role he'd always known he would one day step into, a fundamental piece of his identity. Sam couldn't ask him to turn his back on his family, his legacy. Even if she wasn't the one doing the asking—even if it was all because of the Crown.

Sam had never hated her position more than she did in that moment.

"Hey, it's okay," Marshall murmured, even though they both knew that it wasn't okay, not at all. He was still holding her hand in his, and Sam had the sudden, anguished thought that this might be the last time he ever touched her.

She turned and flung herself into his arms, burying her face in his shirt, soaking it with her tears. Marshall reached down with infinite tenderness and tipped up her chin, forcing her gaze to meet his.

He kissed her. It was soft at first, gentle—but then Sam was pressing forward, wrapping her arms around him and digging her fingers into his shoulders. She kissed him passionately, with every ounce of regret and longing within her, trying to memorize the feel of him.

They both knew that they were kissing each other goodbye.

When they finally broke apart, Sam took several deep breaths. The moon hung like a cold, cruel spotlight in the middle of the sky, illuminating the sorrow on Marshall's face, which mirrored her own.

"I . . . um . . . I guess I should leave," he mumbled.

Sam gulped and nodded, not trusting herself to reply.

When he was gone, she crumpled to the ground and hung her head in her hands. The tears came freely now, ugly sobs that racked her chest, making her ache all the way down in her core.

She wasn't sure how much time had passed when Beatrice's voice made her look up. "Sam? Are you okay?"

"Marshall broke up with me," she said flatly.

"Oh, Sam." Beatrice sank onto the sand and put an arm around her, pulling her close. Sam leaned gratefully against her sister's shoulder.

Through her sobs, she explained what had happened— that there was no possible future for them, because Marshall would have to give up his future as Duke of Orange.

Beatrice nodded. "I know this is hard to hear, but maybe it's for the best. If you were going to break up, it's better that it happened now, before . . ."

"Before I got hurt?" Sam asked sarcastically, and Beatrice winced.

"Sorry. That was a dumb thing to say; of course you're hurting. I just meant, before you got any more hurt than you are now." She hesitated. "Marshall was going to have to choose between you and his family eventually."

"And you didn't think to warn me?" Sam asked wearily.

"I guess I thought you knew. And I didn't realize that you and Marshall were in love."

Sam scooped up a handful of sand and let it sift through her fingers. "You know what? Being a princess isn't really that great."

"Wise words. Should I embroider them on a throw pillow for your sitting room?"

Sam laughed, but it came out as more of a sob.

"I'm sorry," Beatrice said again. "Trust me when I say that

I know how hard it is, losing someone you love because of who we are."

Sam swallowed; her throat still felt raw. She shrugged forward and looped her arms around her knees.

"Can I do anything to help? Would you like, um . . . ice cream? Tequila?" Beatrice offered.

Sam's eyes drifted to the ink-dark ocean, and she spoke without thinking. "I know what you can do. You can go in the water with me."

Beatrice made a funny noise in her throat. "The ocean?"

"Why not?" She needed to do something bold and a little bit reckless right now, something to distract her from the ache that was tearing through her body.

"It will be freezing!"

"That's the point!" The cold water seemed suddenly appealing, as if it might wash all this pain from her, let her start over fresh.

Sam rose to her feet and started toward the ocean, not pausing to take off her jeans and black silk top. Soon the water was frothing around her calves, then her waist; she waded forward, arms stretched out. When a huge wave crested before her, she closed her eyes and dove straight into it.

The air burned in her lungs. It was dark under the surface, and turbulent, and bitterly cold. But most of all it was quiet. For the first time all night, Sam couldn't hear the roaring of her own heartache.

20

BEATRICE

Beatrice was in her office the next morning when Teddy knocked on the door. Franklin, who'd been dozing at her feet, lifted his head at the noise.

"Hey, Bee." Teddy adjusted the backpack slung over his shoulder. "I just wanted to say goodbye before I head to the airport."

"You're leaving already?"

He nodded. "Before I go, I was wondering . . . can we talk about something?"

"Of course." Beatrice headed to one of the armchairs by the fireplace, and Franklin trotted along in her wake, to settle on the carpet with an eager thump of his tail.

Teddy cleared his throat. "I was wondering if you've given any more thought to my suggestions about initiatives I could take on."

"I'm sorry, Teddy. I've been so busy lately."

"You're always busy."

"Well, yes. There's a lot to my job."

It came out a bit terse and defensive, but why did Teddy feel the need to criticize her right now? Didn't he see that she was already stretched thin?

He shifted in the velvet armchair. "That's part of what I'm saying. I want to help, take some things off your plate."

"I know. But, Teddy, I can't just hand out my job responsibilities like I'm doling out candies from a box! They're not even mine to give out. For anything serious, I'd have to ask Congress."

"Right. Okay." He sighed. "I just feel so useless right now."

"You're not useless," she protested.

Teddy gave a self-deprecating laugh. "I am, and we both know it. It was different when I thought you would need me—that I would be your emotional support amid the chaos of the conference. But you're doing great." His blue eyes softened. "I'm so proud of you: you're out there making friends, going to meetings, and getting your climate accord passed, while all I've done is attend a few state dinners."

"That *is* helpful! I always dread those dinners, but you make them more bearable," Beatrice insisted.

"I'm glad. But let's face it, I haven't contributed anything of value while I've been at Bellevue. All I've done is go sailing and work on my tan." He tried to crack a smile. "I feel like a trophy husband."

"In your defense, you're very tan and extremely good at sailing. If I was in the market for a trophy husband, you would be my top pick." Beatrice was relieved to see Teddy's smile broaden at that.

Then he sighed. "I just . . . I miss you, Bee. I feel like we're hardly ever alone anymore, that I only ever see you at a reception, surrounded by people."

She knew what he meant. With all the pageantry of the conference, their relationship had turned into something public, as if they were costars in some elaborate, lavish production.

Or, more accurately, Beatrice was the star, and Teddy was a sidekick.

"I miss the island," he added.

"I miss the island, too," she said softly. "Look—I know this hasn't been easy on you, but I promise that after the conference, when we're back in Washington, we'll figure out your role. Even if we have to submit a new proposal to Congress."

Teddy nodded. "I have something that might make it easier for you."

He leaned down to rifle through his backpack, then pulled out a manila folder. Wordlessly, he handed it over.

Inside was a single printed document.

I, Lord Theodore Beaufort Eaton, being of sound mind and body, do absolutely and entirely renounce my position and my titles, together with all their incumbent rights and privileges, their duties and fidelities. I forswear the Duchy of Boston for myself and for my descendants, and name instead as my successor my brother Lewis McKay Eaton.

This is my final and irrevocable decision.

Beatrice looked up sharply. "You don't need to sign this now. We're not married yet." *And we don't know when we will be,* she almost added.

"I want to sign it. It'll stop some of the gossip about our wedding—show people how serious we are. And it'll make things easier on Lewis," Teddy added. "He can't step out of my shadow until I formally remove myself from the line of succession."

"Teddy," she said helplessly, unsure whether she wanted to thank him—or tell him to stop.

Before she could make up her mind, Teddy grabbed a pen from the side pocket of his backpack and scrawled *Theodore* in the blank space beneath the text. Then he passed the document to Beatrice.

Her breath caught as she took it.

She had known from the beginning that Teddy would give

up everything for her. But it felt so much more real now, watching him sacrifice the role he was born for. It was a statement of such deep faith in their relationship, in *her*.

"You didn't have to do that," she said again, and cleared her throat. "But thank you. It means a lot to me."

Teddy stood and held out his hands. When Beatrice took them, he tugged her to her feet, then wrapped his arms around her and pulled her close.

For a long moment they stood like that, folded together so tightly that they seemed like one intertwined person—like a pair of trees planted too close together, and now their roots and branches had become forever entangled. Beatrice closed her eyes, resting her head in the crook of Teddy's shoulder, relishing the steady warmth of him.

"I love you so much," she told him.

"I love you, too, Bee." He took a reluctant step back, running a hand through his hair. "I should probably get going."

Beatrice reached for him. She couldn't let him leave without one last kiss—a soft, lingering kiss that expressed all the gratitude and regret and fear that she couldn't put into words.

"*Now* you can get going," she said, and he smiled.

When he was gone, Beatrice studied Teddy's statement of renunciation for a long time, reading its phrases over and over. Franklin whined softly, as if sensing her mood. "I know, Franklin, I know," she murmured. Though *what* she knew, she wasn't entirely sure.

Finally she set the document to one side of her desk—handling it carefully, as if it might detonate at any moment—before turning to the stack of papers before her.

21

DAPHNE

If Daphne hadn't already hated Gabriella, she would certainly have started hating her tonight. It was hard not to resent any-one who could throw a birthday party this lavish.

Everything was over-the-top, from the glittering gold photo booth to the ice sculpture to the towering display of French macarons in pastel pink and white. "How did you get them here from Paris?" Daphne heard someone ask, to which Gabriella airily replied, "Oh, we didn't bring the *macarons* here! We considered flying them over on the jet, but they were going to get stale, so we decided to fly the executive chef here instead!" As if that were a perfectly reasonable request, to bring a pastry chef from Paris so that he could bake macarons for a college student's birthday party. Though Daphne sup-posed it was more reasonable than chartering a private plane full of cookies.

And, really, this was more than just a birthday party. This party was a declaration: a coming-home party, an *I'm back and I'm here to win* party.

The Madisons' estate, Payne House—not their ancestral home in Virginia, but their massive residence in town—was on the opposite side of Herald Oaks from where Daphne lived. Here, nineteenth-century mansions sprawled on enor-mous lots, their backyards sloping all the way down to the Potomac. Most estates still boasted the private docks their owners' ancestors had once used, back when it was easier to reach the palace by boat than by horse and carriage.

Daphne and Jefferson stood behind the main house, staring down at the massive white tent on the back lawn.

"Thanks for inviting Nina tonight." The prince glanced to where Nina stood, talking with someone from their college class. "It was sweet of you to include her."

Sweet, Daphne thought wryly. It was a word to describe small children, and sugar-dusted scones, and sappy movies. Never her.

"Of course. I really am glad you're friends again," she told him.

Jefferson let out a breath. "By the way, I'm sorry about that photo."

Last week, the *Daily News* had published the photo that Daphne had sold to Natasha. The tabloid had spun a whole article out of it, with a timeline tracking the progress of Daphne and Jefferson's relationship, and eager speculation about when they might get married. Honestly, the engagement rumors had increased in volume ever since Beatrice postponed her wedding to Teddy—as if, deprived of one royal wedding, America seemed determined to plan another.

"It's fine," Daphne said hastily. "I'm not worried about it."

Jefferson didn't seem to have heard. "We should have the palace security team do a sweep of your computer, see if you were hacked."

Daphne's stomach dropped. "I don't think that's necessary."

"Or maybe your phone?" he went on, frowning. "I just don't understand how anyone could have gotten that photo—"

"Please, Jefferson, just *stop!*"

He blinked, startled by her outburst. A few people glanced over with raised eyebrows. Daphne managed a flustered, frantic smile, lowering her voice to a conciliatory tone.

"I'm sorry, I didn't mean to snap at you. I just hate the

thought of some IT consultant raking through my computer, seeing all our personal emails and messages."

Jefferson nodded. "That's exactly why I want to make sure this doesn't happen again. I know how much you hate articles like that—how much you value your privacy."

Hate articles like that? For a moment Daphne wanted to cry out in frustration at how little he knew her. She'd spent the entirety of their relationship trying to *engineer* that sort of article, spoon-feeding gossip to Natasha in exchange for positive headlines.

But then, she couldn't exactly blame Jefferson for believing all the half-truths and lies she'd told him.

"Your Highness!" a voice singsonged, and Daphne barely refrained from rolling her eyes.

Gabriella's outfit was as overdone as the rest of her party. She had on a lavender dress with a high neck and voluminous poufed sleeves, emphasizing the clutter of her jewelry. She looked like she'd raided the family's safety-deposit box and couldn't decide what to take, so she'd taken it all—four necklaces layered one atop the other, dangly diamond earrings, and a thick headband tucked behind her ears. *More doesn't always mean better,* Daphne's mother would have said. But clearly Gabriella's parents weren't in the habit of telling her no.

Gabriella's lips pursed as she gave Daphne's outfit a once-over. Daphne was suddenly glad she'd sold that photo, because she'd used the money to buy this dress, which was so new that the sales associates at Halo had only just received it from the designer. It was a gorgeous deep green, with a flattering scooped neckline and thin shoulder straps.

"I keep hearing that Kelli B is the guest performer tonight. Is it true?" Jefferson asked, and Gabriella preened beneath his attention.

"I'm not telling," she teased. "Some things are worth waiting for."

She lifted her eyes to meet Daphne's. It was abundantly clear that she was goading her, flirting with Jefferson and rubbing it in Daphne's face.

Let Gabriella think what she wanted. Soon enough, Daphne and Nina were going to take her down.

♛

"It's time," Daphne murmured, coming to tap Nina on the arm.

Everyone was crowded into the massive tent, waiting for the DJ to finish, squealing in excitement as they tried to guess the identity of the much-hyped surprise performer.

"Now?" Nina glanced uncertainly at the stage, then at Gabriella, who was surrounded by a fawning circle of admirers.

"The only place to vacation on the Riviera is Antibes, *obviously*," Gabriella was saying. Her posse nodded as solemnly as if she were telling them the secret to eternal happiness—and to them, she probably was. Gabriella went on: "The hotel has this rope swing that goes out over the Mediterranean. If you rent out the whole hotel, like Daddy will do for my wedding someday, then you can go off the rope swing naked." She winked suggestively.

One of her followers giggled. "You think you'll get married on the Riviera?"

Gabriella glanced at the prince. "I suppose it depends who I marry, doesn't it?"

This time, Daphne didn't bother hiding her eye roll.

They were all out on the dance floor; Jefferson was a few feet away, jumping up and down in that delighted, unrestrained way of his. He always seemed so happy in this setting, as if a dance floor was somewhere he could disappear into the crowd and become any old anonymous person, rather than a prince.

Daphne nodded at Nina. "Gabriella is going to be out here soaking in the attention until the guest performer goes on. Now is our best chance to get into her room and look around!"

Nina relented. "Fine. Let's do it."

They headed into the house, acting like any other young women going to the bathroom together. Luckily, the bored-looking butler who saw them just gave them a polite nod. He had no idea that Nina and Daphne were the least likely pairing of anyone at this party.

They were natural enemies, yet somehow here they were: engaged in a temporary truce, working *together*.

If Daphne hadn't had so much to worry about, she would have found the situation funny.

They didn't actually know which room was Gabriella's, but Daphne had been in enough of these old houses to guess the layout: the master suite should overlook the backyard, which meant that Gabriella and her brother were at the opposite end of the hall.

She tried one door, revealing a dark, masculine-looking room, and shut it again. The next opened to a space that could only be Gabriella's, with a canopied princess bed and hand-painted wallpaper. A bookcase sat against one wall, its shelves cluttered with zero books but plenty of framed photos, aromatherapy candles, and a porcelain bust of Gabriella. Even Daphne, who was inordinately vain, couldn't imagine commissioning a sculpture of her own face.

She paused in the doorway, glancing at Nina. "You stay out here. Anyone asks, you can say you got lost looking for the bathroom. If someone is about to come in, cough. That'll be our warning sign."

"What if I actually have to cough?"

"Don't." Daphne stepped inside, shutting the door behind her.

She beelined for the desk, where she pulled a flash drive from her pocket. A few clicks later, she'd downloaded the contents of Gabriella's computer. She withdrew the flash drive from the laptop, pressing it eagerly into her palm. She'd sort through it at home.

Daphne began searching through desk drawers, finding tickets to old music festivals, heart-eye sunglasses, and a collection of fountain pens from hotels around the world—a pink one from the Beverly Hills Hotel, a white one from the Ritz in Paris. Daphne was amused at the thought that someone as wealthy as Gabriella would steal pens whenever she stayed in a nice hotel. Maybe it was a klepto thing. Maybe she squirreled them away as proof that she'd actually been to all these expensive faraway places.

A quick search of the bathroom revealed nothing except an entire storefront's worth of beauty products. Seriously, how many moisturizers and toners did Gabriella need? She only had one face. Daphne was bending down, lifting the bed skirt to check under the bed, when she heard Nina dissolve into a coughing fit.

"What are you doing up here?" It was unmistakably Gabriella's voice.

Panicked, Daphne jumped to her feet and began scanning the room for hiding spots.

"I got lost looking for the bathroom," Nina was saying, but Gabriella cut her off.

"You liar, the bathrooms are downstairs. You're obviously here to snoop!" There was a shuffling sound. "I'm calling security to throw you out."

"Yes, I was snooping!" Nina cried out. "You caught me!"

What was Nina doing? Daphne hurried to conceal herself behind the curtains that lined the floor-to-ceiling windows. Nina was talking faster now, her words a frantic rush. "I just— I've never been in a house like this before," Nina simpered. "You have so many beautiful things. I just wanted to see your bedroom. I wanted to know what it's like to live like this."

Gabriella barked out a laugh. "You're pathetic. You act like you're more *moral* than me because you don't have any money, but you wish you were rich, just like everyone else."

"You're right. I'm sorry," Nina said hastily.

"Get out of my way," Gabriella snapped, but she sounded oddly placated. She threw open the door and flounced inside.

Daphne's heart pounded. *Please don't look at the windows,* she thought over and over. The toe of her high-heeled sandal peeped out from beneath the bottom of the curtain, no matter how hard she tried to hide it.

Fate, or really Gabriella's vanity, must have been on her side, because Gabriella didn't even look in her direction. She headed with swift steps into the bathroom.

Daphne dared a reckless glance around the edge of the curtain. Gabriella stood before a makeup mirror, reapplying her eyeliner and lipstick. She unzipped her wristlet, one of those tiny quilted things on a chain that barely held a phone and ID, and withdrew a baggie of white powder.

She cut it into a line and leaned forward to snort it delicately into one nostril. Then, as she was heading back toward the hallway, Gabriella paused and frowned down at the floor.

Daphne's stomach plummeted. That was her flash drive, its turquoise plastic painfully visible against the peach-colored carpet.

"Hmm." Gabriella tossed it into her wristlet and swept out of the room, pulling the door shut behind her.

Daphne waited, but when Gabriella didn't return, she finally exhaled. She rushed back down the hallway, almost colliding with Nina.

"Daphne! Are you okay? Did you hear me cough?"

"Yes. Though I didn't exactly get a ton of warning."

"I did my best to delay Gabriella! I hoped it would give you time to hide."

171

Daphne was grudgingly impressed. "I heard that. How did you keep her from kicking you out of the party?"

"I just thought about what makes Gabriella happiest: feeling like she's superior to other people," Nina explained. "So I groveled at her feet a little."

"Thank you." The words were clunky and awkward in her mouth.

Nina blinked, looking as surprised by the thank-you as Daphne was. "Did you manage to find anything?"

"I didn't have enough time. And I dropped the flash drive, so we won't be able to search her computer." Daphne sighed. "Not to mention, I saw Gabriella doing cocaine! If only I could've gotten it on video."

To think that they'd come *this* close—had been mere feet away while Gabriella did drugs—only to come up empty-handed. And now they no longer had the flash drive, so they couldn't even sort through the contents of her laptop. At least the flash drive had none of their own files on it, nothing that Gabriella could trace back to them if she ever plugged it in.

"That's too bad," Nina said. Silence fell between them for a moment. Then Nina added, "Should we go get a drink, at least?"

Daphne wondered at her use of the word *we*, as if they might actually be allies now, or at the very least, no longer enemies. What was that saying—*politics makes strange bedfellows*?

"Then we can go our separate ways and go back to hating each other," Nina added, in such a matter-of-fact tone that Daphne chuckled.

"Makes sense," she agreed. "I think we deserve a drink after that debacle."

The two of them headed toward the party as the opening lines of Kelli B's song blasted into the night.

22

NINA

Nina hadn't expected to stay at Gabriella's party this late. When she finally handed her claim ticket to a valet, it was after midnight, and she had at least a dozen texts from Rachel. They were all variations of *How is it?* and *Send pics!* until the last text, which read simply, *OMG ARE THESE POSTS FOR REAL? IS KELLI B PERFORMING?*

Rachel didn't know about Nina's unholy alliance with Daphne; she didn't even know that Nina's financial aid had been withdrawn. Somehow Nina couldn't bear the thought of telling her friends. *That stubborn pride will be your downfall,* her mamá always said. But Nina wasn't ready to see the pitying looks on all their faces. As long as she didn't tell them about it, her situation didn't feel quite *real*.

And she kept hoping, stupidly, that Daphne's ridiculous plan might actually work, and she would find a way out of this whole mess.

After their failed attempt to snoop through Gabriella's room, Nina had almost returned to campus. Except . . . she and Daphne had gotten that drink together before parting ways, and then Nina decided, why not stay awhile? She actually liked Kelli B. She was already here; she might as well enjoy herself at a concert on the Madisons' dime.

By now it had gotten colder, the air heavy with a mist that

wasn't quite rain. As her eyes adjusted, Nina realized that a thin figure stood at the bottom of the steps.

"Daphne? Are you waiting for someone?" She decided not to ask why Jeff wasn't with his girlfriend.

"I'm calling a car," Daphne said happily, clicking at a ride-share app. Nina wasn't trying to be nosy, but she couldn't help noticing that the screen said *No drivers available in your area.*

Nina's car—actually Sam's car, which Sam had insisted on lending her for the duration of the League of Kings conference—pulled up the driveway. A valet hopped out and held the driver's side door open for her.

At the bottom of the steps, Nina hesitated. Perhaps her mamá's voice was echoing in her head, or perhaps it was all her years of Sunday school. Love thine enemy, right?

"I can give you a ride home," she offered.

Daphne narrowed her eyes, swaying a little. "Should you be driving?"

"I barely had two beers." Nina started to say more, but Daphne cut her off.

"I know, I was with you! You dared me to get that second drink!"

"What are you talking about?" Nina asked, bewildered.

"When you told me you were going back to the bar and asked if I wanted another vodka soda!" Daphne's sentences were louder than normal, punctuated with clear exclamation points, and she was twirling a strand of hair around one finger.

Nina realized, stunned, that Daphne Deighton was drunk.

"When I offered to get you another drink, I was trying to be nice," Nina said slowly. "I wasn't trying to challenge you to some kind of *drinking contest.*"

Daphne's mouth fell open in a pink O of surprise. Then

she laughed. "Well, I saw it as a contest, and I had to drink because I couldn't let you win!"

"Daphne, not everything is a competition."

"Luckily for you!" Daphne said cheerfully. "You would lose at so many things! Dancing, standing guard at Gabriella's door, wearing heels."

Nina bit back a smile as she glanced down at her flats. "You think wearing heels is a core life skill, don't you?"

"Of course it is," Daphne said solemnly. "That's how you can tell a lady, because she's great at walking in heels, no matter how high they are. Like this!" She glided forward for two steps, only to trip on the third. A sheepish expression stole over her face as she righted herself, smoothing her dress as if nothing had happened. "Now you know why I couldn't go home with Jefferson. I can't let him see me like this."

"You mean, a drunk mess?" Nina asked, almost amused.

"I prefer the term *overserved*."

"That's it. I'm taking you home." Nina shoved Daphne rather inelegantly toward the Jeep.

Daphne hesitated, then seemed to reach a decision. "Fine. But only because I can't afford to let this dress get rained on."

"Right. Because *you're* doing *me* a favor, letting me drive you home," Nina deadpanned.

"Of course I am. I'm fantastic company." Daphne said it in such a breezy, matter-of-fact tone that Nina choked out an unexpected laugh.

She pulled down the driveway and onto the Madisons' street. Here, the houses were set so far back on their lots that all you could see as you drove past were hedges and iron gates.

"Take a left at Tanglewilde," Daphne said at the stop sign, and Nina obediently hit her blinker.

A sound echoed through the car. It took Nina a moment to realize that it was Daphne's stomach growling.

"When did you last eat?" she demanded, and Daphne bit her lip uncertainly.

"I had an iced latte this morning. Oh, and half a banana!"

"No wonder you got wasted off two drinks! Didn't anyone teach you to carbo-load before a party?" It was something Nina's parents had told her before she left for college: *Always eat pizza before you go out*, Isabella had said, and Julie added, *Or a sandwich! Or frozen waffles! Anything with bread, lots of bread!* Nina had laughed, and told them that they were welcome to send her a weekly delivery of bagels.

She had a feeling Daphne's parents never gave her advice like that. If anything, they were probably buying her a scale and helping her count calories.

"Take a right here," Daphne went on, but Nina ignored her and kept driving. "Nina, what are you doing?"

"We're making a pit stop."

Daphne's green eyes widened. "We can't—I don't—"

"Relax. No one here cares who you are." Nina jerked her head toward the backseat. "There's a hoodie back there if you want it."

Daphne twisted around to grab the hoodie, frowning as she tugged it over her head. "I didn't think you were the type to wear pink tie-dye."

"The hoodie is Sam's. Really, the whole car is Sam's," she explained.

A few minutes later they pulled into a parking lot alongside a stucco building. The sign overhead advertised TACOS! in electric yellow letters, except that the C had burned out, so nothing remained but TA OS!

"Trust me, this is the sobering-up food you need right

now," Nina assured Daphne, who looked deeply skeptical. "You'll thank me tomorrow when you don't wake up with a killer hangover."

The taco place was exactly as it had always been: colored lights strung from the ceiling, peeling plastic booths, and squirt bottles of so-called "special sauce" on each table, though Nina was pretty sure the sauce consisted of nothing more than ketchup and mayo mixed together.

The woman behind the counter flashed them a wide smile. "What can I get you?"

"A taco sampler and an order of nachos, extra cheese." Nina reached for her wallet at the same time Daphne withdrew hers from her clutch. "I'm not letting you pay; you're broke," she said bluntly, but Daphne still shoved her credit card toward the machine.

"You're broke, too!"

"Aren't you two funny!" The cashier clapped in delight. "I remember what it was like to be out with my best friend when we were young and poor. You know what? This one's on the house."

Daphne isn't my best friend, Nina wanted to protest, but there were free tacos on the line, so she said nothing.

A few minutes later they were seated at a corner booth, platters of food heaped before them. "Oh my god," Daphne exclaimed through a mouthful of taco. "What is this and why is it the best thing I've ever eaten?"

"Barbacoa, and you're starving. But also, these tacos are magic."

Daphne nodded, licking sauce from her fingers. Nina was quite certain that Daphne had never displayed such appalling manners in her life. But there was no one else in the entire restaurant, except an older couple who were pushing a dog in a baby stroller and feeding it slivers of beef. Not exactly the type of people who might take photos and sell them to a gossip site.

Nina's phone buzzed; she glanced down at it and frowned.

"Is that your parents?" Daphne asked. "Everything okay?"

"It's Sam, actually." Nina hesitated, but Daphne would learn this eventually from Jeff, if she didn't know already. "Marshall broke up with her last night."

Daphne clucked in sympathy. "Poor Samantha."

"Like you care," Nina replied, to which Daphne lifted one shoulder in a shrug. The pink-and-white hoodie looked so weird over the skirt of her emerald-green dress.

"I may not know Samantha the way you do. But I know what it feels like to lose something you care about."

"Right. How's all of that going?" Nina asked cautiously.

"You mean, the fact that we're poor and on the brink of becoming commoners?" Daphne began shredding a tortilla into tiny pieces, letting them fall over her plate like confetti. "My parents are panicking, and focusing even *more* of their anxiety on me. I wish I didn't live at home," she added in a whisper.

It was hard not to feel a tiny bit sorry for Daphne. She might be a self-obsessed monster, but wasn't it inevitable, with parents like that?

And wasn't Nina using Daphne's self-obsessed monstrousness for her own ends right now?

"What about you?" Daphne asked. "How did your parents react when you told them your financial aid was pulled?"

Nina flinched at the question. She hadn't realized how cash-poor her parents were—they'd poured all their savings into her mom's fledgling e-commerce business, which was growing, but not yet profitable. Now Julie was quietly looking into selling the business.

"You can't sell out to some corporation!" Nina had

protested. Her mom was so proud of her company; she'd been working on it for years, had built it from the ground up.

"Honey, it doesn't matter. Your education is more important," Julie had assured her, but Nina knew she was putting on a brave face.

She needed to take down Gabriella before her mom gave up the company she'd worked so hard to build.

"I don't really want to talk about it," she muttered.

Daphne frowned. "Why not? I just told you about *my* parents."

"I'm not obligated to return the favor." Nina's voice had risen; she fought to lower it. "This isn't one of your negotiations, Daphne. Just because you shared something personal doesn't mean I have to."

"Who said anything about a negotiation? I was trying to have a *conversation* with you, Nina," Daphne said reasonably. "Isn't that what most people do when they hang out and eat tacos?"

"We're not hanging out; we're sobering you up, then I'm taking you home."

Nina was surprised by the hurt that flashed in Daphne's eyes, and even more surprised by her sudden remorse.

"It's all a mess, honestly. My mom might have to sell her company." Nina drew in a breath and explained it all in more detail. When she'd finished, Daphne shook her head sympathetically.

"That's terrible." Daphne looked down as she added, "But . . . your mom must really love you, to sacrifice her dreams for your sake."

Nina felt a strange pang at Daphne's words. She resolved never to take her parents' unconditional support for granted.

"Can I ask you something?" Daphne went on.

"You can ask, but I can't promise I'll answer."

"Why didn't you ever tell Jefferson about me?"

"You mean, about your bullying and threats?"

Daphne looked like she wanted to say something, but she just gave a silent nod. Nina sighed.

"I *did* tell Jeff, the night we broke up, but he refused to listen. He kept insisting that I had misunderstood you, because there's no way you would do anything like that."

Jeff taking Daphne's side had been the *reason* they had broken up that night. Well, one of the reasons.

"He trusts you, you know. And there aren't many people he trusts," Daphne said quietly.

"That's why you hate me, isn't it?" Nina was a little shocked she'd blurted out the question, but it felt good to say it aloud. "Because I'm still friends with Jeff, even though you tried so hard to get rid of me?"

"I don't hate you anymore, Nina."

Nina stared at Daphne, who seemed just as shocked by her own words. Daphne hurried to recover. "It's really not worth the effort, hating you. I'd rather focus that energy on taking down Gabriella."

I don't hate you anymore either, Nina could have said. But she didn't say it, because she wasn't sure whether it was true. Instead she matched Daphne's lighthearted tone.

"I'm sure you'll go back to hating me with a vengeance once we get rid of Gabriella."

"Almost certainly," Daphne agreed.

They both looked down at the remains of their taco platter, which was rapidly getting cold. Nina felt disoriented. She had no idea what to do with this new version of Daphne, whose sharp edges had been softened by something—vulnerability, and maybe loneliness.

"Nina—I know you think I'm wrong for Jefferson, but I really care about him. We have a lot of history," Daphne said softly.

"You really care about him," Nina repeated. "You don't love him?"

She doubted anyone had asked Daphne that before. But Daphne didn't seem offended; she just looked pensive.

"There are a lot of ways to love someone, you know? I do love Jefferson. Maybe not the same way you did, but that doesn't mean it isn't love."

The same way you did. Daphne had used the past tense, as if Nina's feelings for Jeff were long since over—and they *were*, Nina reminded herself. She and Jeff were just friends now. Totally platonic.

Her mind cut to that charged moment the other day, when they'd been fencing, and the shiver Nina had felt at his nearness.

Nope. That was nothing. She had definitely imagined the whole thing.

"Look, Daphne, you don't need to explain your relationship to me," she replied, trying to change the subject. "It really isn't my business."

"So you're not trying to break us up?"

"What?" Nina let out a disbelieving laugh. "How would that even work?"

"You know, keep your enemies close." Daphne spoke as if it were obvious. "I wasn't sure if that was the reason you agreed to help me with Gabriella, because you wanted to break up me and Jefferson."

The way you broke up me and Jefferson when we *dated?* Nina could have asked. But for some reason she didn't.

"I care about Jeff as a friend. Things between us were so messy, I wouldn't want to go there again," Nina said firmly. "So, no, I'm not trying to *break you up.*" She repeated the words with a sarcastic tilt, to emphasize how ridiculous this whole conversation was.

Daphne nodded, satisfied. "Then we need to refocus on Gabriella. Should we try again next weekend?"

"I'm busy next weekend." At Daphne's look, Nina rolled her eyes. "I know this will shock you, but I do have some semblance of a social life. I'm going to a party."

Daphne brightened at the word. "Who's throwing this party? Does it have a theme? Where is it?"

Her questions were as rapid and precise as a round of artillery. Nina tried to match her speed: "The school, decades, Arbor House."

"Arbor House?"

"There *are* parties at King's College that aren't thrown by the sororities or frats, you know."

Arbor House was the dorm farthest from the center of campus, so far that it literally fell in a different zip code. Years ago it had been a hotel called the King's Arms, where students' families stayed for parents' weekend and graduation. When it went out of business, the university bought the property and converted it into student housing.

Perhaps because they felt sorry for everyone who got stuck living there—it was at least twice as long a walk to class as the other dorms—the university allocated Arbor House a much higher "student activity allowance." Naturally, the residents of Arbor House spent it all on a single epic party.

"I'll come with you. I love a good theme," Daphne decided. "And we can keep brainstorming about Gabriella."

"At a party?" Nina pursed her lips, skeptical.

"There's nowhere better to scheme than at a party. It really gets the creative juices flowing," Daphne said solemnly. "Besides, I want to see these mythical non-fraternity parties. It'll be fun."

Had Daphne really just used the word *fun* to describe a night out with *Nina*?

"I . . . um . . . okay. You should come, if you want." It came out like a question, since Nina still wasn't sure Daphne was serious.

But then Daphne smiled. It looked somehow different from all the other countless times Nina had seen her smile: it was tentative, as fragile and gossamer as a butterfly testing its wings. Because, Nina realized, it was genuine.

As strange as it was, she felt an answering smile on her own face.

23

SAMANTHA

It had been a week since the breakup. Sam didn't feel any better, but on the bright side, she was wearing a costume and in the capital, on her way to see Nina.

Reflexively, she glanced down at her phone screen, then wished she hadn't. There weren't any new messages, at least not from the person she wanted to hear from.

Mercifully, the breakup hadn't yet made the tabloids. Sam suspected that Marshall's family was waiting out of politeness, letting the palace be the one to make the press announcement. Or maybe Marshall hadn't even told his parents yet.

She missed him so much. She missed the sly smile he gave her whenever he'd made a particularly silly joke, the way his eyes danced when she called him out on it. She missed their text thread, the way he would randomly send a single emoji, the dinosaur or perhaps the octopus, as if it held some hidden meaning.

When Sam had asked Beatrice for a night off from the conference—and for a plane, so she could fly to Washington and see Nina—she'd been surprised by how readily her sister agreed. Beatrice seemed to understand how much Sam needed a night with her best friend.

She'd immediately called Nina to share her plans, and Nina had explained that she was going to a party on Friday. "We can stay in," she'd offered, but Sam had adamantly refused. A theme party sounded like exactly what the doctor ordered.

The car pulled up outside Arbor House, and Sam hurried out of the backseat. The building still looked like a hotel, with its gabled roof and stone pillars, and iron balconies on some of the higher rooms, the ones that used to be suites. But no hotel would have music blasting this loud, or costumed students flooding eagerly up the stairs.

Sam spared a glance over her shoulder, where her Revere Guard, Caleb, walked a few paces behind her. At first he'd refused to dress up, but after Sam dug through one of the palace's storage closets and found a Hawaiian shirt covered in teddy bears, Caleb had muttered a gruff "fine." Sam suspected that he was secretly thrilled to wear it.

She tried not to think of how much Marshall would love that Hawaiian shirt.

Sam's costume, though, was the real showstopper: a hot-pink dress that screamed eighties prom, with ruffled sleeves, a poufy skirt, and a giant bow at the waist. Aunt Margaret was the only person in their family who could ever have purchased such a gloriously neon masterpiece.

The tables and chairs of Arbor House's dining hall had been stacked against one wall to create a dance floor, where students in poodle skirts and fringe dresses, bell-bottoms and skinny ties, were already crowded. Glittery balloons clustered at the ceiling, their ribbons floating back and forth whenever someone opened the main doors and let in a current of air.

Sam caught sight of Nina across the room, wearing a flapper dress and a peacock-feather headpiece. Without another word, she began walking—really, sprinting—toward her.

"Nina! God, am I glad to see you."

She couldn't say anything more, because tears were pricking at her eyes, but no more words were needed. Nina just nodded and pulled her into a fierce hug. "I'm sorry about Marshall," she whispered.

When they stepped apart, Sam's eyes drifted over Nina's shoulder, then widened in surprise. Jeff and Daphne were headed over, both smiling broadly.

Jeff looked outrageous in a white tuxedo, complete with a blue bow tie and cummerbund that were covered in sequins. Daphne, meanwhile, was as coolly chic as ever in a short dress made of interlocking gold discs. With her high ponytail and oversized gold earrings, she belonged in a 1960s issue of *Vogue*.

Sam hadn't even considered that Jeff might be coming to Nina's college party; she'd just assumed she would catch up with him at the palace later, bully him into sharing her midnight pizza. And she'd certainly never imagined that Daphne would come to an on-campus party in a *dining hall*. Perhaps Daphne wanted to keep an eye on Jeff in case any college girls tried to throw themselves at him.

"Sam! I'm so glad you're here," Jeff said eagerly.

Then Sam watched, stunned, as Daphne turned and said something under her breath to Nina. And Nina *laughed*.

Before she could react, Jeff grabbed her hand and Daphne's, tugging both of them toward the dance floor. "Come on, this is my favorite song!"

They danced in a delightfully jumbled group—Sam, Nina, Jeff, and Daphne. Nina's friends Rachel and Jayne floated in and out of their circle, everyone laughing and letting their dance moves become increasingly absurd. They tried the punch, which, as Sam had expected, was far too sweet, though Jeff proclaimed he loved it and downed three cups.

The best part was, no one bothered them. There were a few excited whispers, a few people elbowing one another in excitement, but no one came over and said anything, or asked for a photo. Jeff hadn't been lying when he'd said that the other students at King's College generally let him be.

Sam tried to enjoy the moment. She was surrounded by people who loved her, wearing a silly costume, and singing along so loudly she felt hoarse. Yet her smile kept slipping.

Nina, sensing her mood as always, grabbed her arm. "I need some fresh air. Come with me?"

Sam hesitated, but Nina had already started through the crowds, dragging Sam insistently after her.

When they stepped into the cool night air, Sam let go of the relentless enthusiasm that had been carrying her all night. She pressed the heels of her hands to her eyes and sighed.

"Want to talk about it?" Nina asked.

They were standing at one corner of a darkened quadrangle. The colonnades were empty, though Sam heard the thump of the bass from the dining hall.

The morning after Marshall had ended things, Sam had tearfully called Nina and rehashed the entire conversation. So she didn't say anything more about the breakup. She just leaned against one of the pillars and confessed, "I miss Marshall."

Nina nodded. "I know. You really loved him."

"I *still* love him!" Sam burst out. "That's the thing about love: you can't just turn it off when it becomes inconvenient, like flipping a light switch. It's not that easy. I mean, how long did it take you to get over Jeff?"

A strange look darted over Nina's face. "What?"

"After you and Jeff broke up, how long did it take you to fall out of love with him?"

"Um . . . I'm not sure," Nina said evasively.

Sam tugged at her tulle skirt, which rustled loudly. "I hate that things ended like this. I obviously wouldn't want Marshall to give up the dukedom, but that doesn't change the fact that I miss him. I haven't heard from him all week," she added.

"Don't you think it's better this way? A clean break?"

"It's not clean," Sam exclaimed. "It's all muddled and confusing. I wish I could talk to Marshall, but I know I shouldn't call him."

"Aren't you going to see him at the photo shoot soon?" Nina reminded her.

"Yeah," Sam said hoarsely. "But it's not like I'm going to walk up to him and ask what's going on in his head."

Nina hesitated. "Even if you did talk to Marshall, I'm not sure it would help."

"What do you mean?"

Nina tucked a strand of hair behind her ear, causing the peacock feather on her headpiece to sway. "Sam," she said gently, "I love you, but you will never know what it's like to be a person of color dating a member of the royal family."

Sam felt heat rise to her cheeks. "You're right," she said clumsily. She should have asked Nina about this long ago. "I . . . can you help me try to understand?"

Nina leaned her hip against the stone archway. "You know how people are always judging you without having met you? They come to an opinion about you based on some stupid tabloid headlines, and then if they ever *do* end up meeting you, it's not with an open mind. No matter what you say, it just reinforces the opinion of you that they've already formed."

Sam nodded. She'd been America's flighty, unreliable party princess for years, and most people still thought of her that way—in spite of the grueling royal tour she'd done this summer, in spite of how much she'd grown up.

"Imagine it like that, but a million times worse, because I'm not a princess *or* white," Nina said bluntly. "The moment people meet me, they've already made a snap judgment about me based on the color of my skin. That was what made it so hard to date Jeff—because now it wasn't just a few racist people in my own life judging me, but every last troll on the internet. They put me and my family under the microscope in ways I couldn't have imagined."

Sam hated thinking of all the ugly, hateful things people had written about her best friend. "I'm so sorry, Nina."

"I can't speak for Marshall, but I can tell you that I didn't have the easiest time growing up. Some of it was because I always raised my hand in class, and had my nose in a book—I didn't do myself a ton of favors, socially," Nina added, with a self-deprecating shrug. "But girls can be so vicious. The CIA could learn a thing or two about emotional torture from middle school cliques.

"I remember this one time, all the girls at my school were carrying quilted designer clutches as pencil cases. I asked my parents for one, because I'm only human, okay? I just wanted to fit in."

Nina had gone to public school, but given its location in the most affluent part of Washington—all the grace-and-favor houses where government employees lived were five minutes from the palace—it was as academically stringent and socially competitive as a private school.

"My parents refused to purchase a two-hundred-dollar bag for a sixth grader. But my mamá agreed to take me to the wholesale neighborhood at the end of the red metro line, where the stores carry the cheap fake stuff: you know, purses with the brand name misspelled, that kind of thing."

Nina's eyes drifted away, to fix on something in the distance. "When I came to school the next week, so proud of my fake designer clutch, Nancy Huntington cornered me in the hallway and knocked the bag to the floor in front of everyone. 'That's a fake!' she said triumphantly, like she'd caught me shoplifting. 'I know,' I told her, puzzled. 'My mamá took me to get it on the east side.' I'd thought the whole thing was so fun, like it was this private adventure that Mamá and I had shared.

"Nancy just sneered and said, 'The east side? I should have known. That's where people like you shop.' And all the girls laughed and marched off." Nina's voice was thick. "I didn't carry the clutch again after that."

Sam made an outraged noise in the back of her throat. "Oh my god, who *are* these girls? I'm sending Caleb to hunt them down and slash all their tires!"

That elicited a ghost of a smile from Nina. "It's okay, it was all a long time ago. And who knows, maybe it was easier for Marshall, since he's a man, and he's so good-looking and athletic. I bet everyone in middle school loved him."

Actually, there was a streak of loneliness—of insecurity—in Marshall, too, Sam thought. But she didn't want to interrupt.

"When I got to King's College, it was a fresh start. No one cared that I'm Latina or a huge nerd, or that I have two moms. Everyone just accepted me for who I am." Nina sighed. "Until I started dating Jeff. Sometimes it was overt, like people debating my skin color in the comments, but a lot of times it was more subtle and more personal. Like when Robert Standish told me that I'm a more *elegant* public speaker than he had expected."

"Wait, *what?*" Sam made a mental note that Robert Standish's tires were going to get slashed, too.

"Think of all the coverage Marshall got when he was dating you. The headlines never said they didn't approve of him *because* he's Black. Instead they focused on his playboy reputation, calling him the 'bad-boy duke' or 'Hollywood royalty trying to mix with real royalty.' I don't know how it was for Marshall, but for me, those articles—and all the ugly comments that people wrote underneath them—crystallized every insecurity I've ever felt." Nina swallowed. "When I read those things, I was thirteen years old again, standing there in the hallway while Nancy knocked my bag to the ground and told me how pathetic I was for even trying. It felt like a reminder that *people like me* can never really belong."

Of course you belong, Sam wanted to cry out, but she knew better than to say it aloud. Clearly, there was a large part of the world—far too large—that didn't share her opinion.

"Nina, I'm so unbelievably sorry. I wish the palace had protected you better when you and Jeff were together. I wish I had done more."

"I'm not saying this to make you feel guilty, Sam. I'm just trying to make you understand. Marshall loves you, but he also has the media coming at him from every angle, not to mention his family and this legacy that they've held on to for generations. I can understand how hard it would be for him to give that up. Especially with all the millions of people of color who are looking up to him, who see him as an example."

Sam's heart ached that Marshall and Nina—two of the people she loved most—had gone through all of this. No wonder Marshall had felt like he couldn't take it anymore.

Sam wrapped her arms around her torso, warding off the chill. Now that she'd spoken to Nina, she longed to talk to Marshall even more. She wanted to say how sorry she was for failing to understand the pressures on him, for being blind to all the problematic parts of their relationship. She'd taken Nina for granted for years, and now, apparently, she'd done the same thing to Marshall.

If only she could have one more chance, so that she could do things better this time.

"Should we head back?" Nina asked. "They're probably all looking for us."

Samantha glanced over. "You know, when you texted me

and said 'We're all going to the decades party,' I thought you meant you, Rachel, and Jayne. Since when do you and Daphne make plans together? Are you friends now?"

Oddly, Nina didn't deny it. "We've been spending more time together lately. Daphne isn't quite as bad as I thought."

Sam was struck by an idea. "Nina, will you come to the League of Kings closing banquet with me? I'm allowed to have a plus-one."

Nina grimaced. "I don't know . . ."

"Please? You're such a good date to these things!"

"I'm a terrible date. I stand to the side and ignore everyone and eat all the passed appetizers."

"Exactly. You're my ideal date," Sam agreed. "Pretty please, come with me?"

"Fine," Nina said reluctantly. "Now come on. There's a sweaty, gross dance floor inside with our names on it."

They headed inside, arms linked, just as they used to do when they were children and felt capable of anything.

24

BEATRICE

The next day, Beatrice was in her sitting room, nestled in the corner of the love seat while Samantha recounted her whirlwind trip to Washington.

"Can you believe it?" Sam had just related Nina's story about being a person of color dating a royal. "I knew it wasn't easy on Nina, and on Marshall, but I never realized how fundamentally we failed to protect them. Maybe we need new press protocols. Maybe we need to start hiring security for our significant others!"

Beatrice felt queasy at the thought of how terribly the media had treated Nina and Marshall. "Those are good ideas. You could run them by Marshall when you see him at the photo shoot."

Her sister flopped onto the love seat next to her, letting her head fall into her hands. "I'm not ready to see Marshall. Can I call in sick?" she pleaded. "You can Photoshop me in later!"

Beatrice leaned forward. "Sam, you can do this. You're the strongest person I know."

Sam groaned. "Fine, okay? But for the record, I hate when you use that . . . that *look*!"

"What?"

"It's the same way Dad used to look at me, when he said he was proud of me, or that he believed in me."

Beatrice felt heartsore and happy all at once. There was so

much of her father that she consciously tried to imitate; it was nice to think that she'd picked up other things without even realizing.

"I am proud of you, and I do believe in you," she said softly.

They both looked up at the sound of a knock.

"Béatrice?" Louise peeked around the edge of the doorway, then flung it all the way open when she saw them. "Oh good, Samantha, I'm glad you're back. I have news!"

Beatrice noted Louise's black jeans and studded leather jacket with amusement. "You don't look like you're dressed for . . ." She checked the schedule on the side table for tonight's guest lecturer. "How the Mind-Body Connection Is Rewiring International Relations."

"That's because I'm not going to that thing." When Louise was excited, her French accent became even more pronounced: *zhat sing.* "I'm going to a party on the tsar's yacht, and I hope you'll come with me."

"No," Beatrice said, at the same time Sam exclaimed, "Oh, *yes!*"

Beatrice shot her sister a look. "Honestly, Sam, a little guided meditation might be good for you right now."

"I disagree wholeheartedly," Louise cut in. "After a breakup, Samantha doesn't need some person spraying incense and telling her to visualize a perfect circle. She needs music and champagne out on the water."

Beatrice shifted her weight uncomfortably. She wasn't sure she wanted to see the tsar, after he'd roundly rejected her attempts to garner his support for her climate accord. Not to mention that as the host monarch, she should probably make an appearance at the evening's official event. But Sam was looking at her with such a hopeful puppy-dog expression that Beatrice gave up.

"All right, fine. We can go."

Louise nodded fervently. "Excellent. But of course, you cannot show up at a Romanov party looking so . . ."

"Boring," Sam offered.

"Buttoned up," Louise corrected.

"Frumpy!" Sam chimed in, and Beatrice tossed one of the couch's silk cushions at her.

"I am not frumpy!"

Sam acted like she hadn't heard. "Meet downstairs in ten? I know what to wear; you don't need to worry about *me*," Sam added to Louise, who smiled broadly.

"I never do."

They exchanged a complicit, knowing look, like two parents making eye contact over their toddler's head. It made Beatrice laugh in defeat. "Fine, I can fight one of you, but not both. Just tell me what to wear."

Louise beamed. "I was hoping you'd say that."

She disappeared into Beatrice's closet, emerging a few minutes later with a slinky black dress—which Beatrice had only ever worn with tights—and over-the-knee boots. Once Beatrice had changed, Louise put her hands on her shoulders and led her to the vanity.

"Close your eyes," she commanded. Beatrice felt an eyeliner pencil, then a dusting of shadow along her upper lid. "Now open them," Louise told her. Beatrice stared up at the ceiling as Louise brushed wet mascara over her lashes.

"Look at us. We're two of a kind."

Beatrice glanced to where their faces hovered in the mirror. Despite their obvious differences—Louise's hair a pale blonde, Beatrice's dark brown—they looked startlingly similar. They had the same dark-rimmed eyes and smoky lashes, the same red lips.

Beatrice looked nothing like her usual demure self. She looked like a new Beatrice, powerful and a little bit dangerous.

The tsar's yacht was at anchor in the bay, its lights dancing over the water. When they reached the dock, they all lowered themselves into a motorboat, and the driver sped off.

Beatrice glanced back at Bellevue. She so rarely saw it from this vantage point. On one side its beaches curled into the ocean; on the other, cliffs fell in a sheer drop to the crashing surf. The turrets of the main house rose up in stone splendor, lights glowing like fireflies behind the windows.

When a crew member helped them onto the *Xenia*, Beatrice nearly gasped. The doors to the great room were open, revealing an indulgently opulent space, its surfaces covered in gold leaf and baroque tracery. Chandeliers cast glittering light over dark wood furniture and silk couches. It could have been a room lifted straight from a palace, except for the enormous windows that overlooked the water. The sun was setting, orange whorls of flame descending into the ocean and turning the water a molten yellow-gold.

There must not be anyone at tonight's official programming, since this yacht was packed with people.

"Your Majesty, Your Royal Highnesses. Welcome." Tsar Dmitri stepped forward to greet them. He was a bear of a man, tall and imposing, wearing the Romanovs' signature dark red.

Louise and Sam each gave a slow curtsy. Beatrice knew it bothered Louise, but since she was technically still a princess, she was required to give way before monarchs.

Beatrice, of course, did not curtsy. She inclined her head to the tsar, her nod just low enough to be polite but not so low that it would be mistaken for submission.

Dmitri waved at a footman, who came over bearing a tray of crystal flutes. Beatrice accepted one and took a sip, then nearly choked. It wasn't champagne, but vodka.

The party was clearly in full swing. Kings and queens were spilling onto the promenades that encircled the boat, exchanging rapid stories in a variety of languages. The queens of Mexico and Morocco perched on the edge of the hot tub, feet in the water, loudly instructing one of the staff about how to prepare some frozen cocktail that involved bananas and cream. "Just bring the blender up here and I'll make it myself," Queen Monica exclaimed, at which Queen Leila squealed, "It'll be like old times!" Farther down the deck, the kings of Spain and Nigeria were bent over a phone, tugging it back and forth as they fought over the playlist. No one else seemed to care that the music was switching frenetically from one song to another. Princess Maria of Italy was carrying around a large shopping bag, tossing out glow bracelets and ring pops that she'd apparently purchased at a dollar store. And here was Prince James, walking around with the top half of his shirt unbuttoned.

Feeling Beatrice's gaze on him, Jamie grinned and sank into an absurdly low bow, so that his shirt fluttered open and revealed his tanned chest. "Your Majesty. A pleasure to see you, as always." He eyed Beatrice's diamond watch and added, "What time is it, by the way?"

Beatrice glanced down at her wrist. "Six."

Jamie crowed in delight. "It's time, then! A button an hour! A button an hour!" To Beatrice's shock, all the men on board—except Dmitri—obediently unfastened another button of their shirts, which now hung half-open. Beatrice saw the chests of far more kings than she'd ever expected to see in one place.

"Seriously, Jamie?" Sam rolled her eyes.

Jamie just laughed, unbothered. "You're welcome to join in, of course, Samantha."

Beatrice bristled, but Jamie was already heading off to harass someone else. And Sirivannavari, Bharat, and Alexei had started toward them, wearing dopey smiles and glowing necklaces and, in Alexei's and Bharat's case, shirts with the top few buttons undone.

"Really, boys?" Louise teased.

"A button an hour. I don't make the rules, I just obey them," Bharat said flippantly, but Alexei must have caught Louise's disapproval, because he hurried to redo his buttons.

There was a loud thump from outside, and they all turned. Alexei shrugged. "Don't worry, that's just some drunk idiot trying to unhook the lifeboats. Happens every time. They're securely fastened," he added reassuringly.

Louise leaned over, nudging Beatrice's shoulder with her own. "Told you. The Romanovs really know how to throw a party."

♛

An hour later, Beatrice ducked from the terrace back into the great room.

The party had, impossibly, gotten even rowdier. Bharat and Alexei had broken into the pool closet and unearthed a huge crate of squirt guns, and now all the royals were engaged in an all-out water fight, their expensive silk dresses and custom-fitted shirts soaking wet. Beatrice just wanted to catch her breath for a minute, escape all the chaos.

"You're not enjoying yourself?"

She almost jumped; she hadn't seen the tsar sitting on the couch, reading a stack of documents as if he were in his office, not in the middle of a wild party.

"I just needed some quiet," she said carefully.

She thought again of everything the tsar had said last week, when she'd pitched the climate accord to him. At least, unlike some monarchs, Dmitri had done her the courtesy of listening to what she said.

He was smart, and he was stubborn, and no matter what arguments she laid out, he was always ready with a counterargument. How could he agree to something that would eliminate so many jobs, especially among the poorest communities in his nation? Had Beatrice even considered how expensive this proposal would be? She hadn't lived through the bitter cold of a Russian winter; she didn't know what she was asking, telling him to increase taxes and build a series of wind farms he couldn't afford.

Now, looking around at the lavish interior of the *Xenia*, Beatrice found it hard to imagine that there was anything the tsar couldn't afford.

Her eyes drifted to a poker table set up along the opposite wall; she hadn't noticed it before. Dmitri followed her gaze and smiled wolfishly. "Do you play?"

Beatrice flashed back to those rainy afternoons at the country house when her father had taught her and the twins the basics of poker. They used to bet on silly things: the winner got the largest slice of chocolate cake at dinner, or picked which movie they all watched that night.

"Only a little." And maybe it was the contagious energy of the party, or the fact that she was dressed like a braver, brazen version of herself, but Beatrice added, "Should we play? We could add a wager."

"I'm listening," the tsar told her, intrigued.

"If I win, you'll vote for my climate-accord bill."

Dmitri gave a low whistle. "That's quite an ask, but very well. I accept."

A thrill coursed through Beatrice's veins. This was how things were done at these conferences, wasn't it? Forget the debates, forget the protocol, forget the massive delegations and assemblies. Sometimes the world changed in smaller ways: a boat ride over ink-dark water, the flip of a card.

Dmitri threw open the doors to the terrace, his voice booming over the clamor. "Beatrice and I are about to play a hand of poker!"

There was a roar of excitement at his words, and the other monarchs all quickly streamed inside. Half of them were missing shoes or articles of clothing, or, in the case of the queens of Mexico and Morocco, seemed to have traded outfits entirely.

Sam and Louise came to stand near Beatrice. "What are you doing?" Sam hissed.

"Honestly, I'm not sure. I'm sort of . . . making it up as I go along?"

Sam stared at her, an eyebrow lifted. They both knew that Beatrice never acted on impulse; she was always motivated by facts and data and logic. But it felt good to act out of character, to be spontaneous—to be more like Sam—for once.

"Now, if I win, what do I want?" the tsar mused, thinking aloud. "Perhaps you could break your engagement to Theodore and marry one of my sons instead. Not Alexei—he has to rule Russia someday," he added, waving at the tsarevich. "But I have three other boys, all of whom would be more than happy to renounce their titles and move to America for you. You can take your pick!"

Beatrice stared at him blankly. Then the tsar clapped her back, laughing uproariously. "Your face is priceless! Beatrice, you must know that I was joking!"

Was he? Beatrice had the sickening thought that political marriages had been negotiated like this for centuries, probably on boats just like this one. Lives and loves gambled on the throw of the dice, or negotiated as part of an economic treaty.

"Unfortunately for your sons, I'm not available." She smiled, but there was an edge to her words.

"All right, then. What about that tiara you always wear? Anastasia keeps raving about how beautiful it is."

"The Winslow tiara isn't actually mine. It belongs to America."

"Then I suppose if you lose, you'll have to buy it from your own country," he declared, and chuckled at his own words.

Gamble the Winslow tiara? Beatrice's every instinct rose up against the suggestion. And yet . . . For years she had lived by the rules, dotted every i and crossed every t. Maybe it was time she allowed a little bit of risk into her life.

"Agreed." She held out her hand, and the tsar shook it.

They crossed the room to the gaming table, already set up for play with two armchairs and a deck of cards. The other royals gathered around, clutching cocktails or glowing necklaces or water guns that dripped onto the expensive carpet, but Dmitri clearly didn't care.

One of the footmen fanned the cards back and forth, shuffling them, then began to deal. Beatrice remembered her father saying that with fifty-two cards in a deck, there were over three hundred million possibilities for a hand of poker. With some trepidation, she studied her cards.

It wasn't so bad: an ace and a nine.

The dealer flipped over three of the center cards, and Beatrice's heart skipped. An ace, a seven, and another nine. Luck was on her side tonight. She had two pairs already: aces and nines.

"We can call off the bet now, if you're having second thoughts," Dmitri said, watching her expression.

Beatrice slid her cards carefully onto the green baize of the table. "No."

Juan Pablo, the King of Spain, was clutching a cigar; smoke gathered overhead, casting the room in a dim haze. Conversations and gossip fell silent. Beatrice was suddenly aware of even the quietest background noise: waves lapping against the side of the yacht, the hum of the electricity.

The dealer flipped over the fourth card. It was a king.

"Shall we up the stakes?" Dmitri suggested. A low murmur swept around the table, like wind rushing through leaves.

"How so?" Beatrice asked coolly.

"If I win, you ask your Congress to eliminate the taxes on Russian companies operating in America."

Beatrice glanced back at her cards, rapidly calculating the odds. Unless he had a pair of kings, which was highly improbable, there was no chance his hand could beat hers. He had to be bluffing.

Yet his features were stern, revealing nothing. She imagined this must have been what his ancestors looked like when they mounted their armored horses and rode into battle—resolute, emotionless, impassive.

Well, *her* ancestors had gone to war, too. She could be every inch as tough and unreadable as he was.

"Then, if I win, you need to help me get more votes for the climate accord."

"I already promised you my vote."

"That's not enough. I want you to help me drum up support. Become the climate accord's greatest champion."

Dmitri grinned and looked out over the room. "As you can see, we have a bit of a wager going. In the event Queen Beatrice wins, will you all agree to vote for her climate accord?" He laughed in a way that managed to convey how deeply unlikely he considered Beatrice's victory.

Some of the observers pursed their lips, clearly reluctant to promise their support, but some—enough—nodded or cheered in agreement.

The footman flipped over the final card in the center of the table. It was another ace.

Dmitri let out a cry of excitement and threw down his

cards. "You'd better polish that tiara," he exclaimed as the other monarchs burst into raucous shouts.

Beatrice blinked, stunned. He'd had a pair of kings after all.

"Full house." He swept a stack of chips, which they hadn't even gambled on, forward in his eagerness.

"You're right. You do have a full house," Beatrice said slowly. "But so do I."

She set her cards down and watched as Dmitri registered what had happened. He had a full house of kings, but Beatrice had a full house of aces, and in poker, aces counted higher.

He stared at her cards for a moment, shocked, then tipped his head back and laughed uproariously.

"Only in poker can anything outrank a king! Well done, Beatrice. I mean—Your Majesty."

Beatrice smiled, gratified. "So you'll vote for my climate accord?"

"Of course I will, and I'll make sure everyone here does as well. I gave you my word, and a Romanov always keeps his word," he said gruffly.

Beatrice watched Dmitri disappear into the crowd, accepting condolences and commentary on the game. Her body was coursing with adrenaline, as if she'd just completed some impossible task, scaling Everest or running a marathon.

"That was amazing," Louise exclaimed.

Sam pulled Beatrice into a tight hug. "I don't know if I've ever been so proud of you! That was an epic display of girl power—like nineties-girl-group-level girl power! It makes me want to put on a glittery wig and belt out pop songs."

"We can go sing in the karaoke room, if you want," Alexei offered. He turned to Beatrice. "That was impressive. I've been gambling against my father for years, and I've never beat him."

Then Sirivannavari was high-fiving her, and Bharat was twining glow necklaces around her neck, and they were all heading down the hall.

"You have a karaoke room on your yacht?" Sam was asking.

"Well, it's also a golf simulator," Alexei said, as if that made the whole thing more reasonable. "You can use it for any sport, really. A tennis simulator, or skiing . . ."

Beatrice smiled and let herself be swept along with the group. She felt giddy, unstoppable. She had gone up against monarchs far older and more experienced, and she had prevailed.

Maybe she was starting to get the hang of this queen thing after all.

25

NINA

The world must be turning upside down. There was no other explanation for the fact that Nina was pulling into the Deightons' driveway: venturing deep into enemy territory, straight into the lion's den. A month ago, if you'd told her that she would come to Daphne's *house*, Nina would have laughed in your face.

Before she could ring the bell, the door swung open.

"Nina. Hey." Daphne sounded like she'd almost expected her to cancel. Nina had certainly considered it.

When they reached Daphne's bedroom, she glanced around with anthropological curiosity. She'd expected something bland and traditional, but the room was full of surprises: a wooden desk that Nina recognized from a chain store because she had the exact same one; a lamp with a pebbled surface that looked vintage and somehow mermaidish. Three of the walls were white, but the fourth was a dusky blue-gray accent wall, its lines just uneven enough to suggest that Daphne had painted it herself.

On the bedside table, in the place of reverence where most girls kept their phones, Daphne had a stack of books. Nina saw one of the Kingmaker novels, a paperback thriller—which surprised her—and a copy of *Middlemarch*, which didn't.

Then she registered her own thoughts and wondered when she'd developed an opinion on Daphne's taste in literature.

Daphne gestured toward the armchair. But Nina decided to provoke Daphne, just a little, by plopping onto the bed instead, pulling one of the fluffy pillows into her lap. Daphne hesitated, then took the chair.

"I remember that trip." Nina nodded at a photo on the bedside table, of Daphne and Jeff on the ski slopes. Actually, she felt like she'd seen the picture recently. Daphne had probably posted it as a #tbt or something.

"Oh, I—um, I forgot that photo was still out." It was an odd thing for Daphne to say. She seemed to realize that, and hurried to recover. "It's funny that you and I were both in Telluride, but we never really spoke to each other."

"It's not *that* surprising. I went out of my way to avoid you."

There was a beat of awkward silence. Then Daphne said, "Because I was with Jefferson, and you were jealous?"

Yes, Nina thought, but there was no point in digging up old feelings. "Because you were so irritatingly perfect."

Daphne made a strangled noise. "Please. You of all people know how far I am from perfect."

"Look, there's yet another thing we can agree on. We're finding more and more of those these days," Nina quipped. "What I meant was, you *fit in* on those trips, while I clearly didn't. You had the right clothes; you knew the names of all those people at the New Year's Eve party; you were even better at *skiing* than I was."

"You thought I fit in?" Daphne shook her head. "I was constantly checking my etiquette book, terrified that I would do or say the wrong thing."

"At least you *had* an etiquette book! Everything I learned about etiquette, I learned from Jane Austen."

"That sentence should be the title of your memoir," Daphne observed, and Nina surprised herself by chuckling.

It was strange to think that Daphne had been just as nervous on the Washingtons' vacations. Daphne projected such unassailable confidence that Nina had always assumed she was a spoiled aristocratic brat: that she was numb to the Washingtons' staggering wealth, that the sight of liveried footmen around every corner was as commonplace to her as it was to the royal twins.

She was learning, now, that she'd been wrong about a lot of things. Maybe she should reexamine her tendency to make snap judgments about people and their backgrounds.

"Anyway. About Gabriella." Nina felt suddenly desperate to get them back on task. It was disarming, sitting on Daphne's bed like this, looking at photos as if they were normal people—as if they were friends.

"We need a new plan," Daphne agreed.

"Should we break into her room again? It kills me that we don't know what was on her computer," Nina said, but Daphne shook her head.

"Even if we figured out a way to get inside, there's no guarantee we would find anything. It's too risky."

"It was risky last time, and we did it then!"

"That was at a crowded party," Daphne insisted. "How would we explain ourselves if we got caught?"

Nina's brows drew together. "You saw her do cocaine. Can we find a way to report her, get the police to do a search of her house?"

"You know the police won't search someone like Gabriella Madison based on an anonymous tip. We need proof."

"What we *need* is Gabriella's Achilles' heel," Nina mused. "What's her weak point, and how can we use it to trick her?"

Daphne smiled. "You sound like me."

It was true; at some point, Daphne's way of thinking had rubbed off on her. Nina found that slightly disconcerting.

"Tell me everything you know about Gabriella," she decided. "Maybe there's something we're not thinking of."

Daphne recounted the Madisons' family history, which

Nina already knew, and a lot of things Nina had never heard: A rumor that Gabriella wanted to be an "influencer," only to quit when her parents cut her off in retribution—they thought it was tacky. Stories from high school, about girls Gabriella had bullied and trouble she'd gotten into, which her family had then promptly gotten her out of. When Daphne told her that Gabriella had failed physics at her lycée in Paris but had gotten into King's College anyway, Nina frowned.

"That can't be right. A passing grade in high school physics is *required* in order to matriculate," she said angrily. "At the very least Gabriella should've had to take summer school."

"The university made an exception for her, because apparently 'science is different in France.'" Daphne lifted her hands to make little air quotes around the phrase, rolling her eyes.

"Are you kidding? Science is not different in France! That is literally the core tenet of physics—that its laws are universal!"

"Don't you know by now that laws aren't universal? They're different for people like the Madisons."

Nina sat with that for a minute, then gave an angry sigh. "We're not any closer to figuring out a plan. What makes Gabriella tick? Aside from her massive ego."

Daphne's head snapped up. "That's it. Her ego!"

"Yes, she's so full of herself that she literally owns a statue of her own *face*. How are we going to turn that against her? Tape a mirror to the bottom of a swimming pool?"

"We're going to do what you did at her party, when she caught you lurking in the upstairs hallway. We'll flatter her into a false sense of security."

"How?"

"It has to be me this time," Daphne said slowly. "I'll pretend to be her friend, make her believe I want to be part of her entourage, and get her to reveal something incriminating."

"You want to sweet-talk your way into Gabriella's inner circle? That could take *years*."

"It won't, because I'm going to really sell it. I'll make Gabriella believe that I think she's superior in every way—smarter, better, prettier."

"You're not capable of groveling that convincingly. We should probably practice."

"Very funny," Daphne said lightly, though her mouth curled upward a bit. Then she glanced at Nina with an unreadable expression. "You're right, though. I'm not very good at giving up attention. That's always been my real flaw."

"I'm sorry, we're limiting ourselves to *one* flaw?"

"As if you're perfect," Daphne retorted, and Nina shrugged.

"I never said I was."

"I should hope not. You're unbelievably stubborn—"

"Okay," Nina cut in, "that's the pot calling the kettle black—"

"You're incapable of taking feedback or constructive criticism—"

"*You* care too much what people think!"

"*You're* too nice!"

Daphne's words were followed by a ringing silence. Then Nina let out a breath. "Look, we can't just sit here pointing out each other's flaws."

"You're only saying that because you've run out of material." Daphne looked up with a sly, teasing smile. "I, for one, could keep going all night."

What was happening right now? Were she and Daphne actually making *jokes* at each other's expense?

Nina leaned back, bracing her hands on the mattress. "You really think you can make Gabriella trust you?"

Daphne nodded. "She won't be able to resist lording it over the prince's girlfriend. Come to think of it," she said slowly, "maybe I shouldn't *be* the prince's girlfriend for this conversation. I'll ask Gabriella for a moment alone, get her advice about my breakup with Jefferson."

"Your breakup?"

Something sizzled through Nina at the thought of a newly single Prince Jefferson.

No, she reminded herself. She and Jeff were friends now; that was all.

"I'm not actually breaking up with him, of course," Daphne was saying, oblivious to Nina's sudden turmoil. "I'll just make it seem that way. If Gabriella thinks our relationship is on the rocks, she'll draw me close in the hopes of getting all the sordid details."

This sounded like a risky plan, but Nina knew Daphne well enough by now not to underestimate her. "Good luck," Nina said uncertainly.

"Good luck? You're coming with me. This is still a two-person operation," Daphne informed her. "Someone has to record Gabriella once I've made her trust me."

"Record her?"

"So that we have *proof,* of course."

"When exactly is this all going to happen?"

"We'll figure something out," Daphne said confidently. "I'll keep you updated once I've found a way to hang out with Gabriella."

Nina winced. "I'm glad it's you and not me." The thought of voluntarily spending time with Gabriella was abhorrent.

Though she would have said that about Daphne once, and look where they were now, teaming up to help each other.

She and Daphne, a team. It wasn't as outrageous a thought as it used to be.

♛

The next day, Nina sat in the library with Jeff, reviewing his essay for Introduction to World History.

When she'd realized how anxious he was about the class, Nina had offered to read through his essays, and Jeff had taken her up on it. So here she was, trying desperately to focus on Jeff's computer screen, not on the sheer fact of him sitting next to her.

Yet she kept glancing at where his hands were splayed on the table, kept feeling his leg brush against hers. If only he weren't so painfully, effortlessly gorgeous. Except—that was never really what had attracted her, not his looks and certainly not his titles.

She'd never understood girls who were able to kiss someone they'd just met, the way Sam used to in her wilder days. For Nina, the physical was too inextricably tied with the emotional. Back when they dated, Nina hadn't cared that she was with Prince Jefferson; she'd fallen for Jeff, the boy underneath it all.

She forced herself to focus on his screen. At least she'd made it to page four of a six-page essay. "You could have picked a topic that I'm more familiar with," she couldn't resist pointing out. "I know next to nothing about ancient Rome."

"Please, you know everything about everything," Jeff said, with such matter-of-fact confidence that she smiled.

"I could be more helpful if you'd chosen to write about the Tudors, or the transfer of power to the Russian duma."

"Yes, but ancient Rome had *gladiators*," Jeff said, which she had expected, and then he added something she hadn't. "Plus, the structure of their government was so interesting. Did you know our Founding Fathers discussed an elected executive branch, because the Romans elected their consuls?"

An elected executive—how would that work? How could

you possibly get anything accomplished if you were always changing the person in charge?

Nina read through the last two pages, asking Jeff to rewrite a sentence here and there, shuffling the order of a few paragraphs so that the argument built more cohesively. When they'd finished, he pushed his chair back with a sigh.

"Thanks so much, Nina. I really owe you one."

"I'm always happy to help a friend," she assured him.

They left the library, a drizzling mist hanging heavy in the air. Jeff nodded at the sedan in the parking lot. "Can I give you a ride back to the Chalet?"

"That's okay. I want to walk," she said quickly. Better not to spend any more time alone with Jeff.

Yet instead of heading back to the palace, he shrugged. "Then I'll walk you."

"Jeff, it's not very late. You don't have to."

"That's what friends are for," he told her, smiling.

There was nothing Nina could say to that. She was the one who kept reminding them both that they were just friends.

It would have been like any other guy walking across campus with her, except for the Revere Guard several paces behind them, holding an umbrella in case the skies opened into a downpour. And the car that followed, vanishing and then reappearing as it followed the roads that were meant only for licensed university vehicles and supply trucks.

When they reached Nina's dorm, she paused at the doorway and looked up at Jeff. Her blood pinged wildly inside her, bouncing off her skin, making everything buzz and tingle.

His dark hair seemed to glow. In the moonlight he was all shadow and silver, like an old black-and-white photo come to life. Come to think of it, there was something historical in the set of his chin, the resolute way he squared his shoulders.

Nina realized that she'd been lying when she'd told Daphne

that she had no romantic feelings for Jeff. But then, she'd been lying to herself, too.

Whatever part of her had fallen in love with Jeff the first time, it was still there—and in danger of falling for him all over again.

He met her gaze, and Nina caught a flash of nervousness, maybe even of longing.

She took a panicked step back, fumbling for her student ID to hide the shaking of her hands. "Good night, Jeff," she said quickly, and shut the door in his face.

26

SAMANTHA

"Ladies!" Lord Colin Marchworth called out, clapping his hands imperiously.

The ladies-in-waiting, all wearing ivory column gowns and elbow-length gloves, reluctantly broke off their conversations. Colin squinted behind his glasses and began pompously directing the young women into position at the front of the throne room.

"Lady Isabelle, move to the back row; you're too tall. Lady Janet, turn to the side—no, the other way, and drape your arm over the back of that chair—the other arm! Lady Gabriella, a step forward, if you please. . . ."

Gabriella Madison flounced forward. She had the air of someone who expected to be constantly curtsied to, as if she considered herself the highest-ranking person in every room—even now, alongside the queen.

Sam's palms felt sweaty inside her gloves; she tugged absently at the bodice of her gown, a cloying pink chiffon that her stylist had assured her would be salmon-colored, but instead made Sam feel like a little girl playing dress-up.

Her eyes kept sliding nervously toward the door. The photo shoot had begun with only the ladies-in-waiting—because of course, ladies first—but any minute now the lords attendant would show up. Which meant she would see Marshall.

Beatrice reached over to give her hand a squeeze. "You'll be fine."

"I know," Sam murmured back, unconvinced.

The ladies-in-waiting clustered around them in a perfumed huddle of whispers and rustling dresses. Beatrice kept her eyes trained on Colin, who was fiddling with the tripod of his camera. "I can always pretend to faint, like Jeff did that time in Telluride, if you want to call off this whole thing."

"I think Jeff pretended he was going to vomit, actually," Sam recalled, a corner of her mouth lifting in reluctant amusement.

Colin had been the royal family's official photographer for three decades now. He took all the Washingtons' official pictures, the ones intended for postcards and coffee mugs and their Christmas photo. When they were children, the royal siblings had posed every year in matching outfits—red-and-green beribboned dresses for Sam and Beatrice, a collared shirt and knee socks for Jeff—usually out in a grassy meadow. As if by taking their Christmas photo outside the palace, they could convince everyone that they were a relatively ordinary family.

"Smile, ladies!" Colin exclaimed, and they all settled into position.

A few minutes later, when Sam felt half-blinded by the flashbulb, raucous male voices sounded down the hallway, and the lords attendant burst into the room.

And there was Marshall.

His eyes flicked up and met Sam's as if drawn there by magnetism, by gravity. Then the floor seemed to fall out from beneath her, and bile rose up in her throat, and it all came rushing back in a nauseating whirl. The raw anguish in his voice when he'd told her, *I won't walk away from the dukedom, not even for you.*

She'd worked so hard to distract herself—with the trip to see Nina, and by focusing on the League of Kings, trying to support Beatrice—but seeing Marshall, Sam knew that she hadn't healed in the slightest.

Beatrice squeezed her fingers again—just the slightest pressure, a brush of support and sympathy—and it gave Sam the strength to tear her eyes from Marshall's and paste a smile on her face.

She let Colin arrange her in various positions, placing her hands on the back of Beatrice's chair or sitting on the steps of the dais, her pink skirts poufing around her. Her smile never faltered, though the entire time she was hyperaware of Marshall in her peripheral vision.

She kept smiling until Colin finally stepped away from his camera, lifting his hand in a dramatic flourish. "Well done, well done! I'll have the final proofs next week, and will be sending them all electronically. . . ."

Sam couldn't wait an instant longer. *I'll be right back,* she mouthed to Beatrice. Not daring to look in Marshall's direction, she stumbled out into the hallway, grabbing fistfuls of her pink skirts.

Her chest felt tight; her breath was coming in shallow gasps. Sam ran through the East Gallery, where tapestries of Roman gods and goddesses stared impassively down at her; then through the Blue Chamber, painted with a fresco depicting the Battle of the Chesapeake. King Louis XX had commissioned it when he built Bellevue, as a symbol of Franco-American cooperation. Sam had long ago given up counting the historical inaccuracies.

She turned another corner and came face to face with a wooden door whose placard read HER MAJESTY.

Beatrice wouldn't mind if Sam escaped into her office, just for a minute. No one would bother her there.

Beatrice's massive desk stood on the opposite side of the room, stacks of paper arranged neatly on its surface. Sam pulled out Beatrice's chair and collapsed into it, then closed her eyes and groaned.

Maybe it was good that she'd been forced to see Marshall today. They were bound to run into each other eventually; better that their first encounter post-breakup be here, amid the stiff formality of a photo shoot. As much as it hurt to see him again, it would have been even worse to run into him without warning.

When Sam opened her eyes again, they landed on the paper tucked to one side of Beatrice's desk.

I, Lord Theodore Beaufort Eaton, being of sound mind and body, do absolutely and entirely renounce my position and my titles . . .

This was Teddy's statement of renunciation.

Sam read the document once, twice, in a dull sort of shock.

When she heard a low voice ask, "Sam? Are you in here?" she thought at first that she'd dreamed it, that she'd been worrying about Marshall so much she'd hallucinated him. But there he was, standing hesitantly in the doorway.

"Sorry," Marshall added clumsily. "I'll leave you alone. I just saw you rushing out of the photo shoot, and you seemed upset. . . ."

I was upset because of you, she thought. Because it hurt so acutely to see Marshall and know that he wasn't hers anymore, that she couldn't reach over and touch him the way she used to. That they had to behave like strangers now.

"Wait!" Sam blurted out, before he could turn aside. "You don't have to go."

Marshall took a single step into the room, then shifted his weight as if he wasn't sure whether he was allowed any farther. "Um . . . I saw you went to a party with Nina and Jeff last weekend. How was it?"

Sam was still sitting behind the desk. She reached to tuck back a wisp of hair, only to realize she'd loosened the tiara pinned there. "It was nice to see them."

"That's good."

There was another awkward silence. "How's Rory?" Sam asked, hating how stilted it sounded.

"She's good."

Silence again.

Sam couldn't take any more of this. She wasn't sure what Marshall had expected, coming in here and checking on her, as if they had anything to say to each other anymore. They'd said it all on the beach that night, and now there was nothing left.

"Look, I should probably be getting back." She pressed her hands on the surface of Beatrice's desk and stood, but Marshall cut her off.

"Sam."

"What?" The single word came out sharp.

Sam had been fine—or at least she'd been able to pretend she was fine—when they were out at the photo shoot, with all those people around as human buffers. But now it was just the two of them, alone in this room, with no one to diffuse the impact of seeing him. No one to distract Sam from the fact that her entire body was humming, as if it had been dormant and only woke up again in Marshall's presence.

"I'm sorry," he said clumsily. "I know I've forfeited my right to ask how you are, that I have no claim on you anymore. . . ."

Sam's next words came out soft, like a sigh. "Marshall. You'll always have a claim on me."

He nodded slowly. "And you on me."

There was so much packed into those four words. Sam knew that he was opening a door, ever so slightly.

"Sam," he said uncertainly, hopefully. It struck Sam that she'd never seen Marshall, who usually projected such unabashed confidence, hesitate like this.

No, she should tell him. *Nothing has changed. You're still the future duke, and I'm still the princess.*

Instead she whispered, "Yes?"

"I miss you."

She said nothing, letting him continue.

"Being without you this week, I realized what a mistake I'd made. I hated that I couldn't just pick up my phone and text you some funny thing I had seen, that I couldn't hold you ever again. I kept telling myself I could handle it—" His voice broke; he shook his head. "But life isn't something that I should have to *handle*, is it?"

At some point they had crossed the room, step by slow step, to stand next to each other. Marshall reached out to cup Sam's face in his palm. "I miss you," he said again.

Then Sam was burying her face in his chest, wrapping her arms around his torso. Marshall pulled her close and tucked his head over hers.

They stood there for a long moment, just breathing, holding each other as tightly as if they were the only two survivors of a shipwreck, each other's safe haven in a storm.

Things always felt so simple when it was just the two of them. The rest of the world vanished into a distant haze, and all Sam could think about was Marshall—the rumble of his laugh; the fluttery heat of kissing him; the way he made her feel, warm and gooey and at the same time flush with strength, as if she'd become the best possible version of herself.

But the rest of the world hadn't vanished, and they both knew it.

Sam forced herself to step away, then reached for the paper on Beatrice's desk. "Marshall—you need to see this."

As he read Teddy's statement of renunciation, Sam felt an ominous dread gathering in her stomach. This was it. Once he read that document, Marshall would say again that there was no future for them.

He lowered the paper, running a hand absentmindedly through his hair. "I'm not surprised that Eaton went and did this, even though he's not required to until after the wedding. It's a nice gesture, shows how committed he is to Beatrice, and that he's stepping aside to make room for his younger brother."

"I don't care about Teddy," Sam said impatiently. "I was talking about you, Marshall! The fact that if we stayed together, you would someday have to sign a document just like this! I don't want you to do that."

"Neither do I," he agreed.

"Then what are we *doing?*"

"I don't know, okay? All I know is that I can't lose you again!"

Marshall ran his hands up and down Sam's arms, as if he couldn't bear to let go of her. "Things would be so much easier if we were ordinary people, without titles or positions. I wish we could escape for a while and actually live like that, that we could date without our families or the media breathing down our necks. But we are who we are, and that isn't going to change." He sighed. "I know that the logical thing to do is stay broken up and live our separate lives. And I tried to do that, I really did. Then I saw you today, at the photo shoot, and I missed you so much. It was torture, being so close to you but not being *with* you. I love you," he said helplessly. "I know we'd have to face . . . well . . ."

"The geopolitical and dynastic ramifications of us dating?" Sam finished the sentence for him, and he grimaced.

"Yeah."

"You know I love you, too," she said urgently. "Where does that leave us?"

His dark eyes gleamed. "It leaves us where we were before—facing an impossible situation. But this time, we'll face it together."

27

DAPHNE

Daphne circled the great hall of Washington Palace, studying the place cards with furious intensity. The guests would start arriving for the military reception in less than an hour, and she was determined that everything be perfect.

The tables were covered in starched white tablecloths, hemmed so that their lace trim just brushed the floor. The candles weren't yet lit, but once they were—when the overhead lights were dimmed, because only candlelight was soft and stately enough for a room like this—the silverware would gleam. Folded napkins sat crisply at each place setting; wineglasses had been polished, ready for cabernet to be poured from crystal decanters. It was as if this banquet hall existed outside of time itself, untouched by the modern world.

When her phone buzzed, Daphne glanced down and saw that Gabriella had posted a new photo: after her conversation with Nina, Daphne had set up alerts to notify her each time Gabriella shared something. In order to defeat an enemy, you had to first know that enemy.

In the selfie, Gabriella pursed her lips in a blasé non-smile. Oversized earrings dangled from her ears, and she was wearing another of those enormous velvet headbands. *Back from the League of Kings and ready for a night out!* she'd captioned it. The comments were already filled with dozens of variations on *You look gorg!* and strings of fire emojis.

Swallowing her pride, Daphne began to type out a comment of her own.

Stunning! she wrote, because she just couldn't bring herself to say "gorg." *Let me know where you're headed, maybe we can all meet up later!*

Hopefully she was right in assuming that Gabriella would jump at the chance to hang out with Jefferson.

Then, biting her lip, she typed out a quick text to Nina. *I may see G later tonight. Will keep you updated.*

Good luck and godspeed, Nina replied almost instantly.

Daphne didn't know what to make of her interactions with Nina lately: their late-night tacos after Gabriella's party, then the afternoon that Nina had come over and hung out in her *bedroom.* When they'd first pulled up to the taco place, Daphne had assumed Nina had an ulterior motive. Surely she was trying to lull Daphne into a false sense of security, then trap her in some kind of confession. Or maybe Nina assumed someone would take an unflattering photo of Daphne stuffing her face with queso?

It crossed Daphne's mind that Nina might simply be a nice person. But that didn't make sense. Nina must be tricking her somehow, wearing her niceness the way Daphne did hers: as armor, as a disguise, as a way to disarm people.

Daphne certainly wasn't fool enough to actually *trust* Nina. She trusted no one, especially not other women. Her mother had repeated it often enough throughout the years: other women were her competition, and they would fight dirty. At least when a man wanted to hurt you he was open about it. Women pretended to be nice, then stabbed you in the back.

Yet for some reason, *Daphne* was the one who'd said that she didn't hate Nina anymore.

She must be losing her touch.

She turned back to the table, lifting one of the calligraphed place cards and tapping a manicured finger against it. Daphne nodded to herself as she switched the card with another.

"Who did you just trade for Annie McClane?" asked Queen Adelaide, Jefferson's mother.

Daphne hadn't seen her come in. Startled, she sank into a deep curtsy, but the queen waved away the gesture.

"Please, it's just us in here." Adelaide had on jeans and a draped cashmere sweater, the kind that cost over a thousand dollars, though she wore them around the house like T-shirts. An enormous diamond cuff bracelet glinted incongruously on her wrist.

"I thought that Ms. McClane might not want to be seated near Lord Furless. I know they dated a long time ago, but from what I heard about their breakup, it sounded . . . messy," Daphne said tactfully.

Queen Adelaide's face was impassive. "And who else have you moved?"

Daphne swallowed. "I moved Sarah Clemens next to Sergeant Jeffries. She studied Arabic at Cambridge, and he was posted in the Middle East for so long, I thought they might have something to talk about."

Adelaide smiled, and Daphne nearly collapsed with relief. "Well done. Those are good changes." The queen pulled out one of the Chiavari dining chairs and took a seat, gesturing for Daphne to do the same.

Daphne slid her gown carefully beneath her as she settled onto the chair cushion, so that it wouldn't wrinkle.

"This is a big night, isn't it?" Adelaide glanced to the front of the room, where a table was arranged perpendicular to all the others. Six places had been set along one side, so that its occupants could eat in full view of the room. "This is your first time at the head table, in my usual spot."

"Your Majesty, I didn't—"

"Don't apologize," the queen assured her. "I'm actually headed to the airport soon. I'll be spending the week with my parents."

Queen Adelaide's father, the twins' and Beatrice's grandfather, was the Duke of Canaveral—and until her marriage, Adelaide had been set to inherit that duchy, as well as the Duchy of Savannah through her mother's side. The Double Duchess, people had called her. She'd forfeited her rights to both titles when she married George IV and became a future queen.

In Daphne's mind, she'd traded up. Being queen was far better than being a duchess, even a duchess twice over.

"I'm sure you're ready to get away, after everything that's happened this year." Daphne hesitated, then added, "I can't imagine how difficult it was, losing His Majesty so unexpectedly."

"And now, in a way, I'm losing my children, too."

"You haven't lost them," Daphne said, a little puzzled. But Adelaide's eyes were fixed on some point in the distance, as if she'd forgotten Daphne was even here. As if she were talking to herself, or her late husband.

"They're outgrowing me," Adelaide said softly. "They don't need me anymore, not in the way they used to. That's the hardest thing about being a mother. When your children are little, they rely on you for everything: for food and safety and clean underwear; for guidance, and love. And then they get older and learn to wipe their own butts and form their own opinions, and one day you look up and realize that they don't really need you anymore. That, actually, you're the one who suddenly needs them."

Daphne was still reeling from hearing the queen use the word *butt*. "Your children need you. Jefferson needs you," she insisted, and the queen's eyes flitted back to hers.

"Jefferson has you, Daphne," the queen replied. "Beatrice is struggling with the weight of the crown, which is something I'll never fully understand. Even Sam has to deal with being the other sister, the not-queen. She'll need to carve out a place for herself, since there's no defined role for her." Adelaide picked up a dinner fork; its handle was stamped with the Washingtons' crest. "It was different for me. I married into this family, so I was an outsider when I came into it. Like you."

Jefferson's mother had never spoken to her like this. She'd never really paid much attention to Daphne at all, treating her with the same politeness that she did everyone.

The queen smiled wistfully. "Watching you, I'm reminded of how I felt when I was first navigating all of this. It's strange, isn't it? A family that is also an institution, a living part of history. You remind me in so many ways of myself. You're so smart and thoughtful. You look beautiful tonight," she added warmly.

Daphne's cocktail dress was gorgeous, its champagne tulle embroidered with lamé mousseline petals. It was the sort of delicate, wispy thing that a princess should wear.

Daphne tried not to think about what she'd done to get it.

This time, she'd made sure that the photos she sold were more generic, almost anonymous: a candid shot of Jefferson in his school uniform from Forsyth Academy, laughing in the hallway; another of him playing football, which she'd taken from the sidelines. The photo was so high-resolution that you could see each bead of sweat.

Those photos had been taken in public places; anyone could have snapped them. There was no chance that they could be traced back to Daphne.

"Thank you," Daphne told the queen. "Your family has always been so welcoming to me."

Adelaide smiled approvingly. "You'll do fantastic tonight, Daphne." She tilted her head, considering. "There's something missing, though."

Daphne watched, speechless, as Adelaide loosened her diamond bracelet and handed it over. "You probably know I'm not allowed to lend out anything from the Crown Jewels collection, but this one's my own personal property. George gave it to me for Christmas one year." The queen winked. "A bit of sparkle never hurts, does it?"

"I . . . thank you." Carefully, Daphne fastened the delicate clasp. The bracelet seemed to glow on her wrist, as if each diamond were a shard of white-hot fire. It weighed surprisingly little, yet it still felt heavy with significance.

All night, as Daphne circulated through the party—as she sat in the place of precedence at the head table, next to a five-star general—she felt people staring at Queen Adelaide's bracelet. She saw their eyes darting to it, the flash of recognition as they realized what it meant.

Daphne had been accepted into the royal family. At last, she belonged.

♛

It was after ten when the final guests departed. They did so reluctantly, with much clearing of throats and gentle nudging by the footmen; at events like this, people often had to be kicked out. They were loath to leave the glamour and magic of the palace and return to the real world.

"Thanks for doing this with me tonight," Jefferson told her, once the great hall was empty. He nodded toward the stairs. "Hey, didn't the new Max Anderson movie just come out? We should watch it."

"Max Anderson? Really?"

The moment she said it, Daphne wished she could swallow back the words.

Jefferson seemed puzzled. "I thought you liked those movies."

Daphne hated those movies. They were full of explosions and car chases and juvenile jokes, but for years she'd pretended to like them, because Jefferson did. Again she felt a wave of useless frustration, that she'd fabricated a persona of a perfect girlfriend that was so very different from her real self.

She wondered what Jefferson would say if he knew just how fundamentally she'd lied to him. She'd been lying from the start, in large ways and a thousand small ones. She had lied deliberately, ingeniously, creatively. If lying was an art, she was its grand master.

And a part of her was beginning to feel so weary of it—of this great lie underpinning her entire life.

"Of course I love Max Anderson!" She laughed airily, then grabbed her phone from her clutch. Jefferson was starting to say something else, but her attention had fixed on the new message from Gabriella.

We're heading to GSM. You and Jeff should come meet us.

Daphne looked up. "What if we went out instead? The night is young!" Then she added, as if the idea was just now occurring to her, "I think some of our friends are at GSM, the wine bar that just opened on Lafayette."

Jefferson shrugged good-naturedly. "Sure. I'll have Matt do a security sweep, and in the meantime I'll put on some jeans."

"Don't change," Daphne said quickly, resting a hand on his forearm.

He gestured to the medals scattered over his sash. "Daph, I'm in full ceremonial dress."

That was exactly the point. Dressed like this, all crimson

and gold braiding and fringed epaulets, he looked every inch a prince.

Unbeknownst to him, Jefferson was the bait that Daphne would be dangling in front of Gabriella.

"We never go out like this, all dressed up. It could be fun!"

"If you want," he said slowly, unconvinced.

When they walked into the bar—Jefferson in his formal blazer and regalia, Daphne in her floating cocktail dress—everyone turned to stare, just as Daphne had hoped.

GSM was one of those small, trendy spots that could only exist in the capital. Most of the space was taken up by a dark wood bar that curved along one wall, a whitewashed brick arch soaring overhead. Bowls of blood oranges, lemons, and limes sat behind the bar, alongside crystal tumblers and a half-full bottle of Aperol.

Gabriella was perched on the central barstool, wearing the black crop top from her earlier selfie, which she'd paired with a full salmon-colored skirt that cascaded below her knees, and electric-blue pumps. Her face lit up hungrily at the sight of Jefferson.

"Jeff! You made it!" she trilled, sliding down to pull him into a possessive hug. When she stepped back, she stared unabashedly at his outfit. "Don't you look handsome."

"We had a military banquet earlier," Jefferson explained, and Daphne was so grateful for the way he said *we*, casting her in his royal glow.

Gabriella looked over and halfheartedly added, "Daphne. I'm glad you came."

Jefferson stared around at the bar. "What does GSM stand for, anyway? It sounds like a sex thing," he added, and Daphne nearly choked in amusement.

Gabriella laughed indulgently. "GSM are *grapes*, of course! Grenache, Syrah, Mourvèdre: the varietals they use to make wine in the Rhône. This place serves only *French* wine. Obviously."

"That's not very patriotic. America makes wine, too," Jefferson pointed out.

Gabriella laughed again, as if the idea of drinking American wine was just too funny for words. "Michel! Can you get a glass of the eighty-two Latour for His Highness?" It was clear from the way she spoke that she absolutely relished the chance to say *His Highness*.

Jefferson shook his head. "Actually, do you have any beers on tap?"

But the bartender had already poured a glass of red wine, so dark it seemed almost purple. "This one's on the house," he said gruffly, which might have been the stupidest thing Daphne ever heard. If anyone deserved a free drink, it was not people who were already extremely rich.

Daphne forced herself to smile despite Gabriella's blatant attempts to ignore her. "Gabriella, how was the photo shoot at the League of Kings?" She tried to inject a simpering envy into her voice as she added, "I'm so jealous that you were there. How fantastic that you get to be a lady-in-waiting!"

For a moment she worried that she'd laid it on too thick, but Gabriella seemed pleased by Daphne's question.

"It was fine." Gabriella sighed, as if attending the photo shoot had been an imposition on her incredibly valuable time, and turned to Jefferson. "Honestly, your family needs to hire a new photographer. Colin is just so old-fashioned! He asked everyone to smile with their *mouths open*."

Gabriella's friends, who were all listening intently, gasped at the horror of it.

Jefferson frowned, puzzled. "What's wrong with smiling? You have perfect teeth."

"Oh, Jeff!" Gabriella laughed, and her audience laughed with her, like a pack of couture-clad hyenas.

Here was another chance for Daphne to worm her way in. "No one smiles in their photos anymore, Jefferson," she said, a bit too sharply. "Haven't you been on social media lately?"

People like Gabriella didn't smile because they didn't want to seem like they actually cared about anything. Their photos were all lazy smirks and posed candids.

Gabriella's eyes drifted to Daphne's wrist, then widened. "Is that the Kimberley diamond cuff?"

"Her Majesty lent it to me for the night." Daphne had used Queen Adelaide's title for emphasis—to remind Gabriella that she was in with the royal family—but it came out a little pretentious. She saw Jefferson's lips press together. Still, she forged ahead.

"Do you want to try it on?"

"*Yes,*" Gabriella breathed.

Daphne tried not to look at the prince as she slid his mother's bracelet off her wrist and passed it to Gabriella, who clasped it on with a voracious, greedy excitement.

The other girls immediately formed a cooing semicircle around Gabriella. Daphne turned aside, feeling weary and sick.

"Daph—I'm going to head home," Jefferson told her. "I'm actually kind of tired."

Daphne heard the silent question folded into his words: Did she want to come back to the palace and put this all behind them?

She should go back. She *wanted* to go back. There was nothing she liked about this place or these people, except the opportunity that she could get out of it, if she played her cards right. If she could reel Gabriella in, slowly, an inch at a time.

Behind her, Gabriella was quiet, clearly watching their exchange. Daphne swallowed.

She needed to choose Gabriella over Jefferson, to prove her loyalty.

"I think I'll stay out. This place is fun!" She laughed hollowly.

Jefferson's eyes flashed with hurt, but he nodded. "Okay, I'll see you later."

Then he was walking out the door, still looking resplendent in his military outfit. The room felt a little dimmer when he left, as if there had been a spotlight trained only on him, and now he'd taken it with him.

Daphne felt short of breath. A current of fear roared up within her, threatening to engulf her completely. But she looked up and saw that Gabriella was watching her with an alert, curious expression.

"You're staying," Gabriella repeated flatly.

Like Nina had said, Daphne needed to really sell this—to be so convincingly in awe of Gabriella that Gabriella would stop viewing her as a threat, and start seeing her as another of her minions.

She smiled hesitantly, the way she did when she was trying to charm the surliest paparazzi. "Of course I want to stay. It's been ages since I had a girls' night out!" She looked at Gabriella with rapt attention. "Gabriella, tell us more about the photo shoot. Who was there?"

Gabriella stared at Daphne, assessing her. Then she waved at the girl on the neighboring barstool. "Stephanie, you stand. Daphne is taking your seat."

To Daphne's surprise, the girl didn't argue, just did as she was told. "Thanks," Daphne murmured, taking the abandoned barstool.

Gabriella snapped at the bartender. The queen's bracelet glittered ostentatiously with the gesture. "Michel!"

He hurried over, poured Daphne a glass of wine, then retreated. Gabriella glanced back at Daphne, her tone briskly matter-of-fact.

"You'll be at the League of Kings final banquet, right? We should coordinate our outfits."

"Coordinate?" Daphne had the bizarre mental image of her and Gabriella showing up in matching gowns, like twins from a horror movie.

"Yes, coordinate," Gabriella said impatiently. "We can't wear the same color, *of course.*"

Daphne took a sip of wine to keep from choking with laughter. "Of course."

"I don't know which gown I'll wear yet, but most likely a purple one that Nigel designed for me. He says it's my color."

Gabriella tilted her head, looking expectantly at Daphne. Belatedly, Daphne realized that Gabriella was waiting to be flattered. "Oh, definitely. You look fantastic in purple!"

Gabriella nodded, pleased. "Well, Nigel always tells me that, but I'm not sure I'm convinced, you know? So I also had him make a gown in red, green, blue, black, and silver. Which means you really shouldn't wear any of those colors," Gabriella commanded. "We wouldn't want people comparing us."

It took every ounce of Daphne's willpower not to laugh at the absurdity of this demand. "Of course not," she said soothingly.

Now that she had Gabriella's attention, she needed to get closer—and find out when she and Nina could lay their trap at last.

"I'm sure I'll see you before the banquet, though, right? What are you doing this weekend?"

Gabriella shrugged. "I'll be at Lord and Lady Dalton's End of Session party. Maybe I'll see you there?"

Bingo. Lady Dalton was Chief Justice of the Supreme Court; she and her husband threw a huge party every year when the court went on recess. Daphne hadn't been invited, but that wasn't a problem as long as she showed up with Jefferson.

Royalty had an unwritten standing invitation to every party.

As Gabriella chattered on, Daphne stole a few glances at her phone. Jefferson hadn't texted her good night, the way he always did. She had a sinking, panicked thought that she might have risked too much. That in trying to take down Gabriella, she might have driven a very real wedge between her and Jefferson.

It would be okay, she told herself, as long as her plan worked.

And her plans always worked.

28

BEATRICE

"Hey, Louise." Beatrice answered the phone with one hand as she finished getting dressed for breakfast. She couldn't believe they were nearing the end of the conference, that the farewell banquet would be in just over a week's time.

"Béatrice, I just got a call from my father's doctors in Paris."

Beatrice fell still. "Is everything okay?"

"He may be improving," Louise said, and Beatrice realized that the tension in Louise's voice wasn't sorrow, but a raw, anxious hope. "I need to go see him right away."

"Of course." Louise would miss a day or two of the conference, but everyone would understand—

"Will you come with me?" Louise begged. "I know it's a lot to ask this late in the conference. I should probably just call Siri or Bharat or Alexei. But they wouldn't understand."

Of course. Beatrice knew, to her own great sorrow, what it was like to lose a parent—and then succeed that parent as ruler. To feel like you were stepping out onto a vast stage, alone and terrified.

"Please," Louise said again, clearly unnerved by Beatrice's silence. "I can't do this without a friend."

A friend. Beatrice had never had one of those, not the way Sam had Nina. To be honest, she'd always been jealous of those two: the way they could talk about anything without explaining the backstory, could launch into an anecdote with oblique references that no one else understood, yet that made perfect sense to the pair of them.

"Of course I'll come," she promised.

As she was throwing some clothes into an overnight bag, she called Teddy.

He hadn't mentioned his statement of renunciation since he'd arrived in Boston, and Beatrice certainly wasn't about to bring it up. It felt like a silent, hulking presence at the fringes of all their conversations—something she skirted around, because she didn't know how to acknowledge it, now that it had happened.

Beatrice had always known that whoever married her would have to give up everything. Yet each time she saw that document, it hit her in a way it hadn't before. Teddy was sacrificing his role, his purpose, his *identity* in order to be with her, while Beatrice's life remained completely unchanged.

It made her feel slightly dizzy with guilt.

"That's great news, that Louise's dad is better," Teddy said, once Beatrice had explained that she was heading to France. "But, Bee—are you sure that this is the right time to leave? You're supposed to be hosting hundreds of world leaders right now."

"It's just for a night, and Sam can handle things in my absence."

After the photo shoot, Sam had told her that she and Marshall were trying to figure things out. Beatrice wasn't sure what that meant, exactly—the fundamental imbalance at the core of their relationship was still there—but she tried to be happy as long as Sam was happy.

She was rooting for them, even if it meant that Sam would eventually face the same problem Beatrice had, and end up asking the man she loved to give up everything for her.

"Louise is my friend," Beatrice went on, willing Teddy to understand. "She needs me, and I want to be there."

"Then that's all there is to it," he agreed.

Gratitude flooded her chest. "How are things at home?"

Teddy talked for a few more minutes—about how Lewis and Livingston had both used a dating app under fake names and ended up going out with the same girl; about how a pipe had burst, flooding Grandma Betty's house, and everyone in the family was so relieved that she would finally buy new furniture, except she replaced it all with the same floral pattern from the seventies. "They don't even *make* that fabric anymore," Teddy recounted. "Grandma Betty called the manufacturer and bullied them into producing some especially for her, so she could reupholster her new furniture to look just like the old."

Beatrice joined in his laughter, but a nervous apprehension flickered deep in her gut. Teddy was pulling back. He stuck to light, easy subjects, never mentioning the work of the duchy or the fact that he was handing over his lifetime of knowledge and training to his younger brother.

She hoped that she hadn't asked too much of him. But every time she thought of bringing it up, the words froze in her throat.

"I have to go," she told him at last. "I love you. I'll call you when I'm back from Paris, okay?"

She could imagine the warmth of Teddy's smile as he replied, "Love you, too. Travel safe."

Within the hour, Beatrice was on the Bourbons' plane, flying to France—the quick way, straight over the Arctic Circle. When they reached Paris, they touched down in a private airfield and transferred to a waiting car.

She glanced over at Louise, who'd been uncharacteristically quiet for the entire flight. Shortly before landing she had changed into a long-sleeved dress and tights, not applying any makeup except a sheer lip gloss. Without her signature leather jackets and burgundy lipstick, she seemed younger, more vulnerable.

Actually, she looked a lot like Beatrice used to, before she'd started imitating Louise.

Beatrice could tell that her friend needed space, so she waited until they reached the ornate golden gates of Versailles before speaking. "Are you okay?"

"I don't know." Louise's voice shook. "I haven't spoken to my father, truly spoken to him, in so long."

Beatrice wondered exactly what that meant. Had King Louis emerged from a coma after some debilitating injury, like Himari, the girl who'd fallen down the palace's back staircase? Or was it a mental illness?

The palace rose up before them, stately and serene, afternoon sunlight flashing in its hundreds of windows. Stone cherubs and gods peered down at them from the roof, which was lined in gold tracery as delicate as lace.

Their car hadn't even come to a complete stop before Louise threw open the door. The staff were lined up outside the front steps, row upon row of footmen and maids and chefs and valets, all wearing the Bourbons' blue-and-white livery. Louise sprinted up the front steps without even a pretense of dignity, ignoring the way they all swept into curtsies and bows at her arrival.

Beatrice found Louise in the north wing, at the end of a hallway. A nurse in cream-colored scrubs was speaking to the princess in rapid French.

"He's anxious to see you," the nurse explained as she opened the door to a sitting room. Beatrice lingered, not wanting to intrude, but then Louise turned to her with a raw, pleading expression.

"Come with me, Béatrice?"

Beatrice's first thought was that this room didn't belong

in the soaring grandeur of Versailles. The furniture was simple, all plain white wood and colored cushions, with framed seascapes on the walls.

And there was King Louis XXIII, sitting in an armchair, a newspaper unfolded before him.

He looked older and thinner than Beatrice remembered, but after all, the most recent photos she'd seen of him were nearly five years old. He still had his famous curling mustache, though it was entirely gray now.

"Father," Louise whispered, bobbing into a curtsy.

"Good. You're here." The king gave the newspaper a shake; the crinkle of its pages sounded frighteningly loud in the silence. "Apparently you let the country go to complete shit in my absence."

Louise glanced back over her shoulder at the nurse. "Who gave him a newspaper?"

The nurse threw up her hands. "He ordered me to bring him one. How was I supposed to refuse? He's the king!"

Beatrice's stomach twisted. She watched, mentally translating their speech, as Louise turned back to her father. "I'm so glad you're feeling better. We've all been praying for your recovery."

King Louis ignored her and jabbed at the newspaper. "What were you thinking, allowing this sort of infrastructure bill to pass? France doesn't need more bridges or highways! You're going to tax our citizens to death!"

Louise sighed, apparently giving up on her efforts to avoid discussing current events. "Actually, we funded the bill through taxes on corporations. We *decreased* the tax level in the lower income brackets."

The king scoffed. "A ridiculous notion. The next thing I know, you're going to suggest that *we* start paying taxes."

There was a silence, and then he looked up, his jaw tight with anger. "No. Tell me you didn't."

"Father, it's only fair! How can we ask something of our people that we don't do ourselves?"

"Because we are *Bourbons*! Our lives are already dedicated to their service! Do we need to pay half our fortune back to them as well?"

"Most other monarchs have been paying taxes for years," Louise reminded him. Kings had traditionally been exempt from their nations' tax laws, but many royal families, including the Washingtons, had revoked that right in the last century.

"Most other monarchs are weak. As are you," King Louis said stiffly. "Stop pandering to public opinion and stand up for yourself for once."

Beatrice felt like she'd stumbled into a twisted alternate reality. Was this really how the king was going to greet his daughter, now that he'd returned to health?

She couldn't stay silent any longer. "Your Majesty, with all due respect, the Princess Louise has done a fantastic job managing the country during your illness. France owes her a debt of gratitude."

King Louis looked up as if noticing Beatrice for the first time. "Who are *you*?"

"I'm Beatrice, Your Majesty. The Queen of America."

The king stared at her for a moment, then burst out laughing. "Queen of America! That's a good one." He was still chuckling as he glanced back at Louise. "I like this friend of yours, Marie-Anne. She may not be much to look at, but she's funny enough."

At his last words, all the air seemed to drain from the room. Beatrice didn't even have the emotional strength to be offended by how laughable he'd found the notion of an American queen. She was staring at Louise, whose face had gone pale.

The king had just called Louise by her mother's name.

"Father, it's me, Louise. Your daughter," she said quietly.

Beatrice bit her lip in pained understanding. They were losing him. The king's brief moment of lucidity—and cruelty, she thought—was slipping away. He glanced down at the newspaper, frowned at it as if puzzled by the shape of the letters, then set it aside and looked back at Louise.

"You're not dressed for riding."

"Riding?" she asked weakly.

"Yes, we promised Antoine that we'd go out, didn't we? You know how he is when we keep him waiting." The king glanced out the window at the sun-drenched afternoon. "Oh no, it looks like it might rain."

There wasn't a cloud in the sky.

Louise's expression was filled with such yearning and disappointment that Beatrice had to look away. "You're right," Louise agreed, her voice wavering a little. "It does look like rain. I'll tell Antoine that we'll play baccarat instead."

The king's eyes drifted back to Beatrice, and he frowned. "Your ladies-in-waiting need to learn more respect. This one hasn't curtsied to me since the moment she entered the room."

It was true, Beatrice hadn't curtsied, and she marveled that Louis, through the evident murkiness in his mind, had noticed and clamped on to that fact. "You don't have to," Louise whispered, but Beatrice was so heartbroken for her friend that she didn't even protest.

She nodded and swept a brief curtsy. "My apologies, Your Majesty," she told him in French. The king nodded, mollified.

When they headed back into the hall, Louise whirled on the nurse. "You told me he'd gotten better! I came all the way from America, only to find that he's the same as ever!"

"He *was* better! I'm sorry, Your Royal Highness. I really thought he'd recovered this time. He'd been himself for a whole day. That was the longest it's lasted in years!"

"I know." Louise ran a hand over her features. "You're doing your best, of course. I just thought . . . I hoped . . ."

Beatrice was excruciatingly familiar with that hope. It was the same hope she felt most mornings, when she woke up and, for a fleeting instant, forgot that her father was gone. Then reality would crash back around her, and she would remember that she'd lost him—that the weight of the crown was now hers alone.

In some ways it must be harder for Louise, to get her father back for brief snatches of time, then lose him over and over again.

At least King George had been unwaveringly supportive and loving. He'd never belittled Beatrice; his criticisms, when they came, were measured and fair. He had always been Beatrice's father first, and her king second.

If that brief glimpse of King Louis was indicative of his true nature, then he clearly thought of his daughter as his successor, his *employee*. Small wonder that Louise stormed through life with such a commanding, glittering persona, hiding her feelings behind detachment, surrounding herself with friends, yet always keeping a piece of herself back from them. She was terrified to reveal any vulnerabilities, for fear that her father would pounce on them.

Beneath all the bravado, Louise was still just a girl who longed for her father's approval.

"I'm so sorry," Beatrice said quietly.

Louise walked a few dazed paces into another room, a vast living room that was just as grand and imposing as the rest of this grand, imposing palace. She sank onto a love seat, her head falling into her hands, her dress crumpling around her like wilted flower petals.

"I'm the one who should be sorry. I asked you to come all this way, and my father isn't even better."

"Don't apologize." Beatrice rushed over and took the seat next to the princess.

"But I am sorry, because it's awful. It's all so awful!" Louise exclaimed, and began to cry.

There was nothing pretty or princess-like about her tears: her chest heaved with ragged, ugly sobs. Beatrice made small *shh* noises and rubbed Louise's back in soothing circles, the way she'd comforted Samantha when they lost their own father.

Beatrice's eyes stung, and she felt tears running down her cheeks, too. She was crying for Louise and the French king, for herself, and for her dad, who should still have been there, hosting the conference he'd looked forward to.

Look at us, a small, sad part of her thought. Two of the supposedly most powerful women in the world, crying as forlornly as lost children.

"It's okay," she kept saying in low soothing tones. "I'm here. It's okay."

Louise had to get all her tears out now, because she could certainly never cry like this in public. The moment they returned to Orange, she would have to arm herself in her usual smiles and lipstick, and face the world as confidently as always. They both would.

The world didn't allow its queens the luxury of tears.

29

DAPHNE

"I never realized that Supreme Court justices *party* like this," Nina said, staring around the rooftop of the Daltons' house.

Daphne gave a wry smile. "The End of Session party is usually at Justice Dalton's estate in Middleburg, but this year the Daltons decided to throw it in town. Which meant that everyone RSVP'd yes." People had been dying to get a look inside this townhouse for years.

"Apparently, they've all forgotten how much they hate each other." Nina nodded across the patio to where a pair of justices—whose views were diametrically opposed, who had never voted the same way on a single case—were sipping cosmopolitans and laughing like old friends.

Daphne shrugged. "People tend to set aside their rivalries for the sake of a good party."

"Except you," Nina observed.

"Except me," she agreed, almost cheerful. Nothing excited Daphne more than the prospect of a good takedown.

Ever since the night at the wine bar, she'd been playing her part with Gabriella: writing sycophantic comments on Gabriella's posts, texting her with questions, as if Daphne actually valued Gabriella's stuck-up opinion on anything.

For tonight's event, Daphne had gone directly to the palace's social secretary and asked her to RSVP to the party on Jefferson's behalf, as Prince Jefferson plus two guests. It was a mark of how far she'd come that the secretary took Daphne's word for it. And just like that, the party was added to Jefferson's social calendar.

Now she and Nina could finally enact the last stage of their plan.

She glanced around the crowded rooftop, where politicians and judges, courtiers and businesspeople, all elbowed for space. Daphne heard more conversations than she could ever hope to eavesdrop on, flirtations and feuds beginning and dissolving all around her. She wondered what the party looked like from street level: the roof illuminated with golden lights, laughter and jazz music drifting down in tantalizing snatches.

"Gabriella's here," Nina whispered. "Ten o'clock, by the tall woman in red."

"That's Miranda Abbott. The representative from Salt Lake in the House of Tribunes," Daphne said absently, though her eyes had cut straight to the cluster of people surrounding Jefferson. Gabriella Madison, of course, was one of them.

Daphne hated what she was about to do, but what other choice did she have?

Jefferson smiled when he saw her coming, stepping aside to create space for her in their circle. "Hey, Daph," he said warmly. "I heard there's a mac-and-cheese bar on the first floor. Should we go check it out?"

"Actually, can we talk?" She started toward the balcony, then slowed; she had to remind herself that for once, she actually wanted to be overheard. Jefferson followed, puzzled.

Daphne's stomach twisted as she pulled her phone from her purse and held it toward him. "What's this about?"

It had been shockingly easy to find an incriminating image. No matter how hard Jefferson's Revere Guard tried to prevent it, Jefferson still inevitably ended up in the background of people's photos. Daphne had searched through various pictures from the decades party until she found one with Jefferson in the background, talking to a brunette in a poodle skirt.

"I guess that's a photo from last weekend," he said, clearly confused.

Daphne thrust the phone wildly toward his face. "Who is she? Why are you looking at her like that?"

"Um—because I smile at parties?" he said slowly. "I don't even remember that girl's name; she just introduced herself and said hi. Besides, you were right there with me."

Daphne felt like she was picking at a scab, scratching and scratching in an attempt to draw blood. "Why do you think I went to the party with you? I don't trust what goes on when I'm not around!"

Jefferson looked bewildered. "You think I'm cheating on you? Daph, I would never do that. I love you."

He made it so difficult to pick a fight with him. Daphne had no choice but to bring out the big guns. "But you *have* cheated on me," she said quietly. "I know you were with someone else last year, the night before you and Samantha left for Asia."

She'd never told Jefferson that she saw him that night, never forced him to admit to his betrayal. After a while, Daphne had stopped worrying about who he'd been with. So much had happened since then.

Jefferson's eyes cut guiltily across the rooftop. Daphne followed his gaze but couldn't tell what—or who—he was looking at in the crowd.

"I'm so sorry," he said helplessly. "That wasn't fair to you. But I don't understand—if you've known this whole time, why didn't you say anything?"

Because she'd been holding it in reserve for a moment like this.

"I wanted to trust you," she told him. "And I did, until you started at King's College. I feel like I'm losing you now, like there's some part of you that you're holding back from me."

All Daphne had meant to do was escalate their fight, to keep hurling accusations at him until it seemed plausible to everyone watching, namely Gabriella, that they might break up.

Yet as she spoke the words, Daphne wondered if there was some truth to them.

Hadn't Jefferson been pulling away from her lately? Or—even worse—was he being pulled *toward* someone else?

"I don't know what you want from me, Daphne," Jefferson said, now a little frustrated, and Daphne knew she was in trouble from the way he said *Daphne* and not *Daph*. "Am I supposed to text you my every move? You're the one who decided not to come to school this fall."

"Forget it." Daphne spun around and began cutting through the crowd.

When she collided with Gabriella, she gasped as if it had been accidental. "Oh—Gabriella! Thank god."

"Daphne. What's going on?" Not *Are you okay?* but *What's going on?* As if all Gabriella cared about was the fuel she could give the rumor mill.

Well, Daphne was about to give her some.

"Will you come to the ladies' room with me?" Daphne put a hand on Gabriella's arm. "I could really use a friend right now."

Gabriella gave Daphne's hand what she probably thought was a reassuring squeeze. "Of course."

As she and Nina had discussed, Daphne headed down to the third floor. "I need some privacy," she murmured, bypassing the bathroom line and opening the door to a guest room. She flicked a light switch, revealing a queen-sized bed and a cabinet filled with curios: a bowl painted with tiny gold whorls, a silver thing that looked like a bird's nest.

Pushing aside her lingering regrets, Daphne sank onto the

bed and slumped forward, cradling her head in her hands. "I don't know what to do," she breathed.

"What happened?" Gabriella asked eagerly, then seemed to realize she needed to sound more sympathetic. "If you want to talk about it, I'm here. I won't tell anyone," she added, perching on the bed next to Daphne.

What a liar. The only secrets Gabriella Madison had ever kept were her own.

"I feel like Jefferson is hiding something from me." Daphne had feared that this part might not sound convincing, but in the moment it came out very real.

"Hiding something?"

"Or hiding some*one*."

Gabriella's eyes shone with eagerness. "You think he's cheating on you?"

Daphne stared down at her hands, twisting the signet ring back and forth. She could feel Gabriella's gaze on it like palpable heat. "I don't know. Of course, Jefferson would never fall for just anyone," she added, trying to stoke Gabriella's ego. "It would have to be someone he knows well. Someone he trusts."

Gabriella frowned. "Not necessarily. He got involved with that tacky charity case of Samantha's, after all. What was her name? Lena?" As if Gabriella didn't know perfectly well what Nina's name was—as if she hadn't sabotaged Nina's *financial aid*.

It took every ounce of Daphne's considerable willpower to keep from slapping Gabriella across the face. *You're the tacky one, in spite of all your money and titles*, she wanted to say. *Nina is worth a hundred of you.*

Instead she shook her head. "I just worry about what happens when I'm not around. There are always women throwing themselves at Jefferson. He's only human, after all. Eventually he'll stop saying no to them, don't you think?"

Gabriella made a vaguely sympathetic noise, as if she weren't one of the women Daphne meant.

"I guess I should get back out there and face the damage." Daphne sniffed, then glanced hopefully at Gabriella. "I wish I had a little . . . help. Something to take the edge off things, you know?"

There was a momentary flicker of interest on Gabriella's features, but then it was gone. "You're right. We should get back to the party."

Daphne silently cursed her misstep. She'd overplayed her hand; now there was nothing left to do but keep on overplaying it. She would have to grovel, prostrate herself before Gabriella, make herself pitiable and small.

"Wait!" She swallowed, lowered her eyes. "What do you think I should do?"

Gabriella paused. "Are you saying you might break up with Jefferson?"

"I'm asking your advice. You know him as well as anyone." It wasn't hard for Daphne to make herself cry; she'd been close to tears already. She felt the hot wetness in her lashes, trailing mascara down her cheeks. "You'll watch him for me, won't you? Keep an eye on him at school?"

Gabriella flashed a catlike, knowing smile. Daphne had just given her free license to flirt with Jefferson. "I'll keep an eye on him."

Daphne wiped furiously at her eyes. She felt queasy and unsettled, like when she'd skipped too many meals in a row. "Thank you," she forced herself to say, and glanced back at the door. "Ugh, I'm such a mess. Sorry. I just—I feel so overwhelmed by it all."

Finally, Daphne had sacrificed enough to win the dubious honor of Gabriella's trust. She watched as Gabriella opened her clutch and withdrew a tiny baggie of white powder. "Want a pick-me-up?" she offered.

Daphne nodded as if indicating that Gabriella should go first. Gabriella leaned onto the bedside table, cutting a line with her platinum credit card, then sniffed it up one nostril. Her motions were quick, efficient, in a way that suggested she'd done this many times.

When she turned toward her, Daphne laughed nervously. "I'm fine, thanks."

Gabriella didn't bother hiding her condescension as she rose to her feet. "Whatever, your loss."

She started toward the hallway—just as one of the shuttered doors to the closet unfolded.

Nina stepped out. "Before you go, I think we should have a little talk."

"Nina?" Gabriella demanded, and Daphne couldn't help feeling oddly satisfied that she so obviously knew Nina's name. "You little creep. Why were you spying on us?"

"I was spying on *you*, Gabriella." Nina smiled. "What do you think people will say when they find out about your recreational activity?"

Gabriella shrugged noncommittally. "They won't believe it, coming from a nobody like you."

"Except that I have proof. I got the whole thing on video."

For a moment Gabriella just stared at Nina. And then, to Daphne's utter shock, she lunged forward.

She and Nina crashed to the floor, grappling wildly as they wrestled for Nina's phone. They were a tangle of elbows and hair and muttered curses, like something out of a bad reality show. Daphne flew forward, trying to pull them apart, a bit incredulous. Somehow she hadn't expected things to get so physical.

When Gabriella rolled to one side, clutching Nina's phone fiercely to her chest, Nina just laughed. "Go ahead, delete the video. I've already emailed it to multiple people, any of whom will blast it out to the world as soon as I say so."

Gabriella scrambled backward like a crab. She looked nothing like a socialite right now; her hair was an auburn frizz around her face, and the hem of her dress had ripped in the tussle. She looked ruthless and ragged and wild, like an animal focused on self-preservation.

"You can't post that." For the first time all night, Gabriella seemed afraid.

Daphne hurried to jump in. "We won't do anything with it as long as you back down. Get Nina's financial aid reinstated, and protect my father from the Conferrals and Forfeiture Committee."

"I don't know what you're talking about," Gabriella said unconvincingly.

"Don't you?" Daphne reached out to snatch the phone from Gabriella's hand. "Or would you rather I share this video with the *Daily News?*"

Gabriella's eyes narrowed. She hesitated, seeming to consider her options. "You're seriously blackmailing me?"

"We're *negotiating,*" Nina corrected. It was such a Daphne-esque thing to say that Daphne smiled a little.

Gabriella stood, brushing off her wrinkled dress, adjusting her gold belt. "To think that I was actually going to invite you to Antibes this summer if you kept behaving," she said to Daphne. "You're clearly just as low-class as your low-class father. He deserves to lose his title. And as for *you,*" Gabriella went on, rounding on Nina, "you shouldn't be at King's College if you can't even pay for it. Why don't you go somewhere you can actually afford?"

"The fact that you just said that is appalling," Daphne interjected, seething with anger.

Gabriella just sniffed.

"I'm serious, Gabriella. You have until next Saturday to fix what you've done." Next Saturday, when they would all be together at the League of Kings closing banquet.

Gabriella's eyes glittered with hatred. "I don't know why I wasted my time trying to ruin your lives when you're both so capable of doing it on your own."

Well, at least she wasn't denying it anymore.

At the doorway she paused, whirling around to toss out one last barb.

"You know what, Daphne? I should have realized something was up when you said you could use a friend. You don't know the first thing about friendship." She laughed harshly. "No one has ever wanted to be your friend. Not at St. Ursula's, and certainly not now."

"That's not true," Daphne tried to say, but the words came out as more of a whisper.

Gabriella cast her a withering look. "It's sad, watching you go to such lengths to protect your pathetic little baronetcy. As if anyone even cares about a rank that low! Honestly, we're all confused why Jeff is still with you. You have no money, no breeding, nothing to offer except a nice ass."

The room was deadly silent as Gabriella swept out, shutting the door behind her with a click.

Nina glanced over, her voice warm with concern. "Are you okay?"

Daphne was mortified to feel her eyes stinging again. She couldn't remember the last time she'd wept, let alone twice in one night.

And she couldn't remember the last time anyone had looked at her and asked, as if it was such a simple question, *Are you okay?*

"God, Daphne—don't cry." Nina seemed as startled by her tears as she was. "Gabriella isn't worth it. You can't listen to her."

"No, Gabriella is right." The words ached as Daphne spoke them, yet it was a relief, too. "I don't have any friends except Himari, and I pushed her away. I'm too proud and too mean."

"You haven't pushed *me* away," Nina said softly.

"Only because we teamed up against our common enemy!" Daphne burst out. "That doesn't count. We don't actually hang out in real life."

"So let's change that." Nina looked like she couldn't quite believe what she'd said.

"You—what?"

"We're all going to the League of Kings closing banquet next weekend, aren't we? I don't know about you, but I have nothing to wear." Nina seemed close to smiling as she added, "We just got dirt on Gabriella, after all our hard work. We might as well celebrate by shopping."

"I don't think you've ever uttered that sentence in your life," Daphne said weakly.

"Not really. I hate shopping," Nina admitted. "But it's kind of your hidden superpower, isn't it?"

Daphne stared at her, shock transitioning into a wary confusion. "I *am* the best shopper in town. I know when inventory turns over at Halo, and how they run their sales—"

Nina laughed. "Oh, we're not shopping at Halo. We're shopping *my* way."

"What does that mean?"

"You'll see," Nina said vaguely. "Now, come on—let's get back out there."

As they headed out the door, Nina surprised her with one more comment: "Gabriella was wrong, you know."

"About Jefferson?"

"About everything!" Nina paused. "Except maybe her comment about your ass. Don't let this go to your head, but I've always been jealous of it."

It was such an unexpected comment from Nina that Daphne laughed, grateful and oddly touched.

30

BEATRICE

Beatrice lay in the guest room near Louise's chambers, staring up at the carved garlands that looped around the walls. She couldn't sleep; her body was still on Pacific time, and this room felt so vast and intimidating. At home, she and Samantha used to joke that they lived in a museum, but at least it was *their* museum, its corridors and state rooms comfortingly familiar. The sheer scale of Versailles dwarfed Washington Palace, made her feel insignificant and small—which was precisely what Louis XIV had intended when he'd built it hundreds of years ago.

Earlier, when her tears had finally dried up, Louise had suggested that they get straight back on the plane and return to the conference. But Beatrice could tell that her friend was upset. "Let's stay for a night," she'd suggested. "We came all the way here. Maybe you'll be able to see your father again."

Maybe he'll have another flash of his real self, she meant, but Louise had just nodded gratefully and thanked her.

Footsteps sounded in the hallway. Beatrice padded across the room and opened the door, about to ask for a glass of water—but it wasn't one of the staff; it was Louise, who'd been retreating into her own room.

"Louise? Are you all right?" Beatrice asked, then cursed herself for asking such an inane question. Of course Louise wasn't all right.

"I was with my father," the princess said. "For a few minutes he was . . . alert again. He remembered me."

The hallway was dim, lit only by sconces every few yards. Beatrice could barely see Louise's face.

"I'm glad you got more time with him," she said delicately.

The door to Louise's room was open. Beatrice noticed, a little puzzled, that a faint glow came from the ceiling. It was *stars*, she realized—the plastic glow-in-the-dark kind meant for children's rooms. The sight of them was so incongruous with the grandiosity of Versailles, she couldn't help but stare.

Louise followed her gaze. "Oh, those are my stars," she said, speaking as casually as if she ruled the entire sky and not just France. "My mother hung them. She got out graphing paper and star charts, made sure it was accurate. We used to stargaze all the time."

"That sounds lovely."

There was a purring sound from the corner, where a fluffy Siamese sat imperiously on a cushion. "I take it this is Geneviève?" Beatrice asked, venturing forward.

"Don't bother. She won't come outside with us."

"Outside?"

Louise nodded, having reached a decision. "We should go stargazing, shouldn't we? Unless you're tired," she added.

Beatrice cast one last glance at the cat, who returned her stare impassively. "Stargazing sounds perfect."

The gardens of Versailles were spectacular at night, especially the fountains. Arcs of water glittered in the moonlight, falling from mermaids' tails and satyrs' horns into massive stone basins. As Beatrice walked past, burrowing deeper into the jacket she'd borrowed, a few droplets sprayed onto her ponytail. She took in a breath, inhaling the scents of roses and cut grass.

Louise fell back onto the lawn with childlike abandon, stretching her arms to either side as if she were making a snow angel. Beatrice settled next to her and looked up at the stars. They were scattered like teardrops against the velvet tapestry of the sky.

"Is this your version of meditation? To remind you how big the world is, how small your own role in it, all of that?"

"Don't be silly, Béatrice. My role in the world is not small, and neither is yours."

"You know, I've always hated meditation," Beatrice mused. "Like at the end of a yoga class, when they make you lie there in Savasana with your eyes closed? I spend the whole time making lists in my head, thinking of everything that I should be doing *instead* of lying on a yoga mat."

"That's the reason I don't do yoga. It's an inefficient way to work out," Louise said crisply, and Beatrice bit back a smile. "Stargazing was never about meditation for Maman, either. It was about spending time together. Romping around in the grass, letting me feel like an ordinary child for once. She knew all the constellations and the myths that went with them—Ursa Major, Cassiopeia, Charlemagne and his belt."

"Charlemagne is a constellation?"

Louise lifted a hand to point at three stars in a row. "See those three? They're his belt."

"I hate to break it to you, but that's Orion, not Charlemagne." Beatrice was trying very hard not to laugh. How utterly French of Queen Marie-Anne, to see her own forebears in the night skies.

"Don't be ridiculous," Louise huffed. "Of course it's Charlemagne. Where else would he hang his sword, if not on a belt?"

Beatrice decided not to press the issue. "So your mom is into astronomy?"

"My mother is the smartest person I know, yet she can be so foolish." Louise plucked a blade of grass, then let it fall back to the earth. "She has so much to give—intellectually, personally—and still, she spent *years* chasing fad diets and plastic surgery, hoping that if she could somehow get skinny enough or beautiful enough, she might actually make my father love her. She thought she could get him to stop his endless string of affairs and actually stay with her."

Beatrice had heard rumors of Louis XXIII's wandering eye, but it was another thing to hear Louise talk about it so bluntly. Beatrice's parents had genuinely loved each other and had hoped their daughter would marry someone she loved, too—which was more than most royal marriages ever aspired to.

Many kings and queens assumed infidelity from the outset. They treated their marriages with the cynical detachment of a business venture, coming together only when duty required it.

"It's sad, how unhappy she ended up," Louise went on, in a detached voice. "I always wonder what she would have done with her life if she hadn't been born to be queen."

Beatrice blinked. "What do you mean, she was born to be queen?"

"Everyone knew she and my father would marry, since they were both children. Her family are the Ducs d'Uzès; her parents are close friends with my father's parents. It was just assumed. Like you and Theodore, yes?"

"I love Teddy!"

"Oh." Louise sounded a little surprised. "Well, I'm glad for you. Most queens are not so lucky."

Beatrice wasn't sure how to answer that.

They both stared up at the stars for a long minute, letting the enchanted folds of night settle around them. Finally, Beatrice asked, "Does your mother come here often?"

"She and my father have separate households. She's lived at Chenonceau since I was ten. I got to visit her on holidays," Louise said stiffly.

"I'm sorry. That sounds hard, living here with only your father. He seems . . ." *Strict, callous, harsh.* "Demanding," she said aloud.

"He's disappointed in me."

"That's absurd! What reason can he possibly have for being disappointed in you?"

"Why do you think?" Louise said wearily. "The same reason everyone has been disappointed in me for my entire life. I wasn't born a boy."

Beatrice shifted onto her side. She suddenly wished that she could see her friend's face, but Louise's profile was shrouded in darkness.

"It's not the Middle Ages; people don't think that way anymore," she protested.

Louise scoffed. "You really expect me to believe that there is no one in America who wishes that Jefferson had been born first? Does every man in your country support your position as head of state? 'Fantastic!' they all exclaim. 'A woman telling us what to do! We should let her do her job without interfering or complaining!'"

"Well . . . no," Beatrice said haltingly. "I have plenty of critics, men and women alike. But I'm not sure it's sexism."

"Really? What is it, then?"

Beatrice hesitated. Because it *was* sexism, wasn't it? Beatrice's detractors never said it aloud, never authored op-eds that stated *Beatrice shouldn't rule because she's a woman.* They just criticized everything she did. If she wore a new dress, she was extravagant; if she recycled an old one, she had no style. If she was photographed holding a glass of wine, she was a lush; if she didn't drink at an event, she was pregnant, or boring, or rude to her hosts. If she was caught in a photo unsmiling, then she wasn't likable; if she smiled too broadly, she was trying too hard.

"You're right," Beatrice said slowly.

"It's the same for me. You know the French have never had a queen regnant before. Unless you count the *eight weeks* that Eleanor d'Aquitaine ruled between husbands, in the twelfth century," Louise added sarcastically. "My father never said it aloud, but he didn't have to. He feels uncomfortable with the fact that a woman will succeed him."

Something fell on Beatrice's hand; she realized it was a blade of grass. Louise was plucking them like flowers, one at a time with the relentlessness of a bulldozer, then letting them drift back down.

"My parents tried and tried to have another child. It wasn't until I was twelve, when it became clear that no little brother would ever emerge to save the day, that the Assemblée Nationale changed the laws of succession. I went from being an heir presumptive to an heir apparent," Louise explained. "Otherwise the throne would have gone to our closest male relative—my fourth cousin Pierre, the Duc d'Anjou."

"I don't know him," Beatrice admitted, and Louise barked out a humorless laugh.

"He tried to have a career as an artist. A *performance artist*. Lots of glitter and eggs and body paint," Louise said flatly. "His last so-called performance was appearing at the Eiffel Tower in nothing but a red Speedo and red wig, dancing a Scottish jig to a soundtrack of the Vienna Children's Choir. He got arrested for public indecency; my father called the chief of police and quietly got him released."

Beatrice couldn't help chuckling at the image. "As far as art goes, that must have been quite memorable."

"And yet my father still considers asking the Assemblée to change the law back, pass the throne to Pierre instead of to me."

Beatrice's laughter stilled. "Louise—I'm so sorry."

At least her own father had never made her feel like a second choice.

Louise made an impatient noise. "This is precisely why I'll never marry. It's hard enough facing opposition from the country; I can't face it from my husband, too. I'll be like Elizabeth I. The Virgin Queen of the twenty-first century! Except . . . well, you know."

Beatrice couldn't tell how much Louise was joking. "You don't mean that. It would be so lonely to rule alone."

"It can be even lonelier if you marry the wrong person," Louise said simply. "My parents are the loneliest people I know."

That was such an achingly sad statement that Beatrice couldn't really answer.

"What about Theodore?" Louise asked, after a moment. "He doesn't mind that you'll always outrank him, that he'll come second in his own marriage?"

"He knows what it means to be with me." Beatrice thought of the signed declaration on her desk, and her heart sank. She wished that she sounded more certain.

"What is he going to *do* all day, deal with charities and nannies? All the things queens consort used to do?" Louise propped herself on one elbow, seeming genuinely curious.

"Maybe? I don't know!" Beatrice sighed. "Teddy is sweet and selfless. We'll figure it out together."

Louise had a point, though. Teddy's position was uniquely strange—and even though he was a smart, loving, empathetic man, he was still a man. Would he really be happy when they had a baby someday and Teddy was outranked by his infant child? Would he feel emasculated by the fact that their children would all take her name?

"Then he is special indeed," Louise told her. "The only man I ever got serious about . . . he ended up breaking my heart."

"I've had my heart broken, too."

Beatrice had no idea why she'd admitted that, but the words were out and there was no taking them back. Perhaps she simply needed to say it aloud, since she'd never really spoken it before.

"Really? Who was it?"

"My Revere Guard." Beatrice had never told this to anyone except Sam; the whole story had spilled out of her after their father died, when she and Sam were both crying over his grave. It felt like a very big secret to tell Louise.

"No!" Louise laughed, a lighthearted sound that made Beatrice's confession somehow less weighty. "Oh, I had no idea you had it in you! To think, you're just as cliché as the rest of us."

"I . . . what?"

Louise was still swallowing back a giggle. "You're hardly the first princess to hook up with her bodyguard. It's practically one of our job requirements."

"It was more than that!" Beatrice insisted, stung. She and Connor hadn't just been *hooking up*; they had loved each other, even if was a first love and not a forever love. "He was my friend, too. One of my only friends."

Except that Connor had never *understood* Beatrice, not really. He'd always tried to fit her into a space where she didn't quite belong. And then Beatrice had outgrown that shape, because that was what people did as they got older: they grew and changed. And instead of growing together, their lives twining ever more tightly together, she and Connor had grown apart.

"I'm sorry, I didn't mean to tease," Louise went on. "But it's nice to know I'm not the only one who's had their heart broken by . . ."

"By a bodyguard?"

"By a friend."

Beatrice ventured a guess. "You're talking about Alexei, aren't you?"

Louise sat up so abruptly that her hair whipped over her shoulder. "He told you?"

"No, I just suspected." Beatrice had wondered for a while now if there was something between those two; she'd sensed it from the quick way Alexei always looked to Louise for approval, the way she teased him more than the others, as if to prove he didn't matter.

"How observant." Louise seemed grudgingly impressed.

"I don't understand, though. If he broke your heart, how are you still friends? Isn't it painful to be near him? Unless . . ." Beatrice groaned. "You're still seeing him, aren't you?"

"Well, what do you expect!" Louise exclaimed. "It's very rare that Alexei and I are in the same country, let alone on the same private island! You can't blame me for having a little secret fun."

"I don't understand why it has to be secret, though. Can't you just date?"

"We're both future monarchs. How would that work? What exactly would Alexei and I do if we ever got married, merge Russia and France into a single nation? They aren't even contiguous!" she added, as if geography were the only flaw in that plan. "There's no future for me and Alexei," Louise concluded, speaking almost to herself. "He would have to give up Russia and come to France as my king consort, or I would have to leave France and go to Russia as his tsarina. There is no way that we can rule our respective countries and be together."

Beatrice thought of Teddy again, and felt heavy with guilt. She tried to speak her next words lightly. "To think you fell for the one prince you can't have. Who knew you were such a hopeless romantic."

"Oh, shut up," Louise teased, but her lips curled upward all the same. Beatrice was just relieved to have coaxed a smile from her.

She laced her hands over her stomach and stared up at the stars. For once, she did feel rather small, in the scheme of things.

It wasn't a terrible feeling.

31

NINA

Nina was out with her roommates on Embassy Row, the neighborhood near campus that, despite its pretentious name, was lined with dive bars boasting shot-and-a-beer deals and BYO restaurants. They were at one of those restaurants now, platters of pad thai and fried rice scattered on the table before them.

Jayne sighed enviously. "I can't believe you're going to the League of Kings banquet. Your life is unbelievable."

"Ooh—while you're there, you should ask Princess Louise what'll be in style next season," Rachel chimed in. "You know she personally sets *every* fashion trend."

Nina snorted. "I'm not going to the League of Kings to gossip about fashion with some princess I don't know."

Rachel reached for a potsticker with her chopsticks. "Speaking of fashion, Nina, what are you going to wear?"

"Oh, um." Nina coughed. "Actually, this is sort of random, but I'm going shopping with Daphne?" The sentence ticked up at the end, becoming a question.

Rachel's eyebrows shot up, and Jayne choked on her drink. "Daphne Deighton?"

"We don't know any other Daphnes, so, yes."

Jayne cut in. "How did *that* happen?"

Years of rivalry, a strange alliance as they decided to take down a mutual enemy, a slow thawing toward each other, a wary truce, and then . . . Nina didn't know what to call their relationship anymore.

There were entire pieces of her life, now, that she didn't show to anyone but Daphne. Secrets that she and Daphne had made together, which Nina shared with no one else.

"It's complicated," she said vaguely. "I've seen Daphne more often lately, now that I'm friends with Jeff again."

Nina's phone rang from a number she didn't recognize; she ignored it, glancing back up to see Rachel's dubious expression.

"And that's all you are with Jeff? Friends?"

Nina wasn't sure. Lately, she'd become acutely conscious of Jeff's every move: of the way his shirts fit over his shoulders, of the warmth of his arm when it brushed hers as they walked across campus. The spark in his eyes when they met hers, the way his laugh shivered through her.

Before Nina could figure out how to reply, her phone rang again. Puzzled, she answered. "Hello?"

"Nina, this is Matt. His Highness's Revere Guard."

"Is everything okay?" Nina asked quickly, alarmed. Surely there could be no good reason for Jeff's Guard to be calling her directly.

"Sorry to bother you, but I could use your help." Matt sounded sheepish, almost embarrassed. "Prince Jefferson has had a lot to drink, and he refuses to go home."

Shouldn't you be calling Daphne? Nina was about to ask, but Matt's next words stopped her. "His Highness keeps asking for you."

Nina felt a traitorous flush of excitement, which quickly gave way to guilt. She wondered if the fight Daphne had staged with Jeff at the End of Session party had escalated into an *actual* fight—if taking down Gabriella had put Jeff and Daphne's relationship on the rocks.

She cradled the phone closer to her ear. "Where should I meet you?"

♛

The fraternity house was a white monolith on the corner of the Street: that was what everyone at King's College called the road lined with frat and sorority houses, as if no other street were worth mentioning. Stone columns rose up before its entrance, making it resemble a national landmark or perhaps a bank building. Nina hadn't been inside since last year, back when she and Jeff were dating, when they'd gone upstairs in the middle of a party to discuss their relationship.

As she got closer, Nina realized that the people gathered on the grassy front lawn weren't college kids drinking beer from plastic cups. They were paparazzi, milling about with their cameras, glancing periodically at the door as they waited for someone to emerge.

Clearly that someone was Prince Jefferson.

Nina hesitated. No way was she about to let the press take photos of her, start bullying her family again, pry into her personal life—everything they had done when she and Jeff dated.

Except . . . they would only do that if they considered her worth their attention. Nina glanced down at her wide-leg jeans, ratty sneakers, and navy King's College hoodie. She looked like a schlumpy student on her way to the library, not like a girl who belonged in a headline with Jeff.

Because she *wasn't* that girl, not at all.

She pulled up the hood of her sweatshirt and started forward. Sure enough, the paparazzi hardly spared her a glance as she headed toward the entrance.

The foyer was empty, a massive staircase with gold railings curving up to the second floor. The low thump of speakers

266

emanated from deeper in the house, where Nina assumed she would find the party. She started forward, then heard voices in a room to her left. One of those voices belonged to Jeff, she realized, who was drunkenly singing the theme song to a children's cartoon.

"Jeff?" she called out, and the door swung open.

"Nina. I'm so glad you came." Matt took a step back, revealing a billiards room. The blinds had been drawn over the windows, and the other three walls were lined with photos of old fraternity pledge classes, each labeled with the graduating year. It looked like they went back a century.

Jeff sat on the edge of a pool table, swinging his legs like a child on the edge of an actual pool. He brightened when he saw her.

"Nina! You came! I wanted you to."

Unlike people who got surly or sad when they'd had too much to drink, Jeff was always a sweet, affectionate drunk. His smile was boyish and eager, his hair disheveled and a little damp. Nina suppressed the urge to reach back and smooth the unruly curls behind his ears.

"He refuses to go home," Matt explained. "And as much as I'd love to spend the night on this billiards table, our chief of security insists that I get him back."

"I can't leave!" Jeff chimed in, outraged. "I'm . . . I'ze . . . it's a party!"

Nina fought back a laugh, and Matt glared at her. "Look, we have to get His Highness out the front door and into the waiting car."

"Isn't there another entrance?"

"The paparazzi are out back, too! Someone must have tipped off the press that Jefferson was here." Matt sighed. "I'm legally authorized to use force on him in extreme situations, but I don't want to resort to that."

"Use force?"

"Knock him out, then carry him to the car fireman-style," Matt told her, and Nina winced at the image. He nodded. "Exactly. That photo would be all over the internet tomorrow, and aside from ruining my career, it would get the prince in trouble."

Jefferson glanced slowly from one of them to the other, as if he was trying to follow their conversation but struggling to keep up. He frowned endearingly. "Matt, you're not gonna punch me. You're too nice for that."

"We have to convince him to walk out the doors," Matt said to Nina, as if Jeff hadn't spoken.

"I'm not leaving!" Jeff said again.

All at once, Nina knew precisely what to do.

She leaned her hands on the pool table behind her, then jumped up to sit next to him. "Jeff, I need your help. We can't win the race without you."

He looked up sharply. "Race? What race?"

"The race to the car! We have to go now, or the other frat will win."

Her lie worked almost too well. An instant later Jeff was hurtling toward the front door, ready to sprint to the car. Nina had to grab his arm and insist that the rules required them all to stay together. Which was how she and Matt managed to walk on either side of Jeff, acting as human shields.

In the photos, the figure in the middle would be an indistinguishable blur, unrecognizable as Prince Jefferson.

♛

At the palace, Nina helped Matt get Jeff upstairs and into his sitting room. But when she started to turn toward the door, Jeff's voice stopped her.

"Don't go. It's still early!"

Nina cast a pleading glance at Matt, but he'd already

retreated down the hall, probably just glad to have gotten Jeff home in one piece.

This isn't a big deal, she told herself as she settled onto the couch. *We're just friends.*

As if to prove that fact, she flicked on the TV and surfed the channels until she found one of her favorite old rom-coms.

"Wait." Jeff reached across her for the remote. "Can we check the score of the game?"

"Nope. The second I let you start watching sports, you'll never stop."

"You've seen this movie a hundred times!"

"And it's always good, every time," Nina said firmly.

Jeff pretended to lunge across her and reach for the remote, but Nina scooted back, straining her arm as she held it out of reach. They were both laughing, the sort of bright, silly laugh that had defined their relationship when they were kids.

Then somehow Jeff had grabbed Nina and tumbled backward onto the couch, and she was falling onto his chest, and neither of them was laughing anymore.

Nina's focus centered on her hips, her stomach, everywhere that her body was touching Jeff's. She knew she should move, but her body felt liquid and heavy.

"You tricked me," she whispered, and she wasn't sure whether she was talking about this moment with the remote or something much bigger.

"Did I?"

Jeff's arm had looped around the curve of her back. She'd taken off her sweatshirt during the car ride, and his hand just barely grazed the band of skin between her black tank top and her jeans. A shiver ran down her spine at his touch.

"Jeff." She meant it as a warning, but it didn't come out that way.

"Nina."

Neither of them moved. They didn't scoot back, but they didn't draw closer, either. As if by staying utterly still, they could somehow maintain the fiction that this was a wholly friendly interaction.

Nina's hand seemed to move of its own volition, reaching for the damp strands of his dark brown hair. "You smell like beer, you know."

Jeff smiled drowsily. "That makes sense. It was chug-one-to-get-one tonight."

She could feel the thud of his heartbeat beneath her chest; it picked up speed, and her own quickened to meet it. Everything felt hushed and still, as if they'd fallen inside a snow globe and there was nothing left in the world but the two of them.

Then somehow reality snapped back in. Nina pushed herself from Jeff's chest and scooted a few feet along the couch. She had every intention of ignoring this whole thing, pretending it had never happened, but Jeff spoke up.

"I'm sorry," he said huskily.

Nina flushed. "Jeff, it's okay—I didn't—"

"Sam told me not to, you know."

"She . . . what?"

"She said if I wanted to date you again, I had to be careful or she would pummel me into a thousand pieces. And Sam throws a mean punch." The words came out thick and slow. It dawned on Nina that Jeff might be drunker than she'd realized. She scooted a little farther away, her mind spinning.

Was Jeff saying what she thought he was saying?

"Jeff, you're with Daphne," she reminded him.

His face scrunched up in an adorably confused way. "Things with Daphne have been weird," he admitted, then shook his head. "Sorry, I shouldn't be talking about this with you."

The rush of excitement that had flooded through Nina quickly dissipated. "If this is about that fight at the End of Session party, I think there's more to the story," she said guiltily.

"Maybe, but it's not just that. Daphne is different, lately." Jeff looked up at Nina. "I get this feeling that she's hiding something from me."

Of course she is, Nina thought. Daphne had spent years hiding secrets from Jeff, including the biggest secret of all: what she was really like.

For so long Nina had dreamed of the moment when she could tell Jeff about his girlfriend's manipulations. Yet now, when that moment had finally arrived, the words died in her throat.

If Daphne was different lately, it was because the facade she'd shown Jeff for years was starting to erode, and he was catching glimpses of the real Daphne underneath it all. A Daphne that Nina might actually *like.*

Because underneath the manipulating and scheming and double-dealing, Daphne was . . . well, she was Daphne. There was no simple way to describe her. She was complicated, determined, brilliant. She protected the people she cared about with her own twisted but fierce brand of loyalty.

Daphne and Jeff didn't belong together, but it wasn't Nina's place to say so. Their relationship would come to a head without her interference. Better to let them reach that conclusion on their own.

Especially now that she and Daphne were allies, or almost-friends, or whatever they were.

"This is between you and Daphne," she told Jeff. "I know better than to get in the middle of my friends' relationships."

That word, *friend,* hung in the air between them like a challenge. It seemed to sober Jeff up a little. He held Nina's gaze, then nodded slowly.

"Okay," he said.

"Okay," she repeated awkwardly.

Jeff was still staring at her. "Nina—as my friend, you would tell me if something was going on with you, right?"

Nina feigned ignorance. "What do you mean?"

"If you were dealing with a problem, you'd let me know?"

Jeff had clearly sensed that she was troubled about something. For a moment, Nina was tempted to tell him everything—about her financial aid, and Daphne's plan, and Gabriella.

"Everything is great, I promise," she assured him. "Now, are you going to put the game on or what?"

Jeff relented with a smile. "You have no idea what game it is, do you?"

"Not a clue," Nina agreed. "Baseball? Wrestling?"

He closed his eyes and groaned. "All the years we've been friends, and you still don't know that wrestling is a match, not a game?"

Friends. Now he'd said it, too. Hopefully it would get easier and easier to say.

Nina leaned on the pillow between them, relieved that they'd retreated to their usual safe banter. This she could handle. There was nothing wrong or illicit about this.

"Fair enough. Why don't you tell me about the game."

Jeff turned it on and began naming football players, as casually as if that charged moment between them had never happened.

Which was exactly what Nina had wanted.

Wasn't it?

32

SAMANTHA

The upstairs ballroom had been transformed for the heirs' info sessions, filled with wooden tables where everyone sat behind name placards. Sam was at one of those tables now, staring up at the screen, which read: *The Law of the Sea: Oceans Beyond National Jurisdiction.*

"I think our topics are getting *more* boring," she whispered to Alexei, who sat next to her.

Before he could reply, a woman with short dark hair stepped up to the podium and began the lecture on maritime law. Bharat and Sirivannavari, who sat at the next table, flipped a binder to a blank page and began a game of tic-tac-toe. Sam wished phones were allowed in these sessions; it would be so much more bearable if she could text Marshall under the table.

They had been taking things slowly since the photo shoot, spending time in the seclusion of Bellevue rather than going out together in public. No need to draw attention to their relationship, at least not until they'd figured out their next step.

Apparently, when Marshall had explained that he and Sam were back together, his grandfather had pursed his lips but said nothing, as if he could make the problem go away by ignoring it. He was unbearably stubborn—but so was Sam. And she was determined to find a way for her and Marshall to be together, without estranging him from his family.

Sam smiled at the thought of the surprise she'd planned for Marshall that evening. She'd been thinking about what he'd said last week: that he wished they could escape for a while and live like ordinary people, without titles or positions, without the media breathing down their necks. They might not be able to do that for real, but Sam could give them a taste of it.

She clicked her pen absentmindedly, letting the lecturer's words drift over her.

"The sovereignty of nations extends two hundred nautical miles beyond the shoreline, at which point a vessel enters international waters and is subject to maritime law. As future monarchs, you all have diplomatic immunity in one another's nations and on the open seas—with the exception, of course, of those nations who chose not to join the League of Kings. So before you follow in Prince Franz's footsteps and run off to the beach with a bag of mushrooms, make sure you know where you are, or you might end up in jail," the lecturer added with a sharp laugh.

Prince Franz. It was the second time this month Sam had heard of him.

When their lecture ended, she glanced over at Alexei. "You were really paying attention to this one." He'd been taking notes the entire session, as assiduously as a high school student preparing for exams.

Alexei shrugged. "Maritime law is fascinating. I learned that the hard way, after my time dealing with pirates." She thought he was kidding, until he explained that he'd spent two years with the Russian navy, chasing pirates off the coast of Somalia.

"Wow. That's really impressive. Though I can't believe your family allowed it, given that you're first in line to the throne," Sam pointed out. Beatrice wasn't allowed to travel without her Revere Guard, let alone enter the navy and take down corsairs.

"I was going through some stuff," the tsarevich said vaguely. "My father hoped that sending me away would shock sense into me, make me realize how good I had it. I think he worried I would—how did that professor put it?—run off to the beach with a bag of mushrooms."

"Right! She mentioned Prince Franz," Sam jumped in. "I don't think I've met him."

"Probably not, given that he died thirty years ago." At Sam's puzzled frown, Alexei went on, "You've never heard of Franz? He was the younger son of King Auguste of Flanders, back in the thirties."

"What did he do?"

"Fell in love with a showgirl from Paris and decided he didn't want to be a prince anymore, so he moved to Hawaii."

"Because it isn't part of the League of Kings?"

Alexei nodded. "Hawaii isn't *hostile* to foreign monarchs; they just don't recognize foreign titles."

America had approached Hawaii in the nineteenth century and asked if the island nation wanted to join the United States, as Orange had done when Marshall's family renounced their sovereignty so that Orange could accede to the union. Unlike Marshall's great-great-great-grandfather, the Queen of Hawaii had politely but firmly declined America's invitation.

Even now, Hawaii maintained a coolly neutral distance from other nations. It signed the biggest international treaties, and maintained a healthy tourism industry. But every five years, when the invitation to the League of Kings arrived on Queen Liliuokalani's desk—as it did for every monarch who wasn't an official member of the league—she ignored it. The Hawaiian queen evidently had no interest in networking with a bunch of foreign royals she didn't care about.

"What happened to Franz?" Sam asked.

"He and the showgirl lived in Hawaii for the rest of their lives. They opened a bar. It became famous in the seventies as, basically, the international capital of the psychedelic drug movement. Hence that comment about mushrooms," Alexei joked. "Franz was arrested for possession on multiple occasions, and since his diplomatic immunity wasn't recognized in Hawaii, he went to jail every time."

"Wow." For once, Sam was at a loss for words.

They'd made their way out into the hallway; Siri and Bharat were waiting for them, clearly eager to head to lunch. "Can you imagine?" Alexei added as they headed toward their friends. "Going from life as an heir to living in a beach cottage? I don't think I could handle it."

"Yeah," Sam said absently. "I guess not."

♛

Marshall pulled out his phone and held it before him like a mirror as he turned his face back and forth. "This is amazing. I don't even recognize myself."

"I know!" Sam swept her hand to indicate the football stadium, the ant-sized players swarming far down on the field. "It's so much more fun up here, isn't it?"

When she'd shown up at his apartment in LA this afternoon, a makeup artist in tow, Marshall had stared at her in blank confusion. It wasn't until the woman explained her job—she worked on that new zombie show—and began pulling beards and wigs from an enormous trunk that he understood what was going on.

"Wait a second," he'd asked Sam, eyes glinting with mischief. "Are we going out in *disguise*?"

They had both watched in amazement as the makeup artist used bronzer to thicken Sam's nose, shaded her jawline to make it look square. Once she'd added sunglasses and tucked Sam's hair into a cropped strawberry-blond wig, she'd transformed the princess into a completely different person.

"I do wish my disguise didn't involve a beard," Marshall said now, tugging at the furry monstrosity that was stuck to his face with adhesive.

"You look like one of the characters from that Viking show." A smile curled at Sam's lips. "I wonder what R.J. and Ashley would say if they could see us."

"They would probably wonder what we're doing up here. R.J. and Ashley seemed like the type who'd rather watch from one of the suites."

Sam and Marshall were up in the nosebleed section, in the second-to-last row of the stadium. No one else was around except a few teenage boys, and Sam and Marshall's protection officers in a neighboring row. Sam had to admit, it was much better this way: no private box, no tour of the locker rooms, no meeting the players or shaking hands with the team's owner or being gifted a custom jersey. No one snapped photos or even spared them a second glance. They were just two fans sitting outside on a fall afternoon to watch a football game.

Marshall laced his hands behind his head and leaned back lazily. "This must be what it feels like to be an ordinary person."

Sam tilted her head, considering. "If we *were* ordinary people, what do you think we'd be like?"

"Well, we both know I'd be a movie star, so I'd be famous either way."

"I seriously doubt you can act," Sam pointed out.

"Just look at this face." Marshall stared at her, making such a funny expression beneath the beard that she laughed. "I wouldn't need to act. This face alone would get people into theaters."

Sam nestled her head onto his shoulder contentedly. He smelled clean and warm, like summer and sunshine.

"What would you be?" Marshall asked. "A professional scuba diver? Oh, I know—you would lead those haunted ghost tours in New Orleans!"

Sam smiled, but for some reason, she didn't want to engage in the fiction of it anymore.

"When I was younger, I was so jealous of Beatrice. I used to wish that I was the future queen instead of her. I didn't want to become . . ." She swallowed. "Irrelevant, I guess. I didn't want history to forget me."

An awful part of Sam had been relieved when Beatrice postponed her wedding to Teddy, because it meant that the appearance of little mini-Beatrices—Sam's eventual nieces and nephews, who would push her ever further down the pecking order—was delayed. It meant that Sam was still *important*, for just a little while longer.

Marshall's gaze met hers, his dark eyes intent. "Do you still wish that you were the queen?"

A whistle blew on the field; Sam didn't even glance down at the game.

"Honestly . . . I don't know." She turned the question back on him. "What about you?"

He spoke slowly, searching for the right words. "I don't know either. My whole life I've taken for granted that I'm the future duke, but it's all been tied up in anxiety, because I knew my grandfather was disappointed in me."

And now *she* was yet another reason for the duke's disappointment, Sam thought guiltily.

"I'm so happy at the Napa house," Marshall admitted. "If I wasn't me—I mean, if my family weren't dukes—then it would be nice doing something like that full-time. Planting seeds and watching them grow, worrying about rains or droughts instead of, you know, whether I'm an adequate symbol for

America's racial dialogue." He sounded almost wistful as he added: "I'd be outside all the time. Chop my own firewood, cook burgers on a grill, become friends with the neighbors. Hopefully there would be an ocean nearby, so I could teach the kids to surf."

He flushed; that last part, about kids, must have slipped out accidentally. Sam secretly adored it. She so rarely got to see this side of Marshall, the sweetness beneath all the snarkiness and wit.

"You want to be a farmer?" she asked, because she realized she needed to say something.

"Doesn't have to be farming. I just wish sometimes that I could live a quieter life. I mean, look at what we're doing now—can you imagine being able to live like this all the time? To go places without worrying about what kind of impression you'll make, or whether it will reflect poorly on the duchy. To just stay in the same place all year, actually feel grounded."

Sam thought of what Alexei had said about Hawaii. Maybe it wouldn't be all that bad, to do what Franz had done.

It was strange: she used to daydream about stealing the spotlight from Beatrice, and now here she was, wondering what it would be like to live the completely opposite sort of life, one that was wholly private. Maybe that was part of becoming an adult. When you were thirteen you felt so sure of everything, so certain about what you wanted and what you thought the world owed you—but what you wanted as a teenager wasn't the same as what you wanted at twenty, or, Sam guessed, at thirty.

Maybe growing up meant letting go of the desires that no longer fit you, and discovering new ones buried in layers of yourself that you hadn't known existed.

"Marshall," she said, tugging his gaze away from the field. And because she didn't know how to articulate all of this, she did what she always did: let her actions speak for themselves.

She looped her arms around Marshall's neck and lifted her face to his, kissing him right there on the lips. In public, in front of the entire stadium.

And no one looked their way.

They stayed like that all afternoon, just enjoying each other, soaking in their temporary cocoon of privacy.

33

NINA

"You expect me to go shopping *here?*" Daphne stared incredulously at the sign that read CECE'S CLOSET, then pulled her sweater higher over her shoulders, as if worried someone might catch her slumming at a vintage store.

"Like it or not, Daphne, you're broke," Nina reminded her.

Daphne rolled her eyes. "I take it you're my own personal Virgil, guiding me through this dismal underworld of fashion?"

"Abandon all couture, ye who enter here," Nina agreed, and pushed open the front door.

Cece's Closet had the sort of blithe, blatant disregard for inventory management that Nina normally associated with used-book stores. It looked like someone had attempted to organize the clothes based on occasion, or perhaps decade, only to switch their system partway through. A basket labeled DESIGNER JEANS, $30 EACH was plopped next to a rack that held a bright red miniskirt, a fluffy mink coat, and a polka-dotted bikini top that was mysteriously missing its bottoms.

"There are some good things here, if you're willing to roll up your sleeves and look." Nina beelined to one of the racks and began sliding items toward her one by one.

Daphne sniffed imperiously. Nina watched as she wandered over to a dresser, which was scattered with random objects: a beaded evening bag, a quilted belt with an oversized buckle. "Is this a real Edwardian cookie jar?" she asked, holding up what looked, to Nina, like nothing but a plain blue jar.

"Um—I think so?" she guessed.

"How did you find this place?" Daphne's curiosity was clearly piqued.

"My mom brought me here for my prom dress." Nina smiled at the memory. "We went to the mall, at first, but the salespeople were so snobby, and the dresses were either ridiculously overpriced or . . ."

"Or too short?" Daphne offered.

"Or generic. I didn't want to be another girl wearing a spaghetti-strap metallic dress." Too late, Nina realized that Daphne had almost certainly been one of those girls. They had all looked the same, a battalion of girls armed in shimmering gold thread or sequins.

She held one of the gowns up to her chest, and Daphne gave a strangled cry of protest.

"Stop, you *cannot* wear that shade of green!" Daphne threw up a hand as if to shield her eyes. "Quick, put it away before it blinds us."

"What about this?" Nina asked, amused. She pulled another from the rack, a chiffon thing with a fluffy tiered skirt.

"You'll look like a soufflé that flopped in on itself. God, you're hopeless." Daphne elbowed her aside. "Let *me.*"

Daphne began sliding the hangers toward her one by one, studying each dress as if she were a general assessing her troops before battle. For a moment, Nina thought of the last—and only—time she and Daphne had gone shopping together. Daphne had called the store afterward to cancel Nina's dress order, in an attempt to sabotage her and Jeff.

Nina squirmed at the thought of Jeff. She'd tried to act normal when she saw him at lunch yesterday, but their relationship felt confusing now, more charged. Their almost-kiss from that night on his couch felt as persistent and tangible as if they *had* kissed. Nina couldn't stop thinking about it, turning the memory over and over in her mind.

"Start with these," Daphne commanded, arms full of garments on hangers, and Nina looked up guiltily.

"You'll try on a few too, right?"

Daphne hesitated, and Nina pressed her advantage. "Come on, we defeated Gabriella! We should celebrate by showing up at the banquet in fantastic new dresses."

At the mention of Gabriella, Daphne chuckled. "Did I tell you that Gabriella tried to coordinate outfits with me, that night at the wine bar?"

"I'm sorry, what?"

"She told me I couldn't show up to the League of Kings ball in the same color that she did. And since she was choosing between red, green, blue, black, silver, and purple, I was banned from all of them." Daphne tossed her hair, doing an admirable impression of Gabriella's bored, condescending drawl. "Nigel says that purple is my color, so I'll probably wear that, but really, you should steer clear of all the colors. Just in case."

Nina snorted. "Wow. I can't believe her minions actually put up with these demands."

She and Daphne hadn't heard from Gabriella since the End of Session party, not that they'd expected to. They assumed that Gabriella was convincing her father to carry out their demands. If she hadn't done anything by Saturday, they would confront her at the League of Kings banquet and tell her that she needed to act now, or else.

But Nina doubted that things would reach that point. She'd seen the fear in Gabriella's eyes when they got her on video; Gabriella had too much at stake, and granting their demands would cost her nothing.

"You know what?" Nina added, glancing at Daphne. "We need to find you something purple. Just to remind Gabriella that she can't personally *own* a *color*."

Daphne grinned. "I like the way you think."

It was both enlightening and amusing, shopping with Daphne. She was full of opinions about how Nina should dress to accentuate her best features: "You can get away with strapless, take advantage of that," or "Sorry, you're just not tall enough to pull off an uneven hemline."

And whenever either of them tried on a dress that she didn't like, Daphne offered up a scathing critique.

A black satin gown with leather detail on the shoulders: "What are you going for, Count Dracula?" A dress with real feathers along the hem: "National Geographic called; they want their birds back." A lemon-yellow gown: "Why don't you just eat a yellow Starburst and wear the wrapper?"

After that last failed dress, Nina leaned back against the wall and closed her eyes. "This is exactly why I hate shopping for black-tie events," she moaned.

Daphne made an exasperated noise. "Nina, this isn't a black-tie event. It's not even a white-tie event! The attire for the League of Kings banquet is *full decorations*."

"Meaning?"

"Meaning the guests wear their medals of honor and crowns. It's the most formal type of attire that exists."

"Right. Let me just give my tiara a polish," Nina muttered.

"All I'm saying is, this yellow"—Daphne hesitated, searching for the right word—"*ensemble* you have on won't work. We'll just have to keep looking," she added, seemingly cheered by the prospect.

Nina waited until Daphne had helped with the zipper before she asked something she'd been wondering for a while now.

"Daphne . . . if you're so worried about money, why don't

you work? I'm not saying you should flip burgers," she hurried to add. "But you're smart, and people love you. There has to be something you can do with that."

"What, sell an exclusive tell-all interview?"

"You know that's not what I mean," Nina insisted. "What about something less personal? Can't you work at an art gallery? Write a children's book? I can see it now—something with girl power and glittery shoes."

"None of those are options for me. I'm not allowed to take on any kind of sales-related job, even at an art gallery, because it would reflect poorly on the royal family. Anyone who bought a painting from me would be accused of trying to buy their way into the Washingtons' good graces." Daphne shook her head. "And I *definitely* can't write a book, even a picture book about magical shoes. The NDA made it very clear that I was relinquishing my right to write or sell anything, ever."

Nina blinked. "You signed an NDA?"

"Of course I did. Plus multiple riders and amendments."

"Seriously?"

Daphne seemed much less upset by this than Nina. "The palace made me sign something when Jefferson and I were first dating, of course. Then after he broke up with me, they clearly worried I wouldn't consider myself bound by the contract anymore—that I might publish a salacious memoir—so they sent over a contract amendment that very morning." Daphne sighed. "Jefferson dumped me, and then hours later, a messenger from the palace's legal department appeared on my front step. I was crying so hard, I pretty much signed the document without reading it."

Heat flooded Nina's face. She knew the exact morning that Daphne was talking about, because *she* was the reason Jeff had broken up with Daphne—or at least one of the reasons.

The night before, she and Jeff had hooked up for the first time.

"Doesn't it bother you, having a contract about your relationship?" she asked.

It was an intrusive question, but Daphne didn't flinch. "You're thinking about this wrong. The contract isn't about our relationship; it's about what I'm allowed to disclose about the relationship."

Nina shook her head. "It was about your relationship. Even if they didn't state it explicitly, the palace kept trying to dictate what I could wear—" She broke off uncomfortably, but her meaning was already abundantly clear.

"The palace asked you to sign an NDA, too," Daphne said quietly.

Nina got angry all over again, thinking of how Robert Standish had shown up at her parents' house, telling her that if she and Jefferson were together, she could no longer wear *sweatpants*.

"I didn't sign it." Nina's relationship with Jeff had been over before it got to that point.

"Really?" Daphne sounded impressed. "I guess I just assumed that was the cost of dating him."

"Oh," Nina muttered awkwardly, because she had no idea what else to say.

Daphne hesitated, sucking in a breath. "While we're on the topic, Nina . . . last year, when I did all that stuff to you . . . I might have overreacted."

A slow, incredulous smile stole over Nina's face. "Wait a second. Did you just apologize?"

"I don't think so. Did you hear the words *I'm sorry*? That's the technical definition of an apology," Daphne countered, but she was smiling, too.

"You apologized!" Nina crowed. "It happened! I heard it!"

"Look, I just—I wanted to clear the air between us." Daphne ran her hands over the skirt of her gown, absently tracing its tulle layers. "Jefferson told me how you helped take care of him the other night. I'm really glad you were there."

Nina's amused joy was quickly overshadowed by guilt. She'd been trying not to think about what had happened between her and Jeff. Nothing *had* happened, she reminded herself, not really; she and Jeff might have flirted with the line, but they hadn't crossed it.

Yet she knew deep down that her excuses were flimsy. Here was Daphne—apologizing, trying to make things right between them—while Nina had been on a couch with her boyfriend, late at night, practically cuddling.

She resolved not to do anything like that again, not as long as Jeff and Daphne were dating.

"It wasn't a big deal," she muttered, but Daphne didn't seem to have heard.

"Things have been strained with me and Jefferson lately." Daphne stared at the floor as she spoke. "Ever since school started, I've felt him drifting away. And that fight I picked in front of Gabriella didn't exactly help things." She lifted her gaze, flustered. "Sorry, I know you probably don't want to hear any of this—but what I'm trying to say is that I'm glad you and Jefferson are friends again."

Nina realized, stunned, that Daphne *trusted* her.

And Nina had violated that trust. Even if she and Jeff hadn't actually kissed, they shouldn't have put themselves in a position where they might. It wasn't fair to Daphne.

"Of course. You know I'll always help Jeff. We've been friends forever," Nina managed to say.

When they had finally worked their way through the stack of dresses, Daphne decided on a violet gown that they both agreed would wipe the smile from Gabriella's face. Nina, meanwhile, was torn between a black one-shouldered gown and a dress of ecru silk with stitched rosettes.

She and Daphne stared silently at the pair of gowns, which hung side by side on the fitting-room wall.

"Normally I would say you can't wear anything white or off-white after Labor Day." Daphne fingered the delicate embroidery. "I think this might be an exception, though. It's so beautiful."

"The black one is safer," Nina pointed out.

"Since when do you play it safe? Especially with your fashion choices."

There was something almost envious in Daphne's tone, as if she wished she could occasionally dress a little more like Nina—or *behave* a little more like Nina, doing what she wanted instead of what she thought other people wanted her to do.

"You're right," Nina agreed. "Meet you at the register?"

She waited until Daphne was checking out before dialing her mamá's number. Isabella picked up on the second ring.

"Mamá?" Nina pulled the curtain shut, lowering her voice. "Sorry to bother you; I just need your advice."

The clicking sound of her mamá's typing fell silent. "I'm listening."

"Do you think people can change?"

She could practically see her mamá's puzzled smile as she replied. "Do you want to tell me what this is really about?"

Nina looked at her reflection as she answered, as if she was addressing this to herself as much as Isabella. "I've been spending time with someone I used to hate, someone who really hurt me. But now, I don't know. I feel like we're . . . friends?" she said hesitantly. "Do you think that's possible?"

"Anything is possible," her mamá assured her. "And of course people can change. What kind of world would this be if they couldn't? We need to believe that, or there's nothing worth fighting for."

"I just never expected this," Nina admitted.

Her mamá chuckled. "Oh, Nina. The world can be funny like that."

34

BEATRICE

Breakfast this morning was served out on the lawns, since the great hall was already set up for the League of Kings closing banquet. When Beatrice had walked past earlier, she'd seen dozens of staff bustling about, polishing crystal wineglasses and setting out place cards. One footman was measuring a place setting with a *ruler*; another knelt at the base of the table, holding a handheld steamer over the tablecloth.

As if Bellevue weren't crowded enough already, even more people were arriving for tonight's event. Every royal in attendance could invite a plus-one, and while some hadn't bothered to make the trip, a surprising number of guests had arrived, from queens consort and crown princes to boyfriends and casual dates. There weren't many occasions that brought together nearly *all* the world's royals, after all. You could hardly expect them to pass up the chance to preen and show off for one another.

Jeff, Daphne, and Nina were arriving this afternoon, too, plus all the lords attendant and ladies-in-waiting and their families. But the only plane Beatrice could really think about was the one bringing Teddy here from Boston. They hadn't been apart this long since they had first fallen in love, and Beatrice knew that so many things remained unspoken between them.

She shoved aside her worry and glanced around the lawn, where royals lounged at cedar picnic tables and gossiped contentedly. A buffet table along the side of the gardens held breakfast pastries of all kinds, from sugar-dusted doughnuts to dumplings to Greek butter cookies. The sun glittered tantalizingly on the water, the way it used to dance over the Charles River when Beatrice was at Harvard. Actually, today felt oddly like the last day of school: it had the same eager energy, the sense of looming freedom after one last exam—or, in this case, one more day of voting. The monarchs lounging in Adirondack chairs had the same blithe carelessness that college seniors did when they sat around before graduation tossing Frisbees and drinking beer.

Unlike at her Harvard graduation—when Beatrice had attended receptions with the university president and school board, being curtsied to and congratulated, while her classmates went to off-campus parties—Beatrice felt like she was in the center of things.

Ever since she'd returned from Versailles, the other queens and kings had looked at her differently. They respected her, or at the very least were intrigued by her. It was as if the magnetic aura that surrounded Louise had expanded, pulling Beatrice into its golden glow.

She headed to where Alexei, Bharat, and Sirivannavari sat at a picnic table. She wasn't sure where Louise was, but she had a feeling Samantha was with Marshall. They'd been seeing a lot of each other lately, mainly here at Bellevue to avoid the media and Marshall's family.

"When does Raj arrive?" Beatrice asked Bharat, sliding onto the bench opposite him.

Bharat grinned. His date was an up-and-coming Bollywood star, famous for his killer dance moves. "Last night. He's already out by the pool."

Sirivannavari gave a dramatic sigh. "I can't believe you invited a date when this is our last night together for *months*! When are we next going to see each other, anyway?"

"Verbier?" Beatrice suggested.

Alexei shook his head. "We shouldn't wait until ski season; let's do something sooner."

Beatrice smiled. Now that her suspicions about him and Louise had been confirmed, she understood exactly why he'd said that. "Have any of you ever celebrated an American Thanksgiving?"

The conversation went on like this. Beatrice let the waves of it lap over her, chiming in occasionally, her mind still half-focused on the upcoming climate-accord vote.

Louise didn't appear until the end of breakfast, her gaze hidden behind cat-eye sunglasses. "Louise. There you are," Beatrice said warmly, standing up.

Her friend greeted her with her usual double kiss, but she seemed oddly distracted. "Shall we go inside? We have a lot of voting ahead of us."

♛

The morning was a strange blur, in that way that time can seem to both speed up and slow down when you're prickling with nervous energy. Beatrice tried to focus on each proposal as it came up for a vote: a massive trade agreement that renegotiated tariffs, a recommitment to global disarmament. Now the assembly had just finished tallying its votes on a resolution called "Responsible Investment in Agriculture and Food Systems: A Fight to End Hunger."

There was a brief interlude of shuffling papers and muttered conversations; then King Frederick, still the league's chairman, made eye contact with Beatrice. "Next up for a vote is item thirty-one, 'Protection of the Global Climate for

Future Generations,' proposed by Her Majesty the Queen of America."

He cleared his throat and began reading the summary of her climate accord:

"The global nature of climate change calls for international cooperation. This proposal aims to reduce greenhouse gas emissions, as well as reexamine each nation's effective contribution . . ."

Beatrice tried not to squirm nervously in her seat. For weeks she'd been drumming up support for this proposal, cornering her fellow monarchs in small-group sessions or at dinner to persuade them of her reasoning. She'd even asked Queen Maud of Sweden to join her on a walk with Franklin— she was famous for loving dogs—and invited King Takudzwa of Zimbabwe on the sailboat one morning, since he was an avid fisherman.

What surprised Beatrice was how many people made conditional promises, agreeing to vote her way as long as someone *else* did. Bharat's father had promised her his vote, provided that it didn't anger the Queen of England. Queen Irene and King Juan Pablo had hemmed and hawed, then told her they would vote her way as long as Louise did. And of course there were all those monarchs at the party on the yacht, who'd sworn to give her their votes after she beat Dmitri at poker.

"We shall now begin the voting," Frederick said gruffly. "Albania."

It was so tedious that they voted this way, each country casting its vote one at a time, but Beatrice had stopped questioning protocol at this conference.

"No," King Zog of Albania said decisively.

What? Beatrice had assumed Albania was a shoo-in; King Zog usually voted however the tsar did. Hadn't Dmitri talked to him?

A minute later Beatrice was in a cold, sweating panic. So

far Finland and Canada were the only ones who'd supported her. It was all okay, she told herself; they still had so much of the alphabet to go.

"France," Frederick called out.

It took a moment for Beatrice to realize that Louise wasn't saying anything.

Silence stretched across the room. Beatrice glanced over and saw that her friend's eyes were closed, as if she felt dizzy or faint. *Stop the voting,* she was about to call out. Couldn't everyone see that Louise needed a doctor?

Then Louise opened her eyes and looked straight at Beatrice, her features etched with regret. Beatrice's stomach swooped in sickening understanding as Louise finally spoke.

"No."

The rest of the vote went by in a whirlwind. The room had gone blurry, but Beatrice gritted her teeth and held her chin high, swallowing back her tears even though they burned at her eyelids. Louise had deserted her.

Louise, her confidante, her *friend,* who'd taken Beatrice under her wing and made her feel warm and glowing and worthy. Louise, who'd begged Beatrice to come to France with her because she couldn't bear to face her father alone. Who'd cried on her shoulder, told her secrets out under the stars.

Louise, whom she'd made the mistake of trusting.

The *nos* cascaded after that, stacking one atop the other in a devastating landslide of rejection. Tsar Dmitri voted in favor of the accord, as promised—a Romanov always kept his word, didn't he—but by then it didn't really matter. The rest of them kept on denying her, one king or queen after the other.

Beatrice felt everyone casting avid, curious glances her way. Whispers rumbled through the room. *Did you see her face?* they were probably asking one another. *She thought she had the votes, and look how wrong she was. Even her best friend didn't support her.*

Not to mention that the newspapers would eat her alive. They would take this vote as more proof that Beatrice could never accomplish anything, that she couldn't hold her own amid more experienced rulers. That she was flighty and young and irresponsible.

Beatrice kept her gaze resolutely forward. She couldn't bear to look at Louise and risk bursting into tears at her friend's betrayal.

She'd thought they were friends, but in the end, what she'd told Teddy all those weeks ago was true. Hers was a lonely and isolating job, one that didn't really allow for friends. It had been a mistake, letting her emotions get in the way, thinking she could rely upon Louise.

Beatrice had never been able to rely on anyone but herself. She was in this role alone, and she always would be.

35

DAPHNE

There really was nothing so wonderful as a formal state ball, especially one filled with the most glamorous and influential people in the world. It made Daphne feel almost dizzy, as if she were drunk, or at altitude—and in a way she was both. Drunk on success, and at altitude because she'd ascended to the highest of social heights: the League of Kings farewell banquet.

The last time this party had taken place, Daphne hadn't been dating Jefferson yet. She'd still been a nobody, saving up to buy every last magazine at the newsstand and stare at the photos. The royals had all looked so breathtakingly untouchable: the men in jeweled sashes over the crimson or navy of their blazers, the women in tiaras and gowns that glittered like fire. And now Daphne was one of them, a character on the world's stage.

"There she is," Nina breathed. Daphne followed her gaze to where Gabriella stood across the ballroom.

Gabriella looked up as if she'd heard them. Her eyes darted in their direction, and she stared at them for a slow, smoldering moment before turning aside.

Daphne smiled, jubilant. Gabriella was wearing the purple gown Nigel had custom-designed for her; and even though it had probably cost a hundred times more than Daphne's vintage find, Daphne's was classic and tasteful. Unlike Gabriella's, which was covered in flounces and had a plunging V-neck.

It just went to show that *more expensive* didn't always translate to *better.*

Daphne looked at Jefferson, who was chatting a few yards away with the crown princes of Austria and Greece. Daphne had apologized profusely for that fight at the End of Session party, and Jefferson had said not to worry about it, but she could tell that things were strained. She'd hurt him, publicly, and violated the most valuable thing she had—his trust.

She glanced down at the signet ring on her hand. Its weight felt reassuring, its gold *W* gleaming with promise and possibility.

She may have made a mistake, but she could still fix it. She had done worse to her relationship with Jefferson before, and she'd always managed to fix things in the end.

Daphne knew she should head over to where Jefferson stood. Yet as strange as it was, she found that she would rather stay with Nina than go out there and charm people.

If Daphne's mother were here, she would have slapped her for her foolishness. But they had defeated Gabriella and saved her family's title. Didn't Daphne deserve a few minutes off from the endless, relentless climb that was her life?

"Do you know who all these people are, anyway?" Nina asked, glancing around the cocktail hour.

Daphne rolled her eyes indulgently. "Yes. And so should you." She nodded toward the stately white-haired woman in a shimmering cheongsam. "That's Empress Mei Ling. She's an *icon.* They say she invented the evening bag."

"That cannot be true. People have been using bags to hold their belongings since ancient times."

Daphne sighed. "She was the first person to carry a clutch with an evening gown. It's thanks to her that you're wearing a cute bag right now, instead of an embellished fanny pack."

Nina visibly brightened at the prospect of an embellished fanny pack, so Daphne hurried to continue. "That man with the dark mustache is Sebastian, the King of Chile. He's in some feud with the King of Bolivia, though no one knows precisely what it is. And that woman with the blond updo is Princess Louise of France."

Nina stared at Louise with idle curiosity. "Sam says that Louise and Beatrice have been hanging out a lot."

Daphne nodded to where Samantha stood with her boyfriend. "Speaking of hanging out, how are Samantha and Marshall?" For once, she wasn't trying to fish for gossip. It had just surprised her how readily the two of them had broken up, then gotten back together.

"It hasn't been easy on Sam. The whole situation is . . . complicated." Nina glanced over. "I'm guessing you saw the most recent *Time* magazine?"

Just yesterday, Sam and Marshall had been on the cover of *Time* under the headline WHAT HAS HAPPENED TO RACE RELATIONS IN AMERICA? The article featured interviews with a number of thought leaders, who were fiercely divided between adoration of Samantha and Marshall—they believed that America was overdue for an interracial royal relationship, that it was a powerful and important symbol of the changing times—and outraged cries that the relationship was a symbol of oppression, since Marshall would have to sacrifice his claim to the duchy if he and Sam ever got married. This group clamored that Marshall needed to dump Samantha publicly—because *that* would be an empowering gesture, far more than dating her would be.

Daphne couldn't relate to the pressures Marshall was under. She didn't have a position to renounce when she and Jefferson got married someday, and she certainly didn't carry the weight of an entire community on her shoulders. She stood for no one, except maybe little girls who twirled around in princess costumes and daydreamed about marrying a prince.

The realization was oddly distressing, actually. Shouldn't

she represent something bigger than the characters in animated movies?

Before she could voice this to Nina—if she could even figure out how—Daphne looked over and saw that Nina was tapping at her phone. "Put that away!" she hissed. It was poor form to be texting at an event like this.

Nina clearly didn't register what she'd said, because she looked up with a broad smile. "My financial aid was reinstated! The school just notified me by email. Said they were sorry for the mistake, that they reviewed my situation and updated my status, et cetera."

"That's amazing." Daphne had hoped that they wouldn't need to threaten Gabriella a second time. It was a relief to know that she'd actually done as they'd asked.

"It's all because of you! Thank you," Nina exclaimed.

And then, to Daphne's shock, Nina *hugged* her.

Daphne couldn't remember the last time someone had hugged her, at least not like this. A real, arms-around-torso, excited hug. Jefferson hugged her occasionally, but that was different. Her only real friend, Himari, wasn't exactly the hugging type, and Daphne's parents *definitely* weren't.

For a moment she just stood there stiffly, uncertain how to react. "Um . . . you're welcome," she said awkwardly, patting Nina's back.

When Nina stepped away, she was grinning ear to ear. "Oh, yum!" she declared as a waiter walked past with a tray of mini polenta cakes.

Why not? Daphne thought, and reached for one, too. "Now that my family situation is resolved, I think I'm going to start at King's College in the spring."

It was the first time Daphne had spoken those words aloud. She hadn't even mentioned it to her parents yet, but she assumed it would be okay. Now that their title was safe, surely she could find a way to enter school.

"I'm so glad. You're going to love it there," Nina said eagerly.

Daphne felt her phone vibrating in her purse, but ignored it. She shifted, searching for how to word this next question. "I was wondering if I could meet your friends sometime. If you don't mind, that is."

"You want to hang out with my friends?" Nina repeated, as if Daphne had spoken in a foreign language.

"It's not like I'm going to hang out with Gabriella and her gang."

Nina hesitated. "Daphne—my friends and I don't go to parties at Supreme Court justices' houses, or hire Kelli B to play our birthdays. We watch Jane Austen remakes on the TV in our room, and drink cheap wine out of paper cups, and go to parties where no one has a title."

"I can do all those things. You know I love Jane Austen," Daphne pointed out, and Nina laughed.

"So now that I've taken you vintage shopping and you've seen how the other half lives, you realize it's not all bad?"

"Maybe I've realized the benefit of being around people who are actually nice."

They were both silent for a moment. Then Nina said, "You know, there are only three of us in the room."

"Wait. Are you asking if I want to be your roommate?" Daphne didn't know whether she was appalled or fascinated by this notion.

"Oh god, no!" Nina hurried to say. "You would *hate* that."

"It's a terrible idea."

"We could never share space."

"We would destroy each other," Daphne agreed.

"What I meant was, the draw groups are four people, and we only have three." At Daphne's blank look, Nina explained. "A draw group means you enter the room lottery together. You could join us next year and put in for a single. We'd still

300

be in a triple, but you could live on our hall. So you'd be nearby, but still have privacy for, you know." Nina shrugged, her eyes twinkling. "Whatever witchy voodoo magic you need to do in your own space."

A room on the same hall as Nina and her friends. That should have seemed like an absolute nightmare, yet for some reason it didn't. Daphne barely registered that her phone was buzzing once more.

"Would I have to use a communal bathroom?"

"They're really not bad," Nina assured her.

"And eat in the dining hall?"

"Also not bad. Especially now that I know how you can put down a plate of tacos."

"On special occasions only," Daphne clarified, though she was smiling. "I don't know. That sounds kind of nice."

Daphne knew what her mother would say if she overheard this conversation. *It's a trap!* Rebecca would exclaim. *You can never trust other women, Daphne! They're all out for themselves, and will take any opportunity to tear you down.*

She was starting to think that her mother had been wrong. Perhaps because of everything she and Nina had been through together—because Nina had already seen everything Daphne was capable of, the good and the ugly—they could be honest with each other in a way that most women couldn't.

When her phone buzzed a third time, Daphne finally broke protocol and unclasped her clutch. She glanced down at the screen and sighed. Speak of the devil; it was her mother.

"Sorry, I need to take this." She held the phone against her dress and ducked into the hallway, waiting until she was past all the lingering royals and bustle of servers before she answered.

"Mother? I'm at the ball."

"I'm aware." Rebecca Deighton sounded angrier than Daphne had ever heard her; each word was as clipped and

301

vicious as the pluck of the harp strings inside the ballroom. "I just thought you'd like to know that your father has been stripped of his title."

No.

Daphne's mouth formed the word, but she hadn't actually spoken it aloud. She closed her eyes, clutched the phone tighter in her hand, and whispered, "No. That's not possible."

"I assure you that it's true," Rebecca snapped. "A messenger just arrived at the house to let us know the committee's verdict. And to collect our things."

Daphne knew precisely which *things* her mother meant. Her parents' coronets, their ermine-trimmed robes, their papers of nobility.

"Daphne," her mother went on, and somehow her voice had gone even sharper and icier. "What did you do?"

"I didn't do anything!"

It was an automatic response, the same thing Daphne used to say when she was a child and her mother slapped her for reaching for a cookie, or tracking mud in the house, or any of the other thousand transgressions she was constantly committing.

"Why did you get involved? I *explicitly* told you to speak to *no one*! Your father and I were handling it, but then you had to go antagonize Gabriella and ruin all our hard work!"

Daphne turned aside, leaning against a doorframe and lowering her voice. "I don't understand. Gabriella said she would get her father to drop the charges."

"She clearly lied to you!"

"But that can't be right; Nina got her scholarship back." Why would Gabriella have carried out Nina's request but not hers? Was it because she saw Nina as an irrelevant nobody, whereas Daphne was Jefferson's girlfriend, and an actual threat?

"What are you babbling on about? How is any of this related to Nina?" Rebecca spoke the name like a dirty word.

"I . . . nothing. Never mind." There was no use explaining her plan to her mother, not when it had gone so horribly wrong.

"You made a real mess of things, Daphne. You kicked the hornet's nest, and now the Madisons are out for blood. You should have come to me for advice before you tried whatever moronic scheme you came up with!"

"I was trying to help," Daphne said weakly.

"You failed! Peter was lobbying the committee members one at a time, trying to get them on his side. If you hadn't gotten involved, he might have had a fighting chance. But since you went after Gabriella, Ambrose Madison spoke out against Peter—and after that, there was no hope."

Daphne felt sick to her stomach. "I'm sorry."

"*Sorry* doesn't make up for the damage you've done. *Sorry* doesn't win us back our title. Do you even understand what position we're in now, Daphne? We're common! We aren't entitled to attend court events, our names don't appear in the social register, we're a plain *Mr. and Mrs.* now! We might as well be dead!"

"That's a bit of an overstatement, Mother." For some reason, Daphne thought of what Nina would say to all of this. "We're all healthy and safe, and things could certainly be worse."

"Healthy and safe? Things could be worse?" Rebecca repeated. "What is *wrong* with you? I would rather you were in the hospital, critically ill, than that you had disappointed me like this!"

Daphne recoiled as if she'd been slapped. She had always known that Rebecca wasn't the warm and cuddly, bedtime-story type. Yet it stung, hearing how little she cared about Daphne as anything but a vessel for her own ambition.

"Does everyone know?" Daphne whispered, eyes already cutting back down the hall in the direction of the ballroom.

"Technically the news shouldn't be released until the next Court Circular goes out, but you know how word travels. People are probably already talking," her mother snapped. "Daphne—what do you think Jefferson is going to do when he finds out? What about his mother? You expect Adelaide to let a common nobody marry her only son?"

"I'll figure this out. I just need time," Daphne said blindly, frantically.

"Time is the one thing you don't have. You'd better act tonight, before everyone learns of our disgrace." With that, Rebecca hung up the phone.

Daphne stood there for a moment, staring numbly at some portrait of a man in a wig and ruff without really seeing it. Her vision had gone blurry; she felt like she didn't dare take a step or she might vomit, pass out, tumble to the floor, scream.

What a traitorous snake Gabriella was. She'd assured Daphne that she would speak to her father, when clearly all she'd told him was that Daphne was harassing her, and that the Deightons needed to be taught a lesson.

Well, now Gabriella would learn a lesson of her own: that Daphne followed through on her threats.

Her breath coming in short gasps, Daphne logged onto the dummy email account she'd been using for the past months, every time she sold a photo to Natasha.

The Daily News *might be interested in this footage of Gabriella Madison,* she typed, and then attached the video, cropped so that only Gabriella was visible, snorting cocaine.

If Gabriella wanted to ruin Daphne's life, then Daphne would drag her down too.

SAMANTHA

"You really are a great date at events like this," Sam told Marshall as they walked in a slow loop around the ballroom. She'd discovered that as long as she kept moving, no one bothered her, because they all assumed she was headed to talk to someone else—but the moment she and Marshall fell still, a princess or king or another of the lords attendant would come say hello.

"Yes, obviously. But which of my many stellar qualities are you talking about?" Marshall quipped. "Because I'm tall, or well dressed, or a fantastic dancer?"

Sam smiled, though she saw that his heart wasn't fully in their banter. For the past week, she and Marshall had both been pretending that the rest of the world didn't exist. Aside from their afternoon at the football game, and a couple of events for the duchy—where he dodged questions from reporters about their relationship—Marshall had lain low, coming to visit Sam here at Bellevue.

And now they were on the cover of *Time* as the faces of America's problematic dialogue about race.

It felt like to America, she and Marshall were no longer people at all. They were symbols, whose value and purpose were decided by newspaper editors, by online commenters and movie directors, by the hundreds of people shouting each time they made an official appearance. By everyone, really, except for themselves.

Here at Bellevue, surrounded by royals who had their own countries to manage, they were able to skate by relatively unnoticed. But the real world was looming, and eventually they would have to face it.

"Sam, Marshall!" Nina hurried toward them. "Has either of you seen Daphne? She left about fifteen minutes ago, and I'm getting worried."

Sam frowned, confused. "*You* are worried about *Daphne?*" She knew they'd seen each other more often lately, because of Jeff, but when had they become friends?

"Her phone rang, and she got this weird look on her face and then disappeared. I have a bad feeling about it."

"I'm sure she's fine." Sam wondered if Jeff and Daphne were fighting again. Jeff had mentioned Daphne's strange behavior at the End of Session party.

For a moment, Sam hoped that Jeff would break up with Daphne, if only to divert some of the relentless speculation and attention from her and Marshall. Then she felt instantly ashamed of the thought. As much as she wanted freedom from the scrutiny, she certainly didn't want it at her brother's and Daphne's expense.

Besides, it shouldn't work that way. She and Marshall should be able to breathe without offering up her brother and his girlfriend as bait.

"I didn't know your aunt Margaret was coming," Marshall remarked, and Sam looked up. There was Aunt Margaret, walking into the ballroom in a one-shouldered gown of tie-dyed silk, still a West Coast hippie, even in formal attire.

Marshall took a step back. "Nina, want to take a lap with me? We can find Daphne."

Sam shot him a grateful look. She had a feeling that Aunt

Margaret had come for *her*, because she knew her niece could use some guidance right now.

When Aunt Margaret reached her, she pulled Sam into a hug. "How are you holding up?"

"Um, I don't . . . I'm not . . ." Suddenly Sam felt close to tears.

Aunt Margaret took her by the elbow. "Why don't we go get some dinner."

"Dinner isn't being served yet."

"That's why we should go now, before everyone else shows up," Margaret said crisply.

When they headed into the great hall, its long banquet tables arranged with goblets and gold plates polished to a shine, a few servers in uniform startled. Margaret ignored their reaction, waving her fingers at the closest young man.

"Excuse me! Can we get a grilled cheese?"

The footman shot Sam a panicked look. "Dinner will begin in thirty minutes. The main course is a choice between salmon and filet mignon—"

"A grilled cheese would be lovely." Aunt Margaret smiled charmingly. "Please? I know you have bread and cheese here."

He flushed a beet red and sprinted off. Margaret headed to a table and pulled out a chair, blatantly ignoring the folded ecru seating card, which read PHILIP, KING OF GREECE. Sam hesitated, then took the neighboring chair, where LAVINIA, QUEEN OF ITALY was apparently supposed to sit.

"Do you want to talk about it?" Aunt Margaret asked, shifting toward her niece.

Sam leaned her elbows on the table and braced her forehead in her hands. The words burst out of her, as if she'd been holding them back with a makeshift solution of Scotch tape and shoelaces that had broken at last.

"I don't know what to do! I want to just date Marshall

without worrying about the rest, except that clearly isn't possible. Our relationship has ballooned into this—this *thing* that's far bigger than either of us. People are treating us like some kind of symbol for our generation, as if the future of race relations in America hinges on our success as a couple. Not to mention this unresolved issue about the duchy, and Marshall having to renounce his title if we ever got married . . ." Sam faltered, let out a breath. "However hard this has been on me, it's infinitely worse for him."

Aunt Margaret nodded. "It's not easy for people who date us, is it? And Marshall faces all kinds of pressures. Because of the color of his skin, because people are ignorant and prejudiced, and because you're the spare."

"What do you mean?"

The footman reappeared with a grilled cheese on a gold-rimmed plate. "Thank you so much," Margaret said brightly. She took the butter knife from King Philip's place setting and cut the sandwich into quarters.

"It's different for someone who marries the heir—like your mother, or Teddy," she explained. "Don't get me wrong, being king or queen consort is still a thankless and taxing job. But being married to the *other* royal sibling . . . you're a secondary character in the history of this family, yet you're still required to give up your own role and titles in order to join it. No wonder it's so hard, finding someone who's willing to take that on."

Sam had always assumed that Aunt Margaret had dated so many men in her youth because she kept losing interest or meeting someone else. She'd never realized that Margaret's position, not her personality, might have been the problem.

"Were you—did someone break up with you because they didn't want to marry the spare princess?"

Margaret took a bite of grilled cheese, then set it back on the plate. "As I grew older, my royal responsibilities became increasingly second-tier. I had to open the out-of-the-way rural hospitals, deal with local Rotary clubs and Girl Scout chapters instead of members of Congress or boards of directors. I wasn't doing anything that actually mattered." She sighed. "Enjoy the royal tours and League of Kings conferences while they last, because soon enough you'll be out of the spotlight. Why do you think I moved to Orange and started making all these movies? At least my life belongs to me."

My life belongs to me, too, Sam wanted to say, but the words stuck in her throat. Aunt Margaret was right. No one in this family had a real purpose except for Beatrice—the only Washington who truly mattered.

Someday Beatrice would get married and have babies, and those children would become her heirs, not Sam. Sam's career would have peaked at the ripe old age of nineteen.

She smoothed her hair over one shoulder and ventured a question. "Did you ever consider doing what Prince Franz did, just leaving it all behind?"

Margaret blinked. "Prince Franz. There's a name I haven't heard in a while."

"You knew him?"

"I met him years ago, when I followed in his footsteps and ran away to Hawaii. He was in his seventies by then."

"You . . . what?"

Margaret handed her one of the grilled-cheese squares, and Sam popped it into her mouth whole. It had been made with truffle oil.

"It didn't last long, obviously," her aunt went on. "I ran off for a few months, lived on the beach. Worked a rather boring job at a boat-rental company."

"You had a job?"

"No need to look so shocked! I just worked the front office, mostly answering the phone. It's funny," Margaret reminisced. "In Hawaii, no one really cared who I was. They didn't treat me like a princess, or like a celebrity, or like a villain. They didn't treat me like anything at all, really, except an ordinary person."

"Why did you leave?"

Margaret traced her fingers over the delicate gold rim of the plate. "I was lonely. And I suppose I wasn't brave enough to live anonymously. As much as I felt constrained by all the pomp and circumstance in my life back home, there was something reassuring about it, too." She looked plaintively at Sam, willing her to understand. "Being a princess was the scaffolding that had defined my entire life. Once I no longer knew *what* I was, I had trouble figuring out *who* I was."

Sam sat in silence for a moment, letting that sink in. Leaving her family, her role, everything she'd trained for her entire life—no wonder Aunt Margaret had been scared.

But then, wasn't that precisely what she would be asking of Marshall, if they got married someday?

"What should I do?" she asked, her voice small.

"Oh, Sam." Margaret reached over to squeeze her hand. "Only you can answer that question."

"I don't want to come between Marshall and his family. They don't approve of him dating me."

"They don't approve of him dating a *princess*," Margaret corrected gently.

"Well, that's who I am. Unless—"

Unless she gave it all up.

Sam felt suddenly guilty that she'd never considered it until now. This whole time, she'd assumed that Marshall would renounce his identity, because that was what people had done for centuries when they married into the royal family. But what if *she* was the one to walk away from her life?

If she wasn't a princess anymore, all their problems would be solved.

Aunt Margaret had said it herself: being the spare royal

sibling, or the spouse of a spare sibling, wasn't a fulfilling job. Certainly not the type of job worth sacrificing a dukedom for.

Sam felt newly energized, slightly exhilarated, utterly terrified.

"Thank you." Her voice was raw and throaty with emotion. "I just—I never felt like I had a lot of choice in my life, you know?"

"You always have a choice, Sam. No matter what your name is or what family you're born into, that is the one thing you have control over—your own choices. And as important as it is to honor legacy, it can't come at the expense of your own happiness."

Sam nodded. History was history, wasn't it? It was important, but only insofar as it informed the future.

And while she didn't know what her future held, she hoped it included Marshall.

Margaret slid the remaining half of the sandwich toward her. "Here. I've found that while a grilled cheese won't solve my problems for me, it makes them a bit easier to manage. Don't you agree?"

37

BEATRICE

Beatrice glanced at the mirror in the downstairs bathroom, removing a pin that had fallen loose from the nest of pins anchoring her tiara in place. She could make it through the rest of this dinner. Just a few more hours of people staring at her with naked curiosity—wondering why the vote on her climate accord had gone so wrong, and what had happened between her and Louise.

Even Beatrice didn't know the answer to that one. Louise had been texting and calling ever since the vote this afternoon, but Beatrice had left her messages unanswered. She'd even come into the great hall before dinner—and caught Sam and Aunt Margaret sharing a grilled cheese, which brought a smile to her face—in order to switch the place cards, moving Louise to a table far from Beatrice.

At least Teddy was back from Boston. When he'd arrived a few hours before dinner, Beatrice had told him everything. He'd assured her that she shouldn't blame herself, that it wasn't her fault. But Beatrice was having a hard time believing that.

"Béatrice. Here you are."

Of course, she thought dully. She should have known Louise would follow her in here.

"What do you want?"

Louise winced at her tone. "I wanted to apologize for what

happened with the climate accord. I know it meant a lot to you." She smiled tentatively. "You should bring it up again at the next conference; this was a good way to get it on everyone's radar, and you'll have a much better shot the second time around."

"I don't want to try again next conference. I wanted it to pass *now!*" Beatrice realized that she sounded childish and shook her head. "Why didn't you support me?"

"I did support you; I just couldn't give you my vote. Politics is full of difficult choices."

"And apparently people who go back on their word."

"You think I didn't *want* to vote for your climate accord?" Louise asked, her voice rising. "Unlike you, I am not a queen, just a lowly princess! I don't have the luxury of always choosing how I act!"

Louise's words echoed around the bathroom, bouncing off the shagreen wallpaper, the pair of lounge chairs that no one ever actually sat in. She stared down at her hands, studying her various antique and priceless rings as if one of them might hold the answer to all her questions.

"Remember how I spoke to my father late at night in Versailles, when he was more . . . himself?" she went on softly.

"Your father told you to vote against my climate accord?"

"My father told me to do a better job guarding the interests of France!" Louise burst out. "He has always scolded me for being weak and easily swayed. He says that I need to think of France first, and the rest of the world second. He was angry when he found out about you."

"You mean, when he found out that I wasn't actually your lady-in-waiting?" Beatrice said sarcastically, and Louise almost smiled at that.

"Well, yes. When I told him that you're the Queen of America, and my friend, he was displeased."

There was a cold hard stone in Beatrice's throat; she

swallowed past it. "I don't know if we're friends. A friend would have at least warned me, instead of voting against me in public like that. Letting me be a laughingstock to everyone."

Their eyes met in the mirror. They stared at each other, these two women who had each, in different ways, been born to rule.

"I'm sorry," Louise said again. "As long as I'm still a Regent, I don't have full control over my decisions. I wanted to vote in your favor, but I kept thinking of what my father would say when he came back to himself and learned what I'd done. He would have been livid."

Beatrice's anger ebbed, leaving nothing behind but a desolate sadness. "You're the one who always says we should stand our ground, that people will try to marginalize us because we're young women! But then you betrayed me because you're scared of your father's disapproval?"

"I don't expect you to understand. Your family is so supportive, so warm and cuddly. But I've always been alone in this."

I feel alone, too, Beatrice wanted to say. *That's why I was so desperate to be your friend.*

Louise bit her lip. "I've been fighting all my life for a shred of my father's approval, and I never manage to get it."

"If he's that awful, then why do you care what he thinks?"

"He's still my father, and my king. And, like a fool, I kept hoping that he would wake up one day and say, 'What a wonderful job Louise has done during my illness!' I thought he might be proud of me for once."

Again, Beatrice felt so grateful that her own father had built her up—taught her to believe in herself—rather than torn her down.

"I looked up to you, you know," she told Louise. "You always seemed so independent, so *badass*. The type of person who voted according to her own beliefs, not someone else's."

"That's just the version of me that I want the world to see. I'm not actually that brave. Not like you," Louise said sadly.

To think that it had all been a mirage—that under the lipstick and black leather and flippant sarcasm, Louise was as insecure as anyone.

"Thank you for explaining things, I guess." Beatrice started out into the hall, and Louise chased after her. The lights from the sconces shimmered on the lamé panels of her gown.

"You're still upset with me; I can see it. But we need each other, you and I," Louise was saying. "We're the same."

Beatrice halted in her steps, whirling around to look at the French princess. "That was what I thought when we first met, but I was wrong. You and I aren't the same. I would never betray someone like this."

"You already have! Didn't you get rid of that bodyguard, the one you were in love with?"

Beatrice felt like the wind had been knocked out of her. "What does Connor have to do with anything?"

"Because *he* is the tough choice you made in the name of America, just like I made a tough choice for France," Louise insisted. "You got rid of the bodyguard so you could be with someone like Theodore, who is—what did you call him— 'selfless and sweet'? The type of man who will be your support system while you take the spotlight?"

"I love Teddy," Beatrice said fiercely, and Louise threw up her hands in a frustrated gesture.

"I never said you don't love him! But Theodore will never understand the sacrifices you have to make. I do, because I've already made them."

In that moment Louise looked far older than her twenty-eight years, her blue eyes vivid with longing and heartbreak. It saddened Beatrice, to think of everything that must have happened to put such shadows in those eyes.

"I'll see you around, Louise." She turned wearily back toward the great hall, only to fall still.

Teddy was standing there.

"How much did you hear?" she whispered as Louise brushed past.

"Enough."

"Teddy, I'm sorry." She reached for him, but he recoiled from her touch.

"You never told me he was your bodyguard." His words were hollow.

"I—what?"

"I knew that you were in love with someone before me, but you never told me who it was. I didn't realize it was your Revere Guard."

"What does that matter?" Beatrice asked, bewildered.

"I'm supposed to be your *fiancé*, and you've known Louise for, what, a month? Yet you told her something you've never shared with me."

"I'm sorry." Beatrice wasn't sure how to explain it. There had been something profound, almost sacred, about the way she and Louise had shared secrets that night, staring up at the stars. "We were having a serious conversation, and I knew I could trust her. I knew she would understand."

"Because I will never understand your life? Because I don't know the sacrifices you've made for the Crown?"

"Louise said those things, not me!" Beatrice exclaimed, frustrated.

"It's what you think, though, isn't it?" Teddy's eyes were like blue fire. "Look, I may not be queen, but I've made sacrifices for the Crown, too. A lot of them."

"I didn't ask you to do that!"

Instantly Beatrice knew she'd said the wrong thing. She reached once more for Teddy's hand, but he took a swift step back.

"That's true. You didn't," he said flatly. "I gave up the dukedom all on my own."

"Teddy, I didn't mean—"

"I thought we were on the same page, that we were building a life together. That it was you and me now."

Beatrice ached at the memory of when he'd said those words to her, the night she first started to love him, at his family's house in Boston.

"I always knew that I was signing up for a life of being your coworker," he went on. "But I hoped we were more than that, too. I thought you and I were figuring it out together, making each other stronger." He sighed. "It turns out I'm just your sweet, selfless, silent support system."

"When I told Louise that you were sweet and selfless, I meant it as a good thing!" Beatrice felt close to tears. She needed things to be right between them.

Teddy's face was closed off, but he held out his arm, his gesture stiff.

"They're about to serve dessert. That's why I came looking for you; people were starting to wonder where you'd gone."

"I'm sorry. Please, let's talk about this," she insisted, but it was like he'd turned to stone.

"We can talk later."

As they walked back into the ballroom, Teddy was smiling his glazed, distant smile: the one that he used to wear in front of paparazzi, before they had fallen in love. The sight of it nearly broke her.

Somehow, though it sent agony down every last fiber of her being, Beatrice managed to set aside her anguish and paste a smile on her own face, too. Because she was a Washington, and this was a state banquet, and that was how things were done.

38

DAPHNE

Everyone knew, didn't they?

Daphne was on autopilot, chatting with Prince Bharat's date—a Bollywood star with a blinding smile and easy charm—but she hardly registered what he was saying. She felt everyone staring at her, whispering that she was a nobody now. They were clearly delighted at her family's disgrace, though they masked their glee in tones of honeyed pity. Daphne wasn't sure how they'd all found out; probably Gabriella had been circling the room all night, sharing the news. Even if she hadn't, word would still have spread. A good piece of gossip always finds its way.

The guests were still here in the great hall, though many of them had left their seats to mill about. They had reached the dessert portion of the meal; footmen appeared at the table with platters of three types of cake: a chocolate raspberry, a lemon chiffon, and a crisp white cake with almond frosting. Daphne wondered numbly if these had been the flavors of wedding cake at the reception Beatrice had canceled.

She caught sight of Gabriella a few tables over, deep in conversation with her father, who looked more arrogantly smug than ever, and the Emperor of Japan. Gabriella must have felt Daphne's gaze on her because she glanced up, and a slow, eager smile spread over her red lips. She looked like she'd been expecting this conversation all night: looking forward to it, even.

Gabriella murmured something to her father, curtsied deeply to the emperor, then cut across the room. "Hello," she said sweetly, pulling out the empty chair next to Daphne.

Bharat's date—Daphne had already forgotten his name—said hi to Gabriella, then excused himself to go hunt down more cake. Maybe he felt the tension gathering in the air, thunderous as a summer storm.

"How dare you?" Daphne was still smiling, because at an event like this you never knew who was watching, but her words were like daggers. "I thought we had an agreement."

Gabriella laughed, a sound like a crystal champagne flute smashing into pieces. "That was your mistake. I never agreed to anything."

"No, *your* mistake," Daphne seethed. "I would have actually held up my end of the bargain and deleted that video if you'd protected my family's title. But instead you came after us, so I went after you. I sent that video to the *Daily News*, Gabriella. What do you think your parents will do when they see it? Send you to rehab? And what about your adoring public?" Daphne lowered her voice, adopted a slightly mocking tone. "Now you'll never be able to fulfill your lifelong dream of modeling for Nigel!"

"Poor Daphne," Gabriella said slowly. "Don't you realize that my parents couldn't care less about that video? I've been getting drugs from Daddy's dealer for years."

Daphne blinked, and Gabriella laughed that high-pitched, strident laugh again. "Daddy always made up these flimsy excuses about why Julien was showing up at the house, pretending he was an intern with sensitive documents, when we all knew those folders were filled with cocaine and weed. When I asked Julien to start bringing some to *me*, he didn't even flinch. So I hate to break it to you, but my parents already know, and they can't be bothered to do anything about it."

That might have been one of the saddest things Daphne had ever heard.

"Still, I didn't exactly want that video making the rounds of the internet. I have a reputation to uphold, especially with my many philanthropies. Like the Youth Charity League." Gabriella made a disapproving *tsk* noise. "But when you were blackmailing me, you made the mistake of mentioning the *Daily News*. Come on, Daphne, don't you know that Daddy has been golf buddies with the owner since college? That paper would *never* slander our family."

She stared at Daphne with such caustic disdain, it transformed her beautiful features into something ugly. And Daphne wondered, suddenly, why the world rewarded people like Gabriella, people who inflated their own self-image by making others feel small. What right did Gabriella have to look through other people like they were invisible?

"I feel sorry for you," Daphne told her.

Vaguely, she remembered Nina saying the same thing to her once, when Daphne had treated Nina just as cruelly as Gabriella was now treating her.

Nina, who approached everyone with empathy and warmth—even Daphne, her sworn enemy. Nina, who placed an intrinsic value on other people for the simple fact that they were *people*, and had feelings that could hurt.

It struck Daphne that Nina was more a lady than Gabriella would ever be, no matter how common the world might say she was.

"You feel sorry for *me*?" Gabriella scoffed. "God, you're even stupider than I thought. I knew exactly what you would do tonight, Daphne, and you played right into my hands."

Daphne looked up at that. "What?"

"I *wanted* you to send in that video. When you mentioned

the *Daily News* last week, it got me thinking about all these never-before-seen photos of you and Jeff that have leaked recently," Gabriella said smugly. "I told Daddy that someone would email in a video of me tonight. That if it came from the same email address all those photos had come from, we'd know the culprit was you. And I was right."

"I have no idea what you're talking about." Daphne sounded braver than she felt.

"You thought all I was going to do was strip your father of his miserable little title? Daphne, *no one* messes with me and gets away with it." Gabriella was still smiling, her teeth bared. "I'm not done yet."

Daphne liked to think that she was prepared for anything. She always had a plan; and if that failed, she had a backup plan; and in the worst-case scenario she had an escape route.

Yet for once her mind was utterly blank.

She felt like one of those women in an ancient myth who'd been turned into a statue, unable to move or speak as Gabriella braced an arm on the back of her chair and twisted her torso around, letting her hair fall in a glossy cascade down her back. "Hey, Jeff! Come sit with us!"

It was a violation of protocol to shout across a party like that; a few queens and princes sniffed disdainfully. But of course Jefferson didn't mind. He bounded toward them, then sprawled easily in the chair across from Daphne.

"Hey, guys. How's it going?" When neither woman spoke, his smile faltered a little. "Um . . . did I miss something?"

Gabriella didn't waste any time. "What you've missed is that your girlfriend has been selling photos to the press."

Jefferson looked at Daphne, his brow furrowed in confusion.

She swallowed. "I—it's not like that—"

"I'm sorry, what is it like?" Gabriella said crisply. "Did you or did you not sell photos to the *Daily News?*"

Daphne's mind whirled at hyperspeed, searching for a way out of this, but came up blank. Jefferson was staring at her, stricken.

"Daphne?" he prompted.

How many times had she lied to him? And yet, when she needed to most, she couldn't bring herself to tell another lie—not to Jefferson, not anymore. Maybe she was weary of all the subterfuge and deceit.

Maybe she'd started to realize what it meant to be a decent human being, even if she'd come to that realization far too late.

"I did," she confessed, and he recoiled as if stung. Daphne leaned forward. "Please, let me explain."

"What possible explanation could there be? Daphne, I trusted you!"

While she and Gabriella had been talking in near whispers, Jefferson had raised his voice angrily. A few people glanced over, intrigued, sensing the tension in the air. Daphne felt the low rumble of gossip spreading outward from them, but strove to ignore it.

"I'm sorry! I was desperate. My father was going to lose his baronetcy and my parents told me I can't go to college and I felt overwhelmed." Daphne narrowed her eyes at Gabriella. "That's why Nina and I teamed up against Gabriella. We just wanted her to stop attacking us!"

"Nina? How is she involved in any of this?" Jefferson cut in.

Daphne remembered that Nina's scholarship had been reinstated, and she wondered, yet again, why Gabriella had done precisely what Nina asked, yet drawn out the big guns to destroy Daphne. A sticky, sickening suspicion began to coalesce in her chest, but she ignored it.

Nina wouldn't betray her like that.

"Gabriella told her father to take away my family's title, and she tried to get Nina kicked out of King's College, so

Nina and I spied on her," Daphne said urgently. Jefferson looked at Gabriella, who feigned shock.

"Those are outrageous accusations," Gabriella said gravely. "Why would I do anything to hurt Nina? I hardly know the girl."

This was wrong, all wrong. Daphne realized she was babbling; she felt her credibility slipping away, felt Jefferson staring at her with mounting disapproval.

"We caught Gabriella doing cocaine!" Daphne fumbled to pull up the video on her phone, then shoved it toward Jefferson.

None of them said anything as he watched. Daphne was certain more people were staring at them, but for once, she didn't care about public opinion. She was far too worried about Jefferson's opinion.

When the video finished, he slid the phone back across the table, then shook his head at Gabriella. "Honestly, Gabriella, you need to cool it with that stuff. You're not in France anymore."

There was a momentary flash of irritation on Gabriella's face, so lightning-fast that only Daphne noticed it; then her features melted into a mask of contrition. "I know, you're right," she simpered. "Actually, I almost never get high anymore, but Daphne asked me if I had any. She was trying to trap me!"

"Because *you* were trying to trap *me!*"

Gabriella turned toward Jefferson. "Daphne got some upsetting news tonight, and I'm afraid she hasn't taken it well. Her father's baronetcy was taken away because he engaged in some *ungentlemanly behavior.*"

Gabriella's concern was false—Daphne could see straight through it, all the way to her false, lying core—but she couldn't deny what had happened.

"It's true. I'm not noble anymore." She held her breath, waiting, tormented and anxious.

And Jefferson shrugged.

"So?" he asked. "What does that have to do with anything?"

"She's a commoner, Jeff!" Gabriella said *commoner* as if it were an especially nasty disease.

"Gabriella, can you give us a moment alone?" Jefferson asked quietly.

"Of course," Gabriella purred. She flounced off in a tossing of hair and swishing of skirts, practically crackling with self-satisfaction.

Daphne's heart was thudding as Jefferson turned back to her, his voice heavy with disappointment.

"I'm sorry about your dad," he said carefully, "but, Daphne, when has someone's title ever mattered to me? You know I couldn't care less about that."

Some part of Daphne had known this, hadn't she? Jefferson wouldn't have broken up with her because of her family's loss in status. If she'd been honest with him from the beginning, he would have stood by her—and his support would have protected her, until everyone had forgotten the scandal and moved on.

"I don't care about titles," Jefferson went on, "but I *do* care that you've been colluding with the press, selling photos and secrets. Why would you do something like that?"

"I needed money," Daphne whispered. She was past the point of lying anymore; as if, now that she'd started telling Jefferson the truth, it was a faucet she couldn't turn off.

"So you sold photos of our private moments, in order to . . . what? Buy a few new dresses?"

You don't get it! she wanted to cry out in helpless frustration. Jefferson would never understand how it felt to worry about money, or his position, or, as frivolous as it might seem, what he should wear. He could show up in the same suit to everything, and it wouldn't matter! Whereas Daphne faced an army of fashion bloggers who scrutinized her every outfit piece by piece, down to speculation on her *underwear*.

She'd just wanted to look the part of a princess, as everyone expected her to. She hadn't meant it to come at the expense of Jefferson's feelings.

"I know I messed up. I just . . . I didn't want you to be ashamed of me," she said hoarsely.

"I'm ashamed of you now."

She sucked in a shaky breath. "Let me fix this, please."

"I don't think you can," Jefferson told her. "You haven't been acting like yourself for a while now."

As if he even knew what it was like when she *did* act like her real self.

"I've been dealing with a lot," she started to say, but Jefferson spoke over her.

"We're all dealing with a lot, Daphne! I lost my dad this year! That doesn't mean I have free license to take advantage of the people I love," he said darkly. "I've been trying to make excuses for your behavior, but I don't know how to explain this. For years, you have been one of the few people I trusted, and I thought you appreciated what that meant."

"I'm sorry," she repeated, because there was nothing else to say.

Jefferson stood and ran a hand over his hair, looking wounded and bewildered. "I have to go."

Daphne knew better than to chase after him. She just sat there and watched as he walked away.

39

SAMANTHA

Samantha found Beatrice at the front of the ballroom, surrounded, as always, by a cluster of people. Though she noted,
surprised, that Teddy wasn't one of them.

"Bee! Do you have a minute?" Sam couldn't handle the
clamor of her own thoughts anymore. She had to talk this
out with someone, and as amazing a friend as Nina was, she
needed her sister right now.

Especially because some of what she was thinking—
hoping—was a problem that only Beatrice could help solve.

"Of course, Sam. What's going on?"

Sam was so eager to unload all her confusion on Beatrice,
it took a moment for her to notice that her sister didn't look
quite right. Her gown was spectacular, a deep gunmetal gray—
much more sophisticated than Beatrice's usual pastels or
champagne-colored choices—with metallic embroidery scattered over the bodice. Its shimmer echoed the diamonds that
flashed at her throat, in her ears, atop her dark brown hair.

But there was something mechanical and forced about Beatrice's smile. She kept glancing around the room, distracted,
and there were purple shadows beneath her eyes.

Sam frowned. "Are you okay?"

"It's been a long night," Beatrice said evasively. A few wisps
of hair had come free from her sleek updo, which wasn't at all

like Beatrice; Sam reached up to fix one, feeling guilty. She'd been so swept up in her own problems that she hadn't exactly been a great support system for Beatrice lately.

"Forget it. We can talk later," Sam started to say, but Beatrice shook her head.

"You know I always have time for you. Should we go somewhere a little more private?"

Beatrice led them out of the ballroom and down the hallway, where she pushed open the door to her study. Sam realized that she hadn't been in here since the day of the photo shoot.

Beatrice settled into an armchair, but Sam wandered restlessly over to the desk. She picked up a clay hedgehog that she'd made for her father in second grade, which he—and now apparently Beatrice—used as a paperweight.

"I remember when I made this hedgehog for Dad."

"That's a hedgehog? I always thought it was a skunk," Beatrice said, with a hint of a smile. "Or a rat?"

"Why would I have made a rat sculpture?"

"Beats me. It just seemed like something eight-year-old Sam would have done," Beatrice replied. She had a point.

Sam moved the hedgehog restlessly from one hand to the other. "I miss Dad so much."

"So do I, Sam. All the time."

Their shared sorrow hung in the air between them. It was easy for Sam to think of her grief as something she carried alone, like a locket she could never take off, the weight of its chain forever there on her chest.

But of course, it wasn't like that at all. They were all grieving for her dad: she and Beatrice, Jeff, their mom, the entire *world*. It was more accurate to think of their grief like the swell of the ocean, its soft rumble always in the background, something they could all sense, and share.

Sam felt Beatrice looking at her and came to sit in the opposite armchair. Still she kept fidgeting, setting the hedgehog on a glass side table and picking up a book, fanning idly through its pages. Beatrice was patient, waiting for her to speak.

"I talked with Aunt Margaret tonight."

"I know—I saw you two in the great hall. I went in a few minutes before dinner to switch some of the seating arrangements," Beatrice explained.

"That's shockingly rebellious."

"I've been throwing protocol to the wind a lot more often these days."

"Looks like I'm finally rubbing off on you." Sam hesitated, trailing a finger over the book's gilded spine. Some of the embossed letters of the title were peeling. "Did you know that when Aunt Margaret was young, she ran away to Hawaii for a while and worked at a boat-rental company?"

"I didn't know, though I'm not all that surprised."

"It sounds kind of nice, doesn't it?" Sam asked.

"Renting out boats?"

"Being normal."

Beatrice was watching her with the quiet focus their dad used to use when making a decision. Sam swallowed and continued.

"This week at the football game, when Marshall and I were just sitting up in the stands like an ordinary couple . . . it felt amazing," Sam explained. "Like we were free for the first time in months." Free of people's expectations and snap judgments, free of the paparazzi, free of the demands of their positions.

Beatrice nodded. "I feel that way about me and Teddy sometimes. That if we were different people, everything would be so much easier, less complicated." She attempted a laugh, but it didn't come out right. "To be fair, if we were different people, we might never have met."

"You and Teddy are great together," Sam said fiercely.

"Sam—you should see this."

Beatrice headed over to her desk, then shuffled through the papers until she found Teddy's statement of renunciation in one of the stacks. She handed it to Sam, who pretended to read it for the first time.

"You should be relieved that Marshall hasn't done anything this drastic," Beatrice added, her voice breaking.

Sam jumped to her feet. "Bee, it's okay," she exclaimed, pulling her sister close.

Beatrice sagged into the hug, resting her head on Sam's shoulder, messing up both their neatly styled curls. Sam thought she felt tears on the skin of her collarbone.

"He's so angry with me." Beatrice's words came out muffled.

"Teddy?" Sam clarified. "What could he possibly have to be angry with you about?"

Beatrice stepped back, so that Sam's hands fell to her sides. "I took him for granted. My role as queen . . . it's driven something of a wedge between us."

Which was exactly what Sam's position as princess had done to her and Marshall.

As usual, when she wasn't sure what to say, Sam fell back on what she knew best—history and humor. "This is the modern version of the Prince Albert problem."

"The what?"

"Queen Victoria's husband, Albert," she explained. "It was a recurring issue in their marriage that she had all the power and he had none. He'd given up his German estates—to be fair, they were pretty minor estates—to move to England and marry her, and then he had nothing to do."

Beatrice blinked, her eyes still glassy. "Did they figure out a solution?"

"Albert found other ways to keep busy aside from governing. He was the chairman of Cambridge University, and a total science nerd; he supported modern medicine and built the Victoria and Albert Museum. . . ." She trailed off at the expression on her sister's face. They both knew that wasn't really a solution.

"Marshall and I are dealing with a similar issue," she went on. "Except in some ways it's worse."

Because it was racially charged. Because unlike the Eatons, who adored Beatrice and the Crown, Marshall's family resented her. And because Sam wasn't the queen.

If they stayed together, and he married a princess, Marshall would be giving up a dukedom for a role even less impactful than Teddy's.

"Sometimes I just wish we didn't have to deal with all of this." Sam swept an arm to indicate her tiara, her gown, her sash and jewels. "It makes everything so much more complicated. It would just be easier if—if—"

Beatrice finished the sentence for her. "If you weren't a princess."

"Exactly," Sam said quietly.

"Sam, that's who you are. Unless . . ." Beatrice paused, comprehension dawning. "Unless you're saying that you want to walk away from it all. Renounce your place in the line of succession to be with Marshall."

Sam's heart thudded as she answered. "I don't want to make your job harder than it already is."

Beatrice grabbed her wrists, circling them to clutch Sam's hands in her own. "You listen to me, okay? This is about you and Marshall, not me or the fact that I'm queen. I'm not King Louis. You may be my successor, but you're my sister before anything else."

Sam didn't understand what Beatrice meant about not being King Louis, but she stayed silent.

"Sam—I'm going to ask you something that probably seems unfair," Beatrice went on. "A normal person wouldn't have to think like this, but as we've established, you and I are far from normal. Our family has always made major decisions at a young age. So I need you to think, and think hard." She squeezed Sam's hands for emphasis. "Is Marshall your forever?"

"My forever?" Sam repeated.

Beatrice's eyes were blazing. Sam realized that this was how her sister had looked when she'd stared down Robert Standish, when she'd postponed her wedding and gone out for a balcony appearance alone. She was adamantly fierce, resolute. Sam would have gone into battle for her without a second thought.

"If Marshall is really your forever—if you want to build a life with him—then you're right. You can't be a princess. And I will support you in that decision every step of the way. I'll take your renunciation bill to Congress myself; I'll train Jeff to be my new heir; I'll be your greatest champion and your strongest advocate."

Sam knew this was true, because that was what it meant to have a sister.

"But, Sam, walking away from the role you were born to: that's a monumental choice. You cannot make it lightly. And I won't support you unless you're unquestionably, totally sure. Unless you can look me in the eye and tell me that Marshall really is your forever."

Hearing that phrase, *your forever*, was sobering. But Sam knew her answer. She'd known it this whole time, hadn't she?

"He is. I'm all in."

"Then so am I," Beatrice said simply, and let go of her hands.

Sam cleared her throat. "Wow," she said, and it came out scratchy. "I mean—that was easier than I expected."

"What did you think, that I was going to pull rank on you?" Beatrice asked. "Have a little more faith in me."

"No—I just mean, I thought you might tell me to give up on Marshall. The way Dad told you to give up on Connor."

A shadow passed over Beatrice's expression. "Why is everyone bringing up Connor today?"

"What?"

"Never mind," Beatrice said quickly. "Sam, obviously I would miss you, if you were no longer a princess. Knowing that you're my heir, that you have my back—that's one of my favorite parts of this job. But more than anything, I want you to be happy. You love Marshall, and if this is what it takes for the two of you to be together . . ." She sighed. "Love comes first."

"Even before family?"

"Even before duty," Beatrice corrected. "You and I will always be family, whether you're a princess or a duchess or the captain of a speedboat in Hawaii. Hey, don't cry," she said softly, seeing Sam wipe at her eyes. "This is a happy decision."

"I just . . . I don't know what's going to happen," Sam said helplessly, and her sister nodded.

"No one does. That's the fun of life."

For the first time, Sam pictured a world she'd never given herself permission to imagine before—one where she wasn't a princess. Someday, in the future, she could marry Marshall and become a duchess.

Or she and Marshall could both walk away, together.

What if she could become someone else, someone entirely new, someone she hadn't yet discovered? Who would she be if she wasn't Her Royal Highness, the Princess Samantha?

This new self unfurled within her, stretched its leaves eagerly toward the sun.

40

BEATRICE

When she and Sam returned to the ballroom, Beatrice's eyes immediately landed on Teddy, who was talking with Marshall and a few other lords attendant. Sam smiled and started toward them, but Beatrice hung back. She was reeling from everything that had happened tonight—with Louise, with Teddy, and now with Samantha. Was Sam really going to walk away from the monarchy?

Beatrice didn't know whether she was happy for her sister, or afraid for her, or a tiny bit jealous. Even if she wasn't going to follow Sam's example and renounce her position as queen, part of her envied the freedom Sam might someday enjoy, if she really went through with this.

But then, Sam had always been the braver one. Beatrice was supposed to be older and wiser, yet the truth was that she looked up to Sam: her vibrant, passionate, determined little sister, who loved with her whole heart. Sam loved as easily as she breathed. Unlike Beatrice, who always held a piece of herself back, from Connor and even from Teddy.

She hadn't *meant* to; it was just the way she'd been trained. How many times had her father emphasized that this job was lonely and she needed to be self-sufficient? So Beatrice had relied on herself, and her new friendship with Louise.

In the process she'd managed to isolate Teddy, make him feel like someone who worked *for* her rather than *with* her.

For some ridiculous reason, Beatrice wished she could talk to Louise—the Louise she'd known before the treaty vote. She wanted the Louise who'd drawn eyeliner over her lids, taken her stargazing on the lawn of Versailles, spoken with such authority about men, and how women in power needed to stick together. That version of Louise would have understood the tension between Beatrice and Teddy, and known exactly what Beatrice should say to repair the damage.

But Beatrice realized, now, that she'd given Louise too much sway in their dynamic. She'd been so thrilled to enter Louise's circle of friends and feel like she belonged that she hadn't acted like the queen she should be.

Perhaps that was what prompted Beatrice to lift the hem of her gown and start up the stairs to the stage.

The band members exchanged glances, clearly unsure whether to keep playing. One by one they fell silent. Beatrice made eye contact with the cellist, who scooted back so that she could speak into his microphone.

"Hello."

There was a screech of feedback from the mic; she winced and looked out at the crowd. Their various conversations quickly cut off; everyone was staring at her with naked curiosity, wondering how she would embarrass herself next. She saw a few blinking lights as people got out their phones and began recording. It wasn't typical for the host monarch to give any kind of closing speech, especially not after the seated dinner, when the night was escalating into party mode.

"Hello, Your Majesties, and esteemed guests." Beatrice felt her face curling automatically into a smile, then squashed the impulse. Who had decided that women were supposed to smile during a formal speech anyway? She would be as serious and stone-faced as any man, and let them call her names for it.

"As you may know, this was my first time at the League of Kings conference as a queen, and the experience has been . . .

illuminating," she said carefully. "And surprising. And, in many ways, disappointing."

Eyebrows shot up at that remark; a few people exchanged whispers. Beatrice ignored them.

"I have always believed in the League of Kings. I believe that we can achieve what our forebears intended when they founded this institution. They wanted to combine efforts and make the world a better place, because they knew we could accomplish so much more together than any of us could as individual nations.

"I came here expecting a community of nations, yet what I have seen instead are disjointed groupings of monarchs, each of them jealously guarding what they see as their own resources, their own interests." She thought of King Louis XXIII as she added, "I have seen people motivated by fear, sometimes to the detriment of those they love. I have seen a sense of competition and petty jealousy lurking beneath conversations, when we should be striving toward the collective good.

"The modern world is more connected than ever. To the monarchs who say that the business of other nations doesn't concern them, I say that we are all global citizens now, and we need to act that way. We need to work together for the good of the earth and all its people, not just the people who call us their king or queen.

"I pledge to you that America, and I, remain committed to the goal our ancestors believed in over a century ago. And I hope that the next time we meet, we can all continue the good work that we started this year."

Beatrice looked at the far wall rather than the faces in the crowd, because she didn't want to see everyone's disapproval or pity. She had said what she needed to say, as naïve and earnest as it might have been.

If nothing else, at least she'd ended this conference by being true to herself.

She turned toward the side of the stage, but before she could make her way down, a voice rose high and clear into the silence.

"France makes a motion that the gathered assembly hold a new vote on item thirty-one, 'Protection of the Global Climate for Future Generations.'"

It was Louise, speaking with the formal language they had used during all their plenary sessions, asking for a revote on the climate accord.

Beatrice saw contrition and hope in Louise's eyes. She was trying, in her own way, to make things right between them.

There was a rumble of shock through the room, everyone turning to one another with eager commentary.

"This is highly irregular," Empress Mei Ling cried out. A footman sprang forward with a cordless microphone—Beatrice wondered where he'd gotten it—and the empress snatched it from his hands. "Voting cannot happen outside the general session! This is a social gathering with—with—*wine!*" she exclaimed. "We cannot vote!"

King Frederick reached for the microphone. Empress Mei Ling passed it to him, probably assuming that he would echo her sentiments.

"Germany seconds the motion proposed by France," he said instead, gruffly.

"But there are people present who aren't *monarchs!*"

Before the empress could say more, the tsar stepped forward. "Russia moves that the assembly vote by show of hands rather than roll call." He didn't need a microphone; his voice boomed loud and confident over the gathered crowds.

"Very well." Frederick had taken charge again, and this time, no one made a move to stop him, though Empress Mei Ling's lips were still pursed in disapproval. "Let us begin voting on item thirty-one, 'Protection of the Global Climate for Future Generations,' proposed by Her Majesty Queen

Beatrice of America. Of the monarchs here assembled, will all those in favor of the proposal raise their hands."

Beatrice watched, hardly daring to breathe, as hand after hand rose into the air. Something she'd said must have resonated with everyone, because they were all voting in her favor. King Joaquin of Argentina shrugged and lifted his hand lazily; the Queen of England smiled at Beatrice with a mischievous sort of glee, as if she was secretly delighted to see some drama at these conferences for once.

Finally even Empress Mei Ling sighed and lifted her hand, unwilling to be the single vote against Beatrice's proposal.

Beatrice felt close to tears, gratitude and disbelief warring in her chest. She couldn't believe that finally, after everything, it was actually happening.

Through the roaring of adrenaline in her ears, she heard Frederick saying, "And so it is decided. Item thirty-one has been adopted by this twenty-fourth convocation of the League of Kings. This session is now officially adjourned."

When Beatrice made it down the stage, Louise was standing there.

"Your speech was impressive. And inspiring," she said quietly. "I didn't have the honor of knowing your father well, but I have a feeling he would have been proud of you."

Beatrice nodded, because the thing was, she knew that her father *was* proud of her. She'd felt his presence in the room as clearly as if he'd been standing next to her, a comforting hand on her shoulder, telling her that she was strong enough to do anything.

The crowds had begun jostling toward her, everyone clamoring for her attention. Now that she was no longer a pariah—was, in fact, the unexpected star of this year's conference—they all wanted to get in her good graces again.

"Thank you for proposing the revote," she told Louise.

They were drifting apart as more people streamed toward

them, but Louise smiled tentatively and asked, "Maybe we can catch up before I leave tomorrow? We could take Monseigneur Franklin on a morning run?"

Beatrice nodded, smiling. "That sounds nice."

Perhaps they could be friends again, though not in the same way they had been. No more would Beatrice trail after Louise, letting her pick their outfits and set their agenda.

If they rebuilt their friendship, it would be as equals.

41

NINA

It was getting harder and harder to avoid Jeff at this banquet, the way Nina had promised herself she would.

She'd spent most of the evening on the dance floor with Sam, and therefore with Marshall. It was better that she keep a safe distance from Jeff, so they wouldn't verge on flirtation again. Especially not while Daphne was here.

Nina worried that something had happened to unsettle Daphne tonight. She'd been acting the way she always did at a party, all smiles and small talk, but Nina knew her well enough now to see the frantic energy behind her facade. She wanted to get Daphne alone and ask about it, but Daphne was constantly surrounded by people—or with Jeff.

Which was as it should be, since Daphne was Jeff's date. Not her.

The party spilled out the back steps of Bellevue and into the gardens, everyone eagerly awaiting the fireworks that would start at midnight. The band kept playing inside the ballroom, and the doors had been thrown open, so that music drifted down to them like an enchantment. Torches lit the gravel walkways, their golden light reflected on countless jewels and crowns. The breeze from the ocean picked up the skirts of women's gowns, making them flutter, as gauzy and iridescent as the wings of moths. Most people stayed to the well-lit main paths, but there were pools of darkness in some of the groves and side gardens, the sorts of places that seemed meant for a forbidden tryst. The scents of flowers and salt and perfume hung heavy in the air.

Nina caught sight of Sam and Marshall across the patio. As she watched, Sam leaned closer to Marshall, letting him loop an arm around her waist. Nina's heart ached for them both. She knew how much they loved each other, but it was hard for her to see everything Marshall was going through—the microscope he'd been thrust under, the way people ruthlessly and relentlessly went digging into his life. It reminded her of how she'd felt back when she was the one dating Jeff.

"She's your friend, right?"

A young man had drifted toward her, a brow lifted as he followed Nina's gaze. He was undeniably handsome, with high cheekbones and a sculpted jaw, his golden-blond hair curling softly around his ears. A ceremonial sword hung at his waist, and he wore a vest trimmed in dark gray fur that matched his wolfish smile.

The prince of somewhere, Nina guessed. Or maybe he was just a guy in a vest and a sword, not actually a prince at all. Daphne would know who he was, Nina thought fondly. She probably could recite his family tree back a dozen generations.

"Yes," Nina said cautiously, answering his question. "Samantha is my best friend."

"I thought so. I would have noticed you if you'd been at one of the other League of Kings conferences." He held out a hand. "Dance with me?"

Nina cast a confused glance around the terrace. "No one else is dancing."

"All the more reason for us to start the trend."

There was no harm in dancing with a handsome, charming stranger, was there? Yet some foolish part of Nina was reluctant to put herself in the spotlight like that, in case Jeff saw and misread the situation.

Not that Jeff had any right to be jealous, since they were just friends.

"I'm a terrible dancer," Nina said. "I would step all over your toes."

The stranger grinned, undaunted. "A risk I'm willing to take. I'm extremely brave when it comes to beautiful women."

Nina choked out a laugh, amused in spite of herself by his outrageous vanity. "How courageous of you."

"I'm the very soul of valor," he agreed cheerfully. "You should see my collection of medals and awards. Now, shall we dance?"

When Nina still hesitated, he lowered his hand slowly. "My mistake. You have a boyfriend."

She felt color rising to her cheeks. "It's not—"

"Nina?"

Jefferson crossed the terrace toward them, his expression darkening as he took in her companion. "Jamie," he added stiffly.

Jamie? He must be James, the Canadian prince who was always in the headlines for some misadventure or another.

Jamie glanced from Nina to Jeff and back again, a knowing glint in his blue eyes. "Ah. I see," he murmured, so softly that only Nina could hear.

"It's not like that!" she hissed, flustered. The last thing she needed was for some foreign prince to rekindle the gossip about her and Jeff.

"Not like what?" Jeff came to stand next to her. "What are you two talking about?"

"Nothing," Nina said helplessly, but neither young man was listening. They stared at each other: Jeff's face impassive, Jamie's alight with impish glee. A strange tension crackled in the air between them.

Then Jamie took a step back, his smile fading. "Nina, it was a delight to meet you. Jeff . . ." He hesitated, clearly uncertain what to say, then shrugged and left without saying anything.

When he'd gone, Jeff turned to Nina with an unreadable expression. "What were you doing with Prince Jamie?"

"He just came over and asked me to dance! I have no idea why," Nina insisted, unsure why she was explaining herself.

"He asked you to dance because he's Jamie, and because you look beautiful," Jeff said gruffly.

Standing here with Jeff in the moonlight, Nina *felt* beautiful. Her dress was perfect for this occasion, classic and sophisticated with its stitched rosettes and scoop neckline. The embroidery had an ethereal shimmer, distracting from the fact that Nina, unlike most people here, wasn't wearing a tiara, or really any jewelry to speak of. A simple pair of pearl studs gleamed in her ears—they belonged to her mamá, who'd bought them for work meetings because she insisted that they matched everything.

Their gazes met, and the look in Jeff's eyes filled Nina with a sudden liquid heat.

It was so hard, in this moment, to maintain the fiction that they were just friends.

You didn't daydream about running your hands over your friend's chest, tangling your hands in the back of his hair, and tipping his face down to yours. You didn't get so nervous about talking to a friend that your chest fluttered.

Nina took an abrupt step back, scanning the crowds for Daphne, or Sam and Marshall. She would even welcome an interruption from *Gabriella* right now, if it kept things safely platonic between her and Jeff.

"Should we walk in the gardens?" Jeff asked, jarring Nina from her thoughts.

She longed to say yes. But then she thought of Daphne— bulldozing her way through the racks of the vintage store, standing before Nina like a human shield when Gabriella confronted them, looking vulnerable and lonely over a plate of tacos. Daphne, who was prickly and proud, who wouldn't hesitate to go to war for the things she cared about.

Nina couldn't walk off into the dark with Daphne's boyfriend. Not after what had happened the last time they were alone.

Some part of her registered how completely the world had upended, that she was turning away from Jeff to protect *Daphne's* feelings, but what had her mamá said? The world was funny like that.

"I should really get back to the party."

"Nina . . ." Jeff sounded hoarse; he swallowed. "Please, just for a minute. Just to talk."

Just to talk. It was as close to an acknowledgment of that night on the couch as either of them could afford to make. Anything more would be a confession of guilt.

Nina couldn't bring herself to walk away from Jeff, not when he looked at her like that.

"Just for a minute," she conceded.

Jeff led her down the steps and onto one of the side paths—the ones wreathed in shadows, which Nina had just been thinking were probably full of couples taking advantage of the darkness.

"Jeff?" she asked hesitantly.

They reached a secluded grove. The sounds of music were soft and muted, overpowered by the roar of the ocean and the spray of a fountain behind them.

"Sorry," he told her. "I just wanted to get away from it all."

Nina's heart was hammering, her breath catching in her chest. "What did you want to talk about?"

"Nothing. Everything," he said confusedly, and sighed. "I just . . . So much has happened this year. It feels like everything is changing."

Nina couldn't help it; she reached out and took Jeff's hand, the way she had a thousand times with Sam. "Of course it's changed. You lost your father," she said gently.

It struck Nina that this was one of those instances where the English language fell short. The word for losing something insignificant—a baseball game, a library card—shouldn't be the same as for losing someone who defines you, someone you love. There should be a word for losses you can recover from, and a different word for the life-shattering losses, the ones that leave you forever changed.

"I thought things would get easier," Jeff croaked. "But lately Beatrice has been gone and I've been the Regent, and suddenly it all feels . . . I don't know. There were things I thought I knew for certain, and I'm not sure about them anymore. I don't know what I can count on."

"You can count on me," Nina whispered.

He smiled hesitantly. "I'm not any good with words, Nina. Not the way you are. You make it look so easy."

Somehow she was closer to him than she'd been just moments ago, her face tipped up to his. "Make what look easy?"

"Saying how you feel."

Her eyes locked with Jeff's, and Nina knew in that moment that they were not friends. That wasn't what this was between them, not at all.

Jeff had clearly come to the same conclusion, because he leaned down and kissed her.

42

DAPHNE

Nina and Jefferson were kissing.

Daphne stared at them in numb shock, her mind scream-ing in silent denial. She wasn't sure what she'd expected when she followed them—for Jefferson to confess that he was wor-ried about Daphne, for Nina to defend Daphne's erratic be-havior. She certainly hadn't expected *this*.

She should have shouted, sprinted forward and yanked them apart, slapped both of them across the cheek. Yet Daphne's vocal cords were stuck. She felt paralyzed by déjà vu, because she realized now that she had *been* here before, in this exact same situation: the night of graduation, a year and a half ago, when she'd come up to Jefferson's room and seen him with someone else.

The girl in his bed that night had been Nina.

At the End of Session party, when she'd accused him of cheating, Jefferson's eyes had cut guiltily across the rooftop. He'd been looking at Nina, hadn't he?

Of course he had. Daphne should have known it was Nina. It was always Nina, back then and now.

She turned and ran off, but this time she wasn't stumbling down the hallways of Washington Palace; she was racing through the gardens at Bellevue, lit by torchlight that flickered and danced in the wind.

At the turnoff to the garden's central pathway, Daphne

paused, then turned again. She couldn't face the crush of the party right now. She felt like someone had split open her chest with a cleaver and now all her raw nerve endings were exposed to the air.

When she found a bench that looked secluded, Daphne collapsed onto it, the folds of her purple dress slippery around her legs. For once she couldn't bring herself to care about snagging her gown. She closed her eyes, trying to ignore the monster of truth that kept roaring from within.

You're wrong, she thought at the monster. *Nina wouldn't sell me out. She's my friend.*

The reply came in her mother's voice. *You stupid little fool, Nina was never your friend. She was working with Gabriella to get rid of you.*

No, Daphne insisted, more feebly this time. Nina wouldn't betray her.

Except that she'd just *seen* Nina betraying her.

Daphne dug her hands into the sides of the bench so hard that it hurt, as if the pain might bring things into focus. It all made a savage kind of sense.

Nina had wanted Jefferson from the beginning; that much was obvious. After Daphne suggested that they join forces against Gabriella, Nina must have cast her lot with Gabriella instead of with Daphne. She'd gone with the more powerful ally, which Daphne should have foreseen, because it was exactly what Daphne would have done in Nina's shoes.

Nina had approached Gabriella, and in exchange for Nina going double agent against Daphne, Gabriella had clearly promised to get her financial aid reinstated.

Then Nina had pretended to go along with Daphne's plan, had pretended to be her *friend*, because it was always easier to break something when you were on the inside.

She remembered that when Nina had come over to her room, her eyes had drifted to the photo on Daphne's nightstand, the one that Daphne had recently shared with the *Daily News*. That must have been when Nina figured out that Daphne was selling photos of herself.

And the whole time, Nina had been at college with Jefferson, acting like they were "just friends"—as if two people with romantic history could ever be just friends—and Daphne, like a fool, had believed her. Had *trusted* her.

It had been a lie, all of it. Nina had been acting, and Daphne should have seen it coming, because this was court and they were all actors here.

For so long Daphne had done just fine without any friends. Friends were a liability. Friends made you vulnerable, and vulnerability meant weakness, which meant blood in the water. Friends could hurt you.

And then Nina had come along, with her late-night tacos and her warm smiles and her apparent sincerity, and Daphne had realized just how lonely she really was.

Daphne was surprised to find that she was crying. Not the delicate, polite cry she called up in public, but a raw, ugly cry, full of snot and broken sobs.

She'd lost everything that had ever mattered to her: her rank, her relationship with Jefferson, this friendship with Nina. And even though the friendship hadn't been real, Daphne still felt its loss like a punch to the stomach.

Eventually her sobs quieted. She gave a deep, hollow sigh and let her head fall into her hands.

Her grief—and regret—began to petrify inside her, forming a protective shell around the core of her being. Those feelings slowly gave way to anger, which came as a relief. Anger she could work with. Anger could be a tool, if she was smart enough to wield it.

Nina had played her, and Daphne had let her do it.

She'd let Nina back her into a corner and knock her down, but she still wasn't defeated. Not yet. She was still young and beautiful, still famous, and she had a history with Jefferson. That all counted for something.

She slipped the signet ring off her finger and turned it over in her hands, studying the cool script of the *W.* It reminded her of everything she couldn't afford to lose.

Her hands shaking only a little, Daphne put the ring back on, then reached into her clutch for her compact mirror. She dabbed concealer beneath her eyes, wiped away the streaks of mascara that had run down her cheeks, darkened her lips. When she was done, she assessed her work dispassionately, the way an artist might study a painting in search of its flaws.

Strangely enough, she looked even more beautiful than usual. The tears had made her eyes luminous beneath her thick lashes. The neckline of her gown stirred with her breath, which was steadier every moment. She felt like she'd been under a spell for months.

And now that her mind had finally broken free—returning her to her *real* self at last—she would make Nina pay for her betrayal.

Daphne stood with a toss of her famous red-gold hair. Shadows seemed to gather and swirl around her like a cloak as she started back toward the party with deadly purpose.

43

NINA

Jeff was kissing her. And Nina kissed him back.

She couldn't help it: her body was operating on instinct, on muscle memory, because this was *Jeff*, after all. She had loved him so desperately for so long. Maybe she had never stopped loving him.

Nina's entire body tingled, as if the feel of his lips on hers had ignited a long-forgotten magic. Deep down, she knew that this was what a kiss should feel like—steady and certain, and fundamentally *right*, like you had found your way home when you didn't even know you'd been lost.

It wasn't until she heard a sound across the garden that Nina tore away and stumbled back a step.

She looked over, panicked that they had been caught, but no one was there.

Jeff drew in a breath. "Sorry if I misread things. I thought, the other night . . ."

Nina couldn't bear to make eye contact with him. "Jeff, we can't do this to Daphne. She's your girlfriend, and she's my friend." The strangest thing was, it was true.

How had Nina managed to become friends with her former enemy, the girl whose boyfriend she also happened to be in love with? Why didn't she have an ounce of self-preservation?

Jeff shook his head. "Things are weird between me and

Daphne. I won't get into it with you, but suffice it to say that Daphne and I aren't in a great place."

"You can't just kiss me every time you and Daphne have a fight!" Nina burst out, suddenly frustrated. "It's not fair to me *or* Daphne, okay? Honestly, I wish you would just—"

"Just what, Nina?"

"Just hook up with one of the other countless girls who throw themselves at you! Quit yo-yoing from Daphne to me to Daphne to *me* again! I don't get it—we aren't even that similar! Why do you keep doing this to both of us? Can't you just find someone else to rebound with?"

Jeff stared at her a long moment, and Nina swallowed. She had never really asked what he'd done when he wasn't with her or Daphne, last summer and fall, when he was bouncing around the world with Samantha. Certainly *Sam* had gotten into plenty of trouble on that gap-year trip, and all the royal tours they had taken.

Nina could see it now: Jeff picking up some random girl at a bar in New Zealand, playing darts with her, letting her win because he was that chivalrous. Sneaking her into his hotel room, sneaking her out again the next morning like he'd once done with Nina. That type of girl wouldn't bat an eyelash at being smuggled out in a black car; she would be squealing with glee at the fact she'd just hooked up with a prince. It would give her bragging rights forever.

Maybe it would be easier if Jeff went after a girl like that. At least then Nina wouldn't have to risk losing him all over again.

She wasn't sure if she could handle any more of this twisted love triangle between her, Daphne, and Jeff.

"I'm sorry if I gave you the wrong idea. Kissing you wasn't the best way to start this conversation," Jeff said clumsily. "I told you, I'm not any good with words. Let me start over."

Nina picked up the skirts of her gown and noticed, not

really caring, that her hem was muddy and grassy. She let go, holding her breath.

"I *like* you, Nina," Jeff said bluntly. "Lately, I've felt like there was something between us again. I wouldn't have even said anything, except that the last time we hung out . . . I know I'd had too much to drink that night, but it felt like we came close to kissing."

"You're still with Daphne, though," Nina reminded him.

"Technically, yes," Jeff mumbled. "But I'm going to break up with her."

"I don't want you to break up with Daphne for me!"

"I'm not breaking up with her *for* you, Nina. I'm breaking up with her because Daphne has been . . . different lately. She's not acting like herself."

She's not acting like herself because she's becoming a better person, Nina thought. *Because you two never really belonged together. And now that you're seeing glimpses of her real self, you realize that she isn't the girl you thought you fell for.*

But of course Nina couldn't say any of that.

"I'll always care about Daphne," Jeff went on—the type of trite statement that people usually made in breakups, except that he really did mean it. "It's just that lately, spending time with you, I remembered what it was like. You and me."

He reached out as if to touch her, but Nina took a swift step back. She wasn't ready to commit to this, not yet.

"If you break up with her, it's going to destroy Daphne," she said softly.

"Daphne is stronger than you think. I know you said you're not that similar, and maybe on the surface you're right. But you and Daphne are both strong. You want to know the reason I dated both of you?"

Nina didn't particularly want to hear why Jeff had dated Daphne, but he answered his own question anyway. "You both know your own mind. You're confident. You don't let other people tell you what to do. And I can trust both of you. Or at least, I thought I could," he added under his breath, then looked up at Nina.

"So, yeah, it'll be messy ending things with Daphne, but she'll be okay. Breakups happen."

Breakups happen. He made it sound like this was a garden-variety breakup, and not the Prince of America ending things with a woman who already thought of herself as a princess—who'd probably already picked out her wedding china.

"You gave her your signet ring. Everyone basically thinks of that as a pre-proposal," Nina couldn't help saying.

Jeff ran a hand wearily over his face. "Like I said, I'm not always good at this stuff. I try to use gestures instead of words, because it's easier. But gestures have a lot of different meanings to different people."

"As your friend, I have to agree."

"My friend?" Jeff looked so confused and uncertain that Nina felt herself softening toward him.

"I've always been your friend, Jeff. Even if you don't make it easy."

"But . . . *just* my friend?" He paused. "If I broke up with Daphne tonight, would that change things for us?"

Nina didn't want to, but she couldn't help smiling at him. She seemed to lose control of her reactions when Jeff was around, as if her heart knocked her mind out of the driver's seat and seized control of things. He melted all her resistance, all her excuses.

She needed to go, because if she stayed with him a minute longer she might kiss him again, and she couldn't live with herself if she did that while he was still with Daphne.

"I'm going to head back," she started to say, turning on one heeled sandal.

"Wait, Nina—before you go, can I ask you something?"

She glanced back at him, biting her lip, and nodded.

"Did you and Daphne really try some kind of takedown of Gabriella?"

She nodded, surprised Daphne had told him about that. "I know it sounds absurd, but I wasn't sure what else to do. I was about to lose my financial aid."

"You should have talked to me," Jeff said emphatically. "I could have fixed it, much faster than—"

He broke off, but Nina could finish the sentence for him. Much faster than he'd fixed it now.

"Jeff. Are you the reason my financial aid got reinstated?"

He flinched, suddenly anxious. "I'm sorry if I overstepped. I tried to talk about it with you last week, but you clearly didn't want to bring it up!"

So that was what Jeff had meant, when he'd looked at her with that searching gaze and asked if there was anything she wanted to tell him. Maybe Nina should have just shared the whole story then and there. Like her mamá always said, she was too stubborn for her own good.

Come to think of it, their inflexible pride was another thing that she and Daphne had in common.

"I didn't mean to snoop," Jeff went on, "but I was talking to Dr. Hale about on-campus housing for next quarter—"

"You're going to live on campus?"

"I want to. Now that the League of Kings is over and Beatrice is heading back to the palace, I can be a normal college student," he explained. As if he could ever be normal.

"I asked Dr. Hale if there were any rooms available in a building near yours. Not because—I mean, I didn't assume that we would be . . ." He cursed under his breath and tried again. "I didn't want to walk across campus every time I wanted to see you. I swear I wasn't jumping to any conclusions about whether we would be, um . . ."

"It's okay," she cut in. His confusion was kind of endearing.

"But when Dr. Hale pulled up your student file, she said

your enrollment for next quarter was still pending, that they were waiting on a tuition payment, since you were no longer eligible for financial aid."

Nina sucked in a breath. "Jeff. You didn't pay my tuition, did you?"

"No!" he insisted. "No, I tried to bring it up with you, and you dodged the topic but still seemed upset. So I called Dr. Hale and asked if she could look into your situation, find out why your financial aid was revoked. She called me back and explained that the whole thing had been a mistake."

When Nina said nothing, Jeff's hopeful expression faltered.

"I'm sorry. I really wasn't trying to sweep in and . . ."

"And fix problems with money and status, the way you always do?"

"Yeah. That."

He agreed so readily that she almost cracked a smile.

"I knew you'd hate it if I got involved, but I also know that you would hate dropping out of school even more. You're so smart, Nina, and whatever happened with your aid, it clearly shouldn't have happened in the first place." Jeff hesitated, then added, "If it really was cut off by Gabriella's father, then we should open a formal investigation. That's a flagrant abuse of his position on the board of trustees."

"I don't want a formal investigation," Nina said quickly. She just wanted this whole thing to be done with.

Jeff hesitated. "Are you angry?"

There were a million things Nina could have said, but she settled on the simplest. "I'm not angry. Thank you for helping."

She still felt a little embarrassed that her family's economic situation had been laid bare to Jeff—who had more money than he could ever hope to spend, whose family probably owned the land King's College was *built* on—but looking at Jeff, she saw that he truly didn't care. His eyes didn't gleam with judgment, just concern.

"Okay, then," Jeff said heavily. "I guess I need to go, um . . . handle things."

Nina's warmth evaporated. There was no getting around the fact that this would hurt Daphne.

Maybe if she was careful, and considerate, she could find a way to keep them both—Jeff and Daphne. She could give it some time post-breakup before going out with Jeff, make sure it didn't seem like she was waiting in the wings to pounce on him. Maybe they could find someone else to set Daphne up with. Who knows, maybe Sam could introduce Daphne to some of her and Beatrice's new European friends—Nina could see Daphne being very happy with a Baron von Something-or-other.

And someday everything would be forgiven, and they would all be at the Washingtons' ski house, laughing about how it had all worked out for the best.

Wishful thinking, probably, but Nina had always been an incurable optimist.

44

SAMANTHA

"This party is getting wild," Marshall observed, an eyebrow lifted. "Is that King Zog trying to do a handstand?"

"I can't tell if it's a handstand or a cartwheel, but either way he needs to be careful. Those Albanian pants are extremely loose."

Marshall laughed and reached for Sam's hand, twining his fingers in her own. She loved that about him—how readily he reached for her hand, as if he was only content when some part of his skin was touching hers.

She loved him, more than she loved her title. And with that knowledge her mind was made up.

"Let's walk," Sam murmured. Marshall followed as she moved through the gardens, pausing at a fountain here, a hedge of roses there. This wasn't the palace she'd grown up in, yet she felt a touch of nostalgia, telling it goodbye.

Sam drew to a halt before an enormous stone sundial, its surface covered in etched lines. A metal triangle, carved in the shape of a bird's wing, rose from its center. "Do you know what phase the moon is in?" she asked, glancing upward.

Marshall looked up at the sky. "Um . . . not full?"

"This sundial calculates time in thirty different ways, even at night. But you have to know the phase of the moon."

"I think checking the time on my phone would be faster," Marshall pointed out.

Sam stepped forward to touch the sundial's faceted surface. She was surprised to find that it was still warm, radiating the sunlight it had soaked up all day.

"This was actually a gift from Queen Victoria. She sent her sons here—all four of them, one after another—to propose to Princess Frances."

"Which one did Frances marry?"

"None of them," Sam told him. "She flat-out refused, told her parents that she wouldn't be shipped off to England like a parcel. Her brother George ended up marrying Victoria's granddaughter Alice, so America and Britain got the alliance they wanted." Sam traced the Roman numerals carved on the sundial's surface. "Sometimes I wonder what Frances was thinking. If she ever felt confused about the point of it all."

"The point of what?"

"Of being a princess."

Marshall leaned forward, bracing his palms against the edge of the sundial. "I'm usually good at reading between the lines when you go all history nerd on me, but right now I'm confused."

She took a deep breath. "I've been thinking, and maybe . . . maybe I don't need to be a princess anymore."

"What?"

"I could give it up. Renounce my position in the order of succession."

Marshall stared at her in dumbfounded shock. The ocean crashed in the distance, a low rumble beneath the laughter and voices of the party, the soft chirping of insects.

"I talked to Aunt Margaret tonight. And to Beatrice," Sam explained. "Marshall, so much about this situation is blatantly unfair, not the least of which is the fact that we laid the whole burden on you. We assumed that if you and I stayed together, *you* were the one who would eventually have to renounce your title."

"Of course we did," he said slowly. "That was implicit, because you're the princess. I'm just a future duke."

"Why was it implicit? It shouldn't be."

Marshall took a step back, voice hoarse. "I can't let you run away from your life because of me. That's—that's unprecedented!"

"I don't think of it as running away. More like I'm running *toward* something better." He was still shaking his head, so Sam tried another approach. "And it's not unprecedented. Have you heard of Prince Franz?"

"Who?"

"He ran away from his royal responsibilities too. He was a Prince of Flanders back in the thirties who renounced his titles and moved to Hawaii."

"Sam . . . ," Marshall said slowly, but she talked over him.

"I'm not saying we have to do anything yet. But when the time comes, I can be the one to de-princess-ify myself," she told him, trying to elicit a smile. "Then there won't be any obstacles to us being together. I can move to Orange, be a duchess, the whole nine yards. I'm actually pretty good at shaking hands, opening museum exhibits, headlining charity events. In all honesty," she added, half teasing, "good luck finding another woman in America who's as well trained for the job."

As she spoke, Sam knew this was the right thing. It wasn't fair that Marshall should give up everything for her without them at least discussing the alternatives. He was the Beatrice of his family: the one facing all the pressure, the one who would wear the title someday.

Marshall was silent for a long moment. Finally he looked up, his dark eyes meeting hers. "I can't ask you to renounce your family for me."

No, she thought, panicked. He couldn't be about to break up with her again—

"Not unless I do it, too."

It took a moment for Sam to process what he'd said. Then her lips curled in a smile. She'd secretly hoped he might say this, but hadn't dared suggest it; she could never have lived with herself if she thought she had dragged him down this path.

"What are you saying?" she asked, just to be sure.

"I'm saying, do you want to go all Prince Franz together?"

He reached for her hand again. Sam thought she could feel the thrum of his pulse where their palms touched.

"Are you sure?"

"I've never been more sure of anything than I am about you. Sam, you're amazing. You're complex and dramatic and funny and brilliant." The way he said it, Sam was pretty sure that even *dramatic* was a compliment. "We don't need to do anything irreversible; I'm not ready to sign a formal document of renunciation, and I doubt you are, either. Besides, Rory would never forgive me for dumping that kind of responsibility on her without warning." He let out a breath. "But, Sam, you're not the only one who's always wondered what life would be like away from it all. What if we went to Hawaii and explored what it's like to be real people?" There was a flash of vulnerability in his features as he added, "We should make sure, you know. . . ."

He trailed off, glancing over at her.

"Make sure what?" Sam asked, confused.

"Make sure you still love me, if I'm just a nobody instead of a future duke."

He held his breath, waiting for her reaction. Sam stared at him for a moment, then tipped her head back and laughed.

"Hey, that wasn't funny! I'm not joking!" Marshall protested.

"Marshall, that might be the silliest thing you've ever said. Of course I'll still love you," she promised. "I would love you no matter who you were: a farmer, a firefighter, a high school water polo coach—"

"Oh, good thinking. I should look into being a water polo coach," he agreed.

"I'm just saying, it's *you* that I love, not your titles." She hesitated, then added, "I like to think that we would've found each other eventually, even if we were ordinary people. That we would have crossed paths and known right away that we were meant for each other."

"Maybe not *right* away. You were a little bossy at the start," Marshall teased.

"Just at the start?" she replied.

Hand in hand, they headed back toward the main house.

"So, if we actually went to Hawaii, what would we do?"

Sam knew what he meant: If they were no longer training for the roles their families had given them, who would they be? How would they find purpose?

"Well, when she ran away, Aunt Margaret worked at a boat-rental company."

Marshall made a strangled noise. "Pass."

"Prince Franz himself opened a beach bar."

"Better, but still a pass."

She glanced over. "You told me that you want to teach your kids to surf someday. In the meantime, you could teach other kids. And me," she added. "I'm a terrible surfer."

"I've never understood that! From what I hear, you're a great snowboarder." He paused. "And what will you be doing, aside from learning to surf?"

Making friends, Sam thought. Meeting people who would treat her not as a princess but just as a woman named Samantha. Reading some of the hundreds of books Nina was always texting her about. Making sandcastles, exploring, leading ATV tours or scooping ice cream behind a counter.

Whatever she did, she would be figuring out who she was. Who they both were, free of the obligations and duties they'd always taken for granted.

"I don't know what I'll do, but it doesn't matter," she told him. "As long as I'm there with you."

They reached her bedroom on the second floor just in time. There was a series of notes from a trumpet; then the first rockets of the fireworks rose into the air. Sam and Marshall headed to the windows and threw them open, staring out at the horizon.

The fireworks were a thunderous burst of color, cherry red and electric blue and a vivid gold. The sky looked like it was on fire, as if the world had suddenly become as bright as noon. On and on it went, pinwheels and comets exploding into the darkness.

When the show finally ended in a shower of sparks, a hush fell over the crowd.

Sam went to her desk, grabbed a sheet of her embossed stationery, and began writing a note.

Bee,

Sorry I'm leaving without saying goodbye. I've been thinking about what you said, and I haven't changed my mind. I'm all in. So for now, I need to stop being the Princess of America, and just be Samantha.

I promise I'll be safe. Thank you for understanding, and for letting me choose love over duty.

Love, Sam

Marshall came to stand behind her. "'I'm all in'?" he asked, reading aloud.

"Tonight, when I asked for Beatrice's advice, she told me I needed to decide whether I'm all in. If I'm willing to give up everything for you." Sam turned around to face him. "And the answer is yes. I am."

"You told Beatrice that?"

She rolled her eyes. "Don't let it go to your head."

"Too late. My ego is already inflating, like the Grinch's heart, growing three sizes too large."

Sam folded the note, planning to leave it here for Beatrice to find, and Marshall's smile faded.

"Wait." He untwisted the golden bear pin from the front of his jacket and handed it to Sam. "Put this with the note, so she knows that I'm all in, too."

"In that case . . ." Sam gestured to the tiara atop her head. Marshall swallowed, but helped her remove the pins anchoring it in place. He set it delicately atop the folded paper.

The tiara glittered like fire, matched by the golden gleam of the bear pin. His inheritance, and hers.

It hit Sam all over again in that moment—the sheer magnitude of what they were leaving behind. Centuries of history, and family, and legacy.

She loved Marshall more than all of it.

"We're really doing this, aren't we." He sounded both excited and fearful.

Sam's heart thudded wildly, but when she looked up at Marshall, she was grinning. "Yeah. We're really doing this."

45

BEATRICE

The remaining partygoers were still milling around outside, the sounds of laughter and increasingly rowdy music mingling with the outraged exclamations of guests who weren't ready to leave.

Beatrice cast another glance around the terrace but didn't see Teddy. They still hadn't spoken since their conversation in the hallway. They had just circled the party all night like a pair of polarized magnets, never getting too close, each always aware of the other's territory.

She headed upstairs and knocked on the door that connected their bedrooms. A moment later, she heard rustling sounds from Teddy's side.

"Teddy? Can we talk?"

When he threw open the door, she saw that he'd changed into jeans and a long-sleeved Henley shirt, and that his shoes were on, as if he planned on going somewhere.

"Hey, Beatrice," he said warily.

She started to step inside, but when she saw his closed-off expression, she stayed in the doorway.

"First of all, I wanted to thank you for tonight," she began, striving for upbeat and casual. Maybe if she acted like this wasn't a big deal, Teddy wouldn't either. "It meant a lot to me that you stayed at the party, after everything."

"I promised that I would host the party with you, and I

don't go back on my promises," he said stiffly. "That's why I'm the one you picked out of your parents' binder, isn't it? Because you knew I'd be good at the job?"

There was nothing she could say, because Teddy was right, at least a little. Her parents had included him on her list of eligible suitors for that very reason—because he was smart and mannered, and could chat easily with the sovereigns of foreign nations.

"Teddy . . . ," she began helplessly.

"It's fine. I'm always happy to be your arm candy," he replied, sounding so unlike himself that Beatrice recoiled.

"Stop being like this! You know I love you!"

He sighed, softening, and opened the door wider. "You might as well come in."

It was a lukewarm invitation, but Beatrice came inside. Teddy sat on the edge of the bed, and even though she wanted so desperately to sit next to him, she perched on the edge of the armchair instead.

"I'm sorry," she said again. "You were right, I shouldn't have told Louise about Connor. It was just. . . . I've never had a close friend before, not the way Sam has Nina. And it was so *nice*, taking to someone who's struggling with all the same things that I am."

"It's more than the fact you told Louise about Connor," Teddy said heavily, and Beatrice flinched a little at the strangeness of hearing him say Connor's name.

Teddy ran his hands over the coverlet. "I'm not sure how I fit in your life right now. I always expected you to come first in a lot of things, as queen. But I hoped that I could help—be your ally, your sounding board. That when you wanted to talk things out with someone, you would lean on me."

"I do," Beatrice protested.

"Do you? Lately, it's felt like the times you're happiest are when you're with Louise, doing fun single-girl things. Going to parties on a yacht and playing poker, jetting off to Versailles for the weekend."

A flicker of irritation shot through Beatrice. "Those things weren't as bad as you're making them sound. I wasn't acting like Samantha in her party-princess days, dancing on tables in Vegas. I went with a friend to see her sick father!"

"I didn't mean it as criticism. I'm just worried," Teddy said flatly. "Our political relationship is inherently imbalanced, but that doesn't mean our *personal* relationship should be. I thought we were equal partners in this."

"We are," she insisted.

Teddy's eyes were very blue and very steady as they met hers. "I'm not afraid of the life we're building together. When I signed that document of renunciation, I did it gladly, because I knew it brought us one step closer to that life. But I don't know if I can say the same for you."

This time, Beatrice didn't protest, because she had no idea what to say.

"Relationships always involve a measure of give and take," he went on after a moment. "I'm not concerned about the fact that I need to flex for you and your position, but rather, that I'm flexing without any recognition on your part." He paused. "You never mentioned the document of renunciation on any of our phone calls these past weeks, not even once."

"I'm sorry. I didn't know how to bring it up," she offered, knowing it wasn't enough.

"You could've started with thank you," Teddy said quietly.

"Except I'm not sure I wanted you to sign that document at all! I'm *scared*, Teddy!"

His eyes widened a little at the vehemence of her words. "Scared of what?"

"I'm scared of being queen! I'm scared of feeling lonely. I'm scared my position will drive us apart, create a wedge between us as time goes on." She swallowed. "Most of all, I'm scared of losing you. You gave up everything for me, and we don't even have a job for you to do!"

Her words echoed around the room. Teddy splayed his hands on the mattress and let out a breath. "Why didn't you talk to me about any of this?"

"I wanted to, but I didn't know how," Beatrice confessed. And then some spiteful and awful part of herself added: "I thought maybe you were keeping something from me, too."

Teddy blinked. "What?"

"When we talked on the phone, I had this feeling that you were keeping something from me. I assumed that it wasn't going well—training Lewis to be the future duke, transitioning everything to him. I was afraid to ask, because I didn't want you to admit what was going on, in case it made you resent me."

Something flashed in Teddy's eyes, and Beatrice pressed further. "Was I right?"

"In a way, yes. You're right that I was keeping something from you."

She held her breath as Teddy knelt down to unzip the duffel bag on the floor—which was still neatly packed—and pulled out a black velvet box. "I was hiding this," he announced, and tossed her the box. Startled, Beatrice caught it.

"I was trying to wait for the right moment, but I guess the surprise is ruined. Go ahead," he told her. "You can open it."

Her eyes stinging, Beatrice unclasped the box. Inside was a spectacular sapphire engagement ring. The deep blue stone was surrounded by a halo of diamonds, with sparkling pavé diamonds all around the band.

"It was my grandmother's ring," Teddy explained. "Apparently, when our financial situation was at its worst, my grandfather sold it. No one realized until I came back a few weeks ago and tried to find it in the safe. It took longer than

I expected to track it down and buy it back from the jewelry dealer who'd ended up with it." Teddy's voice was rough. "Obviously, the Crown Jewels vault is full of rings, but . . . I wanted to bring at least one thing to the marriage, or at least, make this one thing about our relationship seem normal. I thought it was unfair that you had to propose and provide your own ring." He shoved his hands into his pockets. "I guess I figured that since you proposed last time, it was my turn."

Beatrice's heart ached. That day when she'd proposed to him—when he'd gotten down on one knee and sworn to be her liege man—felt like a lifetime ago.

How had she managed to ruin everything?

"So, yeah. That's what I was keeping from you," he said flatly. "I would say there are no more secrets between us, but I'm not really sure what else you're keeping from me."

Carefully, Beatrice reclasped the box and passed it back to Teddy. "It's beautiful. Whenever you want to ask, I'll be ready."

"But I don't know if *I'm* ready," Teddy replied, and she went cold all over.

"What do you mean?"

"I have a lot to figure out."

Beatrice shot to her feet. "We can figure it out together! The League of Kings is over; I have plenty of time now. We can brainstorm your role, fix everything that's not working . . ."

Teddy smiled sadly. "This is the kind of thinking that I need to do on my own. I need to figure out what it will mean for me, moving forward, that you only have time for me when your job is on hiatus."

Beatrice realized that she'd said the wrong thing. She shouldn't have made it sound like she prioritized the League of Kings above her relationship.

Except—that was the truth, wasn't it? She wasn't Samantha, free to renounce her position when things got tough.

She was the queen, and the Crown must always come first.

Teddy picked the duffel bag off the floor and slung it over one shoulder. "I'm just going to clear my head, get some space."

You just had *space, for weeks!* Beatrice wanted to cry out. Instead she asked, very quietly, "Where will you go?"

"Nantucket, I think." Teddy pulled his phone from his pocket and frowned down at the screen. "The jetway is clear. If I leave now, I can be there before noon."

"But you and me . . . are we okay?"

Teddy didn't answer for a long moment. "I think the space will be good for us," he said at last. "I'll call you when I get to the Nantucket house."

She stepped forward—to kiss him, hug him, grab a fistful of his shirt and dig her heels in so that he couldn't leave— but Teddy put a hand on each of her shoulders. He leaned forward and kissed her once, on the forehead. The way you might kiss a little sister, or a cousin, or a friend.

Beatrice felt too weak to say anything as he turned and headed out the door. She just slumped to the floor, her hand lifted to the place where his lips had been.

46

DAPHNE

Daphne hadn't left the party. Why should she? She wasn't the one who'd faked an entire friendship, then kissed her so-called friend's boyfriend.

Nina and Jefferson were both avoiding her; Daphne could tell from the deliberate way they were looking anywhere *but* at her. She just tipped her chin up and ignored them. As long as Jefferson hadn't broken up with her or asked her to leave, she still had a fighting chance. She could still make Nina pay for what she'd done.

She'd been weak, and Nina had taken advantage of that weakness, but Daphne wouldn't make the same mistake a second time. She knew better now than to trust anything Nina told her.

Daphne was standing out on the terrace, the tattered remnants of the party swirling around her, when Jefferson approached.

"Daphne. Hey."

"Jefferson." She smiled as if nothing was wrong, as if she hadn't sold photos to the media or seen him kissing Nina. "Are you having a fun night?"

He ignored her breezy tone. "We need to talk."

Those four words had never preceded anything good.

"I—of course." Daphne felt her smile slip as they headed through the double doors.

Already the ballroom looked tired. The magic of an evening like this never really lasted, did it? The dance floor looked scuffed, and half-empty bottles of champagne were sweating on the bar. Even the figures in the marble statues seemed exhausted, as if they longed to close their eyes and take a quick nap.

Daphne felt a brief stab of hope, because Jefferson surely wouldn't break up with her here in the ballroom, but then he ushered her down the hallway and deeper into the palace, to a sitting room she'd never seen before. An ugly watercolor hung on the wall, so ugly that Daphne suspected a relative must have painted it.

"Daphne, you know how much I care about you."

He'd said *care about you*, not *love you*. Daphne tried not to panic.

"Things between us have gotten weird lately," he went on, and Daphne cut in.

"I know, and I'm sorry! It's my fault. I should never have betrayed your trust like that."

"You did, though," he said bluntly. "Maybe it's this situation with your family's title, which I'm really sorry about. But you've been acting strange for a while. It makes me wonder if we're a good fit anymore, or if we've maybe . . . drifted apart."

Drifted apart? More like he drifted *into* Nina and decided he was through with Daphne. *Again.*

Daphne was grateful that she'd seen Nina and Jefferson earlier, had already let the hurt storm violently through her, then ebb. Staring at Jefferson now, all she felt was a cold determination not to lose him.

She refused to let Nina and Gabriella win.

What could she do—throw a fit, burst into tears, and accuse him of cheating? Jefferson might stay here and comfort her for a while, but he wouldn't take her back. Maybe she could tell him that Nina had betrayed her, pretended to be her friend and sold her out to Gabriella. Except that he was so starry-eyed when it came to Nina, and Daphne didn't exactly want to remind him of Gabriella, and of the photos she'd sold.

She shuffled through every bit of gossip she knew, every last secret she'd accumulated during her years at court, but none of them would make Jefferson stay if he really wanted to leave her. Daphne knew how to gently steer him in one direction when he was torn—she'd been doing it for years—but she wasn't powerful enough to *force* him into something he didn't want to do. No one could do that, except his family.

Then it hit her, in a terrible, deadly flash of inspiration. The one way she could keep hold of Jefferson, now that all else had failed.

Some lingering sliver of conscience, left over from her fake friendship with Nina, reared its head for a moment. Could she really go through with this? Wasn't she going too far?

If her mother were here, she would say that nothing was too far, no sacrifice too great. Not for the good of their family. If Daphne had to journey to the gates of hell itself to get rid of Nina and win Jefferson back, Rebecca would send her on her way and wish her luck.

At the thought of Nina, Daphne's resolve hardened. She wasn't doing anything worse than what Nina had done to her—twisting someone's emotions for her own purposes. Lying to someone she ostensibly cared about.

"You're right. I *have* been acting weird."

It wasn't hard for Daphne to start crying. She was on edge, and afraid, risking her entire future on one last gamble. She would be staking everything on this hand, and if it failed . . .

She couldn't let herself think about that. If she didn't

look the possibility of failure in the eye, then she could keep outrunning it.

"Daphne, it's okay." Jefferson put a hand on her shoulder, patting her awkwardly, and Daphne sobbed all the harder.

"I've been acting weird because I'm terrified," she said brokenly, tears streaming down her cheeks. "I wanted to tell you, but I didn't know—I'm not sure—"

She had to be careful with her words. The key was to babble incoherently, so that later, Jefferson would never be exactly sure what she'd said.

"I didn't know how you would react; I thought you'd be angry or upset. People are going to think that I was trying to *trap* you or something."

Jefferson's hand went still. "What are you talking about?"

Daphne lifted her tear-streaked face to his. "I'm late."

"Late?" he repeated.

"I'm late," she said again. "I might . . . I mean . . ."

She saw comprehension sink in. His expression flickered from stunned shock to a brief flash of dismay or maybe guilt, but then it all melted into a hesitant concern.

"You're pregnant," he breathed, and Daphne said nothing. "With a baby. Our baby."

"Are you angry?" she whispered.

"Oh, Daphne. Of course I'm not angry."

It was such a typically Jefferson response, so warm and sweet, that Daphne felt her resolve waver. Another guy might have asked more questions, or thought to make her take a pregnancy test, but Jefferson was so goddamned trusting, and his emotions were so easily swayed. He saw Daphne's fear— which was very real—and read it as proof of her words. Then he took that fear and made it his own.

He retreated a step and began pacing around the room, muttering more to himself than to her.

"I can't believe—I mean—Beatrice is going to freak out—Mom is going to freak out—"

Eventually he drew to a halt before Daphne. He seemed calmer now, more settled.

"It'll be okay, Daphne. Don't worry. We'll figure this out, I promise."

Her voice quavered as she whispered, "You're not leaving me?"

"Of course not."

Daphne felt herself start crying again, and Jefferson pulled her close, his hands closing around the small of her back. She buried her face in his shirt and sobbed into his chest—real, raw, painful tears.

She couldn't believe she'd lost her composure twice in a single night. It had obviously shattered something deep within her, when she'd realized that Nina had never cared about her at all. But the detached, cool part of her brain thought that just this once, it was okay for Jefferson to see her true emotions. It lent credence to her lie.

"It's okay," he kept murmuring in a low, soothing voice. "I'm here. Don't worry, it'll be okay. I'm here, and I'm not going anywhere."

"Thank you," she whispered.

Jefferson took a step back and looked at her, his whole earnest heart in his eyes. "What did you think, Daphne, that I'd leave you to do this alone? My parents raised me better than that. I'm taking responsibility for this baby—for both of you. It's the right thing to do."

The right thing to do. He wasn't staying with her because he wanted to, but out of a sense of obligation. Still, it was better than nothing.

He kept talking, saying something about how they would figure this out, that maybe they should tell their parents together, but Daphne wasn't really listening. Relief was flooding through her body like a drug, and in its wake came a sense of victory.

The part of herself that had stirred to life in her friendship with Nina, the part with a conscience—the part of her that still felt guilty—was steamrolled over by the great lumbering machine of her ambition as it creaked back to life.

"Thank you," she murmured over and over, and "I'm sorry," and "I love you." And with every lie she spoke, a measure of strength flowed back into her veins. She began to feel a familiar sense of control, of mastery—over herself and Jefferson and the narrative she was spinning around them both.

Of course, her solution was only a Band-Aid. Eventually someone would make her take a pregnancy test, and it would be abundantly clear that she wasn't, in fact, expecting. But Daphne had been careful in her choice of words. She'd simply told Jefferson that she was late, and cried some frightened tears, and let him fill in the rest. She'd never claimed that she was pregnant for *certain*.

No one could blame her for an honest mistake.

And in the meantime, he wasn't breaking up with her. As long as she hadn't lost him, she could figure out the rest later. She would just have to make him fall in love with her again. She didn't doubt that she was capable of it.

After all, she'd done it twice before.

47

BEATRICE

Beatrice stumbled into her room. Franklin, who was curled up in her closet, barked his excitement at her arrival.

"Oh, Franklin," she said softly, and sank in a defeated puddle to the floor.

He whined, nuzzling his head against her, licking at her face as if puzzled by her tears. Beatrice let out a ragged sob and ran her hands over his warm golden fur. She wished she knew what to do.

She needed to talk to Sam—the only person who would understand.

Beatrice hurried to her sister's room, then paused at the door to knock. She didn't want to intrude if Sam and Marshall were in there together. "Sam?" She waited, then tried again. "Sam? Are you here?"

Tentatively, she pushed the door, and it swung inward on silent hinges.

The room was clearly empty: the bed crisply made, the curtains drawn. Beatrice started to turn away, but a flash of light caught her eye. Sam's tiara was on the surface of the writing desk.

As Beatrice walked closer, she noticed that something gold was nestled by the tiara. Marshall's grizzly-bear pin, the icon of the Dukes of Orange.

He and Samantha had both left their family heirlooms, the symbols of their positions, here on the desk.

Her hand trembling, Beatrice reached for the note that was folded next to the tiara, though she already knew what it would say.

Sam was choosing Marshall. *I'm all in,* she'd written. She'd placed her own desires over the Crown.

Most of the monarchs at this conference would have viewed Sam's choice as a sign of weakness, a character flaw. Once upon a time Beatrice might have agreed. Now, though, she couldn't bring herself to criticize Sam's choice.

At least one of the Washington sisters was able to choose love over duty.

Since she was a child, Beatrice had been told that the Crown took priority—that if she and the Crown wanted different things, then the Crown must win, always. That she was a queen first, and a young woman second.

When she was with Connor, she'd been all girl, and not enough of a queen. Then Teddy had come along and made her feel like she could be both at once. He didn't just love "off-duty" Beatrice, in the brief snatches of time when she felt like an ordinary person; he loved her all the time, even when she was queen. Connor had loved her *in spite of* her position, whereas Teddy loved her in a way that made her feel more *secure* in that position.

Yet somehow Beatrice had still let the Crown come between her and Teddy.

She wondered how her parents had done it. Though, as unfair as the situation was, things had probably been easier for her mom, since there was a precedent for queens consort. Whereas Teddy didn't have a clear role in her life.

And now Samantha was riding off into the sunset with Marshall, ignoring the demands of the Crown altogether. Beatrice realized that no matter what her fellow monarchs might say, Sam's decision wasn't weak at all. It showed powerful self-determination and courage. Sometime in the past year, Sam had forged herself into a woman to be reckoned with—a woman who knew her own mind.

Maybe Beatrice should take a page from Sam's book and go *all in* on her own relationship.

She wasn't about to renounce her title and run away to Hawaii, but she knew, suddenly, that she should fight for Teddy. Beatrice's heart sank as she recalled the desolate look in his eyes when he'd kissed her on her brow and said goodbye. Increasing the distance between them wouldn't solve things; it would only push them further apart.

All she wanted was to be with him. Sitting next to him, lying alongside him, her arms wrapped around his chest, their breaths intermingling. He was her anchor amid the storm, the only solid thing she could cling to in this whirlwind of a world.

Beatrice set down her sister's letter, leaving it neatly folded next to the tiara, then hurried into the hall and down the stairs.

There were a few bedraggled partygoers spilling onto the path that led to the guest cottages. When the valets saw Beatrice emerge through the main doors—still wearing her gown and heels, not even clutching a purse—they glanced at one another in confusion. "Your Majesty, can we help you?"

She felt like a character from a movie making a sweeping romantic gesture as she said, "I need a car, now. We have to reach the airport before Lord Eaton's plane takes off."

To her relief, a Revere Guard stepped away from the front steps and nodded toward one of the sedans. "I'll drive, Your Majesty."

The ferry ride was torture. Beatrice kept staring from her phone screen to the tinted window, counting the minutes, hoping she would make it in time. Finally they were on the mainland and cruising along the freeway toward the private airstrip.

"Are we close?" she asked the Guard, leaning her forehead against the cool glass of the window.

"Less than ten minutes, Your Majesty."

A fresh wave of optimism washed over Beatrice. It would all be okay, once she saw Teddy. He would take one look at her expression and know what she was thinking, the way he always did. He would pull her into his arms, tell her that he loved her and that of course she hadn't lost him.

The crash happened in the blink of an eye.

One minute they were driving, the surroundings passing in an indistinguishable blur of coastline, and the next moment there was the violent thud of impact, the screeching of tires, the shattering of glass. The world lurched sickeningly upside down, and Beatrice *hurt*—

Then everything went dark.

48

SAMANTHA

Sam and Marshall walked down the sidewalk of the beach town hand in hand, inhaling the salt air and the morning sunshine. Palm trees swayed against the blue sky overhead. The stores they strolled past—painted in bright colors, with open porches and handwritten chalkboard signs—were just throwing open their doors. Only a few cars wound slowly along the streets; everyone was walking or riding a bike, children in pigtails and shorts racing each other to school.

Sam had on wraparound sunglasses and a wide-brimmed hat over her hair, which was still half-curled and crunchy with hairspray from last night's event. It was surreal, to think that just twelve hours ago she'd been at the League of Kings final banquet, and now they were here.

Once she'd left her note for Beatrice, Sam had tossed a few things haphazardly into her weekend bag and started off. She wanted to leave quickly, before anything happened to make her or Marshall lose their nerve.

She'd gone straight to Aunt Margaret—who was, unsurprisingly, one of the last people lingering out on the terrace—and drew her aside.

"I need your help," Sam had said, cutting right to the chase. "Do you know a way that Marshall and I can get to Hawaii without anyone finding out?"

For an instant, Aunt Margaret looked shocked. Then a

slow, proud grin spread over her face. "Hawaii," she repeated. "Good for you. And, Sam . . ."

She'd folded her niece in a hug, squeezing her tight. "Good luck."

Whatever strings Aunt Margaret had pulled, she'd gotten them onto a plane within the hour. Soon enough they were landing at a private airport in Hawaii and being greeted by an immigration agent, whose name tag read BEN. Sam handed him her passport with a shiver of trepidation.

He looked down at it, yawning, and then his eyes shot open. He glanced at the photo, then at Sam, then at the photo again.

"Samantha Washington?" Ben asked slowly, disbelievingly. He'd used the common version of her name, no *Your Royal Highness*-ing, no bowing.

"Yes?"

He blinked, then began fumbling with a stack of papers in a file cabinet. "Hang on, there's a protocol I'm supposed to follow if this ever happens, but I don't have it memorized—I never thought it would actually— Sorry."

When he found what he was looking for, he sucked in a breath and read aloud:

" 'You are aware that Hawaii maintains cordial relations with the United States of America. However, if you choose to enter these borders, you will not be greeted as a visiting dignitary. You will not be invited for a private audience with Queen Liliuokalani. You will not be granted any special treatment from the police or state department, as the Kingdom of Hawaii does not recognize diplomatic immunity for any foreign royalty. During the duration of your stay, you are subject to Hawaii's laws and legal system.' In other words," Ben added, evidently going off script, "you will be treated as a private citizen, not as a princess."

Sam marveled at the fact that enough young royals had

come here that Hawaii had created an official *speech* for the immigration agent to give them upon arrival.

"I'm not here to break any laws," Sam said.

"Then why are you here?"

"Um . . . to learn to surf?"

He cracked a smile at that, stamping her passport. "In that case, welcome to Hawaii."

That had all happened an hour ago. Now Sam and Marshall were walking down the street, their weekend bags slung over their shoulders. And no one cared.

A few of them had recognized her, Sam could tell; it wasn't as if no one in Hawaii knew who she was. But they had no desire to come over and ask for a photo, tell her that they loved her or hated her or that they were *shipping* her and Marshall. They didn't seem to care what she did, as long as she didn't bother them.

Ahead was a sign: SUNRISE BEACH HOMES: SHORT- AND LONG-TERM RENTALS. "Should we take a look?" Sam suggested.

Marshall held out a hand in a chivalrous gesture. "After you."

Inside, a young woman with pink hair sat behind a desk strewn with papers and brochures. The walls were taped with real estate listings of cheerful beach cottages, some with BOAT INCLUDED! written on top.

Her blood rushing, Sam cleared her throat. "Hi. We're looking to rent a place on the water."

She waited for the realtor to gasp in recognition, but the woman just smiled politely. "Anywhere in particular?"

"Far from town," Marshall cut in. "Somewhere remote. Very quiet."

"How long will you be staying?" The realtor pulled up a blank form on her computer and began typing.

"We're not sure." Sam held her breath and took off her sunglasses. Still the realtor didn't react.

"There are a few cottages on Molokai that might interest you," she said brightly. "Can I have your names?"

Sam blinked, but the woman was looking up at her, hands poised over the keyboard, head tilted expectantly.

It had been a very long time since someone had asked Sam for her name.

"Martha," she said firmly. It was one of her middle names, after Queen Martha, the very first American queen.

And as an alias, it probably carried a bit of good luck. After all, she'd used it once before—the night of high school graduation—and she hadn't been caught then.

"Martha?" Marshall whispered, coming to stand closer to her. "Is that your Hawaiian alter ego?"

"Maybe. Why not!"

There was a dimple at the corner of Marshall's mouth; she wanted to lean forward and kiss it. And so she did. She kissed him right there in the rental office, and no one took a picture or catcalled them or spun an article out of it. It was exhilarating, liberating, wonderful. It was such a simple thing.

Here they weren't a duke and a princess, or the symbol of a social movement, or the repository of their families' legacies. Here they were just a boy and girl, renting a house on the beach, the way countless young lovers had done before.

49

NINA

Nina gave a bleary-eyed yawn, glancing at the clock on the bedside table. Her eyes widened in surprise. Was it really after ten a.m.? She'd expected Sam to have come in by now, to throw Nina's drapes open and beg her to come downstairs and eat waffles.

She wondered how it had gone last night between Jeff and Daphne. That was the only thing popping Nina's bubble of happiness: the knowledge that her newfound joy came at her friend's expense. As the night wore on, Daphne had probably wondered why Nina was avoiding her, given that they'd been attached at the hip earlier. Nina knew she was an abject coward, but she couldn't bear to face Daphne after Jeff had kissed her. She wasn't a good enough actress to pretend that everything was normal, not when guilt twisted inside her gut.

Now that they were broken up, though, Nina would find Daphne and apologize. She doubted Daphne would be very understanding. But maybe if Nina explained everything—her history with Jeff, that she hadn't meant to fall for him but it had just happened—maybe there was a chance they could preserve their new friendship.

Nina rolled onto her stomach, reaching onto the bedside table for her phone. Aside from the usual check-ins from her parents and Rachel, both Washington twins had texted.

Jeff: *Hey, can we talk?*

And Sam: *I'm sorry, I had to leave! I'll explain later, but you won't see me for a while. Thanks for being the best friend ever. Love you.*

You won't see me for a while? That probably meant that Sam had left town with Marshall. Nina shook her head, amused. There was never a dull moment with the Washingtons—this dramatic, complicated, wild, wonderful family. Nina loved all of them.

It felt like they were *her* family, too.

She hurried to get ready, throwing on a pair of dark jeans and a plum-colored top. It was a surprisingly tailored outfit. There were no ripped knees or frayed hems on the jeans, no writing on the shirt. She remembered what Daphne had said at the vintage store when Nina had pulled out a T-shirt that said LOVE in stitched red letters: *Nina, you can't wear a shirt with writing unless you're an athlete in your team jersey! Text gives people something to interpret, and they will always choose to interpret it in a way you didn't intend.*

It was funny that she was now quoting Daphne-isms to herself.

When she reached Jeff's room, the door was wide open, the room clearly empty. Nina's steps slowed.

She saw a flash of dark hair at the end of the hall—that was Anju, Beatrice's new chamberlain. Nina began jogging toward her.

"Excuse me?" Really, she should know the proper form of address by now.

"What?" Anju's head snapped up, but when she saw Nina, her expression softened. "Nina, right? You're Samantha's friend?"

Nina nodded. "I'm sorry to bother you, but do you know where Samantha or Jeff is?"

Anju stared at her. "You haven't heard?"

That was when Nina realized how eerily silent it was. The morning after an event, Bellevue should have been humming with noise: vacuums, tables being wiped down, a temporary stage being disassembled, thousands of flowers being carted out for donation to the local hospital, as the royal family always did after an event. There should have been clinking forks from the foreign royals eating one last breakfast, goodbyes called out in a hundred different languages before they headed to the airport.

Yet it was silent—the tense, uneasy silence that falls after an earthquake.

"What happened?" Nina asked. It came out in a whisper.

"Her Majesty was in a car accident."

"What?" Beatrice was hurt? How had that even happened? Nina swallowed. "Oh my god, is she okay?"

"She's at the hospital in LA, in intensive care. I'm actually headed there now, if you want a ride." Anju glanced at Nina again. "Any chance you've heard from Samantha, by the way?"

"I think she might be with Marshall?" Nina guessed.

"That was what we assumed as well. She left this note in her bedroom, next to her tiara and the Davises' ducal pin."

Anju handed Nina a folded sheet of stationery. Nina began scanning the message, then looked up, stunned. *I need to stop being the Princess of America? Thank you for letting me choose love over duty?*

"Is this . . ." She didn't know the phrase she was looking for.

"It's a note for Her Majesty, obviously." Anju pursed her lips. "But the courts may view it as an official statement of renunciation."

Now Nina understood why Sam had vanished in the middle of the night. Wherever she and Marshall were, they hadn't just escaped for the week or even the month. They'd run off indefinitely. This was a big decision, and one with serious consequences.

Sam hadn't told her where she was going because she didn't want to implicate Nina, or put Nina in a position where she would have to cover for Sam. The less Nina knew, the fewer lies she'd be forced to tell once people started asking questions.

Like Anju was doing right now.

"I don't think Sam wants to stop being a princess *forever*. Just temporarily," Nina explained, panicked.

"Then you should try to call her from the car. None of us have been able to get through, but she might answer for you."

Numbly, Nina followed the Lady Chamberlain into the backseat of a van. Anju was talking rapidly the whole time, snapping at various people in a tone that managed to be both hushed and frightening at once. Nina tried calling Sam a few times, but it kept going straight to voice mail.

"Yes, we'll have to make a statement soon enough," Anju was hissing into her earpiece. "It's a miracle we've been able to keep it from the media this long. I was hoping to get Her Majesty's condition a little more stable before we let everyone storm in with their questions and conspiracy theories. . . ."

Nina hadn't even spared a thought for the media; she was too shocked by the fact that Beatrice was seriously hurt. If only to keep her mind busy, she flicked over to the major news sites on her phone. They were all still reporting the usual mix of political updates and splashy celebrity pieces about the League of Kings.

Certainly there was no indication that America's queen was currently on life support.

Then they were being shuffled through a side entrance to the hospital, and into an elevator, and Anju finally clicked off her call and glanced down at Nina. "Samantha didn't answer?"

"I'll try her one more time," Nina offered, though she wasn't optimistic.

In the private wing of the hospital, they paused outside a waiting room. As Nina held the phone to her ear, trying Sam yet again, she heard Jeff's voice from inside.

"You're sure I'm supposed to do this? It feels wrong, while Beatrice is still . . ." Jeff hesitated before saying *alive.*

"Jefferson, I don't know if you have a choice," Daphne murmured softly, soothingly.

Why was *Daphne* here?

Anju had breezed through the door, clearly forgetting about Nina in the face of more urgent matters. Nina edged closer and peered inside.

It was one of the private VIP waiting areas, with plush armchairs and an expensive glass coffee table. Jeff was there, and Daphne, and an older, distinguished-looking Black man whom Nina didn't recognize—along with Anju and a few other people in suits, who were palace staff or PR people.

Beyond, Nina saw a hospital room filled with beeping machines. Beatrice's dark hair spilled over the pillow, though her face was covered in a breathing mask, various tubes stretching from her wrists and nose.

Tears stung Nina's eyes, and she hurried to wipe them away. God, this was like last year, when the king had been in the hospital, except this time it felt worse because this was *Beatrice.*

Beatrice, who'd been an older sister to her in so many ways. Who'd winked and shown eight-year-old Nina the concealed door behind the credenza so that she could win hide-and-seek against the twins. Who'd sat patiently with Nina one day in high school, explaining all the various pieces of silverware so that Nina wouldn't embarrass herself at her first state dinner. Who'd given Nina so many things: advice on her college application, a set of first-edition Brontë novels for her eighteenth birthday, the conviction that she shouldn't ever hide her nerdiness in order to fit in.

Nina sniffed, wishing that Sam were here. It felt surreal that Sam didn't even know what had happened to her sister.

A figure shifted in the chair by Beatrice's bed. It was Teddy, Nina realized. Dimly, she wondered why Beatrice was on life support, while Teddy had escaped the car crash unscathed.

"It's okay, Jefferson," Daphne murmured, drawing Nina's attention back to the waiting room.

Jeff's back was to Nina, so he didn't see her, but Daphne looked up and met her gaze. Her stare was filled with such bitter hatred that Nina recoiled.

Clearly, Daphne had found out about Nina and Jefferson. Nina had no idea how, but this was Daphne, who always knew everything. Except . . . the look on Daphne's face wasn't one of hurt confusion. She wasn't just upset with Nina; she *despised* her.

Last night, after he'd kissed her, Jeff had said that he was breaking up with Daphne and wanted to be with Nina. Had he not actually meant it? Or had Daphne convinced him to change his mind somehow?

It made Nina wonder if Daphne had ever been her friend at all.

Daphne had said it herself, the night they got tacos: she'd turned to Nina and asked, *Aren't you hanging out with me to try to break us up?*

What if, the whole time, *Daphne* had been the one pretending? It made sense; she'd been threatened by Nina and Jeff becoming friends again. So she'd pulled Nina into her fold and kept an eye on her, ready to strike if Nina became too much of a threat. Keep your enemies close and your rivals even closer, right?

A bitter, ashen taste filled Nina's mouth. She was surprised how much it hurt, realizing that Daphne had never cared about her. The whole thing had been a charade, a great game of pretend, and Nina had fallen for it. She'd let Daphne play her like a pawn in her scheme, just as Daphne was playing Jeff.

She should have known that Gabriella was right—Daphne wasn't capable of a true friendship.

"Let's get started," Anju said, with a nod toward the man Nina didn't recognize. "In the absence of a Supreme Court justice, a senior peer can swear you in. Lord Orange is here to read you the oath."

That must be Stephen Davis, the Duke of Orange, Marshall's grandfather. He stepped forward and bowed. "It's a great honor, Your Highness."

Jeff looked at the people around him, eyes pleading. "Shouldn't this be Samantha?"

"We still can't find her," Anju said gruffly.

Lord Orange cleared his throat. "Given what she wrote in that note, Samantha and my grandson may not want to be found. Some people would interpret her message as a renunciation of her title," he added, his tone unreadable.

"Jefferson," Anju added, "in her Declaration of Regency, Beatrice named *you* as her contingent heir. Should anything befall her during the period of regency, which it has, then you become Acting King." Nina could practically hear the capitalization in those words.

Finally, her mind caught up to the scene unfolding before her. Jeff was about to take the Oath of Accession to the Crown.

She thought dazedly of what he'd said just last month, when he'd explained that Beatrice had named him as her Regent. *It's just a bunch of parties and ribbon-cuttings,* he'd joked. *Hey, at least I have more excuses to wear my ceremonial sword.*

He hadn't anticipated this, but then, no one could have.

Once or twice over the years, Nina had wondered what

might happen if Beatrice abdicated her position and Samantha became queen, for no real reason except that Sam was her best friend and she wondered what kind of queen her friend would make. But never had any of her what-ifs or imaginings brought her here, to a situation where *Jeff* would be the one in the Imperial State Crown.

Daphne put a hand on Jeff's arm in reassurance. "You can do this, Jefferson. You're ready."

From the way she touched him, Nina saw that Daphne was in full control of herself—and of Jeff—once more. It was like his moment in the garden with Nina had never even happened.

Stunned, Jeff nodded. Nina watched as Anju handed a book to Marshall's grandfather. A Bible, she realized. The tattered, paperback kind that you could always find in a hospital somewhere.

The duke held it before the prince, his face grave. Jeff placed his right hand atop it.

"Your Highness. Do you solemnly swear to govern the United States of America according to its laws and principles?"

Jeff's voice was surprisingly steady as he replied, "I do."

"Will you faithfully execute the Office of King, for as long or as short a time as you may need to hold such office, on behalf of Her Majesty Queen Beatrice, long may she reign?"

Long may she reign, Nina thought with a pang. She glanced back toward the hospital bed, where Beatrice lay still.

"I will," Jeff promised.

Nina felt Daphne's gaze on her again. For a moment Daphne's perfect mask dropped, and her face was alive with greed and ambition.

Of course Daphne would be thrilled at this turn of events. As long as her fate was tied to Jeff's, then his swearing-in meant her triumph. If Daphne had anything to say about it, she would ascend to greater heights than even she had dreamed of.

Forget trying to become a princess—now Daphne had set her sights on being queen.

"And will you preserve, protect, and defend the Constitution of the United States?" the duke finally asked.

Jeff nodded. "All of this I promise to do, so help me God."

The Jeff that Nina knew was so very unkingly, with his boyish humor and easy charm. But as he lowered his hand from the Bible, she saw that there was something different about the set of his shoulders, the firmness of his jaw. Already he was more distant, more regal—not like her playful Jeff at all, but a figure from one of the glossy postcards sold in the palace gift shop. Too distant and high-ranking to touch.

Here he was, the boy Nina had loved for more than half her life. Maybe he loved her too, or maybe he loved Daphne, or maybe he loved them both at once—this was Jeff, after all, who had a bigger heart than anyone Nina had ever met, except maybe Samantha.

But in the end, Nina's love for him wasn't enough, not when so many forces were tearing them apart: Jeff's position, and Nina's aversion to the spotlight, and Daphne's ruthless determination to have Jeff for herself.

A sense of weary, stifling defeat settled over her.

If Nina couldn't handle being with Jeff the prince, there was no chance she belonged with Jefferson the Acting King. She'd be subjected to a thousand times as much scrutiny, would be picked apart and judged and found wanting by the entire world. Her family would be thrust under a microscope, her past raked through. Nina couldn't go through that again. She couldn't go up against *Daphne* again, not when it kept ending in such heartache.

"You win," she whispered, too softly for Daphne to hear. Not that it mattered. Daphne already knew she was the victor.

Blinking back tears, Nina hurried down the hall before Jeff could see her.

By the time she descended the front steps of the hospital, a few reporters had gathered near the entrance. Word of Beatrice's accident must have finally leaked. There was a collective intake of breath as Nina pushed open the main double doors, but when they saw her, they all glanced away in disappointment. They'd probably been expecting a member of the palace's PR team.

Then one of them called out, "Hey! Aren't you Samantha's friend, the one who dated Prince Jeff?"

The cameras rose into the air, their metallic clicks multiplying like the drone of wasps.

And suddenly they were all shouting questions at her: *Where is Samantha? Is it true that Beatrice is on life support and Jeff is king? Was the car crash really an accident, or did someone try to murder the queen?*

"The only thing I know for sure is that it's all changing," Nina said, her words tight with a raw, hot emotion. She refused to let herself cry in front of the cameras.

"*What's* changing?" a reporter called out.

"Everything." Nina hurried down the last few steps, then glanced over her shoulder. "I don't know what's going to happen. But when it's all over and the dust has settled, this country will never be the same again."

ACKNOWLEDGMENTS

I can't believe we made it to a third book! This series has been a joy to write, in no small part because of the many talented and wonderful people who've made it all possible.

Caroline Abbey, I'm so lucky to work with you. Thank you for your thoughtful editorial notes, your sense of humor, and most of all for believing in this series so fiercely that you helped us get a third (and a fourth!) book. Here's to more royal adventures to come!

I'm grateful to the entire publishing team at Random House, especially Michelle Nagler, Mallory Loehr, Kelly McGauley, Caitlin Whalen, Kate Keating, Emma Benshoff, Jenn Inzetta, Elizabeth Ward, Adrienne Waintraub, Tricia Lin, Jasmine Hodge, Morgan Maple, and Noreen Herits. And special thanks are due to Alison Impey and Carolina Melis for yet another spectacular cover.

Joelle Hobeika, you make my books better in countless ways! Thank you for your patience, for your creative brilliance, and for keeping us on schedule despite my maternity leave. Thanks also to the entire team at Alloy Entertainment: Josh Bank, Sara Shandler, Les Morgenstein, Gina Girolamo, Kate Imel, Kendyll Boucher, Romy Golan, Matt Bloomgarden, Josephine McKenna, and Kat Jagai.

I'm lucky to work with an incredibly talented foreign sales team at Rights People. Charlotte Bodman, Alexandra

Devlin, Harim Yim, Claudia Galluzzi, Hannah Whitaker, Jodie O'Toole, and Amy Threadgold: Thank you for bringing *American Royals* to so many languages around the world. Special thanks also to Naomi Colthurst, Alesha Bonser, and the rest of the team at Penguin UK.

Writing can be a lonely job. I don't think I could do it without my friends, who are always willing to debate royal history, help me think through story problems, and intervene with a taco dinner when necessary. (Alexandra and Eliza, the American royals owe you a margarita!) Sarah Mlynowski, I'm grateful to have you as a mentor and friend.

Mom and Dad, you have been my greatest champions from day one. Thank you for believing in me, supporting me, and babysitting William all summer so that I could finish this book! John Ed and Lizzy, I love and miss you both so much. There are parts of this book that were written for each of you—you know which ones.

Alex, I can't believe we agreed that I could tackle a book with a newborn during a pandemic. (Let's never do that again!) I couldn't have managed it without you. Thank you for your calm in the face of chaos and for making me laugh with your outrageous story ideas. You and William make everything worth it.

Finally, I want to thank the readers. To everyone who has shared, posted, reviewed, or simply enjoyed the American Royals books—*Rivals* exists because of you. It is a rare privilege to get to continue a series to a third installment. You are the ones who made it possible! Thank you for believing in the American royals, and for all the love you have given these books. I can't wait to see where the journey takes us!

LOVE

POWER

SCANDAL

BETRAYAL

AMERICAN ROYALS IV

Coming in 2023

The title is still a secret, but like all good secrets, it's there for those clever enough to find it. . . .

Here's a clue for royal insiders: *The title is hidden within these pages—in chapter 1, in chapter 9, and twice in chapter 49.*

Think you can be the one to spill the tea? Share it on social with #AmericanRoyalsIV. But of course, real insiders know . . . American royals drink coffee!